How Not to Drown

How Not to Drown

A NOVEL

JAIMEE WRISTON

alcove
press

Copyright © 2021 by Jaimee Wriston Colbert

Published in the United States by Alcove Press, an imprint of The Quick Brown Fox & Company LLC.

Alcove Press and its logo are trademarks of The Quick Brown Fox & Company LLC.

Library of Congress Catalog-in-Publication data available upon request.

ISBN (hardcover): 978-1-64385-557-8
ISBN (ebook): 978-1-64385-558-5

Cover illustration by Olivia Holmes

Printed in the United States.

www.alcovepress.com

Alcove Press
34 West 27th St., 10th Floor
New York, NY 10001

First Edition: May 2021

10 9 8 7 6 5 4 3 2 1

In Memory of Sarah Abigail Ferguson Pratt
my great grandmother

The courage, compassion, and triumph of her life's journey,
From Prince Edward Island to Honolulu,
And whose family's migration from the Isle of Skye to PEI,
Having lost their home in The Clearances,
Was inspirational to me in writing this novel.

And for my dad, Arthur James Wriston, Jr.
My first storyteller

There's always a siren singing you to shipwreck.

—Caitlin R. Kiernan, *The Drowning Girl*

From each crime are born bullets
that will one day seek out in you
where the heart lies.

—Pablo Neruda, *"I Explain a Few Things"*

Wherever snow falls, or water flows, or birds fly, wherever day
and night meet in twilight, wherever the blue heaven is hung
by clouds, or sown with stars, wherever are forms with trans-
parent boundaries, wherever are outlets into celestial space,
wherever is danger, and awe, and love, there is Beauty . . .

—Ralph Waldo Emerson, *The Poet*

PART I

AUTUMN

◆ AMELIA ◆

Last night Amelia felt a floating sensation, as if her bed had become part of a vast body of water, then a sudden desperate need to breathe as Gavin came drifting down beside her like a parachute, a jellyfish, or something shot, arms reaching out in surrender. She swam under him, pushed him up toward the surface, where she could see the blurred shape of a woman kneeling on a rock above them, peering down. The woman's hands parted the water like a curtain, as if she could move it aside and touch him. Her mouth was open. Calling his name? Or just taking what he could not anymore, a breath and then another.

Afterward, Amelia lay in her bed sweating, forcing her own breath in, out, in, out, her heart beating against the wall of her chest like something caged. Was it a dream? Her sheets felt dank and clammy. A gray dawn crept through the window and she willed it to slip back into darkness so she could sleep. Earlier Amelia had downed half a Xanax—just half—but usually it plunged her into a darkness too profound for dreams. In the greasy light of dawn she fumbled about on her nightstand, knocking over the bottle of Xanax, an almost empty cup of water, and his picture, which fell to the floor. Amelia was left with this upon waking: her son didn't fight it; he didn't fight to stay alive.

★ ★ ★

Three hours later an intense fall sun slices like a blade into her kitchen windows, exposing layers of dust on the window sills, lurking like dandruff. *You lounged by your pool and ignored us, but here we are, your personal detritus, waiting for you.* Not that Amelia *lounges.* She spent the summer fighting for custody of her son's twelve-year-old daughter, whom she'd never met, then panicked when it was granted. How could she take care of a twelve-year-old, for God's sake? What had she been thinking? What would she feed her, how would she entertain her, what do twelve-year-olds even *do* these days? What can she teach this child about a world where what happened to her father happened . . . Plus—let's admit it—she thinks now, having his child here will hardly bring back Gavin, now will it? She shakes her head, a foggy sensation like cobwebs behind her eyes. God, did she end up swallowing both halves of that Xanax somehow? Well, the upshot is that none of it matters. The girl is moving in today. Her *granddaughter.*

"There's an innocence about her," the social worker had said on the phone last night, her obligatory call announcing the next day's *ETA*, she called it.

"Meaning she's good, well-behaved—what exactly?" Amelia asked.

"Hah, no. More like she's taken herself out of time, if you will. Happens sometimes with kids subjected to an adult world they're not ready for."

"My my, taken herself out of time, *if you will*? I'd like some tips on how *that's* accomplished!" Amelia said.

"This child has been deprived of a normal childhood. Naturally the state hopes you'll give that back to her," the social worker rambled on, missing or ignoring Amelia's sarcasm entirely. "Since she will be living in your home in Massachusetts, the state of Maine requires periodic progress reports so we can review her acclimation."

"Acclimation?" Amelia had sighed. "She's hardly moving to the Amazon, is she? She won't need immunizations to live in Massachusetts."

"Well," the social worker said, "it's a heap of paperwork, I'll tell you that."

"The state of Maine gives a rat's ass?" Daniel had said when she told him about the call, talking through the crack in his bedroom door. *Selective* Tourette's—he only speaks this way to her. Then again, since her older son never leaves his room, he doesn't have a whole lot of conversations with anyone else. His dad, when he calls, though lately Leo's been going on about how his phone's been wiretapped, Beijing and Moscow spying on him, Google drones hovering, all of them just waiting for him to make a call they can listen in on, he's convinced—so he doesn't call much. Amelia sighs. *Shrug it off,* she orders herself. But honestly, is everyone around her certifiable?

She fixes herself a cup of ginger tea to combat the sourness curdling in her stomach whenever she remembers the dream or whatever it was, that moment when she's in the water underneath him, needing to breathe, needing *him* to breathe, pushing him up the way she once pushed him out of her, and once again he does nothing to help, not even his arms pump—wouldn't you at least pump your arms if you were trying to live? She stares out the window over the kitchen counter, the late September sun lighting up what's left of her garden: two deeply red overripe tomatoes, a tangle of cucumber vines climbing up a trellis, and her flowers. The houses closer to the ocean in her Sandy Hills neighborhood don't have green lawns. With the increasing severity of nor'easters, tidal surges kill the grass and leave beach stones in their wake, but she prides herself on her flowers, making these at least grow.

Amelia rubs her eyes, their insistent wetness today, careful not to smudge her mascara as a white sedan with Maine plates pulls into her driveway. *Allergies,* she tells herself. She'll let that lurking dust settle. One could imagine its glitter as moments of mica rather than dead skin cells, mites, and debris. Amelia's spent a lifetime putting the decorative spin on things. As a model, and then the *former* model moniker ("Hepburn-esque" they called her), she'd gotten used to a level of worship not conducive to her present stage, the senior generation, next to checkout. I'm *outta here* they used to say, nary a thought to anything this close to permanence.

Once again she shrugs off that foggy sensation from last night, the gnawing sense of loss, of abandonment, Gavin in her *nightmare* for God's sake—never mind a dream; let's call it what it was. She marches down the hall and opens the front door to his daughter, motioning her and the social worker inside.

"Heaven, this is your grandma," the social worker chirps after Amelia shuts the door.

"Oh please. Am I white-haired and stooped? I was Amelia to your father and uncle, so how about you call me *Grand*melia." She nods at the girl, expecting some sort of acknowledgment; it's rather clever, isn't it, this amalgamation of a name with (ugh!) a genera-tional marker? Heaven just stares at the wall, a stocky child with an empty gaze, bland as a bowl of pudding. Or rice? No, rice has some definition to it, an actual structure to the grain, whereas this girl's entire persona emanates unformed flesh. Not like her father at all, Amelia decides, her handsome, charismatic, *murdered* son.

"Heaven! Who names a child that?" she had barked to her for-mer husband, after the court-ordered custody was finalized; the court chose her over Leo, who'd been exhibiting that odd behavior of late, his phone and internet paranoia, wandering and forgetting where he wandered from, forgetting his keys to get back inside once "inside" was deemed spy-free. So a thin victory indeed. "With a mother named Cassiopeia, if they'd had a boy he'd have probably been Mars. Or just cut to the chase with Planet!"

Leo had the audacity to chuckle, as if any of this was a joke.

"*Heaven Can Wait*," Amelia tells the girl standing vacuously in the hallway, waiting for the child to say something, *anything*, citing the name of a film the child no doubt had never seen, not the clas-sic original nor that boy-toy knock-off some years later; let alone for her to acknowledge the clever (Amelia thought so) play on the child's name.

The social worker, who had introduced herself as Peggy Howell, told Amelia on the phone last night that when the police tossed the rental (she actually used that word, *tossed*, like it was some TV cop show) where the family had been living, they found Heaven sleeping in a bed crate, sans the bed. "That's addiction for you," Peggy Howell said. *Not exactly an environment where one might sit and enjoy an old movie*, Amelia thinks now.

She ushers the social worker (*case worker*, Peggy Howell said is the preferred terminology, but a spade's a spade far as Amelia's concerned) and the child into her kitchen, figuring she'll offer an obligatory cup of tea; turns the kettle on then seats herself at the table, motioning for the two to sit. They do not. Heaven, dragging two black garbage bags filled with her belongings, stares into the space over Amelia's head with a sullen, just shy of belligerent expression, a pair of unflattering cropped leggings (first order of business will be to re-wardrobe this girl!), and dirty white socks slung so low into her unlaced sneakers she may as well not have them on at all. Peggy Howell thumbs through her satchel then places a pile of papers on the table, asking Amelia to read them when she has a chance, and if there are no questions just sign and stick in the mail. "Goodbye Heaven, goodbye Amy," she says, sighing like she hates to leave them, one foot already back in the hallway, pointed toward the door.

"Amelia! Do I look like an Amy to you?" Not that it mattered, since what the *case worker,* with her toothy grin, deposited into Amelia's custody is another painful reminder of why the child is here in the first place: Gavin, her younger son, her golden boy, dead at the presumed hands of his wife, incarcerated at the Rock Harbor Women's Correctional in Maine. Presumed, because her daughter-in-law would neither deny nor admit it.

The police had found the *alleged perpetrator,* as prosecution had called her at the trial, stumbling about Rockland's Main Street at three AM, appearing disheveled and disoriented, the glassine envelope with its powdery residue in her jean pocket reason enough to haul her in. Her blood tested positive for a full-on assault of controlled and illegal substances: prescription opiates, PCP, cocaine, and heroin. Two days later after an unusually high tide, a fisherman discovered Gavin's body moored in the shallows off The Ledges, a large welt at the back of his head consistent with a hard whack from a solid object, and that afternoon some kids walking out on the breakwater found a two-by-four with Cassiopeia's fingerprints and Gavin's blood on it, wedged between two large rocks. The *victim's* corpse was autopsied, with similar results in his own blood count, a cocktail of the same illegal substances plus crystal methamphetamine (along with saltwater chemicals and significant shrinkage of blood volume resulting from ocean submersion), and it was determined his death was caused by drowning, the prosecuting attorney alleging that the accused had hit him on the back of his head with the two-by-four, causing him to fall off the breakwater into the ocean. How long he may have been conscious and suffering as the frigid water filled his lungs was up for debate.

"Objection!" Cassiopeia's court-ordered defense called out. "The defendant is too petite for a forceful enough hit on a man's head that would have caused the much larger victim to fall into the water." A board the same dimensions was brought to the front of the courtroom (a travesty, Amelia thought, like the whole thing was some scripted play put on by second-rate actors in a community *theater*—how about we bring in a hunk of wood as evidence!), and the DA invited Cassiopeia to step down from the witness stand and swing it. What that proved was nothing, not a particularly bad nor a good arm. When the DA asked her if that was as hard as she could swing, she shrugged, said she could *probably* still hold her own from playing on a softball team in high school. "I was outfield," she added. Amelia could barely look at her.

The prosecutor, a rod-shaped Amazon with man-shorn hair the color of a storm, proposed that the couple was high on drugs, the alleged perp angry at her husband, having walked in on him in a compromised position with the accused's friend, Mary Barbara Smithers. A witness who was also in the house (the backwash area of Rock Harbor, when the sea rose in a nor'easter the first to flood—not a good neighborhood, Amelia had her own lawyer investigate) confirmed this: Mary Barbara in a lacy red bra and matching thong and Gavin with his pants around his ankles. And right there's your motive, the prosecutor concluded, tapping her spike-heeled leather boot like a gavel.

They had taken their argument into the street, observed by another witness to have headed straight to the breakwater. Mary Barbara was questioned, and yes she had followed them for a while, pleading for Cassie to calm down, apologizing and the like she said—admittedly she'd been a *little* high, what was she thinking? she'd regret it for the rest of her life, but she left when they headed out on the breakwater, too cold, she said, shivering for effect. "You could check with MJ at the Rock Harbor Pub," all smiles now—"I had a brew then went home. He'll tell you that—one suds, I'm gone."

When given a chance to speak in her own defense, what seemed most urgent to Amelia's daughter-in-law was to make it clear that Mary Barbara Smithers was not her *friend*, just someone who shared their rent. She wouldn't deny what she was accused of and she wouldn't confess, claiming not to remember anything beyond their walk out to the lighthouse. Yes, she admitted, they'd been fighting; no, she didn't remember any board out there, hitting her husband with it, or Gavin falling into the sea—just that he was gone. No, no one else was out there with them at the end of the breakwater, so sure, she guessed she *must* have done it.

"You do understand the seriousness of these accusations?" the judge asked, leaning over and peering down at her from his throne.

She nodded, brushing a shag of uneven bangs, like she'd slashed them with a kitchen knife, off her forehead, avoiding his eyes, her own eyes dry, though occasionally Amelia noted her shoulders heaved like she was stifling a sob, probably for effect. "My husband's gone," she said.

"And you don't have anything more to say?"

She was quiet for a moment, then she said something in a thin flat voice that chilled Amelia: "I know I should remember—I have this terrible fear of forgetting—but it's all blank. It's just days passing now, one after the other."

In the end, by virtue of the evidence the prosecutor had com-
piled and proposed to the jury: that Gavin French's death was pre-
cipitated by a blow on the back of his head with a two-by-four that
had Cassiopeia French's prints on it and the victim's blood, causing
him to fall off the breakwater into the water and drown ("Objection, conjecture!" the DA interrupted and was overruled); that the
accused had an established, witnessed motive; that there was no
one else out on the breakwater at the time the incident occurred,
Cassiopeia French was assumed guilty by virtue of an angry act
that led to her husband's death. However, as it was not the clean-
cut case the prosecutor had hoped to pin on Mrs. French, whereby
evidence could prove beyond a doubt that the alleged perpetrator
delivered a calculated and *deliberate* blow to the back of her husband's head with the intent to push him off the breakwater into the
ocean, Cassiopeia was convicted of voluntary manslaughter (they
had both ingested a *plethora* of drugs, the DA argued, and there was
no evidence of anything premeditated), and sentenced to fifteen
years at Rock Harbor Women's Correctional. Cassiopeia hung her
head at the sentencing and swayed a little, but otherwise showed no
reaction, no *regret* that Amelia could see.

At that point Amelia left the courtroom, but her own lawyer, who was sitting within earshot of the Defense, told her that
right before they carted Cassiopeia off to RHWC, the DA had
said to her, "That woman could be trouble." Meaning *her*, Amelia
MacQueen!

Cassie had turned around and stared as Amelia, spine straight like
a pole's stuck up it—her daughter-in-law's *articulate* observation—
flounced out of the courtroom. She turned back, shrugged. "I'm
already going to prison; how could I have more trouble?"

The DA had nodded thoughtfully, as though he was mulling it
over. "Well, I got you manslaughter. She wanted murder one. The
problem is, she still wants it."

"What—she wants me tried again? Aren't you supposed to be
my lawyer?"

He had shaken her hand as two officers approached bearing handcuffs and leg irons. "You've been sentenced, Mrs. French, no appeal.

I got you the lesser conviction, fifteen years instead of thirty or life. If you'd pled guilty at the arraignment, as I advised, could've saved ourselves the trial, and worst-case scenario, you'd maybe get the same sentence, but with her off your tail. I'm afraid we're finished here."

"But I don't *remember* it!" Cassie had howled as she was led shackled from the courtroom, an officer hissing at her to shut it. When Amelia's lawyer went to see her in prison a few weeks later, she confirmed what she'd said at the trial: she didn't deny it, she just didn't recall it.

Fifteen years. The travesty of it! The *murderess* will restart her life in middle age as a free person, a blip on the "Life Table" expectancy these days, and Amelia's son will never see his fortieth birthday. Amelia vowed to make it her mission to force her daughter-in-law's confession, make her forfeit that "I-don't-remember-it" ploy. She had asked her lawyer, and as she suspected Cassiopeia couldn't be tried twice for the same crime, but maybe a civil suit, like the O. J. Simpson thing, something that at the least would exonerate her son's name from this dirty business, the drugs, liaisons with other women—the things they brought up in that courtroom that had nothing to do with an innocent man being killed! *Drug addicts,* the court had declared: *What can you expect?*

Amelia shakes her head now and stares at the girl—Cassiopeia's daughter, her son's daughter, her *granddaughter*—standing dimly in her kitchen, clutching the pull-strings on her garbage bags, one in either hand. "You know, I've never imagined myself as a grand-mother. Never thought about it much. Younger women, *some,* might dream about becoming a mother, but a grandmother . . . I guess you just have to grow into it."

Heaven says nothing. Is the child hard of hearing, on top of her tasteless outfit?

"Well"— Amelia rises, walks over to the boiling kettle, flicks the switch off, turns back toward the girl—"I don't suppose you're a tea drinker?"

Again Heaven says nothing, watching through the window as Peggy Howell's car backs out of the driveway, heading north toward Maine.

"I'll take that as a no. Let me show you to your room. It used to be your father's room, but that was quite a while ago. Your Uncle Daniel is in the room beside yours. You won't see him much, but you'll know he's there. He's *always* there."

★　★　★

Later that afternoon after helping Heaven settle in, instructing her on bed making, room cleanliness, the basics, the girl had still not spoken more than four words to Amelia. "What do you say?" Amelia had prompted her, handing her a clean set of sheets and a basket of toiletries: a new toothbrush, toothpaste, conditioning shampoo, and a lavender-scented soap.

"Yes?"

"What?"

"Yes . . . please?" Her granddaughter's face had wavered between bland and downright morose, although she did show a flicker of interest when Amelia offered to let Heaven keep her portable CD player on a shelf above her bed. "For the time being," Amelia said. "Did you happen to bring any CDs?"

The girl nodded, a slight smile.

"Not after nine PM, and not on a school night," Amelia said. "What do you say?"

"Yes?" the girl said again.

Amelia had sighed. "*Thank you*, for lord's sake! Just say thank you."

Now Amelia sinks into the sectional sofa in her living room, feet up on the glass coffee table, with *The Globe* on her lap, and as she's settling in, her phone rings. She glances at the screen, 207 area code—Maine. Answers, dreading.

"Leo wandered again. They found him in that awful Kennebec neighborhood, the industrial area he likes so well—can't imagine why—it's a wreck! I mean it's not like this building's in a decent neighborhood to begin with, so why does he want to go worse? Taking pictures, only there's no film, he even forgot the film! No film, no jacket, just his T-shirt on, his fingers were like ice, the police said. Looked disoriented, they said. Picked him up and brought him here—they know him by now—expecting me to retrieve him at the door like he's some UPS package, show him into his apartment. Me, the downstairs renter. Not his wife, not nothin' to this guy but the woman who pays him rent. Thought you should know."

Amelia clenches her teeth until her jaw burns. They've had this conversation before. "Well, he lives there doesn't he, Mabel? As in owns the building *you* live in? And by the way, am I his keeper?" Heaven is playing some kind of electronic mess on the CD player; Amelia pictures her sprawled on the bed, thumping her foot against the wall to the music's beat, the way her father used to. Gavin would listen over and over to the same thing, or so it sounded to Amelia, that repetitive beat, and he'd whack it out on the wall beside his bed, thump thump . . . Amelia wipes her eyes again, pain ripping through her chest. Was it really him last night, and was it *her* beneath him in that water? It didn't feel like her, felt almost animalistic, primitive, not quite human, not quite *her*, but the yearning was there, she recognized that, her need to save him before it was too late! Nudge him to the surface so his face could break free and breathe.

"So?" Mabel says. "You there?"

"Listen to me," Amelia hisses into the phone. "I have one son . . . gone, another's not right in the head, and a granddaughter who seems to think she's the reincarnation of Ringo Starr. Don't you think that's enough on my plate?"

Silence. From somewhere a door shuts. More silence. Amelia can hear breathing, the heavy space between his breaths. "Leo? That's you, isn't it."

"I had to wait," he says. "If the line crackles we're not alone. People assume it's the law tapped in on you but no, you see, not always. Russia, China, Nigeria—you name it. If they can hack into a password-protected computer imagine how much easier a phone. You pick it up and talk."

"Oh lord," she sighs. "Leo, be normal, please?"

"Ringo Starr is alive," he says.

"What?"

"You need to pick someone dead if you're going for reincarnated drummer. Spencer Dryden maybe. Remember? Jefferson Airplane?"

She does. Visiting her cousins on Oahu, back when she and Leo were dating, they had all climbed up then down into Diamond Head Crater for an Airplane concert. The day was a wash of colors, indigo sea, Ko'olau Mountains the deep green of spinach behind them, but the crater itself was bone-dry and brown, spears of cactus erupting here and there like acne. They'd ingested something. Mushrooms? Psilocybin? Everything in waves like the heat, she could *see* this heat, every molecule, the band wailing, Gracie howling, shimmying and shimmering in her mini-skirt, those extraordinary legs, Spencer Dryden at the drums. Leo's beside her and then he wasn't, because now she's pressed up against the outside wall of a *lua*, her cousin had called it, kissing some guy, a friend of a friend of . . . well that's what it was in those days, wasn't it? 1967, Summer of Love? When you're high, when you haven't a care, a *friend* of her cousin, eyes the color of the sky, like he'd glanced up and the sky shot down inside them. He's got his tongue in her mouth, tickling the back of her throat, his bare chest pushing against her breasts in her tie-died tube top. Then Leo is there, grabbing her hand, squeezing it inside his massive palm and fingers, pulling her back to him.

Now she feels a wave of despair, that loss again, as if it's not only her son but all of them, drowning. "Leo," she whispers into the phone, "for God's sake, Leo." Heaven shuts the music off and the house is silent.

✦ HEAVEN ✦

I T'S BEEN LESS THAN a month since she was dropped off at this place, and already her grandmother has ordained herself Queen-of-Heaven's-Sucky-Life. "You simply can't go to the Harvest Dance in polyester," Grandmelia declared last night over a mac and cheese dinner. *Grandmelia*—like she thinks that name makes her only half a grandma or something? Whatever, it's not like Heaven *wanted* to call her Grandma. The dinner was Uncle Daniel's request, though Grandmelia had to make it since he won't come out of his room, a side of curly fries and chocolate marshmallow ice cream for dessert, Heaven's favorite. In fact all of it was Heaven's favorite, and she devoured every bit, her grandmother frowning, staring at Heaven's chubby arms, potato cheeks, her *almost* boobs. Okay, the boobs are mostly fat but without that fat, *good Christ* (an Uncle Daniel way of talking) Heaven would have nothing there at all, and Bethany Harrison, a size B *plus* she bragged in the middle school girl's bathroom, would rag her even worse. Yesterday Bethany and her wannabees cornered Heaven in the bathroom and forced her to lift up her T-shirt. "Show us your itty-bitty-titty bra, size triple A *minus*!" Bethany snickered and the flock of blond-headed Bethany *as-ifs* snorted, and Juniper Mayberry (pronounced Mayber*ee*, accent up, she'd corrected Heaven) squeezed out a fart, Heaven in the line of fire.

What world does Grandmelia think Heaven lives in? Not a world where she would voluntarily go to a seventh-grade dance, that's for sure. It would have to be punishment for the worst crime, kidnapping Bethany Harrison at gunpoint, tying her up in the trunk of Grandmelia's car, then dropping her off at the town dump when Grandmelia does her weekly run, all dug out and smelly, seagulls poking about like rats, plus plenty of real rats too! Just another bag of garbage. And this punishment on the heels of Heaven's fingernails pulled out, one by one, or her face pushed into the toilet and held there until it popped or she passes out. Passing out would be better than that dance.

But Grandmelia kept at it, pointing to the flyer: "Meet Your Friends! Dance to Music Selected by our Junior DJ *Rawesome* Ross at the Harvest Dance!" Someone had taped it to the back of Heaven's jacket as a joke. Grandmelia didn't get it. No one expected her to go; no one *wanted* her to go. "Tomorrow the South Shore Mall," Grandmelia declared. "We'll purchase a suitable outfit." Outfit. Even the word wasn't part of Heaven's life. Where she came from in Maine, an *outfit* was jeans and a flannel shirt in the winter, jeans and a tank top in the summer, and both in those indeterminate seasons, her mom called them, when the weather never knew which way it would go, so you'd take the flannel off when the sun got serious, slip it back on when it rained. Her mom with her skinny legs and boy hips could rock that *outfit*—who cared if the flannel was polyester? Her mom wouldn't.

Grandmelia was up for this thing because she figured this was what an almost teenager should be doing with her time. "You're almost a teenager," she said, "so of course you want to go to the school dance. Every girl wants to go to a dance."

"I don't," Heaven said.

"Why not? Are you a lesbian?" Grandmelia asked.

"No. I mean I don't think so. I don't know, I just don't want to go."

"I wouldn't care if you're a lesbian, mind you, it's not a judg-ment. There are plenty of times in my own life when things might've gone better if I preferred women. Men can be trouble, and that's a fact. You must keep your wits about you and outsmart them at every turn. But if you're not, you're not, and if you are *not* a lesbian, then there's no excuse for not going to that dance."

"I could go if I was a lesbian, if I *wanted* to, but I don't." This after Heaven proposed she stick pins in her eyeballs or swallow rocks rather than go. Grandmelia has no clue what it's like at that school for Heaven. She had a brief window, what was left of Sep-tember and one week into October, a honeymoon period when the kids left her alone due to her status as the "new girl," while they figured out her rank in their social order. Then all hell broke loose, an outcast, a fat one at that, according to Bethany Harrison the meanest mean girl in mean girl history, and every day brought some new assault: snarks about her body, mouth farts, tripping her, helpful suggestions like why don't you commit suicide? Posting shit about her on Facebook and Snapchat, which Heaven can't see because Grandmelia *won't get her a smartphone!* And their so-called jokes! Yesterday's was sticking her backpack in the boys' bathroom, where Josh Cunningham said he peed on it; it was wet when he tossed it back to her. "It's a joke," Josh said, "smell test!" someone yelled, then the bell rang for first period and everyone scattered, leaving her standing in the hall beside her wet backpack, late for class.

It's not like Heaven has any talent or hotness or money, or anything at all going for her, like being good at computers or sci-ence so you can be part of the geek squad. Geeks are considered *almost* cool, depending on their geek specialty, music and movie hijacking and computer hacking make the cut; anime, being awe-some at video games, pretty cool; plain old brainy like being good at math, not so much, but they'd leave you alone, except when they made you do their homework. Nope, she's just Heaven, fat girl with the stupid name from Maine, which according to most kids on the south shore of Massachusetts may as well be Min-nesota, Montana, Mississippi, or Missouri—just another M state that isn't their state, so it isn't cool. Of course with a mother in prison and her dad drowned, she really isn't just *any* dumb girl from Maine, but she has to figure out the right time to play that card. Depending on how things go, that will either be the thing she covers up No Matter What, or she'll use it to wreck their white-bread-middle-class-culturally-defunct-suburban lives. She got that one from Uncle Daniel, who last night, when she was crying in her room, did their special knock on the wall, and when she answered, he told her not to fret, that on top of the white-bread culturally defunct thing, they were all a bunch of pampered, self-indulgent, entitled cunts. The boys too, he said, all of them, cunts. Uncle Daniel says a lot of swear words, which cheers Heaven up.

★ ★ ★

Heaven at the mall with Grandmelia. Watch your back, Grandmelia! Inches up behind *who shall be called Grandmelia* perusing a row of dresses in size Much! Too! Big! for a twelve-year-old, according to her grandmother. That spaghetti-strapped velvet's caught her eye (with a puffed sleeved jacket? Oh *good Christ* if she wore that to a school dance she'd be slayed, hung, torn to shreds, just call her dead!). Heaven sets her sites on the cosmetics counter across Macy's aisle. Something for her mom maybe when they visit on Saturday? Scooches across the polished aisle while Grandmelia chats up the salesgirl, looking for a bargain— "these buttons are stitched so poorly," she insists, "they can't teach their underpaid workers in Beijing how to sew on buttons?" Heaven sliding up quieeetttttly to the L'Oréal counter. The lipsticks sit unconquered in an open tray, though she knows cameras are hidden in the ceiling over them like God's little eyes. If she were one of Uncle Daniel's bitchy faeries he tells stories about instead of a fat girl (*solid*, Grandmelia describes her to the salesgirl, like she's a couch), she could fly up and emasculate those cameras. That's last night's cool word from Uncle Daniel. He said Grandmelia did that to his dad, *emasculated* him, so that's why his dad, Heaven's grandfather, doesn't live with them. Heaven wasn't sure what the word meant (cut off his balls, Uncle Daniel said when she asked); she pictured scissors or maybe a knife. She could emasculate a camera with those.

On the way home her grandmother blows through all the little and not so little South Shore towns—Braintree, Quincy, Weymouth, Hingham, Cohasset, Scituate—and finally Seahaven, where they live, a satellite town to Scituate, the *working-class* Scituate, Uncle Daniel said. The area was once known as the Irish Riviera, he said, where a renounced Scot like Amelia MacQueen, might blend. Not so well heeled as its northern neighbor Cohasset with its million-dollar homes, he said, but a notch upscale from Marshfield to the south, with its half-million dollar homes. It's townies like them mostly who live in the flat coastal neighborhoods of Sandy Hills, the ones that flood, older houses, smaller, expendable, according to some, he said. Seahaven and Scituate used to take a backseat to the elite suburbs north of Boston but holds its own now that it's got the train: official commuter community. White-flight suburbia, he said.

Along both sides of the highway, trees are bright red, yellow, and orange, then a barren grove where most of the leaves are already down. Heaven stares at Grandmelia—the set of her chin—glaring out the windshield as she drives. Grandmelia considers highway driving an act of war. You have to have a good defense and prepare to go on the offensive too, she'd said. She'll be pissed when Heaven informs her she won't be caught dead in that spaghetti-strapped dress, tissue-wrapped in a bag by her feet, or maybe that's the *only* way it would get on her, when her body is dead. Grandmelia will snark that she can't imagine how Heaven figures on getting a boyfriend. She pulled that one at their school-clothes shopping fiasco, Grandmelia called it, Heaven insisting on jeans, T-shirts and a black hoodie instead of the "stylish" corduroy pants and jacket Grandmelia tried to get her.

"Want to just murder me first, Grandmelia? Cause that's what they'll do if I show up at school in a corduroy pantsuit. Like who even *wears* pantsuits?"

"Fat girl jeans and a T-shirt—good lord, how will you attract a future boyfriend?"

Heaven had rolled her eyes. She'll study up on how to be a lesbian, she decided. No boys liked her anyway, though the girls didn't much like her either.

Today is a wash of late-afternoon sun, blazing into the windshield, and Grandmelia snaps down the shades as they pull onto 3A. "Almost home," she sighs, nodding with satisfaction like she's accomplished something getting them off the expressway. When they stop at CVS for Grandmelia's meds, Heaven snakes a pen for her mom so her mom can write letters. She's not allowed to use the computer in prison for email, which Heaven figures is the reason her mom isn't writing to her. Cheaper stuff like ballpoint pens have fewer cameras angled on them, and she uses her grandmother's butt to hide behind as they go through checkout; Grandmelia said she has an *uplifted* one, that Heaven might consider doing squats to tighten hers.

Last week Grandmelia took photos of Heaven with her Kodak Sure Shot, following her about one day: Heaven eating her Cheerios; Heaven doing her Grandmelia-enforced chores; Heaven watching a Lifetime special about a teenage girl who falls in love with a boy from a different race—*so* 1950s Grandmelia scoffed; Heaven at her desk, writing a letter to her mom. "I'm mailing these photos to your mother with your letter," Grandmelia said. "Maybe she'll remember she's supposed to be a mom."

Heaven has her doubts. Her mom's in prison, after all, and maybe they don't let you be a mom in prison. Maybe she's forgotten how, Grandmelia said, but Heaven isn't sure there's a set of rules for this sort of thing. Her house wasn't like most houses, and her mom and dad didn't seem like most moms and dads, but they were nice to Heaven, they didn't make her do chores or force her to go to a dance that she'd rather—okay let's throw in toenails too, yank those puppies right out along with her fingernails—than go to.

Besides, what Heaven has figured out is there are two moms now: the one who's in prison back in Maine and the one who lives in her daydreams. "Heaven is always daydreaming," her English teacher told Grandmelia in her biweekly "update" e-mail.

Grandmelia had scoffed at that one. "You haven't mastered how to at least *look* attentive?" she said. Heaven's memories are something else entirely, and sometimes she isn't sure how they fit into things, but the mom in her daydreams can be whoever Heaven dreams her to be, an astronaut maybe, which she'll tell the kids at school when they ask, because she's sure that'll be any day now since Mrs. Rhiner (*Rhino!*) told their English class that Heaven didn't *have* a mom at home she could bring her project to, some lame thing about asking your mom her family history. Heaven can tell them her mom is in Houston, training for outer space. Or maybe she's a movie star who has to live in Hollywood. Or a spy—ha!—spying on terrorists, making the world safer for skanks like Bethany. She overheard that word from Uncle Daniel, arguing with Grandmelia, who was trying to set up dinner with some lady she'd invited to their house, a classmate and former girlfriend of Heaven's dad, if Daniel would only come out of his room for one hour, the time it takes them to eat. "We aren't *The Glass Menagerie*," he told her, "I'm not auditioning *gentlemen callers*. She's a skank!" he snapped when Grandmelia kept needling him, yacking at him through his bedroom door.

When they're finally home Heaven changes into her new bathing suit (too small, has to yank it down over her butt; Grandmelia sees her as the size she wants Heaven to be and buys clothes for that skinnier Heaven), then jumps into Grandmelia's pool where she can figure things out at the bottom. It's not a super deep pool, one of the aboveground kind since the yard is small and has a lot of rocks, but if she sits at the bottom and closes her eyes, then opens them quickly in the milky water she can almost make out a sleek shape. Uncle Daniel told her to look for the one who on land appears as an angel, but in the water she's maybe a selkie from the Isle of Skye. They've been known to help with quests, he said, though watch out for the ones who might lure you down. Heaven figures either way she can't go down too far in six feet of water.

Her quest is to join the swim team, but first she has to teach herself to become the best swimmer ever, which means making herself love swimming again. After her dad drowned, she wasn't so sure about it, even though Grandmelia says it wasn't an accident. "Ask your mother about that sometime," she sniffed. Heaven practices every day in Grandmelia's pool. It's still a mostly warm late October, and on the days it isn't, Grandmelia heats the water. Heaven sits down at the bottom and holds her breath, imagines herself breathing, *in out in out*—if you can breathe you can't drown. She'll get so good they'll have to let her on the team, and then maybe the other kids will like her because she's an awesome swimmer. If they don't, she has a backup plan. She'll be a siren from Uncle Daniel's stories, singing her tormentors to their doom. She'll practice underwater, and when Bethany, who's on the team, least expects it, when she's doing the one-hundred-meter lap, Siren Heaven opens her mouth and out it comes, her drowning song.

✦ DANIEL ✦

"YOU'RE LOOKING PARTICULARLY GLUTTONOUS these days, like you have a lustful appetite for food and sex, a Nero-esque kind of guy, maybe even an appetite for blood!" Daniel tells Him in the mirror. Him stares back. Give me a break, Him says. He doesn't, he isn't. Amelia said it's unhappy fat, the times he'd been forced to let her inside his domain, his *man* cave, his hideout, his refuge, a life's perimeters, his own goddamn room with its miniscule bathroom attached, like stepping into a vertical MRI tube, can't even raise his arms in the shower to wash his hair properly, if he still had enough left to wash. "Who you think pays the mortgage around here? My house, my terms," she snarled. The way she insists on creeping into his private world just wears him the fuck down. "It's 'your life-didn't-turn-out-as-you-hoped' buffer fat," she'd said, "your 'keep-everyone-away-particularly-women' fat." Yeah, whatever *Mommy dearest*, just leave me the fuck alone.

From the room next to his, he hears Heaven kicking the wall. She's been here just five and a half weeks and already she's a cog in their household wheel, like she's always been here, getting on Amelia's nerves. He counts: one, two, three—kick, four, five, six—whap, seven, eight, nine—*pow*. It's their distress code. He told her she had to stop at nine because even numbers are a curse. Nine is odd, he said, three, seven, and nine, all good. Particularly three, magical three, so three successions of kicks, with the slam after nine, means she's serious. She'd been sent to her room by Amelia for, ironically—and he hopes Heaven appreciates this—slamming her bedroom door. The *pow* isn't as insistent as her usual, probably nailed her toe on the baseboard again.

He removes the picture he put of his dead brother over the hole in the wall he created for communication with his niece. Gavin, five years old, clutching a red Lego truck; even Daniel thought him occasionally cute then. Immediately Heaven's owlish face appears, what he can see of it: puffed cheek, one pale eye, and a nose beak.

"Grandmelia makes me so mad!"

"Well fuck fuck fuck," he says three times, and she giggles. He's told his niece that her grandmother thinks he has Tourette's (he doesn't), and Heaven relishes this, thinking maybe he does, maybe he doesn't, but if Grandmelia believes it and is pissed off about it, that's good enough for her.

"Isn't being an agoraphobe enough abnormality, must we ice the cake with Tourette's too?" Amelia had said. He told Heaven how in response he said fuck fuck fuck to his mom, and Heaven howled.

"*Everybody* I know says the F-word," Heaven informed him. "Can't I please come in your room with you?" she asks now.

"Have you figured out the secret password yet?"

"Nooooo. It's too hard!"

"Well, there you go. Back to the drawing board."

"I hate drawing," Heaven whines. He hears her body slump against the wall between them and feels a sudden shock of sadness for her. How will Amelia do it, he thinks, raise Gavin's orphan in a world so damaged? How will she make her feel safe, with temperatures rising, the coasts drowning, and beautiful creatures going extinct every day due to fucked-up human greed. Sure, loot the Arctic for oil, make more greenhouse gasses, let the glaciers melt—who needs them except the polar bears? He places his hand on the wall, imagines he can feel the heat of his niece through it. "There," he whispers.

★ ★ ★

Daniel is the watcher, that's his job. He's poked another hole in the wall—this one for his eyes only, behind the Menehune picture from his Hawaiian cousins. Shift it slightly to the right and voilà, a tiny peephole he worked on for a week with a Phillips screwdriver; these renovated beach houses pretending to be in the big-boys league masking as year-round houses, their walls like papier-mâché. A hole between his and Amelia's room so he can keep an eye on her occasionally, make sure she's all right. He doesn't spy on her, which would be her accusation if she knew. From his miniscule vantage point, he can see her only when she stares at herself in the mirror over her vanity table; what he sees is the reflection of her face. Amelia has become unmoored since Gavin's death, this obsession of hers to make Gavin's wife confess, and sometimes Daniel feels a weight of dread, imagining what it would be like to lose her too.

He loves her more than he'd like to at this point in their lives, wishes some of that love had gone south with his once-taut stomach, his abs that were all rib, Gavin used to joke, but now are just pockets of flesh. He can't justify it, this love he has for his mother, she's such a pain-in-the-butt. Until he sees her when she's let her guard down, gazing at herself in her mirror, touching her face, her lipsticked mouth shaped *Ohhhh*. He still thinks she's beautiful, though he'd never tell her that. He knows *she* no longer believes she is and is in despair over this; when she looks at herself, she told him once, what she sees is what's no longer there. She wouldn't believe him anyway, would tell him he's nuts, like when he told her about the angel. "That's just plain nuts, Daniel," she said. "You hear me, certifiable."

He's pretty sure the angel came last night while he slept. Can smell traces of her, seaweed plus some lemony scent, like she hadn't been on land for a time and had a craving, lemon meringue pie maybe, like Daniel's grandmother made sometimes. His eyes tear up. He misses his grandparents. More holes in his life where something should be. Figures it's got to be the angel, sea or land, whether she flew or swam over the fake wood floor of his bedroom (*laminate*, Amelia insists, like the word makes its imitation classier), because the angel is the one who saved his own butt from drowning.

The night before it happened they'd been gazing at stars, Amelia with Gavin and Daniel on either side of her, still kids, still innocent, perched on a sandy bluff off Turtle Bay where they were staying for the week, north shore of Oahu, a place more secluded and not lit up by the resort's floodlights. She's explaining how they each have their own position. "If we had a star map," she said, "you could stare at the chart and locate them by their angles, their differential from each other. The bigger ones are planets; you can tell because they're brighter," she told them. "But what makes them shine so bright?" Daniel asked. She said nothing for a while, and even Gavin for once was quiet, just the silky sound of little waves slipping onto the shore and the line of breakers further out, crashing against the rocks. Then she laughed. "What makes anything shine, Daniel? By standing out from the rest, of course."

She was young then, her long legs, thick auburn hair, cheekbones sharp as arrowheads. And she glowed, like if you crossed Katherine Hepburn with the sun. People thought she looked like a young Katherine Hepburn, who was aging then the way his mother is now, skin loosening, hollowing out, and sinking back into that enviable bone structure. Amelia was the brightest, Daniel understood that. So of course she loved Gavin more, because he shone like her.

The next day, off Goat Island, ocean the color of sliced turquoise, after he grew tired from fighting the current, nothing to rest his feet on, no reef, no coral heads, just deeper, colder, darker as it swept him out, Daniel went down. When he opened his eyes below the surface, he saw the long sleek shadow, pushing him up.

Up, he thinks now, directing his gaze out the window at the sky, its slow darkening. Almost time for Mercy-in-the-next-door-garage to come home from work. He turns off his own light so he can watch for her entrance, her light switched on, the way she stands in front of the window and takes her work clothes off for him; she knows he's there, the watcher. She'll do it slowly: the white waitress shirt, the black skirt ("what a Mormon would wear to serve meatloaf in," he heard her tell Amelia once, shouting at each other from across their yards, Amelia in her flower bed next to the aboveground pool and Mercy pacing the rocky perimeter of her parents' property). The best are her shoes—the three-inch platform (he guesses it's got to be at least that high) on her right foot, with the glitter tie around her ankle, kicked off; then the other, a plain white sneaker like a nurse's shoe. Then he's watching her limp across the room in her bra and underpants, her beautifully shaped legs, one shorter than the other, she ties on her bathrobe and flops onto the bed. Only then, and only sometimes, does she remember (or care, he dares to hope?) the window. Gets up, yanks the shade down. "Good night!" he whispers. It's simpler this way. He can appreciate her, maybe even love her, without messing things up by actual contact; spoken words, wrong words—even right ones—in the end they are only words. Mercy lets him watch her undress, and sometimes she even dances for him, late at night, when no one else is awake.

Daniel knows the daytime world by its sounds. The mailman's jeep's been needing a new muffler for two years; the school bus dropping off the neighborhood kids, three times in the afternoon: high school, middle school, elementary. His ears are acute. They tell him the world, what he needs to know of it. Some doctors think he may have dived down onto a coral head that day in the ocean off Goat Island, maybe his head even stuck there for a few minutes, a traumatic brain injury of some sort. Perhaps his brain along with his heart was deprived of oxygen for too long. Or maybe the angel couldn't make up her mind what to do with him, his body drifting down like something that belonged there, then finally pushing him up to the surface. Reject, regret, rescue? Once you breathe air you cannot go back.

Window as portal. His eyes, her eyes, he imagines them brown, or maybe light green like new grass—except she's a brown-eyed type, richer, deeper, more real, a staunch, feet-on-the-ground sort, even if one foot needs a little help getting there, not like the pale-eyed liminal Scots of his family. *Mercy!* Single, lonely—she's got to be; he's counted all her visitors for the one and a half years since she moved back home, two women, one of them older and she came a few times, two men who left before dawn.

"Failed adult," Amelia said, had heard that Mercy had a husband, was expecting a baby, then suddenly there's none of it. A diner waitress, his mother told him through his bedroom door; he could picture her rolling her eyes.

"Why is she back home?" he asked.

Amelia couldn't be sure, but something rendered her incapable and dependent on her parents at thirty-seven. "If you'd open your door, you'd see me shrug," she said.

One sticky note pad, one-quarter filled, noting her visitors: the women, friends or more likely colleagues, he decided, fellow waitresses; first guy who left before dawn, then the other, both of them youngish to middle-aged, nondescript, your basic guys. Daniel stayed up to make sure there were no problems after her lights went out. Because he knows *she* knows he's there, watching, making sure. She even did the air high-five in the window after the first one left and Daniel ducked. But later he relived it, imagined her hand stretched all the way across her yard, over his mother's fence with its tangles of sumac and ivy, into his window.

She's home now, garage apartment (fixed up just for *her*, Mercy told Amelia, stepdad number four said she had anger issues, that she'd *harsh his mellow*, being in the house). Harsh his mellow! Daniel grins. Sounds like something his own dad, Leo, might've said at one time. Daniel sees her mosey up to the window now to see if he's watching her, she seems to know that *he* knows when she usually gets home. He peeks out the side of his curtains as she lifts up her shirt, does her little dance. Anger issues, her stepdad said—that's why they'd put her in a garage? Unhealthy to be around, harshes his mellow? Sounds like a classic hippie waistoid, Daniel thinks now, labels all the stupid in his brain *mellow*. Leo wasn't a waistoid, although to hear it from Amelia, she was the breadwinner from the get-go. That garage is refinished, Amelia had said, or maybe refurbished? Re . . . something, because, his mother pointed out, you can't put a car in it.

Now the garage is backlit in the sunset sky, a halo of its light around her head. For a moment he thinks she looks like an angel, and then he wonders if his head too would be backlit; *ha*, he thinks, a peeping angel. Hello freak! she mouths to him, lolling her tongue against the glass. He imagines her calling him that, or maybe Amelia heard her say it? He doesn't mind—in some ways it's almost a term of endearment, more personal to him than her calling him nothing, not even noticing him. She unbuttons her shirt, white diner-wear, tosses it on the floor—he imagines garage concrete with a throw rug, classy as all get out, refurbished his ass; removes her bra, presses her breasts for a moment against the glass window.

Outside a sudden rain shower and with it the smell of the sea through a permanent crack in his own window. Daniel wonders if she can smell it too. Next she kicks her shoe off, her perfect leg, three inches too short, Amelia said. (But what's too short? It's relative isn't it? If the leg was alone instead of paired with a longer one, it would call the shots.) He imagines himself whispering this in the pale dawn light, staring at her face, relaxed in sleep, not a line on her skin, no frown, no fear of every moment outside your own room branded onto your flesh.

Mercy zips on a hoodie, then steps out into the rain for a smoke; he can see its darting light like a tiny torch as she stands hunched under the eaves. The night is misty, dank, and he wonders if it reminds her of Seattle, where she told Amelia she'd lived with her bad choice of a first husband, the wet, the gray, and she'd run across the drawbridge that separated where they lived, their dilapidated apartment building, from the tidier streets that led to UW, to escape his nastiness when the drink got in him.

Daniel shakes his head. It amazes him the things his mother manages to get out of people, private, sometimes excruciating moments from their own lives, and yet they tell her. It's not like she comes across as some therapist type or even remotely empathetic. He figures it's more like an inquisition, and they cough it up because there's something about Amelia—people feel like they have to keep talking to her since she won't feel an obligation to hold up her end of the conversation, and the silence between them would be worse. *Well at least you weren't so angry back then,* Mercy's mom had said after Mercy came home again, this time her doing, husband number two, a good one, too good for her, she had told Amelia.

Daniel watches Mercy step back into the garage, pull off the hoodie, put on an old chenille (he figures) bathrobe. Drags her table in front of the window to show him its busted-up treasures. She's done this before, and he opens his curtain wider so she can see him here, watching. Her Collection of Broken Things. His ceiling light shines down on his mostly bald head. He wonders if she's okay with that, maybe even likes the look, the vulnerability of it, smooth and fragile as an egg. Would a bald man be a jerk to her, think he's hot shit; he's *bald*, right? The table holds her remnants: broken things from former jobs, she told Amelia, shards of dishes, since mostly she ends up waiting tables; the firing fits, or fits when she fired her own sorry ass, pitching water goblets—she displays one, cracked like a rip of lightning across its blue glass sky, then a ceramic oyster plate sliced in half. Her brief stint as an office temp ended up in a laptop hurled, wasn't hers so she couldn't keep the evidence, but she lifts up its fake leather case she snagged, former home of a fifteen-inch PowerBook. Daniel nods, lets her know he gets it, empty of its contents.

Next she displays a broken mirror, which was last night's action. He saw it happen when she flung it against the opposite wall. *Seven years bad luck?* She shattered it good, but its frame looks intact. She points at the gold, flakey stuff around the edge. *Fake!* she mouths. He beams his flashlight at her, he's done this before, blinks it on and off three times; she probably thinks it's some kind of Morse code, like she's supposed to get it.

Lifts a shard of the glass, the biggest part that's still whole, turns it so it reflects herself. Brooding, her furrowed brows look. *How will she attract husband number three?* He could imagine Amelia thinking that, but he rather likes the look, seems a reasonable way to look out at a world that's wounded you. Mercy puts the mirror back down on the table, presses her whole body against the window for a moment, holding her arms out in a crucifixion pose. He flashes his light, three times. She pulls down the shade, shuts off her light, then he turns off his too and stares into the dark of his room.

◆ MAGGIE MacQUEEN, 1851 ◆

O UR PEOPLE BEGAN WITH the Vikings, a conquest of course,
though Da said he preferred it that way; Norse blood, he
said, must've gotten *something* warrior from it. Our sister Abigail
was the tall, strapping type, with those Nordic looks that opened
doors, and indeed she did have a few crack open into a better life,
despite our prospects. Charles too, our older brother, with the same
fair looks as Abigail, managed quite the plunge into a respectable
life, though in his case I suspect it was his cleverness with numbers.
I was more squat, dark-haired, where their hair was the color of
roses and maple, the pale reds and reddish-browns that announced
to the world we were Scots. Aye, but the blue-green eyes all of us
inherited, and the freckly skin (though mine was ruddier), paler
folk, we Gaels of the Isle of Skye. Outer Hebrides people were
darker yet, black eyes and hair, a mystery to me how this was; like
their islands, the way they rose out of the mist, beckoning but
indistinct, as if they're there and yet they're not.

Skye was named the Misty Isle by some, our rain and fog, a
wetness that soaked you through at times, fair enough when the
sun came out. Others believed that the word *Skye* came from an

old Norse word for wings, as its three peninsulas make it look like a giant bird. I rather think it's the birds themselves, the terns and gannets, their great white wings like angels gliding above, kitti-wakes and fulmars too, drifting over the sea, diving for fish, their sharp yellow eyes, settling each spring and summer in our cliffs. I'd wonder what they've seen, where they've been, soaring through the sky, our little angels.

Maybe devils, said Ma when I told this to her, always one to take the opposite tact; keeps us on our toes, said Da. He and I saw the sweet fruit of a thing, and Ma the stony pit. But she was a fighter, and in the end, when we lost our crofts, was many the women who were the strong ones. Tales of those pulled from their burning homes by their hair, tossed outside like so much rubbish, the men in hiding or else on the mainland working—the factor with his posse of cowards, riding out with their torches when it was women and children and the ancient they'd be evicting. The Clearances, some called it. Others called it genocide.

It's the wind I remember best, the way it cut around our little cottage, whistling over the thatched roof, poking its nose between the stones in the walls like a nosey visitor, one who's refusing to leave. Sit down with me if you must, Ma would tell this wind, but keep out of the wee ones room. For Ma, like many crofter's wives, had lost a couple babies, one that never did draw breath and another whose breath was poor from the start, such that pleurisy was his doom.

Ma's clothes were soot-covered from keeping the peat at burn, her hands raw from pounding oats, helping Da with the scythe to harvest them. Curled up between Abigail and wee Molly, pre-tending to sleep so she didn't make me rise and help while it was yet so cold, I'd hear that wind shoving its way down the chimney pipe like some schoolyard bully, the peat smoke wafting up to greet it. The wind whistled, breathed, exhaled like the boil of a steam engine, which I'd not yet heard until Glasgow, where we went for the crossing, but in my memory even now I hear its roar.

★ ★ ★

Our neighbors were emigrating—how much worse can the new world be, they said—with any luck a fair bit better. Food grown scarcer, the factor meaner, more rent, every year 'tis more rent, Da agreed, and what we got for it? This poor land, we broke our backs removing the stones from the field, wasn't even a field before. They left, packed like logs on a vessel, and we never did know if they made it. Not all did, the emigration ships; some sunk and on others the Gaels became sick with cholera and typhus, from being crammed in without enough food, fresh water, barely enough air to breathe.

Da said maybe we could move to a new settlement beside the sea, where they can't graze the sheep, as was rumored we'd be replaced with. Ma said that's a dotty idea; try to feed a family of nine on nothing but fish and limpets, then the factor comes and insists the laird wants half? They bickered over it, Da saying he'd at least like to give it a try, and she said it would be better to send the eldest off—Charles, Abigail, and Maggie—fewer mouths to feed, time for them to find their own situations. This land will starve us yet! said she. Poor Ma, how strong she had to be, slaving away her youth on the croft, wee lasses and lads tugging at her skirt, mouths open, bellies howling.

One evening when Da had too much whiskey inside him, he became all lovey and sad-eyed, told Ma he'd give her a sealskin coat if he could, trap it and skin it and sew it up himself. Ma said don't be daft, that Da knew what the fishermen said, how wearing red was bad luck, but wearing sealskin, that was the worst luck of all. Why so? asked one of the lassies. Aye, because she'll come looking for it, silly! said Ma.

There's a story Da used to tell about the Roanes, majestic seals that were also part human, who lived in a fine palace under the sea. Swam in the ocean as seals, walked the land as folk. Clever and beautiful, they willed you to fall in love with them, then swam you down to their palace, to your marriage bed where there was no breath.

I didn't want a seal for a husband, handsome as they were, the gray and brown ones sunning on our rocky shores, their heads popping up in the waves as they swam about. Though there was something human about them, I saw it even then, such soulfulness in their eyes. I wanted to be with a boy. Wasn't quite sure what for, someone to yell at? Like with Ma and Da, when the food grew scarcer, our stomachs with knives in them, those slashing pains of hunger—and they'd shout at each other over it? My idea of marriage was snuggling, someone to keep you warm at night when the wild winds howled, a softer bed than the thatch we slept on—tangles of moor plants, heather dried up and beat and sewn together, with a wool sheet tucked over it; and warmer than what you'd get with the iron on the fire for a spell, wrapped in a cloth, then placed in bed to warm our feet, the three of us lasses that slept in one, arguing who's turn it was to be closest to it. I liked to imagine warmer feet than an iron on mine—big ones, and softer too.

Dear Diary, I'd scribe in my mind, paper and the talent to use it being uncommon on the croft, but I knew about diaries from Ma, who saw one at our cousin's house in Glasgow. With a sheepskin cover, she said, dyed red! Then I'd imagine some boy sitting with me on the edge of the cliff where Abigail and I perched sometimes after a long trek to Uig, purchasing textiles for Ma at the ferry dock, tweed from Harris most often. There we'd sit, staring toward the outer Hebrides, and I'd imagine what was beyond their shadowy borders: continents, countries with cities, what little I knew of these, the lives I might have there, people I'd know, dresses I'd wear, fancy bonnets instead of the plain white mutch the croft women wore. I wouldn't even know what he looked like, this boy I'd pretend beside me, because the boys from the croft were dense as sand. We lived in Suisnish, and sometimes we'd walk over the moor, along Loch Eishort to the neighboring Boreraig, but the boys were no better there, thick-legged crofter sons and thick of skull too. This is the advantage of a diary in your mind. Blink your eyes and the book is shut.

Across from where we lived was the Sleat Peninsula, lush, almost a tropical forest in comparison to the rest of the island, which, though green from all the wet, was mostly moor, and barren of forest save but a few copses. Lord MacDonald's home was on Sleat, and he was the laird who owned ours, the one who'd force us to leave. A hard land it was, our settlement back from a cliff that overlooked the loch, on down to the stone beach at low tide; otherwise, the waves—how they'd pound, spray blowing up like smoke. The ground was mostly poor for planting, rocky fields, boggy moors, but the peat from the moors kept us warm, and when it didn't, when the land no longer produced enough food for our bellies, still the laird's factor would up the rent, for this and that, until he stopped giving Da any reason at all.

Skye, land of red rock, the Cuillin hills rising like ghosts through the fog, monsters, their steep ridges and peaks like gigantic scales, deep green in the summer, snow covered the rest, great forked tongues when the mists weren't obscuring them. Even the rain had color, silver slashes of it, slicing like needles. Flowers in the spring, bluebells and buttercups, and the heather, a great purple swath of it in the summer over the moors, as though the moors were one big bruise. I'd lie in it sometimes and pretend I was on a purple cloud floating away.

★   ★   ★

Sheep are more profitable. We can sell their wool, lamb, mutton from the old, said the factor when he gave Da his first warning; you can use every part of a sheep.

Then how we supposed to eat? Da said. This after the blight ravaged our potato crop, nothing but oat porridge most mornings and night, bones if we're lucky, thrown into our broth for protein.

The laird wants what's his, said the factor. I was peeking out from our room beside Abigail, the wee ones behind us, and Charles beside Da, his place as first-born son. He avoided Da's naked eyes, pleading they were, what his pride could not allow his mouth to utter; instead, Charles stared at Ma's boots, tied up with twine, laced tight as she could to keep the cold and wet out where the holes be.

Aye, muttered Ma, by our hands and our backs this *grazing* land was made, nothing but rock and stone and bog before.

The factor stared at Da, deliberately ignoring Ma like she's an insect, a small whining annoyance. We'll be back next time to force you out, if you're not gone before, he said. Abigail and I moved from our room then and stood behind Ma, as was expected of lasses, our visitor leaving (though hardly a guest!). Charles was frozen—not even his mouth twitched—waiting for a signal from Da. I could feel Ma's anger gather, the way she stood straight up and bristled, exhaling a slow burning steam.

I'll kill him when he comes, slaughter him myself! she hissed, when the factor was gone. Cook him up, provide meat for a fortnight that greedy, overfed gut of his.

You'll do no such thing, said Da. You heard how bad those that fought got it, old Mary MacLeod choked by the strings of her mutch down in Boreraig when she was refusing to leave. We're next. He sighed, sat cross-legged on the floor by the peat fire, and said nary a word throughout our meager supper. Broth, no bones and but a quarter oatcake each. The wee lassie was crying over it, the pain in her belly, but we elders knew better. Tears could not squelch hunger.

As history will come to show it, The Clearances of our two villages, Boreraig and Suisnish, was in several stages—the ones who went first, burnt out they were, and then those that stayed until the bitter end, 1853, when the rest was destroyed. They came in the dead of winter, when the men were on the mainland trying to make a bit of money, threw the women and children out into the cold where many of them died, having no food or shelter, before their men could make it back, discovering they had no homes to return to.

Ma argued, nagged, pleaded, went rigid with rage, until Da finally agreed to it: Charles, Abigail, and I would go forth. Word was that the Hathaway Shirt Factory in America was hiring; in Maine, Charles told us, though we knew not what that meant. Ma nodded like she knew, and Da scowled as if he knew more and it was not to his liking.

Once there I'll secure situations for Abigail and Margaret, Charles said, using my adult name that no one spoke, but I suppose it was fitting because once a lass leaves her family for a situation, she is on her own. They're good seamstresses both, he said. And that wasn't true, only Abigail. I had always preferred the field and the sea, harvesting where needed, fishing or shelling, picking limpets, even pounding the wash over rocks in the stream—anything but the loom, the cloth, and the needle.

"Best get any notions of anything else out of your head," Ma would say, thrusting a wee one's woolens into my hands to darn. This is the life you're born into, 'tis the only one you've got." But that turned out to not be so.

PART II

WINTER

◆ HEAVEN ◆

GRANDMELIA HAS AN ARSENAL in her bathroom, a full-on war against *old*, her weapons lined up on the updated vanity—updated she tells Heaven, to reflect her current aesthetic of space, light, and emptiness. Grandmelia is all about the current aesthetic. Eye shadows in the greens and purple palette, eyeliners, eyebrow pencils, mascara, false eyelashes "for when you need to bring out the guns," Grandmelia tells her, face makeup, which used to be called *pancake*, she says and Heaven pictures globs of sticky beige frying in a pan, powders for a blushed look—"never get an *actual* tan," Grandmelia warns, "tanning ages the skin, plus you'll get skin cancer"—and lipsticks in a spectrum of reds and violets, a hint of mauve. "Ruddy-toned Scots must never wear orange or pink," Grandmelia says, "and avoid yellow like the plague, yellow makes Scots look dead."

She's yanked Heaven into her bathroom to punish her, Heaven figures, for asking Grandmelia *yet again* to buy her a smartphone. Grandmelia said Heaven should consider herself fortunate to have a *dumb* phone.

"When I was your age, do you think I had a phone beyond the one on the kitchen counter where everyone and their brother could listen in on your calls?"

"A *dial-up*?" scoffed Heaven.

"You dialed it," said Grandmelia.

"But the kids at school tease me because I can't get on Facebook or Snapchat with my phone! They write bad things about me."

"Let them. If you can't see it, it can't hurt you. Don't you think you have enough problems in your own backyard, let alone take on the World Wide Web, missy? Pedophiles haunt the internet for young girls like you. They lurk. Instead of playgrounds, they have chat rooms. Besides, you could get bullied."

"I'm already being bullied! Like maybe *because* I have a lame phone and can't get *on* the internet," Heaven whined, "all the other kids have better ones."

"If all the other kids had chicken pox, would you want that too? You're lucky to have a phone at all. You think poor children in India have them? Somali *refugees*?"

So the conversation went, the way it *always* went. No smartphone for Heaven.

In her giant glass cabinet there are rows of shelves with face creams that read like a supermarket ad: vegetables and fruits for antioxidants, fat from yaks, cartilage from sharks to spread under Grandmelia's eyes and plump up her cheeks, wrinkle-blasting serums and capsules of vitamin E to break open and sabotage those fine lines around the mouth, Grandmelia explains. Heaven would be wise to take heed, she tells her. "Frowning creates the *ugliest* lines, though you won't get off much with a smile either. Life is a procession of lines. The more time you're blessed with, the more track marks cross your face." Grandmelia leans down until she's eye to eye with Heaven. "You see?" She points to her chin. "A map of my years."

"Here's the truth about growing older," Grandmelia says, glaring at Heaven, who figured she may as well sit if she has to listen to this stuff, and had plunked her butt down on the vanity. "I don't know what manners are like where you are from, but in Massachusetts we do not sit on tabletops," Grandmelia says, nodding as Heaven slouches back up on her feet. *Gawd,* Heaven thinks, if only she had her iPod in her pocket, and maybe one of those Bluetooths she could stick in her ear so Grandmelia wouldn't know she's listening to Miley Cyrus, her fave. If only she had Miley's hair!

"Heaven, are you paying attention? Hear me out now. You're young so you believe you're invincible, your future an expressway, think you have your whole life to exit and reenter wherever you please. In ten years you'll come into your own, and maybe that's when you get your bloody smartphone! Fifteen, you peak—your skin, eyes, hair, will never be so lustrous again. A few years later you'll begin to wonder if you've been targeted: everything that was you suddenly seems lessened, rubbed out, eventually erased, and before you know it, you're the only one who's looking. What will that phone mean then, I wonder. You hear me, missy? I did fine, for a time. After the modeling ended, we had enough to live on. My grandfather was a frugal Scot, and I learned how to invest and save from him. But it was done in the blink of an eye; they weren't knocking on the door with any more offers. One day, mark my words, you'll walk by your mirror and you won't recognize the person passing through."

"You don't look *that* old," Heaven says politely, because Grandmelia's nailing her with those lion eyes she gets when Heaven's expected to say something *appropriate*, like she'll pounce if Heaven doesn't beat her to it. What does she know about old people? Her dad never made it to old, and last she saw, her mom still rocked her jeans and a flannel shirt.

"There are *processes*," Grandmelia explains, scheduled appointments for her hair to be cut and dyed every four weeks. "Rule of thumb, as long as your eyebrows aren't white beyond what can be plucked and disguised under an eyebrow pencil, you can continue to dye your hair. It's a cruel act of nature that strips away a woman's hair color after letting her get used to it for forty years. Nature is malleable," she tells Heaven, "like most things subject to influence." Grandmelia is all about defying nature.

Restylane shots for her chin folds every six months, plump up that *gravitational slide*, Grandmelia calls it; legs, underarms waxed at the spa (where they also zap the occasional mustache hair, Heaven figures; she saw Grandmelia going at one once with a pair of tweezers like she was about to yank out a tick); Pilates where Grandmelia practices her cervix pulls to keep "down there" in place; a personal trainer at the Fitness Center once a week to modify her arm weights, keep that arm flab off—otherwise, she takes spin classes. (Heaven imagined Grandmelia twirling like a top until she got dizzy and fell, was disappointed to find out it's a kind of bicycle, and not even one you ride outside!).

She will occasionally do water aerobics in her pool, but that's not kind to the hair or the skin, Grandmelia tells her, frowning at Heaven's daily immersions, she calls them, Heaven plugging her nose and settling down on the bottom of the pool, hair floating out like Medusa, before shooting up to the surface, gasping for air. Uncle Daniel told her the story of Medusa, whose hair was a nest of snakes, and if you looked into her eyes, she could turn you to stone. That could be useful; she'll practice on Grandmelia.

Grandmelia tells Heaven she became so used to men crushing on her back in the days of being an *almost* supermodel—she was an inch too short at five-feet-ten, when the rage was the Russian Veruschka, a stunner at six-three—that she wasn't aware when it stopped. Oh sure she still gets *looks* these days, but mostly they're old men who'd woo you for your nursing skills. Was it all at once? One day her periods stop, pheromones disappear, and that's it? Or a slow shedding like sloughing off old skin. Her skin, once so beautiful despite its Scottish tendency to freckle. "Which is why," Grandmelia says, pushing a bottle of sunscreen into Heaven's hand, "you must use this if you insist on those daily immersions. You aren't starting with all the plusses I had; you clearly don't take after your dad with his delicate bone structure, so you must learn to protect what you do have and use it to its full advantage. Like most plump people you have nice skin. Plumping saves the face from that sallow quality thin people can get."

Grandmelia picks through her arsenal for products appropriate to Heaven's age, skin, and hair color. "I'm going to teach you how to use makeup. Sit down," she commands, "and *not* on my vanity," pointing to the salmon-colored leather stool in front of the giant mirror stretching from one side of her bathroom to the other, built in over the matching vanity. Heaven does, reluctantly. This could get nasty, she thinks, eyeing the products Grandmelia has lined up in front of her. The color of the walls also match the salmon of the stool and the vanity, and Heaven tries to concentrate on that instead of looking at herself in the mirror. "This color reminds me of fish," she says.

Grandmelia shakes her head. "Are you thinking of your next meal already?"

Heaven scowls. "I don't even like fish."

Grandmelia sighs, and for a moment instead of staring at Heaven she's gazing at herself in the mirror; like she's a little sad, Heaven thinks, which makes Heaven even more uncomfortable. She surreptitiously rubs the tops of her chlorine-itchy legs under the vanity (if Grandmelia sees her she'll make Heaven slather Vaseline on them) and peers down at the floor, but then Grandmelia grips Heaven's chin, forcing her to look up.

"Look child, I never had a daughter. I'm not complaining, mind you, just stating. I wanted to do something I might've done with a daughter, something we could do together, you and me. Makeup is something I happen to be very good at. So let's concentrate here, shall we? Good makeup skills will serve you all your life. The first step is a decent moisturizer, how moist depends on your skin type and I suspect yours is oily—most young girls have oilier skin—dryness comes with age. Of course, you're about to enter your pimple years and that's the downside of greasy skin. Next you apply foundation. Watch," she says, squirting a dime-size glob of something beige and gluey into Heaven's open hand, then using Heaven's other hand like she's Grandmelia's puppet to dab and spread it on her skin with circular motions across her face.

"You do have nice eyes," Grandmelia says. "Those come from my family—Scottish blues and greens. Nicely made-up eyes detract from pudgy cheeks. To highlight those we use a tad of purple eye-shadow, then slash a bit of blush underneath, make it look like there's actual cheekbones. A hint of rosy lip gloss for the finish—you have thin lips, and this will create a fuller illusion. Some say you can't trust thin-lipped people."

Heaven shrugs. Her mom's lips are thin, she supposes. Her dad's were like a rosebud, her mom said, always about to open.

"Voilà! We don't want to overdo makeup in the seventh grade, so we'll save the mascara and eyeliner for another time. What do you think of the new you?"

Heaven studies herself in the mirror along with Grandmelia, who has crouched down beside her. Grandmelia's face is long and gaunt, and Heaven's squat and squished looking; Grandmelia's hair is red like bricks, and Heaven's the color of mud. It's in the eyes that Heaven sees it. Their eyes are the same color: blue-green with a sweep of purple shadow on the lids. But it's not that so much; it's something in them, an expression—Heaven wouldn't call it fierce exactly, but not boring either like Bethany's basic blues. It's a look that gets her in trouble, a way of working the world, her dad called it. It's in Grandmelia's eyes too, and she wonders if Grandmelia notices, because she suddenly stands up, exits the bathroom, and Heaven is left staring at herself under all that makeup. She looks like a mime or a doll from a horror movie, but maybe this could be a useful look at school. She'll have to wait and see.

♦ AMELIA ♦

YESTERDAY AMELIA WAS SUPPOSED to have her ten-year colonoscopy, but the doctor was one of those condescending types—technicians with attitude, Leo called them. She's trying to tell him how she doesn't feel like she used to, and he's spouting off colon cancer statistics, regaling her with a PowerPoint of colons *compromised*, he emphasized, with malignancy. So she left, her colon untouched as the rest of her these days, sexuality gone dormant, not extinct but not exactly smoldering either. Now, after driving several hours, she feels that slow burn in her gut. Fishes around in her purse for a Tums.

Her granddaughter pouts in the backseat, having been told there's nothing to snack on but granola bars, and those are for lunch—which isn't at ten thirty in the morning, Amelia added. "Somewhere in the world I bet they eat at ten-thirty," Heaven whined. "Not in *my* world," said Amelia. Now Heaven's plugged into her iPod, earbuds stuck in her ears. They're trapped in the weekend traffic heading north to Maine, even under a bleak February sky, Massachusetts escapees ("Massholes" the Mainers call them). Amelia's annoyed that she has to do this in the first place, ferry this sullen girl for her once-a-month, court-ordered visit to her mother, Amelia's incarcerated daughter-in-law.

"Ahoy there in the backseat!" Amelia barks. Heaven scowls. The stink of too many cars on this highway seeps in through the vents as they idle, and she flips the heat on high, making sure the outside vents are shut tight. "Just checking for life," she says.

"I'm alive, *whoop-de-do*," Heaven says, imitating Amelia when she says it.

"You know missy, you wouldn't even *be* alive if it weren't for me, my genetics. I made your father, then he made you; you bear my history in your genes. So a little appreciation, maybe, once in a while? Some respect?"

Her granddaughter rolls her eyes. "My dad said we're making *new* history."

Heaven's *dad*, the sensation that comes over Amelia sometimes when she thinks about Gavin, almost like he's here with her for a moment, a slight breeze, stirring of the air, then gone, Amelia stuck in traffic, a belligerent granddaughter in the backseat. Of course, when she thinks of *Heaven's* dad, sometimes she just can't help but think of Gavin's dad, his *real* dad. And this traffic, *God*, irritating yes, but not even close to L.A.'s.

Amelia and Leo, roaring up the 105 in a rented Mustang, late for a shoot, LAX to CBS, Amelia, the new model for the Egg Me! brand of diet products, and Leo had been hired for the stills. They'd flown in from New York and the plane was late. She'd worked with him once before, pretty decent for a fashion photographer in what was then a predatory industry, maybe still is, though these days models seem a bit "edgier." In Amelia's day, models were glorified clothes hangers, and most of the fashion photographers were either gay and arrogant, or speed-toxed predators, entitled to whatever they figured was theirs. You hoped for gay.

Leo kept a polite, professional distance that came with being genuinely good. They'd been in a hurry to get to Studio A for the stills shot prior to the commercial, and if they were late, the commercial would lose its place in the lineup. As the traffic suddenly lurched to a hard stop, he thrust his arm across Amelia's chest so she wouldn't hit the dashboard, an intimate, protective gesture. There wasn't much in her that needed protection in those days (that hasn't changed!), yet this gesture and similar moments of concern for her, in the weeks that followed when they started dating, had seemed so natural and unassuming, caring in ways lacking in her usual dating repertoire of New York narcissists—writers, club musicians, ad men, would-be actors if they had any talent—that she ended up marrying him. Better nail him, a model-friend advised; his species is going extinct.

Within months of their wedding Amelia became the face of Egg Me!, the egg diet that was the Atkins of its time. Commercials with celeb fatties, disk jockeys, comedians—even one of Jackie Gleason, standing beside her on a scale: Eat Egg Me! and you'll look like her, not them! *Egg Me!* she'd chant in her seductive voice, as seductive as you can be about eggs anyway. Eggs, the *perfect* food, Haley Long, the diet guru quipped, his bleached-teeth grin, trim as a whip. Eggluscious desserts, eggy lasagna, egg-fu-me-and-egg-fu-you, egg patties on the grill, even packages of crumbled hard-boiled yolk in lieu of blue cheese: eggs, virtuous, nutritious, low-calorie and delicious, an *American* food.

She quit the New York modeling world at Haley's behest and a lucrative contract, Egg Me's! exclusive rights to her career. Leo transitioned into photographing bands (they were required to live in L.A. for the Egg Me! gig, its commercials, and the *Egg Me! Morning Diet Show* on CBS; fashion was New York, L.A. had TV and acid rock). He became a sort of jack of all trades on the music scene when he wasn't behind the camera—he could play a decent, though not exceptional, bass guitar; he could sing decently, though not exceptionally; he could handle percussions; he could handle sound equipment and lighting given his knowledge about cameras, and while Amelia was busy making money for Egg Me!, Leo had become, in addition to photographing bands, a sort of backup man for them, which seemed to Amelia an uncomfortable metaphor, and she grew to resent this in him, that after a reputation as a sought-after photographer he could settle for a behind-the-scenes life. After they had Daniel and it was mainly Amelia's money from

Egg Me! supporting their family, she got mean about it (she'll admit this now, though maybe not to Leo), claimed everything they owned was because of her. Leo said he'd never wanted to own anything anyway.

So they fought, and on the night Leo had a gig for *Rolling Stone*, photographing The Doors in Fillmore West, Amelia, who'd flown up to San Francisco with him, leaving Daniel with a babysitter, made her own little private venture. After too many shots of Remy Martin and God knows what else smoked, snorted, licked, passed around the band room on a Melmac platter like a snack plate, while Leo shot photos in the auditorium she slept with Johnny Keg, lead guitarist for Leaping Lizards (named after a neon-green LSD tab all the rage those days), opening for The Doors. She had slipped backstage while Jim Morrison was doing what he did, lewd, brilliant, their extra-long sets. Enough time to get pregnant with Gavin, who inherited his father's fabulous face and, alas, his appetite for drugs.

Why did she do it? Amelia's asked herself this over the years. Too much Remy? Annoyed with Leo? Because she could? Because sexy, almost-famous men wanted her? But what made her need to prove it with *this* one?

Four months to the night, Amelia, whose periods had never been regular, realized she hadn't had one in a while, along with what she'd assumed was an aggravating "bloat," causing her to one-up her pants size. Within weeks she was shopping for a new wardrobe at Motherhood. She had to confess, too late to consider an abortion, she'd felt its flutters in her womb. "You betrayed me for *vanity*?" Leo said. He hadn't slept with her during the month of conception; they'd been in one of their wars.

Nine years later when Leo and Amelia divorced, it was Amelia paying alimony to Leo—"shut-up money," Leo called it, the only person besides Amelia to know whose son Gavin really was; which bought Leo an even bigger dream than a backup life, a reclusive life where he retired to the Augusta, Maine, duplex his parents left, pursuing the kind of photography he wanted to do, the kind that doesn't pay. He never stopped being a dad to Gavin despite the betrayal of the genes, and part of the shut-up clause was that neither of them would mention to Gavin who his chromosomes provider was: Johnny Keg, whose psychedelic aesthetic refused to adapt to the disco trend and who eventually disappeared, surfacing in a Skid Row motel room a decade later, dead from an OD. It was Leo that Gavin came to for money when he needed it, and Leo who ended up financing two drug habits rather than see Gavin and his wife reduced to junkies on the street. Or so he said.

❖ HEAVEN ❖

Visitors Rules of Conduct

#1 Visitors must dress appropriately: Clothes should be clean and modest, men wear shirts with collars, long pants, women wear long pants or skirts. No outerwear jackets, no hats (exceptions: hijabs, headwear for the elderly, and chemotherapy scarves.) No tank tops, no tight or low-cut tops, no overly tight pants, no shorts, no skirts above the knees, no flip-flops, no hoodies, no sweatshirts with metal zippers, no T-shirts with provocative messages, no extra-long sleeves that cover hands, no gloves.
Hands must be visible (not under the table) at all times.
#2 No ornamentation: No piercings, no jewelry (wedding or engagement rings exempt but will be inventoried at Entrance desk), no hair ornaments or hairpins. Tape over any visible tattoos.
#3 No touching . . .

THINGS HEAVEN HATES ABOUT this boring ride to Maine:

1. Grandmelia behind the wheel, spouting "Look at this! That! Here! There"—trying to get Heaven attendant to the world, she says, instead of *addicted* for lord's sake to her iPod. "You have addiction in your blood," Grandmelia said, "so you should work on fostering *good* habits." Heaven keeps her earbuds in even when the iPod's turned off, so Grandmelia thinks Heaven can't hear her.

2. The traffic, because that makes the whole *ordeal*, Grandmelia calls it, even longer. *Gawd,* she screams in her head, imitating the way Grandmelia says it.

3. Worrying about her mom as they cross over the big green bridge into Maine, with even more traffic chugging up the highway, until they cut off to another highway and then down to the coast, where it's one lane crawling through a bunch of little towns, more bridges, rivers, ocean, the s-l-o-w torture getting closer and closer, *slowly,* to Rock Harbor, the prison where her mom is.

4. What will she say to her this time? No doubt Grandmelia will rat on her, tell her mom how Heaven has to go to detention every day for a week after snipping off a lock of Bethany Harrison's hair. Just a small piece, and with nail scissors for Christmas sake (Grandmelia makes her say that instead of Christ, which Uncle Daniel says has a more satisfying ring: "Christmas is a construct, babe in a manger meets pagan solstice," he said, "*Christ* is the heart and guts"). Math class, boring, boring, b-o-r-i-n-g *Christmas* crap, and it's just dangling there from the seat in front of her, hair the color of Buttercrunch, plus earlier Bethany called her a loser. Lose *this*! she whispered. Just a snip, a wave of blond, and Bethany wouldn't even have noticed, only Robyn—the boy who sits next to her, whom Heaven likes because the other kids tease him too— weird-boy they call him and *faggot* since he wears a girl's skirt, sometimes with lacy socks—Robyn saw and snickered. Which made Brittany, Bethany's friend (the "B-girls" Uncle Daniel called them when she told him about them, Bethany, Brittany, and Brianna—bitches all) look over. She's the one who told on

Heaven, her hand waving like it's the *Christ* American flag. Robyn told Heaven he changed the spelling of his name from Robin with an "i" to a "y" because it's more *aesthetic*. He just shrugs when the others tease him, doesn't give a rat's turd, he says.

5. What if they catch on fire in this steamy sucky traffic— Grandmelia, the car, Heaven in the back where she can't get to water? If she could get out of this car and into that ocean it would save her. Water puts out fire. Water rules.

Grandmelia jerks monster car into a sharp right turn, and there it is: Rock Harbor Women's Correctional, RHWC, the red brick giant on the hill opposite the other red giant on the other hill, separated by a moat off Penobscot Bay. The men's is RHAC, Rock Harbor *Adult* Correctional. "Are women not adults?" Grandmelia snarks, pointing at the sign, and Heaven starts to answer but her grandmother says she meant it *rhetorically*.

"*Shit,*" Heaven whispers under her breath as they step out of the car and Grandmelia locks it, beeping the horn for good measure to confirm it's locked, then motions Heaven to follow her.

Once inside Grandmelia surrenders her purse to a guard at the Entrance desk, Heaven gives him her backpack, and they walk through a metal detector, Heaven first, then Grandmelia, who sets it off. She's patted down by a short, unsmiling, uniformed woman standing sentry beside a barred electric gate, who then makes Grandmelia undo her French twist. "Bobby pins, sharp metal objects," the guard says.

Grandmelia snaps, "Ridiculous!"

The guard points at the Rules chart on the wall behind the Entrance desk. "No hairpins. You take them out or you don't go in, no skin off my back."

Grandmelia mutters under her breath about harassment and fascists and how she shouldn't have to be in such a place, subjected to such indignities, nothing in her life has prepared her for *this*; then they are led with the other visitors in single file, through the barred electric gate that clangs shut after them, down a narrow brick hall into the entrance of the visiting room, where they are told to stand in line until called. Their names are checked off one by one, then they walk through another electric gate, *clang*, and the corresponding inmate is ushered in through a gate on the other side of the room.

Grandmelia and Heaven are told to sit opposite Heaven's mom, at a table that looks like a school desk, one of about twenty such tables, making the room look like a classroom, Heaven thinks, a butt-ugly one with nothing but Rules charts taped to brick walls the color of a bloodstain. Her mom has her head down, her long cinnamon-colored hair hanging down over her face like a curtain. She lifts her head when they are seated, and pushing her hair back with a pale hand dangling from a wrist the size of a toilet paper tube, Cassie smiles blandly at Heaven, avoiding Grandmelia's sour face.

Good move, Mom, Heaven thinks. She's having a hard time with the word because lately she's more about the mom who lives in her daydreams than the one in this place. The mom that lives in her daydreams has a better life, for one. The one in this place looks tired and sad. In one of the few conversations she remembers having with her mom, her mom making pancakes—a good day until they burned and she hurled them along with the pan into the trash—Heaven asked her if she missed her dead mother, and her mom said it wasn't too bad because she could still be alive in her memory. "I can imagine her with us now," she said. "Although"— and her eyes went flat—"she wouldn't like the way I live. She'd like you though," her mom said, and smiled, patted Heaven's head, and that's when the pancakes burned.

Now Grandmelia tells this mom she should hold Heaven's hand, and they both make a face at Grandmelia. "We aren't allowed," Cassie says, "no touching—see the Rules chart on the wall?"

"Well that's just ridiculous," Grandmelia says, "a mother should be able to hold her own child's hand."

"It's okay," Heaven offers, "I have chocolate on my fingers from the granola bars we ate." Instead of stopping for a real lunch! Heaven would like to add, but they already went over *that territory* in the car, Heaven's stomach growling. "Always hungry," Grandmelia

said. "Learn to satisfy your cravings with foods that don't add calo-
ries and excess flesh. Carrots, for one." The mom stares at her own
hands, which Heaven notices look small and nervous, the way her
fingers keep jumping and fiddling around with each other like they
live lives apart from the mom they're attached to.

Grandmelia signals one of the guards, a woman with spikes of
silver hair poking out of her scalp like a wire brush, who saunters
over, no hurry to get to them. "A mother should be able to hold
her daughter's hand," Grandmelia says.

The guard shrugs. "So who's stopping her? You read the small
print on number three? *Except* in the case of biological children
under eighteen."

"Well for crying out loud, you'd think the signage would be in
a size someone could see! And what if they're adopted?"

The guard frowns, "What do you mean?" Then she asks
Grandmelia if Heaven is adopted.

"Oh for God's sake, no, she isn't adopted." Grandmelia glares
at Heaven's mom, who takes Heaven's hand limply in hers, gives it
a quick shake then releases it.

"Were you two just introduced?" Grandmelia snarks.

Cassie picks up Heaven's hand again, then briefly places her
other hand around it like she's palming a softball. Her hands feel
clammy.

"I've got chocolate fingers," Heaven warns. Will this mom
think she's gross?

"Could be I've got a cold," this mom says, sniffing.

"Confess!" Grandmelia hisses, leaning toward Cassie's left ear,
but Heaven can still hear her. "For real this time. A civil suit, you
tell the truth. You won't get more time, it's not about that. It's
about coming clean. Make an honest woman out of you."

"I'm honest *and* clean. I'm also in prison. Or didn't you notice?"

Grandmelia goes quiet for a moment and stares at Heaven's
mom. She scowls, tapping her burgundy-painted fingernails against
the table. "Well, what do *you* think, Heaven—did you happen to
notice your mother is in prison?"

Heaven looks around the room, avoiding Grandmelia's eyes and the mom's eyes, at the other prisoners in their beige jumpsuits (Grandmelia said never wear beige from the waist up or you'll blend into the walls, that it's suitable only for pants or a trench coat offset by a colorful scarf). Their visitors are mostly older women, moms or maybe grandmas, a few kids younger than Heaven, and some men, all sitting opposite their prisoners. Then she looks at the guards, the brush-haired lady and a really skinny man who could pass for a mop handle, also in beige, but theirs is a less ugly beige, more tan, with patches on their sleeves and a pocket insignia that says "Rock Harbor Correctional" on it. She wonders if they're packing guns, or maybe Tasers. She looks at the two entrances to the room, the one they went through and the one the prisoners were led through, floor-to-ceiling metal gates that buzz open from some remote system. "Those gates keep the inmates locked in and everyone else out unless they're on the visitors list," Grandmelia had explained last month when they came here. "What if someone has a panic attack or they're claustrophobic like Uncle Daniel?" Heaven asked. "Now there's an incentive to keep your nose clean and not go to prison!" Grandmelia snarked.

Is this mom claustrophobic? Heaven peers at her now, her flat eyes focused into the distance above Heaven's head. Imagines her pounding her fist against the brick wall, *"Let me out, let me out!"* Which is your garden-variety claustrophobia, Uncle Daniel said, but he never goes outside. Grandmelia said Uncle Daniel is more agoraphobic than claustrophobic, afraid of the whole damn world, she said. Said he'd prefer getting stuck in an elevator to wandering through a busy supermarket like a normal person. Anyway, the mom in her daydreams isn't claustrophobic, Heaven can make sure of that. It's like she can be a god with the mom in her daydreams: *Here ye! You're the most beautiful, sweetest, best mom ever, you love me more than anything* and *you're not claustrophobic.*

A sudden whiff of something beefy drifts into the room through the metal gate, and her stomach growls, loud enough to make the mop-handle guard look over. Both Grandmelia and the mom stare at her. "That child is always hungry," Grandmelia says.

Cassie shrugs, looks sad, or tired, or both, smiles thinly at Heaven. "Maybe hunger isn't the worst thing," she says.

Heaven nods. She tries to look humble like any of this means anything at all, but she's smelling those dinner smells, and what she really wants right now is to go home. But even going home is confusing. She should be able to take her mom's hand, even though they hadn't held hands for a very long time—the moment earlier with granola bar chocolate on Heaven's fingers didn't count—but it's her mom who should be taking Heaven home. If this is her *real* mom, how could she end up in a place like this?

⋆ DANIEL ⋆

Fᴵʀꜱᴛ ᴀʙᴀɴᴅᴏɴᴍᴇɴᴛ ᴅʀᴇᴀᴍ, ᴅᴀɴɪᴇʟ eight, his brother four. For all he knew his parents were in love, that this is what love looked like, two parents and a home in Silver Lake. Amelia supported them (she reminded them of this daily) and Leo, who'd eighty-sixed the rock-star photo biz after Gavin was born, took pictures of food. He'd arrange various cold cuts, knockwurst, wedges of cheese, bunches of grapes, and hot dogs in an aesthetically pleasing, saleable shot for Oscar Mayer, and then do something goofy like stick a shirtless baby doll in the middle of it all, its rubber belly lurching over its diapers, a plastic bottle stuck inside the hole of its mouth. His dad wasn't getting a lot of callbacks. "Want to make me suffer? Fine, hit me," Amelia said, "but let's not starve our kids."

Back to the abandonment dream. Amelia and Leo were hosting a dinner party with Haley Long, the Egg Me! guru, his wife of that year, and a few others from the franchise. Right before the guests showed up, Amelia, her breath already reeking of gin, had taken Daniel aside and told him how he was responsible for Gavin. "Not just tonight," she said—though Amelia insisted Daniel keep the two of them out of her hair until bedtime—but as the older brother it was his duty to make sure his little brother was safe. "Birth order obligation," she said. "Gavin's a pretty boy and prettiness isn't always a blessing. People will resent it and maybe even bully him for it; that's where you step in, his protector. You're solid, dear," she had said, running her hand through Daniel's hair. "You're granite and Gavin's our lovely fragile opal."

An hour past their bedtime, Daniel finally got his brother into bed, cajoling him, threatening him, then offering his Incredible Hulk action figure if Gavin would *shut up* so their mom wouldn't come storming in, Gavin squealing, "Yeah! yeah! yeah!" jumping on his bed. Daniel fell asleep to shrieks of laughter and delicious food smells from the dining room; the boys were fed Salisbury steak TV dinners before the guests arrived. Gavin stole his brownie, so Daniel had to make peace with the runny applesauce for dessert.

The dream began with these good scents, tinkling sounds, Daniel holding Gavin's hand and the two of them in their pajamas, walking outside into a lush green meadow (couldn't be where they lived, not many meadows in L.A., and the ones in the hills or in Griffith Park had scrubbier, desert-like vegetation). Night fell and suddenly the deep green opened like a mouth, sucking Gavin in. Daniel could feel the pull on his hand as he tried to hold onto his little brother, yelling to his parents to come help as the green vortex whirled Gavin away from him. Daniel woke up in a panic to laughter from his parents' party, and cried for them. No one came. He looked over and saw his brother was asleep, but what bothered Daniel was how his hand hurt from trying to hold onto Gavin in the dream, and how when nobody came to help, he's pretty sure he was the one who let go, not so much for the pain, but because of the fear he would be next, sucked into that long green grass, waving, shaking, chattering like teeth. That in fact Daniel would not protect his little brother if it meant he too would be lost.

★ ★ ★

Four years later, just days after Daniel's twelfth birthday, this was put to the test when the boys accompanied Amelia sans Leo to

Hawaii for an Egg Me! tropical shoot. It was to be at the new Kuilima Resort on the north shore of O'ahu, and on the day *it* happened Amelia was doing a commercial for Egg Me's! new line of powdered guava and papaya smoothies and lilikoi breakfast shakes. *How to diet like they do in the islands from the comfort of your own home. Egg Me! takes you there by combining scrumptious native fruits with eggs, dried and powdered for their pure goodness; add skim milk, shake it up real good, and you have yourself a low-calorie, high-protein, oh-so-tasty in the convenience of an eight-ounce-glass meal.* Cut to Haley Long's emery board of a body, his spidery fingers caressing the boxes of powdered drinks in a variety of *scintillating* tropical flavors, yum or *ono*-good as they say in Hawaii. Amelia in a bikini top and a hibiscus-print sarong, standing on the trademark scales placed on the sparkling white sands (swept of all beach debris, coral, shells, seaweed, moments before). *Egg Me!* she'd cry, to the accompaniment of *real* Hawaiian surf and a beach boy strumming his ukulele.

The original plan had been for the boys to visit their cousins who lived in Kaneohe on the day of the shoot, but when that fell through—one of the cousins had the flu—Haley selected from his entourage of *personal assistants* a teenage girl, daughter of his hairstylist, to take care of Amelia's kids. The hotel suggested Goat Island, off Malaekahana and Laie, a mostly flat, rocky slab with a white sand beach and wind-brushed trails. "At low tide you can walk out to the island and collect shells, but make sure you get back to the beach before the tide comes in," the concierge warned.

Her name was Martine, and Daniel remembers thinking she was the prettiest girl he'd ever seen, whining to Amelia about Martine being called his *babysitter.* Though at sixteen she did seem a world apart from his. Some of the locals fishing on the island thought she was pretty cute too and whistled when Martine showed up pulling Gavin on a raft, Daniel picking his way over the reef behind them in rubber reef shoes. She was Chicana, and maybe with her darker skin and hair the locals thought she was one of them, because as soon as she took off her bikini cover-up, spread out her towel on the sand, and told the boys to go play, they were buzzing around her like moths to light and Martine was loving it. So much so she didn't keep an eye on the tide, and by the time she said they'd better head in, waves slapped against the island.

As they fought their way back through crashing whitecaps toward the distant beach, Martine cried to Daniel to grab onto the raft, Gavin sprawled on top, and she'd pull them both. "Hold on!" she screamed as a wave smashed against the raft. They were coming in two directions, and in Daniel's memory they were huge, he was clutching the back of the raft, legs flung out, trying to scissor-kick through them. He was scared and for a moment considered crawling up on the raft with his brother, but it was a one-person size—the hotel had suggested a second, but Martine didn't want to be bothered with extra stuff to carry. "We're going for shells, not rafting," she said.

So when a wave approached that was bigger than the others, a wall of white foam rushing toward him (like in another abandonment dream where he was in bed, and his bedroom wall was moving in, about to crush him, and again no one came when he cried out), he had to make a quick decision. If he held onto the raft, his shoulders and chest pressed against it as he clutched the slippery plastic sides weighing it down, it would swamp them both, and Gavin could be washed off. His brother still didn't swim well, whereas Daniel had taken lessons every summer since he was five. He'd like to remember thinking all this through, mulling it over, then making the decision to let go of the raft at the moment of impact, to save his brother. That's what Amelia would expect him to do. In truth what he remembers is the fierce rush of the water over his head, Martine's shriek, and he let go. Just like that.

He didn't panic at first. He's solid like his mother said; he knew how to swim, and the water, once he got away from the wave action over the reef, was calmer. But when he reached down for a foothold, there was nothing. Don't *worry*, be *happy*, that stupid song Amelia listened to, chauffeuring them around in her Volvo wagon, Southern California, its stucco houses, palms, pools, Disneyland, Hollywood, the hills and canyons where coyotes howled, all of it under smog so thick and a sprawl of lights so bright you couldn't see the stars at night, and that's where Daniel wanted to be. But maybe he was okay here, buoyant if he just relaxed. Paula Brunt his swimming teacher said that about salt water, *buoyant*, even though her lessons were in her backyard pool.

Daniel could hear voices receding, the shrieking of Martine becoming distant, fading like an echo of itself. Paddling his arms, kicking his legs toward the shore in the same direction they'd been going from the island, and yet the shore seemed to be getting farther away. He could feel himself growing tired and scared, his breathing more labored, and he remembered how Paula Brunt said if you get scared or tired, you just flip over on your back and let the water bear you. Which he did, but the problem was the choppiness of the swells, and his own ragged breathing kept making him gasp, which made the water flow into his mouth, down his throat, and he could feel himself sinking.

Again he tried to stand upright, though there was nothing to stand on, and he imagined his head a little coconut bobbing on the water—who would even see him out here? The sounds from the beach and people now completely gone, and he tried to imagine himself part of a different world, of fish and whales and things that live underwater; there was life down there, he'd seen it in the aquarium. But then he'd panic because he had lungs and didn't have a blowhole to blow out the water, and he could feel it seeping inside him like a puddle, like when he'd bathe Gavin at Amelia's request, and Gavin would hurl cups of water onto the floor because he knew Amelia would come in and scold Daniel for the wet spreading across what's supposed be dry.

Foreign matter, flotsam, jetsam, rubbish, things that drift where they did not belong, and Daniel understood that the ocean didn't care about him—who would care as the water flowed inside him and he sank? Opening his eyes underneath the surface, he saw a grainy blue, a soft, milky blue, blue like the sky when they flew here, Gavin in the window seat, but Daniel beside him could see it, a world turned upside down and he's falling, falling, he's just twelve and he knew someday he'd die, he wasn't a fool, the invincible kid thing, uh-uh, Daniel understood it was the nature of things to eventually go bad; but it wasn't peaceful like people said drowning was, he really really *really* wanted that breath, oh! God! would give anything for it! Take his brother! Here, his hand . . .

Suddenly she's under him, a shadow, a shape (later Amelia would tell him it was a hallucination or a dream, that he'd probably passed out), rose up under his sinking body and took him in her arms? flippers? wings?, lifting him toward the surface. Bubbles and a sound blunted by the water, a chopping sound and he's on the surface, eyes closed, head tipped back, but he could hear it, the roar of a motor, a rescue boat, Martine had alerted them and they'd seen him rise, his arms straight up like he was reaching for the sky.

★　★　★

Daniel was in Castle Hospital for four days. He'd suffered severe hypoxia, his lungs filled with fluid, and could be his heart stopped, maybe even brain damage from being starved of oxygen, something happened before a lifeguard revived him and the ambulance came. Because when he emerged from all of it, checked out of the hospital, drove to the airport with his mother and brother and father who'd flown from L.A., his dad whose face Daniel saw first when he woke up in that hospital bed, the oxygen mask secured over his own face like a diver, like he went back down, and when he closed his eyes, then opened them, it was Leo beside him in a chair by the bed, Daniel watching from somewhere else. Him but not him, a ghost hovering above his own body, watching that body work its way back into doing the things a twelve-year-old does—eat, sleep, read his books, listen to his grandfather's stories, even play with his brother when Gavin insisted—but ghost Daniel watched his body do these things with only a mild interest, like he was half there, like the part of him that made him *him* had been left down in that milky blue, perhaps being cared for by whoever it was, *whatever* it was that had saved him.

★　★　★

Darkness now, her silhouette through the window. Daniel sees Mercy kick off that shoe and imagines it's him taking her out of it, its platform making up for the lost inches. He can't tell for sure from this distance but once he used his binoculars (just once, didn't feel right, more like spying than the perfect balance of their relationship, him watching her and her knowing he's there), and he thought maybe it was cork, something spongy instead of the hard sole of a boot, like walking on dirt, the earth, heel down. Maybe one night, shoes removed, she limps across Amelia's little yard, crawls through his window and surprises him, asleep in his bed. Surprises him, because if he thought about her *really* doing this he'd break out in a cold sweat, hands would get clammy and maybe he wouldn't breathe, like when the ocean came inside him and there was that moment when he thought he couldn't do it, take another breath. Daniel knows how lonely she must be, that leg, perfectly formed, a homunculus leg and beautiful to Daniel, setting her apart. If she just appeared in his bed one night, where he didn't have to plan for it, worry about it, anticipate her coming, he'd let her stay.

◆ LEO ◆

Leo french, son of the atomic age, a postwar product not of the meticulously groomed, generic suburbs that erupted in the fifties and sixties like acne, the ubiquitous white flight of the seventies and eighties; not the Boston South Shore *acquired* stability of Amelia's family, but the small industrial cities, Rust Belt, waste belt, their forgotten, neglected histories before America became Teflon, all about the outer shine, plastic veneer, conspicuous consumption economy. Leo's from Augusta, Maine, and that's where he headed back to when his marriage with Amelia was officially over, signed, sealed, divorced.

It was one thing—a pretty *big* thing—knowing you're not the chromosomal father of your second son, but when the first (*real*) son comes back from a near-drowning changed in some way Leo couldn't put his finger on and the doctors denied—you're lucky to have him, they'd insisted, severe hypoxia, fluid in his lungs, damage to his heart—Leo blamed Amelia, her career that came first, leaving the boys with some teenager she didn't know (that nitwit Haley Long, one of his orbiting groupies, he flattered himself into thinking), letting her take them to the beach for chrissake, and not even *just* the beach, to an island off the coast! How could he continue to *pretend* with a wife, a mother, so self-absorbed she let something like this happen? It wasn't a question of whether he loved her; he wouldn't be the first to love someone who'd failed him in all he believed sacred.

Leo dropped the food photography. You couldn't do much with food; they wouldn't let you make it out to be anything other than what it was, fresh or processed, organic or artificially enhanced, grown, manufactured, nowadays out of some GMO lab, then—whammo—you're in a future where they track you coming and going, security cameras on street corners, your phone, computer, and now it's the drones, little computerized crickets whirring about your property, hanging out in the pine trees pretending they're just another cone, recording your every movement.

He set up his photography studio in the basement of his parents' falling-apart duplex on the post-industrial end of Water Street. After they were gone, he did little to stop its gravitational slide back into the land—shutters askew, porch boards sagging, the paint flaking off the wood siding and window casements, a window hanging loose like a dislocated arm—and began his career as a chronicler of decay. Decay was transformative, changing from what was; decay was aging out, people, their things, jobs, industries with their semi-demolished factories, discarded rusting machinery, old basins, chimneys, PVC pipes, joints, things that were a part of other things, gone. He'd prowl the city dumpsters after dark, abandoned playgrounds where the equipment had been left to rust, yard sales, flea markets, places where people discard what's no longer wanted. A blade-bent egg beater from the forties, a Schwinn bicycle seat—rusted springs underneath, scratched forty-fives, a headless porcelain doll, a saw with half its teeth missing on a rusted blade. After each venture out he'd arrange his finds on a picnic table (itself a salvage-yard find) in his studio and take pictures of them, then off to Augusta Public Library, avoiding his PC and Google because that's where they track you, believing one should support the library in the same way he felt all culturally starved, slowly dying institutions should be dignified. There he'd research each object's origins, see if what his photograph expressed had caught a glimpse of its past, its history, its original *essence*—like searching for the child in the face of a very old person, finding her spirit in the eyes.

As the years went by, he sold less of his photography, quit trying to. The beauty he saw in the desolation around him had to do with isolation, things left to chart their own course after being abandoned from their original purpose. Leo saw that this was him too, an aging man surrounded by what once was. He was no longer relevant, and he was okay with that. He wasn't a fan of the current relevance.

Lately though, honoring this isolation has become tricky. Last night he'd gotten a call from the prison, the one he'd been dreading. His daughter-in-law requesting his visit, said it was urgent. "Got your name on Saturday's list, you're cleared. I need to talk to you," she pleaded.

He didn't want to see her; she'd ask for money, what else? Probably for drugs—he doubted she'd gone clean in prison; movies showed prisoners having easy access if they could pay. He watched these on his ancient analog TV, had to use a special box to get a signal into the digital world. The cable company told him it might be cheaper to buy a small flat screen, go digital like the rest of the country. But why let something die when it wasn't even partway gone, turn it on and it's on, plus no telling what they built into the digital TVs: cameras, software tracking what you watch so they could sell you things, so they can know where you are. *Mr. French is home tonight, watching his TV.*

When Leo drives south to chat with his son through his bedroom window, or just watch him from across the street—Amelia doesn't know he does this, he's memorized enough of her life to figure out when she won't be around—he is gratified to see Daniel doesn't have a TV, preferring books and music on the stereo Leo sent him for his birthday five years ago. It's a long drive, but he doesn't like to talk to Daniel on the phone, you never know who's listening in. Besides, he can still drive, that's something Leo can still do.

Route 17 from Augusta to Rock Harbor, through sparse little towns, patches of open field with ponds and falling-apart houses— maybe he can get some shots on the way back? His Canon's in the backseat just in case, hills like long blue bones on either side.

Rock Harbor is on the coast between Rockland and Rockport—the Rock Towns, his dad called them—where the land ends, which makes him nervous. What are the odds? One son almost drowns, then years later the other *does* after being pushed in or hit, something got him in there, maybe all the drugs he was on and everything shut down? Who knows? Leo's daughter-in-law, whatever role she played, but he can't imagine her doing Gavin in. Cassie loved him. The times he saw them together, Gavin was a lighthouse to her boat. He'd beam and she'd chug around him. Though he never let her get too close. Pity any soul who fell in love with Gavin. Gavin was in love with Gavin.

Had to be the drugs, Leo guessed, because in the end those ruled them both. He'd seen them high, then soon afterward hurting with the need to get there again, coming to him for the means. To their credit the child was always somewhere else, but it meant he didn't even know his granddaughter. Leo rubs his eyes. Best concentrate on the destination, focus out the windshield, windswept coast in the distance. Last time he drove out this way, he got lost in his own head and ended up in Northport, four towns over from where he'd been going, most of it poor as a bag of dirt, like a lot of rural Maine.

★　★　★

"I want you to take her," Cassie says, sitting at the visitor's table opposite Leo. She's twitchy, her fingers drum against the laminated fake wood (everything in here metal or fake), and this makes him nervous, her knee bumping against his. Leo pulls his long legs under his chair, wincing at the arthritic pain in his right knee. Straight legs are better for him, but twitch is not a good sign. He'd seen twitch in them both, Gavin and Cassie, and it put him on edge. Twitch is raw, twitch is desperate.

"Who are you talking about?" He'd been prepared for her to ask for money, even had the cash in his wallet, no checks she'd told him before.

"The kid! Heaven. She's better off with you. Amelia makes me nervous."

Leo snorts. "Amelia makes everybody nervous, but that's beside the point. Cassie, look at me. Do I look like a person anyone would want to raise their daughter? I'm not even employed, even if I was still young enough, which I'm not."

She studies him for a moment and Leo pictures what she's seeing: his frayed corduroy button-down shirt, the old Panama covering patches of thinning hair (a guard made him take the hat off, checked the lining for contraband, then let him put it on again); a face still somewhat handsome, he supposes, his former sharp-featured look (Richard Gere, he'd been compared to), crumbling now, that downward journey old faces have, like all things organic, dying back to its roots.

"But Amelia's a bitch," she whines. A loud buzzer goes off and Leo jumps. Cassie twitches. "Midafternoon count. Inmates in the visitors room don't have to; we're counted and searched before we set foot in here, everything short of a fuckin' strip."

Leo nods, "Right. Look, maybe Amelia makes you nervous, let's agree she can be difficult, but the court mandated she's the one, custody of your daughter."

"I have these visions," Cassie whispers. Leo feels like he's in *The Exorcist*, his head whipped around in so many different directions, once again no clue what she's talking about. An image of projectile vomiting, fountain of green. God, of all the things he's started to forget of late, why can't scenes like that make the cut?

"Right," he sighs, figures he's walking into it, but clearly she's waiting for him to ask. "What visions?"

She leans across the table closer to him. He can smell a sort of fruity scent on her, her hair, skin, or maybe more chemical, like a scent you wear to cover other smells up. "Sometimes he's alone in the water, sometimes we're both together."

"Who, Gavin? That . . . night?"

She nods and he sees her eyes are moist, her lips quivering. "Don't you get it? If one of them is real, if ever I remember for real doing *it*, it will fucking kill me."

Suddenly Leo can't look at her and peers around the room instead. Not a lot of visitors, correction officers slumped against the wall on either side of the door. The whole room looks exhausted. He sighs, levels his eyes at her forehead. "Sorry, but I'm not following this."

"Oh for chrissake! Amelia's a pit bull, latches on, you can't shake her off. Says I have to confess to something I don't *want* to remember. It's not that I don't want to confess, like she seems to think. I didn't deny it. Why isn't that enough? I'm here, convicted for chrissake, does she want me executed too? Why can't this be enough?" She starts to cry, bony shoulders shaking, hands, twitching fingers pressed against her face.

Leo feels like he's supposed to say something, or maybe pat her arm, but thankfully he saw on the Rules of Visitor Conduct he's not allowed to touch her. He tries to look sympathetic when she stops, but that nagging sense—he's sitting face-to-face with someone who likely knows something about how Gavin died, the last person to see him alive. Not that Leo questioned anyone getting so upset with Gavin they'd help that along. He wasn't so nice, let's face it. Even Leo could've seen wanting him gone sometimes, the way he treated Daniel, who probably nearly drowned so Gavin didn't have to.

"Look," Cassie whimpers, "I didn't deny it. I'll say I'm sorry to *you* just in case, but Amelia has to stop getting all up in my business and trying to make me say things! It's . . . fuckin' painful. I'm sorry. If I could trade places with Gavin I'd do it, just so I wouldn't have to want him back every crappy minute of my crappy life and know I'll never see him. I'm sorry Leo, damn it! For whatever the fuck I did or didn't do."

He nods, swallows hard, feels suddenly like he might cry too, and he's not even sure why.

"But I need some money," she adds, almost in the same breath.

He nods again, safer territory here, his ticket out. "How do I arrange it?"

"Tell the CO at the Entrance desk it's for my personals account, toothpaste, tampons, the like. I'll deal with it after that."

The buzzer sounds, she stands up and stretches. He sees for a moment into the loose sleeve of her jumpsuit, bruises on the underside of her arm, her veins, like maybe she needled it in? Far as he knew Cassie only smoked or snorted—Gavin was needles, the works, his *vitamin* shot, he called it. Or maybe someone grabbed her hard, yanking her the way you might an errant child, the way he'd seen Amelia once yank Daniel, a few months after the near-drowning when he didn't seem to respond to things anymore; either that or so slowly you could never tell if he'd heard, if he was considering what you said or was somewhere else entirely. Maybe that's why she pulled him so hard, to bring him back. He had those same bruises on his arm, the marks of her fingers around him.

"I'm not as tough as I look," Cassie whispers, following his glance.

Leo feels something crack open inside his chest. He clears his throat and nods. What she looks is goddamn broken.

✦ AMELIA ✦

"Y OU'VE GOT TO BE kidding! You want me to take you to the town pool in March? The *outside* pool?" Amelia shakes her head, sticks her hands on her hips but resists stomping her foot. The girl is serious.

"They just opened it yesterday for adult lap-swim, plus tryouts for swim team tomorrow. I need to practice, but they won't let kids swim laps without an adult!" Heaven whines. "Otherwise, you know, I wouldn't have bothered you."

She has that look she gets, a crafty, negotiating gleam in her eye—Amelia's begun to recognize it, her look when she wants something so bad she's not going to back down and will argue all night until Amelia orders her to bed. Amelia sighs, the child is stubborn, a not unfamiliar trait in this family. "Fine, but for just one hour. I have other things I'm supposed to be doing, like cooking dinner? And what on earth possessed them to open the pool mid-March? It's not even spring."

"Two days it will be."

Amelia shakes her head, grabs her keys. "What do you say?" But Heaven has already headed out the garage door to the car, dragging her towel in her wake.

"Pick up that towel, for crying out loud!" Amelia shouts.

★　★　★

Blessedly they have the pool to themselves, though how many others would be crazy enough to swim on the 19th of March under a mass of gray clouds and that chilly sea breeze pumping up from the coast? The town wants money, that's what this is about; she had to insert her credit card to open the gate to the pool!

Amelia huddles on the bleachers far enough back to avoid getting splashed, pulls her wool poncho closer into her body. Leo gave it to her one Christmas in the early years of their marriage, when things between them were still mostly okay. At first when she unwrapped it she'd felt disappointed. For a renowned fashion photographer he didn't seem to have a clue what a woman might like in an item of clothing, say, a cocktail dress, a silk blouse, even a tastefully designed scarf. The poncho was black and white Houndstooth without style or flair, but the wool was warm and soft. She remembers him wrapping it around her shoulders just before dawn, when she was out on the patio of their L.A. apartment, shortly after she'd given birth to Daniel and they'd both been up all night with his crying. Amelia was crying too, staring up into the dark hills beyond the city, and his hand lingered for a while on the back of her neck. Although prone to donating barely used clothes, regret buys and tacky gifts, Amelia had kept the poncho all these years.

She watches her granddaughter pull through the water, the rise of her rounded shoulders, scissoring of those thick legs. She *is* surprisingly fast, Amelia thinks, as the girl makes it to the end of the pool, does a quick underwater flip, and heads back again. Her own boys never wanted to swim on a team or have much to do with water sports after what happened to Daniel. For a while in high school Gavin had a friend with a sailboat. But Amelia suspected the draw for that was to pick up girls, motor out a ways, drop anchor, and smoke pot; never mind the sailing part. She could smell it on him when he came home, and half the time his swim trunks weren't even damp.

For a brief moment the sun pokes out of the clouds and Amelia lifts her face to its warmth. When she looks at the pool again, Heaven has climbed out and sits on the side, staring at her legs. "Ready to go?" Amelia calls out hopefully.

The girls scowls and shakes her head. "I scraped my knee on the end of the pool, doing the flip turn."

"Well maybe you better not do the flip turn then," Amelia says.

"I have to!" she howls. "I'll lose a couple seconds and won't make time tomorrow. Then I won't make the team."

"So you don't make the team—is that the end of the world?"

Heaven glares at Amelia, grabs her towel and dabs at her knee, then jumps back into the pool.

Amelia sighs, lifts her face again even though there's no more sun, and closes her eyes. How is it she always manages to say the wrong thing to this child? "Would it hurt you to be nice to him once in a while?" Amelia's own mom said to her once when Daniel was . . . God how old was he anyway? Tracking dirt from his shoes across her parents' living room carpet and she'd yelled at him, "You born in a barn or what?" beating her own mother to it, no doubt, so instead her mother took the high road, pretended to be on Daniel's side. Not that Amelia had ever received much modeling from her mother on how one is supposed to *mother*. And truthfully, Amelia didn't take to the role naturally, not with Daniel anyway.

After their wedding Amelia remembers feeling a little shocked at what she'd done. *Married* Leo French. Yes, he was the best at the time, by far, of the types of men who were interested in her, but her generation was making it acceptable to cohabit, sans marriage, the sexual revolution. It was Leo who'd been so hot for them to get married.

Then, married just a year—not happy exactly, she'd never expect *that*—happiness was a myth for poor people to look at rich people and go, yeah, but I bet they aren't happy. She wasn't even close to being poor people, not with her Egg Me! contract, but Leo couldn't give a flying *fut* about the rich, that's what he said, and

she'd liked that in him, at first, chalked it up to a rebellious spirit.
Plus he was a nice guy, nice to her and that's likely as good as you'll
get, her own mom had said. Amelia was never one to get stuck on
the love thing (though he said it to her every night making love.
Amelia! he'd whispered, crazy guy even thanked her for it, kiss him
between his legs and it was him on his knees). *LOVE*, a word like
a vessel made of rubber to stretch or shrink depending on whatever
it is you put in there: Birthday night at the Mark Hopkins in San
Francisco? Weekend chores list? *If you love me, you'll wash out the*
damn sink after you shave.

But then he wanted a baby. "Baby, *baby!*" he said, and he
almost got her thinking it was possible; sure she could do it, be
a mom, even though her own was remote and cool. She remembers feeling herself yielding . . . a family, Leo said. God, but what
kind of a mother would she be? She'd asked him. A good one,
he'd insisted, all cotton-eyed sincere. But who were we kidding?
One night after he'd tucked himself into bed, motioning her to
join him, she kicked off her shoes, thunk they went on the bedroom floor, crawled on top of him and pushed her perfect face (he
used to call it), in his face. "I don't know how to be a mother!"
she'd said. He kissed her lips, gently, patted her flat belly, *baby*, he
whispered, and it was his seed that night—Amelia had clocked it
to the day—that met her egg halfway and made Daniel. A child
conceived minutes after its mother confesses she didn't have a clue
how to be one.

Amelia sighs again, watching her granddaughter doggedly
splash across the pool, forward then back. *She's determined, I'll give*
her that, Amelia thinks. So look what comes of being a mother,
decades later you're a *grandmother!* Remembers how for a couple
weeks before she knew she was pregnant she'd secretly tried *not*
to be. Then Leo discovered her diaphragm; she'd been sneaking
it in, and he was disappointed in her. "But my contract!" Amelia
had cried. "What will Haley Long do about Egg Me!"? Leo had
grinned, almost wickedly. "He'll think of something. He can photograph you from the back, for one, your lovely derriere. Or he can
suck eggs! How about that option?"

At their ultrasound Leo had her almost believing the amoeba-like blob, *our child*, a fried-egg looking entity with a beating heart could be loved and mothered by her, that she would be perfect at it. But what if she wasn't? Amelia asked him later that night. He told her the world was all about odds, about taking chances; take this one for our child, he said. They'd stuck the photograph the ultrasound technician gave them of their little egg-baby on the refrigerator. She'd gone to sleep thinking she could still hear that beating sound, the whoosh of blood from its heart.

A year later when Daniel, a couple months old, wouldn't stop crying, Amelia thought she'd go crazy with it: baby shrieks, baby wails, exploding like a siren in her head. One morning she hauled him outside their apartment, a mostly Latin neighborhood with its Caucasian hipsters, surfers, artsy types, druggies, and endless traffic noise, into the back courtyard. Stood on its patches of dried-out grass near a little flowering bush where the hummingbirds whirred about like it was some kind of Eden and tossed that screaming baby into the air. For a startled moment her son stopped crying, gave Amelia a bewildered look—who *are* you? And of course Amelia couldn't answer other than for damn sure she wasn't a child abuser, so she caught that baby on his way back down. When he cried again Amelia comforted him—there there, Mommy won't do it again, throw baby to the sky and maybe he becomes a bird and just flies away. That would be the smart thing, this creature that had the bad luck to be born her kid.

Could she have known even then, intuited maybe, what would happen to Daniel? The near-drowning, how he was one kind of boy at eleven, then someone else at twelve after it happened? It wasn't his intelligence—Amelia, Leo, Daniel's school, all of them agreed Daniel was bright, maybe exceptionally so, but he seemed to have emerged from his ordeal *frozen,* traumatized is what the school psychologist determined, referring him to a psychiatrist who could medicate. Antidepressants, antianxiety, the various "anti's" were tried and then a stimulant when everything they gave him just seemed to build that wall higher around him, each *cure* adding a new brick.

He'd told her at twelve, after the incident, that he understood love and duty were the same—love was duty, duty was the way he knew how to love. It was his duty to look after his brother, which she'd always stressed to him. Watch out for anyone who might harm Gavin, she'd said. Was it her fault then, the kid never seemed to have his own life? Didn't date, didn't have friends— tagged along with Gavin and Gavin's friends, but told her the things they did, ball games, arcades, parties, even going to a movie felt *frivolous*.

Used to tell her when he slept, he'd reexperience his near-drowning. How in his dreams the water rose up under him, his bed, over his mattress, sheets, that sensation of his feet clawing the water for a bottom that had dropped away. Then he'd utter typical Daniel dogma, what useless appendages feet are, that fins are surer; humans should never have evolved from the sea, he'd say, because the sea will keep trying to reclaim its own. Her other son . . . drowns, and the one who *almost* did, but didn't, says things like *this*!"

Amelia swipes the sudden tears from her eyes, whispers fiercely to herself, *Get a grip!* and watches as Heaven climbs out of the pool, grinning. "Did you see it?" Heaven shouts, though Amelia is just feet away.

"See what?"

"I did it! I made time, twice! I did a perfect flip turn for both! It's JV time but I'm halfway to varsity."

Amelia stands up stiffly and tosses the spare dry towel she brought to her granddaughter, dripping and shivering on the pool deck. "Well, so now can we go?"

Heaven nods, suddenly downcast, and Amelia's breath seizes in her chest. A vision of Daniel, before his accident, climbing out of the pool she used to take him to in Hollywood Hills for his swimming lessons. How happy he'd looked then, proud of some stroke he'd learned that day, excited to tell her. Did she say anything to him in response? Amelia can't recall. She steps down off the bleachers, leans toward Heaven, and tugs the towel back up around the girl's wet shoulders where it had slipped down. "Let's get you into a hot shower," she says, "before you freeze to death. For lord's sake, opening an outside pool in March!"

★   ★   ★

Later that night, Heaven asleep, Daniel doing whatever he does so late in his room—she knows he's up by the bar of light under his door, Amelia crawls into bed to read. But before she can open her book, her eyes grow heavy and she turns off the light.

> *Daylight, ocean glistening under a high sun, floating face-down on its glassy surface (dead man's float it's called, crazy because if she's learned anything it's that dead men don't float, they sink!), we gaze into its shine. "Why not just open your mouth and swallow?" he says. She watches him do it like a whale, taking in the ocean, frothing it out in a white foam through his trachea, his nose, a cartoon bubble of it over him as he sinks and swallows, sinks and swallows, sinks . . . Later when they cut him open, a fine layer of sand will remain in his alveoli, lungs marbled with grays and yellows as they starve for air, ballooning out and out and out until they're ready to burst or pop (your lungs drowning!), until the water fills them completely and they settle into their new weight. When they cut him open, his stomach will bear seaweed and fish and little microscopic things, what's left after he's split, dissected, his blood drained out along with the ocean inside him, everything that's Gavin—oh Gavin!—that once was alive.*

Amelia sits up in her bed shivering, turns on the light, and peers furtively about her room, as if he could be in it. Another dream of Gavin drowning, along with a coroner's report. Did she *see* that, or maybe her lawyer told her? Those terrible days after his body was found, before Cassiopeia's arraignment, seem surreal now. Amelia has trouble sorting out what actually occurred, from her despair, the dizzying weight of her grief. *Was this real . . .?* Her son's life reduced to a report. Amelia reaches for her Xanax, the glass of water, and her book again. Puts the book facedown beside her on the bed, closes her eyes, still wet from the dream's tears.

✦ HEAVEN ✦

HEAVEN ON *DECK*, THE swim coach called it. You go on deck when she calls your name for swim team tryouts: "French lane six!" the coach shouts into her bullhorn. Heaven rushes down the narrow row of bleachers to the bottom row, where of course Bethany Harrison and the B-girls, who are already on the team so they get to sit in front, stick out their feet to trip her. Oops, stepped on Brittany's little pinkie toe. "Pig!" Brittany howls. "Sorry!" Heaven says, head down, don't look them in the eyes. "Yeah, not really," she mutters under her breath. The sky overhead is a hard March blue, with puffy cirrus clouds like smoke rings. A wind picks up suddenly. Heaven shivers. *"It's too cold for them to open the outdoor pool yet, what are they thinking, it's not even spring!"* Grandmelia had bitched yesterday; maybe she was right. Never mind, Heaven thinks, the ocean is deep, dark and cold—she can handle it; she'll *rock* this town pool.

Heaven on the starting block, lane six. Look to her left, lane seven, a small Rachel Something, not a B-girl, not even a seventh-grader yet, so not a threat. To her right a girl who's getting homeschooled; no one seems to know her. Heaven takes a deep breath, practices holding it in like she did in Grandmelia's pool, counts, blows out. Her heart is beating like crazy in her chest like a snare drum's in there, tap tap tappity tap. Sudden mouthfart noise from the bleachers, then Bethany's tinkly fake laugh made louder, so Heaven hears. Coach blows her whistle. "Listen up, girls, positions!"

Heaven and the rest of them on deck, readying themselves to dive in, knees bent, arms out over their heads, chins tucked. "You know the drill! Freestyle, backstroke, butterfly, breast, then out! I want you to go as fast as you can without compromising the strokes—got it? The stroke is all," Coach shouts.

Stroke is all, stroke is all, breathe, breathe (Just concentrate, her dad used to tell her, think it out—that was before his own mind kind of drifted away, but still Heaven hears him whisper in her head), *schweeeeep*, goes the whistle and she's in! Stroke, stroke, breathe, pull, stroke, stroke, breathe pull . . . flip turn, and again, *stroke is all, stroke is all, breathe, breathe.* Heaven swimming, *Heaven swimming!* It's all she wants to do, stroke stroke breathe breathe pull pull, suck in a big breath, flip turn, repeat. She feels great! Like this, right now, this is *her,* Heaven *winning*!

When she's done, she clasps onto the deck at the end of the pool for a moment, catching her breath, and for just a moment she peers up at the bleachers and imagines her mom there, with a couple of the other moms, her *real* mom, cinnamon hair, pale skin, smiling at Heaven. *"You did it sweetheart!"* Not that she ever called Heaven that, but her dad did, sometimes. Her mom probably thought it anyway.

Heaven hoists herself up on the deck as the rest of the lanes finish, one after the other. Rachel is last and Heaven sees her panting, her eyes tearing up through her swim goggles as she clutches the deck. Heaven offers her hand to help Rachel out.

"Swimmers, listen up!" Coach says, walking behind them now on the swim deck. "If I call your name, you made the team; if I don't, that means you keep working your strokes, the stroke is all, then you try again next year." Heaven holds her breath as the coach calls out names of the older girls, who tried out first, the division over the one Heaven's trying for. She peers up at the sky, clouds, maybe even a snowflake or two as that chilly wind picks up again, but that's okay, anything to distract her from the B-girls making fart noises until she hears it: "Heaven French, Division Two!"

★   ★   ★

Heaven racing through the hallway to her room, don't even stop in the kitchen for a snack, toss backpack on bed, slam door, then open it again, closing it s-o-f-t-l-y in case Grandmelia's lurking somewhere in the house and she'll yell at her not to slam her door.

Does the one-two-three knock on the wall plus two more, her five-knock she made up for when she has something important to tell Uncle Daniel. Uncle Daniel said okay to the knock, it's an odd number he said, so he'd honor it, but only if he's available at that *particular* time, otherwise it reverts by default to the standard three-knock, meaning I'm here and would like to speak to you, when you're ready. Uncle Daniel answers by removing the picture that blocks her from seeing him. "What's up?" he says.

"I did it, I made the swim team!"

Uncle Daniel beams at her. "Well now, I'd say that bit of news is worth your five-knock, congrats!"

"But that's not all, "Heaven says quickly, before he puts the picture back up, closing her out. "I've got an answer for you, maybe," she says. "Could've been a dolphin that rescued you when you almost drowned! There are dolphins in Hawaii where it happened. They can rescue people. I learned that in science today."

He peers thoughtfully through the wall over her head like he's gazing back in time to see it again, his drowning, his savior. "Well kiddo, I hope you know not everything is about science. For example, science would say there's no such thing as a selkie. Well I happen to know they have monk seals in Hawaii too, that exist nowhere else. Maybe they evolved differently, like one chromosome splits and suddenly she's part human, part seal, so maybe she had arms."

"You said you weren't sure about her arms, could be fins, you said. Plus selkies are from the Isle of Skye, not *monk* seals. So why would she go all the way to Hawaii?"

"Maybe to save me from drowning. They try and save drowning people. Although there's another similar species that may have evolved into sirens. Sirens are known for their songs that lure people down and make them drown. It's complicated."

Heaven glares at him through the hole in the wall; they've made it wider, so the picture barely covers it. "I *know* about the drowning songs! Plus, if it *was* a selkie and she went all the way to Hawaii and saved you, why didn't she go to Maine, then, which isn't so far, and save my dad? Are you saying a siren sang a song that made *him* drown? So why him and not you? And doesn't drowning take only a few minutes? Like, how could she swim all the way from Skye in, what, five minutes tops, to save you? It's not possible. I reject it." Heaven stamps her foot in that obstinate way, and for just a second Daniel sees his brother in her—his mother too.

Uncle Daniel narrows his eyes, blue-green MacQueen eyes, like hers. "Why you being so argumentative about this, kiddo? Were you there? I don't think so. This isn't a physics debate. It happened. To me."

"I'm just trying to figure it out. It doesn't make sense. Hawaii is really far away. Maybe she didn't like my dad?"

"Why wouldn't she?" Uncle Daniel scoffs. "Everyone else did."

"Because of the drugs. Grandmelia thinks I don't know. What universe does she live in? At school there'd be like all this anti-drug stuff, posters showing what different ones look like, and they'd teach you how bad it was. Then I'd go home and there it all was, the ones you're supposed to say no to, spread out on the coffee table like it's chips or peanuts. And here's another thing." Heaven takes a deep breath like Grandmelia tells her to do before she just blurts something out; take a moment to think about what you're going to say, Grandmelia says, don't just *blurt*. "I want a mountain bike really bad for my birthday, but Grandmelia said I don't need one because we don't have any mountains. I mean what's up with that? First she said no to a smartphone, and she won't let me on the internet unless she's there to track what websites I go to. *Gawd!* It's like she doesn't have a clue about my life. Who uses mountain bikes on mountains around here anyway?"

"Way to change the subject, kid. There aren't any mountains in Seahaven."

"Duh, that's what I'm talking about, Jesus!" Rolls her eyes. Grandmelia doesn't like it when she says Jesus, but Heaven's heard her too when she doesn't think anyone's listening, talking to herself like she does sometimes, or on the phone with her lawyer. Heaven opens her bedroom window, kitty-corner to the hole in the wall, and stares out at Grandmelia's pool. It's become a warmish March afternoon, still technically winter but spring is tomorrow, and Heaven imagines how the air will fill with honeysuckle smells and the drone of bees. "When swim team practice starts, I want to ride it there. Bethany Harrison has a Yeti SB75 and she rides hers everywhere. It's got a turquoise frame and pink inside the wheels. She said it's the best. I want a red and black one."

Uncle Daniel nods. "Sure, I get it. Power colors. Show the bitch up." Heaven snickers. "Yeah, the bitch!" She loves it when Uncle Daniel talks to her this way, as if she's an adult instead of the little kid Grandmelia treats her like. "So that's why I need Grandmelia to get me one."

"Then you make it your quest. Like the Holy Grail. You made the swim team, so now you need a new quest. Amelia is the keeper of the means for the bike, and your quest is to get it from her."

"But she said no," Heaven whines.

"You can't give up a quest. Once it's declared, you have to keep at it until it's accomplished. That's the rules of questing."

★   ★   ★

The next afternoon, a sunny one, Grandmelia's on a patio lounge chair. She'd turned on the pool heater so Heaven could swim, then moved her chair closer to talk to Heaven, who's in the water going down down down, holding her breath, counting, so she can't hear Grandmelia nag her about wearing a bathing cap so her hair won't turn green.

"You'll have to on the swim team, if you don't it will feel like straw!" Grandmelia says as Heaven pops up to the surface with a gasp. "Is that what you want? *Green* straw for hair? How will that fly next fall at the eighth-grade dance?" Grandmelia had given up on the seventh-grade dance after Heaven, refusing to go, cut the straps off the velvet dress (then was grounded without TV for two weeks); so now she's setting her sights on next year.

"I'll probably shave it off so I can go faster. And shave all my body hair too."

"Oh whoop-de-do! You don't even have body hair. You have down like a duck."

Heaven stands up and walks through the shallow water toward Grandmelia. She won't argue because her quest requires focus and strategy. She knows about strategies from watching Robyn on the debate team. He kicks ass with his strategies. "My mom and dad used to take me for ice cream on my birthday."

"Did they now. I'm surprised they had time, what with their busy lives. Not that ice cream is the best choice for your figure, you know."

"Yeah, and then they'd let me get whatever I wanted. They made me responsible for my own gifts, they said, so I'd have what I want." Well, this was *sort of* true: they did let her have whatever she wanted, but mostly it had to be, like, under five dollars, if she was lucky; sometimes they only had about a couple dollars in change. But she could at least get a candy bar or gum. Sometimes they didn't remember her birthday, but mostly they did. One time her mom gave her an awesome blue scarf! It was way up in a tree—probably blew there, her dad said; off of someone's neck! said her mom. But she climbed that tree anyways to nab it, then gave it to Heaven for her birthday. The scarf was the color of the ocean where it's deepest. Heaven wishes she still had it. After Peggy Howell removed Heaven from their house, she returned for Heaven's things. The scarf wasn't there when she came back.

Grandmelia shakes her head under her straw hat, a towel over her legs—why even go out in the sun if you have to put all that camouflage on just to sit in it?

"So," Heaven starts, her quest a shiny beacon in front of her—picture a lighthouse in a dark sea, Uncle Daniel said, and aim the *fuck* toward it—"soon as school's out, the swim team practices every day at six AM. Thank you in advance for all the rides there."

"I don't *do* dawn," Grandmelia says. "Don't think I don't know what you're pulling here, young lady. How about you explain to me, like I'm a person who doesn't know Seahaven and most of the rest of the South Shore is flat as the back of my hand, why you need to have a mountain bike? Why not just a *bike* bike?"

Heaven sighs, a dramatic outtake of breath (her dad called it Heaven's adults-are-retards sigh). She kicks under the water, but not so Grandmelia can see, only if she notices bubbles rising from the disturbance. Keep your cool, Uncle Daniel said. "Because I *need* a mountain bike. It's my quest."

"Uh-huh," says Grandmelia. "Such an articulate argument. No one *needs* a mountain bike in a place where the highest incline is the hill at the dump, unless you are considering ocean cliffs riding, suicide at best. Let me tell you something . . ."

At that Heaven dives back under, inhale it in, sing it out, avoid whatever comes from her grandmother's mouth because she's sure it won't get her that bike. She rolls over and opens her eyes, staring up through the water, Grandmelia's face at the side of the pool wobbling like a hot air balloon.

When she rises again, popping out of the water like a porpoise, Grandmelia stands up, her beach towel tied around her hips in a sarong. "About your uncle," she says, not missing a beat, as if Heaven's been listening to her all this time. "You should understand he's not always emotionally stable. What I'm saying is you should not be taking advice about these *quests* from him. If you insist on a fancy bike, ask your mother. That's what parents are for."

"She doesn't have any money. She's in prison!" Heaven wails.

"So there you have it. Now *that's* a quest."

Heaven watches Grandmelia stroll back inside the house, tossing her hat onto the glass patio table, red hair falling about her shoulders like flames. Like a witch, she thinks, one of Uncle

Daniel's wicked faeries up to no damn good, he's said. Heaven jump-kicks the water and leaps up, her arms outstretched crucifix style then smack down on the surface, arms in front, palms cupped slightly for maximum thrust; face down, shoulders up, legs in a tight scissor kick she speed strokes across the pool in four seconds because it's an aboveground pool (a glorified bathtub Uncle Daniel called it), flip turn, then back again. She'll rule that swim team with her super-breaststroke. If Grandmelia won't buy her a bike, Heaven will snake one. She likes Bethany's.

*   *   *

Her mom told her that her dad was the one who named her Heaven, the ultimate hope he said. "You can fuck up in this life, but so long as you don't kill someone, there's Heaven to look forward to," he said. Like he was religious, which he wasn't, except once when he was tweaking, her mom said, he saw the luminous tunnel; only he said *laminate*, which they had laughed about later, the laminated tunnel to Heaven. He said Heaven would change everything, another one of his lies in the form of a wish, her mom told her. At the time Heaven didn't know what tweaking meant, though she kind of does now from TV shows (before she moved here; Grandmelia never lets her watch anything violent or with drugs). But she had listened to her mom the way you listen to someone you hope is telling you some kind of truth, the truth of her name. She'd always hated her name, but knowing her dad chose it because he thought *she* was special meant something anyway.

Heaven, about to become a teenager. She wonders if her mom thinks she maybe already started her period, wears a bra, shaves her legs, those puberty markers that Heaven knows Cassie's own mom was there for until she wasn't; because she died, though, not caged in a prison like an animal. Little girl Heaven running down Cabrillo Street before they moved to Maine and all hell broke loose, Cassie would say, her mess of hair, flying into her dad's arms (before his arms became attached to the needle).

Heaven, sprawled out on her bed in the room that used to be her dad's when he was the age she is now, tears out a sheet of notepaper from her English class composition book and writes:

Dear Mom,
Is it still okay to call you Mom? Grandmelia makes me call her Grandmelia because she doesn't like grandma and I don't know if when someone goes to prison they become someone else so you can't call them what they were. Uncle Daniel says you're still my mom no matter if you're there and I'm here, and Dad is still my dad even though he's dead. You may not remember my birthday is in nine weeks, I don't know if they have calendars in prison. I know you can't use the internet so you can't find out that way or on a smartphone, well I can't do that either because Grandmelia makes me use a dumb phone. Anyway it is and can I please have a mountain bike? That's all I want, not even cake or ice cream, just a mountain bike. It can be my Christmas present too, even though that's like a lot of months away. But my birthday is SOOOOON. Guess what? I made the swim team and practices start this summer so I can use it to go there. Everyone on the swim team has one, like Bethany Harrison. She isn't the captain, but she acts like she is, and it would help if I had an awesome mountain bike so she can't tease me because I don't have one. I want a YETI SB75 like hers, but I would also be okay with a NORCO Shore 2. You probably wonder why I'm telling you about this since you're in prison and can't go shopping, but Grandmelia said I have to ask you first. She said there's no mountains in Seahaven so I should get a normal bike but what she doesn't get is Seahaven isn't normal, not my school anyway. My school is psycho! And BTW the NORCO Shore 2 has the word "shore" in it not mountain. LOL—which sounds like little old lady. ☺
From Heaven, almost a teenager

◆ MAGGIE MacQUEEN, 1852 ◆

THE DAY THE FACTOR came with the eviction notice was a cold
one for late September. The daylight had been getting shorter
and we'd begun seeing the play of the aurora borealis at night, a
magnificent sight in the clearer skies of autumn, wavy greens, the
rarest reds, curtains of color shimmering in the dark. Ma had just
come off the moor, emptied her creel of peat, built up the fire, and
was starting the porridge for our breakfast, a pan of milk steaming
on the fire.

The factor stomped into the cottage like he owned the place,
though the laird did, not him. We could see his men out front, and
later Da said he was tempted to crawl out the back window, make a
run for the coast to hide in the cliffs like some of the Suisnish men
had already done, the idea being maybe they wouldn't throw out a
woman and her children. Except they would, they did—he knew
it and could not trust Ma with her temper and the sharp words that
came from it. So he stayed in the back room with the wee ones and
Charles, Abigail, and me, with Ma.

Where's your man? the factor asked Ma, waving the eviction
notice in her face.

Ma stood up straight as a shovel from where she was stirring the porridge, her sharp blue eyes locking onto his weasel ones. How dare you, said Ma, snatching it from his hands, and though she couldn't read, we all knew well enough what it said, what they all said, and she crumpled it up and tossed it into the fire.

The factor tipped back his fat head and laughed, exposing a meaty neck, the flesh on it hanging like a rooster's wattle. You think that changes anything, cheeky lass? You're out tomorrow first light, or you'll regret it. I promise that much. Then he grabbed the pan of milk and poured it all over the fire, sizzling, its smoke blooming throughout the room, putting it out. Abigail squealed, then slapped her hand over her mouth. Ma was silent, but this time there was more slump in her spine than bristle. We needed that milk, and now we had none, the porridge would be done this morn and there'd be nothing more, save for some scrappy bits of this and that. And no fire for warmth, as Ma had used up all the peat for this one.

Da, emerging out of the back room after the factor left, surveyed the ruins of the fire, the milk steaming and evaporating over where it had been. We have but a few hours, he said, shaking his head, and then the roof it will be. He pointed up at the thatch, and I remembered when they burnt out part of Boreraig, how it turned the night sky the color of the ribbon candy Da brought us once from a trip to Fort William. That was a good day, enough left over from our barley harvest he sold there for candy.

Ma said, and if we refuse?

Da grabbed her hand, tugging at her wrist. You heard what happened in Boreraig! Elspeth MacCoy dragged out of her burning cottage by her hair, her daughter thrown out on her mattress; giving birth she was, and both died, wee babe and the mother. They said in the next cottage over a girl went mad and now she's living in the Cuillin like an animal, eating tree bark and bugs.

Curse their bloody eyes! said Ma, and she'd do it too. A lot of curses in those days, and plenty of them stuck. One of laird Mac-Donald's men was cursed in Suisnish by an old woman they later shot for her rebellion; she'd wished upon him a terrible disease that would burn out his eyes and leave him childless. Was said that year he got syphilis, and not only did he end up childless and blind but crazed as a hare in winter.

The next morning before the sun pinked the sky we were up, the wind howling, a blow off the sea—ill weather comes behind it, you watch, said Da; ill blessings too, said Ma. We could smell the wet peat, no fire for warmth, no milk, just a handful of oats for our breakfast. Baby Robert cried and Ma instructed Molly, the eldest of the wee lasses, to rock him while she, Abigail, and I finished doling out who carries what: young Dottie with the sieve, she being the smallest that can carry anything at all. Charles would bear the loom we'd inherited from the neighbors when they left for the new world, for it was known the emigration ships allowed just two parcels and a trunk, the trunk for whatever silver they had and tools that could fit inside. We did not have much, though with nine in our family, it was enough to fill our cart twice over, and so the rest we had to carry.

Da gathered us around him and told us about the Kylerhea ferry that would shuttle three of us to mainland Scotland; there we would part and no longer be nine—Charles first, who'd already secured passage on his ship to the new world of Boston, paid by his future employer, then the train up to Maine. Da bought passage on another vessel six weeks after for Abigail and me, an emigration ship to Nova Scotia, but with cargo too, where we'd be packed in like kippers and couldn't bring much, just a trunk between us. We'd stay with our cousins in Glasgow until it departed. The best he could do for his money, Da said.

Abigail wondered how they would manage all that must be carried, particularly when she, Charles, and Maggie were no longer there to help. Ma said they'd manage, that she herself could always bear more. Da turned his back to us, by which we knew not to walk on the other side of him or we'd see his tears.

What about you and Ma and the wee ones? I asked his back, slumped over now to almost a sit, though there was nothing left to sit on in the cottage, the chairs all strapped to our cart by now. Abigail glared at me for asking this, but I wanted to know what

I'd be missing, sniffling a bit, trying very hard not to outright cry, myself but a lass of fifteen and not ready to part from her Ma and Da.

Word is they'll eventually be sending most of the folks from the cleared villages to the new world anyway, Da told us, forcing the ones who resist. Or we could try our hands at fishing, he said, they weren't bothering some that settled on the rocky cliffs and the beaches, places where the sheep couldn't be grazed. He hadn't decided what would be best. Then Da turned back around, put his hands on my shoulders. You must go with Charles and Abigail to the new world, lassie. Make something of yourselves. Carry the MacQueen name to it and do us proud.

I was sniffling now in earnest and about to give in to it despite Abigail's sharp kick to my shin, when there's a knock, and before Ma's halfway across the small room, the factor kicked our door open and stood there, the early morning sunlight blazing over the moor behind him, his fat head lit up by it like his hair is on fire, like it's the Devil himself come calling. We could hear horses and commotion, and suddenly our neighbor's roof burst into flame, a black billow of smoke.

Out now before someone's hurt, the factor said, and Ma snarled something unseemly at him (Da will tell us later the curse she proposed, inviting him to boil in a head-to-toes pox, Da's mouth twitching into almost a smile). Ma's voice was low and harsh. She ordered Abigail to usher the wee ones out, Charles at our cart, guarding the loom. Three of the factor's men came bursting in, snatching at what little we had left inside, tossing it out. One of them grabbed Ma's pretty shawl draped over a chest packed with our dishes and she growled at him to *put that down this instant.* Before Da could stop her she'd grabbed a handful of stones from just outside our door and was pitching them at him, and the factor too, until another of his men came up behind and bludgeoned her with a fire poker, stolen off our cart. Ma fell to the floor of our cottage and the man with her shawl tossed it on top of her like a shroud.

Rebecca! Da shouted, ordering the rest of us out, lifting her up into his arms. She was wobbly, unsteady on her feet, but she made him put her down. I shall walk out of my home the same way I come in it, she said. Blood streaming down one side of her face and the wee lassies, Dottie and Mary, sobbing by the cart. Abigail shushed them, but I just stood there, thinking here is the moment that will change everything: Da helping Ma, bent as a chimney pipe and leaning on him, out across the threshold she'd walked through countless times, carrying whatever it took to make us a home, and now the roof was lit with the factor's torch, the thatch bursting into flame, and it was over.

There was commotion everywhere, people running, scream-ing, stench of things burning. Pa picked up a fistful of Skye dirt, told us all to hold out our hands and dribbled bits of it into them: Here, he said, is your home. Wherever you go, carry it there. He told Ma, make sure when I die, you place it in my coffin. Ma, who had tied a wool rag around her head to staunch the bleeding, said nothing and refused to put her hand out for the dirt. She stood and watched our cottage burn.

Dear Diary, I went in my mind, *'tis our saddest day. We have but the clothes on our person, our cart, and what all it fits, to be home for our family, and with Da and Ma fixing to leave Abigail and me off at the ferry, Charles going on ahead, we won't even have our family.*

★   ★   ★

Though we had walked most of the day, no one dared complain how tired they were, the wee ones set atop the cart when their lit-tle legs would no longer hold. Could've used the horse, Ma grum-bled, which was owned, along with the goats and a cow, by several families on the croft and was all agreed would be left for any that remained. We had hiked down the cliff, Ma tying up our skirts with twine, down to a beach where some families cleared from a settlement on Harris had landed, creating a makeshift shelter out of piled up stones and thatch. Others had joined, a small village of them surviving on what fish they caught, limpets and crab. A vil-lage built on sand, gone with the first winter storm or a full moon tide, muttered Ma.

They had the peat-black eyes of the outer Hebridean folks. Further out still, the St. Kildans with eyes like coal, said Da. But those ones keep to themselves, he said, you won't see any factor bullying them off their island—because no one wants Hirta anyway, said Ma, what's there but birds? We'd heard stories about the St. Kildan boys and men who climbed the jagged cliffs for fulmars in just their knickers, and once I told the Diary in my mind it would not hurt my eyes to see this, bare-chested lads rappelling those cliffs.

I was watching one of the Harris boys as our parents stood chatting with the elders, his shoulders like he bore creels filled with rocks. *Dear Diary, I am in love with the boy whose eyes are a winter's night,* I scribed in my mind. Then Da motioned us forth. What could we do but plod on, down the arm of the peninsula opposite Sleat, where the laird lived, Lord MacDonald, known to have cleared that land first, but not for sheep—a hunting spot, was said, for wealthy lowlanders and Englishmen to come slaughter our deer, seabirds, whatever they could find for the sport of it.

That night, after walking the length of Loch Eisort, finally arriving at the Kylerhea Ferry that would bear three MacQueens off the Isle of Skye, we turned and saw, as the rosy dusk grew, the red sky over Suisnish and Boreraig, where the villages had been set on fire. Beyond the Cuillin Mountains loomed, black as the teeth of the Devil himself.

When we said our goodbyes, we weren't carrying much beyond those fistfuls of Skye dirt. Abigail and I packed ours together in a canning jar to put in our trunk, which was already on the ferry. It did not occur to us that we might have separate homes, or that one of us might not have a home at all. We had on our blue wool skirts, dusty from the track we'd walked all day on, and our everyday linen jumpers. Our Sunday white jumpers were packed away, to save them for church when we found one; Presbyterian said Ma, make certain of that. We weren't obligated to wear a mutch, being unmarried, but Ma told us to drape our scarves over our heads anyway for warmth on the crossing. The weather is kind enough now, she said, but weeks out it will be much worse. Besides, said she, if a sailor sees your long locks and takes a fancy, married to the sea you shall be!

Then Ma gave Abigail her pretty tweed shawl, told her to put it in our trunk when we were in Glasgow and save it for good. Abigail, she explained, being older, was likely to be betrothed first. (And prettier, I could feel Ma willing her tongue to not speak it, but it was true, we all knew it.) Abigail protested but Ma insisted. Do I have use for it anymore, Ma said, without even a home to keep it in? I've husbanded already and look where that got me, she said, scowling at Da's turned-around back. We knew she didn't really blame him, how could she? He had so little left for all his hard work.

The ferryman blew the boarding horn and started the paddles up. Go, Ma said, and I kissed her cheek quickly, then touched Da's shoulders, and his muscles twitched, as his face would too if I could see it. So thin he was; I suppose all of us were those famine years. I grabbed the wee ones, hugging them hard. We had already said our goodbyes to Charles, who'd rushed to catch the earlier ferry, having passage on a vessel the next day.

Abigail and I stood clutching the rail, watching our family recede as we sailed into the loch, swept ever faster away by the strong current there. Behind them the blue hump of Skye in the early evening light, a calm night, even the heavens seemed listless and sad. I knew in my bones I would not see our family again, and I felt such a hollow, sunken feeling I wanted to curl up right there on that deck and sleep it all away. Abigail might've thought the same as she suddenly grabbed my hand and held it to her heart, her other hand clutching our train tickets to Glasgow.

She would, though, as it turned out, see Ma, even live with her a spell, along with two of the four wee ones, having made their own crossing a year later. They had tried that first year to croft some land by the sea in Elgol, but the shore was all rock, and the fish about fished out by others doing the same. So they took one of the over-packed emigration ships to Prince Edward Island, and there was a cholera outbreak on it, which was the fate of many of those crowded ships. Alas, Da and two wee ones succumbed.

Personally, I never did believe it was cholera that got my Da, though the ship's captain logged it that way. He'd never been sick a day in his life. It was his heart that broke, and Ma told Abigail he died clutching that Skye dirt in his fist. But I'm getting ahead of myself here.

★   ★   ★

On a bone-cold late November day, our cousin Martin MacQueen secured Abigail and me passage on a carriage to the Glasgow ship-yard, where some beak-nosed clerk in a stuffy little office checked our tickets with the information Da had posted, to make sure we had paid. Then to the harbor we went, and a barque vessel we were put on for the crossing, the Allen and Brown. Not one of the usual emigrant ships like what the rest of our family went on, packed full of passengers bound for the new world, Australia and Canada mostly, although these countries were not yet independent, still mostly claimed by Great Britain. The emigrant ships kept a mani-fest of all their passengers' names, whether they are male or female and what they did for a living, if they had means to do anything at all. Da might've put down "weaver" for Abigail and me, as the intent had been for Charles to find us a situation at a shirt factory. Or the clerk might've scribed just "F" for female, not much being expected or allowed us beyond our sex those days.

But this vessel was most likely registered as a trade ship, though no one seems to know for sure as history did not seem to record it. The ship carried a fair number of us Gaels, along with other cargo, lumber and dry goods of various sort we weren't meant to know about; not your concern, said the Captain, an ample-armed man, his face rigid as a plank of wood. We were told what we could and couldn't do, where we couldn't go and where we could—up to the deck for air, but only in the daylight, and if the captain called all hands on deck it meant any Gaels must go back down to the hold, crammed in with all the rest that weren't supposed to be on it, an illegal passage in other words, what Da could afford. Thus our names were not recorded, and when we were lost, who would know we existed?

It's common knowledge now about the northeastern ship-wrecks, how the Atlantic can kick up a storm in the time it takes to note clouds are gathering, the sky looking green and poorly. Permit me a brief divergence here, as much of this was unknown when Abigail and myself set foot on this ship, our destiny. It fascinates me how that word, *destiny*, seemed so certain when we were lassies on the Isle of Skye, limited in its outcomes by the station we were born to, a crofter's family. That we were sent off to the new world was already a considerable altering of what our fates should have been, but to get there—crossing a mercurial Atlantic—was its own kind of destiny, unknown by most who'd be passengers, who having been evicted from their homes, the land of their birth by virtue of not having means to own their own land, paid these vessels to bear them to another. I believe it my duty to cast some light on what we were heading into, because when we stepped onto that ship in 1852, it was in darkness.

PART III

SPRING

✦ HEAVEN ✦

"YOU MUST UNDERSTAND, HEAVEN, that faeries are an inscru-
table folk, as likely to hinder as help. We were the Mac-
Queens of Suisnish on a cliff overlooking Loch Eisort, and across
was Sleat, a peninsula surrounded by sea and loch with views of the
Cuillin Mountains, and a great green hill near Dun na Ceard
known as the sithein, faerie hill. There are stories of the craftsmen
who lived on that hill, who with the faeries help, when they were
in the mood for it, could convert any piece of iron or wood brought
to them in the night. You'd hear their lament: 'Oh my distress and
calamity, oh my distress and calamity,' and in the morning whatever was brought had been turned into something else.

"Not far from this is the tiny Port na Faganaich, which means
Bay of the Forsaken Ones. There are grand stones rising out of the
sea, and my great-grandpa, who would've been your great-great-
grandpa MacQueen, told my grandpa, who then told me, how one
night a party of young Sleat fishermen returning late from fishing saw something splashing in the phosphorescent water. They
approached quietly and discovered a group of beautiful seal maidens who'd sloughed off their skins, laid them on the beach, and

were playing with each other in the waves. One of the fishermen took the skins and hid them, and when dawn came and the selkies (for of course that's what they were) went to put on their skins, they were gone. They wept and lamented, but in the end, since they had no skins and could not return to the sea, they married the fishermen and lived as women happily enough.

"Then one night the fisherman who hid the skins had it 'laid upon him' to give them back. That's a magical commandment put into your head while you sleep, and in the morning you have no choice but to obey. That night the sea called to the seal maidens to return. Their husbands were turned into stones, and ever since then, on a full moon night you can see seals swimming and playing around these stones."

Heaven, peering through the hole in the wall at her uncle shakes her head. "Yeah, *right*," she says, imitating the snarky tone the B-girls use. A foghorn wails in the distance, the night humid and thick with haze. She'd like to lay it in Grandmelia's head to get her that mountain bike! She looks around Uncle Daniel's room: a tall wooden bookcase, his bed, a scratched-up old desk, and the mat he's sitting on. "How do you even remember this stuff? Is it in your books?"

Uncle Daniel points at his head. "It's all in here. My grandpa told me stories, his dad before him, and so on; helps me not to think thoughts I don't want to think. If you *tell* yourself you're not going to think about something, then having that thought means you're thinking about it. So you tell yourself something else instead."

"Well, that sounds mental. So how do you know about seals turning into people? Like how does it even happen?"

He shrugs. "Some of them started out as people, drowned then saved by a seal."

"My dad drowned, and he died!" Heaven shouts.

Uncle Daniel presses his finger to his lips. "Shh, your grandmother isn't a fan of seals. It's rumored one of them bit her when she got too close. It's all about transformation. Not everyone can be transformative. Maybe your dad was too handsome. That's the problem with good-looking people. They can't imagine life from the perspective of someone less beautiful. What, are you kidding me, have a body like a floating log and wear wet gray and brown fur for the rest of my life? And that voice, *please*. Sounds like a dog with a tennis ball stuck in its throat."

Heaven rolls her eyes. "You're a dork, Uncle Daniel. Your stories don't make sense."

"Stories aren't supposed to make *sense*. They're supposed to make you not want to bang your head against the wall or take a long walk off a short pier."

Heaven grins. "I wonder what part of Grandmelia a seal would even *want* to bite."

◆ AMELIA ◆

Visitors Rules of Conduct

#4 Modulate your voice—keep the volume down.
Examples: No yelling. No arguing. No speaking loudly or
in a shrill tone. No excessive laughing.

AMELIA IS MAKING THE trek up north, minus the weekend traffic (Thursday) and minus her granddaughter (afternoon swim
practice, and since Amelia wasn't looking forward to another sullen
drive it's as good an excuse for her as it is for Heaven). Pulls off 95
for gas, a large black coffee, and roasted almonds, slipping the kid
at the cash register her AARP card ("Discounts for seniors!" the
sign said), peering around just in case. He takes it without looking
at her; if not for her height she'd be invisible. When he hands her
back her change, he's forced to look up. "Have a nice day," she tells
him, muttering *midget* under her breath, then feels bad noting he
has pimples—probably can't even *get* a girl, let alone someone of
Amelia's caliber.

Never mind, she has a mission to accomplish, a *quest*, as Daniel and Heaven keep spouting. Everything is a quest with those two, and she resents that they are "those two," an almost thirteen-year-old and Amelia's forty-two-year old son who won't come out of his room. They act the same age, secrets whispered—they think she doesn't know about the hole in the wall—what, she's an idiot because she's old? She's held her tongue because quite frankly it entertains Heaven and a Heaven amused is out of Amelia's hair. Daniel's been feeding her those ridiculous tales from the Isle of Skye. Their ancestors abandoned that place for a reason. "Don't you get that your uncle doesn't have enough of his marbles to even leave his room?" she asked Heaven one day. "He can't handle the real world, so he makes one up in his head!" Heaven shrugged. "The real world isn't so great. It's pretty overrated," she said sagely. Like her granddaughter's lived enough to judge.

Takes the turn off 95 onto 295, where she'll pick up the route heading up the coast. If she stayed on 95 she'd end up in Augusta, which makes her think about Leo living there, and what's up with him, anyway? She really doesn't want to get involved, divorce means it's not supposed to be her problem, and yet that witchy Mabel, his downstairs tenant, called again this morning—"He wandered last night, found his way back at two AM but forgot his keys," she griped, "so guess who's got to get up and let him inside his own darn building?" Amelia murmured something by way of thanks, but every time this happens, it's Amelia who feels diminished. Leo, just four years older, her former mate. If he can't handle the logistics of a life anymore, then that makes her . . . what? Is this what she's coming to? Should she be putting her affairs in order before she forgets what they are?

You watch your past peel away, every notable death of someone from your own generation, a chunk of you goes too, but this thing with Leo . . . it's not *death*, nothing so final, more like he's slowly forgetting who he is. Or *where* he is. Then there's his spy paranoia. What should she do about any of this? (Though why must she get involved? She's not legally obligated!) Should she talk to someone, a doctor? But what would she say? My ex-husband, once a renowned photographer, *wanders*. WASPS don't speak of these things. We keep them in a box, tidy and out of sight. Do not open for fear of something exposed, somebody's drug problem, a crazy son, her dad's gambling, her mom's aloofness, hypochondria, her own one-night-stand with *not even a superstar*! Leo had pointed out, a *lesser* star—if he'd been Jim Morrison would her husband have understood? She imagines the conversation: *"Oh sure,* Jim Morrison, *who could blame you?"* Clean up, sanitize, tape the box shut.

A sludge of traffic now inching over the Bath bridge, shift change at the Ironworks, limping along through little coastal towns that, God forbid, wouldn't want to destroy their provincial character by anything as sensible as a stoplight once in a while to control two directions of traffic!

When Amelia finally arrives, she's logy, her thighs hurt from sitting in the car an hour longer than she should have, the beginning of a headache and a *really* bad mood. Going through the metal detector and searched, and on top of that, her purse rifled through even though it stays at the Entrance desk until the visiting hour is over (like she'd slip a file to Cassiopeia for her to break out? She'd as soon see her inside these walls for the rest of her life!); then following a guard along with a line of other visitors through two clanging security gates locking them inside— all this isn't helping her mood. At the entrance to the Visiting Room her name is the last one called, and instead of Cassie seated first, the usual drill, Amelia is seated, and her daughter-in-law is ushered in, handcuffed and shackled at her ankles, a tall, scowling guard pushing Cassie's shoulders down opposite Amelia, forcing her to sit.

"Well for crying out loud, now what?"

Cassie rolls her eyes. "I'm being punished, can you tell? For messing with another inmate. I told them to just cancel my visit with you but nooooo, they put me in restraints for the privilege of seeing you. You suppose they think I'll attack you? Boo!" she hisses, and Amelia catches a whiff of something sharp on her breath.

"Messing with. You mean . . ."

"Oh for chrissake, you think I'm gay? I should've been so lucky. A spat got a little physical, was all. She was supposed to give me something, then she didn't."

"Well you sound like a nine-year-old on the playground! A guard has to lead you in like a little kid."

Cassie shrugs. "Yup, that's about right. It's how we're treated. And by the way, they prefer to be called corrections officers, but I hear you—if it walks like a duck, stinks like a duck—"

"Yes, yes. Can we skip the chat and move on?"

"Look, *mother-in-law*, I know why you're here, and I already told you! I can't remember and I'm getting tired of you messing with my head about it!"

"I'm not messing with your head. How am I messing with your head? You just have to try, period. You were the only one there. That much was established."

"You're messing with my head because you won't get *out* of my head, and it's driving me crazy the way you keep insisting. You'd make a great leech: cling on, suck dry! I didn't deny it. I'm being fucking punished for it—that's got to be good enough."

"My son is dead! Can you understand what that's like, to have a son stolen from your life, from *life*? I just want the truth. That's all I'm left, the truth of what happened that night."

Cassie is shaking all over, a full-body assault. Amelia can feel her knees bumping against the underneath part of the table. Her eyes look wild and unfocused; *like a horse*, Amelia thinks, *a feral, untamable colt.*

"What'll it get? It won't bring my husband back!"

"He was my son before he was your husband—he's still my son! I want his name cleared of all that other dirty business, the drugs, that other woman. The way they made it out in that courtroom it was like they thought he deserved what happened to him."

Cassie snorts, her eyes fill up. "Women you mean, plural. That whore was just the latest. I can't feel enough about her to even call her *that whore* and mean it in my heart. I just don't like using her name, hearing it in the room. She doesn't deserve the attention. She was just another blowjob to him, her big ugly mouth."

Amelia winces at the BJ reference, so coarse, she thinks. "So you killed him. I understand jealousy. I get that. Jealousy is human. The prosecutor held it out as a viable motive, so why can't you just admit it?"

Cassie clears her throat, pales and looks for a moment like she might throw up. Her eyes water, and she swallows hard like she's choking on something. "Viable motive? You're reducing my god-damn life to a *viable motive*? Is that it, Amelia? We change the subject this minute or I'm outta here. They can shackle me to my cot, be better than this."

Amelia sighs, rubs gently under her eyes, careful not to smudge her mascara. They teach you that as a model: powder around and under the lids to reduce smudging and other now useless information, like shading your eyes with dark brown or gray to create depth, how to contour under your cheeks with blush to empha-size the bones. Her face is all bone now, like the rest of her. Her mother, who tended toward a certain heft (*cherubian*, her dad called it), had always warned Amelia that after giving birth, then as she aged, she would put on weight. It never happened; yet another way she was a disappointment to her mother. "So what is it *you* would like to talk about, Cassiopeia?"

"Get Heaven the bike."

"What?"

"You know damn well, for her birthday, when it gets closer. I got her letter, couple weeks ago. You told her to ask me, so I'm telling you. Get her the bike."

"Sure," Amelia snaps. "And with what, may I ask?"

"You can afford it. Be a grandma for once."

Amelia snorts. "And why don't you try being a mom!"

"You should talk, you didn't even come to our wedding."

"You got married on a bloody rock! You call that a wedding?"

"It was Point Lobos, a famous landmark in San Francisco. I cocktailed near it, at the Cliff House," she says proudly, like it's an accomplishment, Amelia thinks.

"What *are* you giving her then?" Cassie's knees are bump-ing the table so hard Amelia feels its tremors underneath her own hands, shaped into fists as if she too needs to pummel something.

"How about I'm giving her a home! A sight more than you ever gave her, sleeping in a crate for lord's sake, the social worker told me."

"That was Heaven's choice. We let her express herself."

"I'm sure that was what it was all about, letting your daughter *express* herself while you and my son got high!"

"Inmate French and visitor!" a corrections officer barks across the room, *"Modulate!"* pointing at the Rules Chart.

Cassie leans in toward Amelia's face, her cheeks prickles of red like match heads, close enough for the officer to shout again, "French, move it back! You've got two minutes! Abbreviated visit today."

"No wonder Gavin never wanted to visit you," she spits. "You're a snake, aren't you? He wasn't a fan of snakes." Stands up, holding out her handcuffed wrists. "Thanks so much for the visit"; her voice tart. "I'd shake your hand but, you know . . ." winking at the CO as he grabs her arm. "I've about had it with you, French!" he snaps.

"By the way, *Grandma*?" Cassie calls out as she's led toward the exit. "Heaven says it's a *mountain* bike she wants. Don't ask me why, I hear there's not a mountain to be found in Seahaven."

Amelia scowls, then smiles thinly at another guard who's come to escort her out. She's about Cassie's size, Cassie's age, maybe could've *been* Cassie in another life if her daughter-in-law wasn't such a complete wreck of a human being! Maybe she could've been the one with the keys, instead of in handcuffs. "Forgive my prying, do you have kids?" The guard shakes her head. Amelia nods, "Bit of advice: keep it that way."

★ ★ ★

Later that night, half-asleep or in a dream he's with her again. Dank and wet, a tangy smell like rotting seaweed, but then the wet starts feeling more airy, ashy like they're swimming through smoke and she sits up choking, gasping for breath as she feels him pull away from her the way he always did when she tried to get too close; she's reaching out, calling his name in the liminal light of her room, it is her room she's in her bed—*Gavin*! Vanished, a comet shooting out of sight, towing the tail of her yearnings like a string of lights, each one winking out the further he goes.

If only she could've reached out far enough, she would've never let him go.

◆ HEAVEN ◆

Heaven doesn't have sleeping dreams, not exactly. Her mom said maybe she wasn't creative enough or smart enough when Heaven told her she didn't dream, but that was after Heaven told her she saw her dad and a couple of his friends give each other shots, and Cassie said she must've dreamt it. "Probably what you saw was a dream and you just didn't know it," her mom said. Heaven's problem isn't when she sleeps, it's what she sees *in between* the part where you're awake then asleep, or you're asleep then you wake up but not entirely. There's a layer of some other thing in between sleep and awake, a kind of half-lit place that's more shadow than light, but the shadows move, and they take on shapes and these shapes *do* things, scary creepy things sometimes, and Heaven's awake enough to know she doesn't want any part of what they're doing.

Last night one of the shadows became an arm, a big arm like on a big man, only it was just this arm rocking back and forth, then opposite the arm comes this small slender hand, a lot like her mom's hand, the mom in prison, when Heaven thinks about this now. The hand kept moving up and down like it was shaking another hand but there was nothing there; up then down and the big arm rocking back and forth. Heaven lay very still in her bed, pretending she was asleep; she didn't call to Uncle Daniel in the next room, because she learned when she lived with her mom and dad that it didn't get you anywhere to call, since most of the time nobody answers. Then the shadows know you're awake.

Now that it's morning the world in between has disappeared, but Heaven can't quite get with the picture, as her mom used to call it when she'd wake up all groggy and slow and her mom's trying to be a mom, she'd tell her, trying to get Heaven *outta here* to school. Thinking of that shaking hand that looked like her mom's makes her not want to eat breakfast, so she sits, her food *growing colder by the minute*, Grandmelia warns her.

"You haven't *touched* your breakfast," Grandmelia says. "I scrambled those eggs, added *white* cheese for you and I will not see them wasted. You can just stay there until you eat something."

Then Uncle Daniel refuses to eat his too, in solidarity, handing Grandmelia his untouched plate through the door. He'd cracked open his door wide enough to pass her his plate, and Grandmelia sticks her foot in the opening so he can't shut it. Now they're arguing back and forth, and not even about her food, while Heaven sits with a plate of cold eggs.

"Will you stop filling her head with those ridiculous stories! She wants her hair long like a mermaid, she told me. Heaven's a chunky girl with a round face and mousy hair; growing mermaid hair is not a rational objective."

"It's her hair. She can do whatever the fuck fuck fuck she wants with it," Uncle Daniel says.

Heaven watches them, like they don't know she's right *here*, where Grandmelia told her to be, in the wide-open dining room, watching. Grandmelia's dining room is the size of their house in Maine's kitchen and living room combined.

"You aren't going to fade away on me again, are you? Is not eating your breakfast about Heaven or some kind of statement? Last time you were practicing being a monk if I recall. Couldn't eat anything but miso. A monk whose bedroom is his monastery!"

Grandmelia stamps her foot, the one not stuck in Uncle Daniel's door, like she expects Uncle Daniel to challenge her, but he just smiles. "Miso is food of the Buddha."

"I doubt Buddha consumed Hannaford brand packages of instant miso."

Heaven sighs, a sound like a breeze wafting through, to see if they remember her. Grandmelia turns around and glares. Her eyebrows have holes in them where she plucks the white ones out, but they aren't growing back, and even if they did they'd also be white, so she'd have to start all over again. She hasn't put her face on yet, because then she would've taken a charcoal pencil and drawn her eyebrows in—who needs *actual* hair, she told Heaven. Was that about eyebrows or Heaven's refusal to get a haircut?

Maybe Heaven is invisible, maybe that's why they're talking about her like she's not even here. Sometimes when her mom and dad sniffed powder up their noses or lit their glass pipe, Heaven really *could* be invisible, watching them when they didn't see her at all. She figured if she kept her eyes on them, they couldn't drift away. Like those shadows from the in-between world when she finally fell asleep, drifting, dissolving, gone. When they return the next night, they will have morphed into something else.

"It's a constant battle," Grandmelia told her hairstylist in Scituate Harbor yesterday, after Heaven refused to let Peru cut her hair, then finally agreed on a compromise, trimming her bangs. Grandmelia was talking about Heaven again like Heaven wasn't sitting right there in that haircut torture chair, but Heaven nodded, all agreeable, gazing out Peru's window at the harbor, flat and metal colored under a gray sky. She'd slipped a tortoise shell barrette from the display shelf into her backpack and didn't want to draw attention to herself after the haircut fuss. It's got gold sparkles and will look awesome when her hair's long enough to clip into a ponytail. Or maybe a messy bun—she'd rock a messy bun.

She told Grandmelia she wanted mermaid hair because she can't tell her what she really wants, which is surfer-girl hair. Uncle Daniel is getting her a secret birthday present that hasn't arrived yet, because he has to figure out a time when Grandmelia won't

be around for FedEx to bring it. A surfboard! All the way from
Hawaii, he said, Waimea where they make the best ones, where
they get the biggest waves in the world. This is way better than
the mountain bike because even though Grandmelia finally broke
down and got her one, even gave it to her before her actual birthday, it's not the brand she wanted, not even her second choice. "It's
not a brand *anybody's* heard of," Bethany pointed out when Heaven
rode it to their first swim practice. Bethany tossed her long blond
hair off her shoulders, called it a ghetto ride. Now Heaven doesn't
want to ride it anymore, but Grandmelia insisted. "You wanted a
mountain bike, you got it," she said, that the option for crack-of-
dawn carpools was closed.

Uncle Daniel's getting her the surfboard because she's become
such a good swimmer and can hold her breath for a super long
time underwater. That's a survival skill, he said. She can paddle the
board out past the lighthouse jetty where the sea turns aquamarine, he said. Who knows? Maybe she'll even see a selkie out there
cavorting with the Harbor seals that swim by sometimes. Plus she
can teach herself how to surf, Heaven added, surfing's cool. Uncle
Daniel said he didn't know about surfing, but he knew how to
paddle, and paddling a surfboard's got to be easier than paddling a
raft. "It's streamlined," he said, "shaped for speed and trajectory."

Heaven was thinking how she could paddle out and dive in
where it's really deep and go way way down to practice her drowning song, then up again, and when a wave comes she could surf it
in! She can't wait for Grandmelia to go to Maine again to see the
mom in prison, which she's doing regularly now, trying to make
her come to her senses, Grandmelia said; she didn't say what senses
her mom needs to come to and Heaven couldn't care less because
that's when Uncle Daniel said would be the best window to have
the surfboard delivered.

Maybe she'll become so good on that surfboard she can paddle
all the way up the coast to where her dad drowned, and maybe it
will be Heaven who finds out the truth of what happened. When
her dad drowned and they locked her mom up, Heaven was put in
foster care before and even for a while after the trial, then Peggy

Howell brought her to Grandmelia. Foster care was some buttoned-up man and a lady with a bunch of kids, and Heaven slept in a bedroom with their daughters. They said grace every night, holding hands, and asked the kids about school, but nobody would talk about why her mom's in prison, like if they didn't talk about it Heaven wouldn't know. "Mistakes were made," Peggy Howell said. Grandmelia blames her mom, but Heaven remembers how they got, her mom and her dad, the stuff up their nose, his shots they didn't believe she saw, her mom's exercise band tied around his arm; all airy like you couldn't anchor them down. So maybe that's what happened, her dad just blew off those rocks into the ocean like a dandelion fluff.

Meanwhile there are other fish to fry, as Grandmelia puts it, meaning when you have additional concerns, she said. These are Heaven's "additional concerns" since turning thirteen last week. (Grandmelia bought a zucchini cake, said it was healthier than the chocolate cake Heaven had asked for—*blech!*) First, her body. At thirteen she expected real boobs instead of the fatty bulbs that haven't changed a bit since she was twelve; her period, which if the girls on the team find out she hasn't gotten yet will be the end of Heaven's life. Since she can hold her breath so long, four seconds longer than Melissa Chang, the second best at holding her breath underwater, they've at least had to admit she's good at something, and not half bad at the breaststroke either, her stroke. (Bethany said it's because Heaven has extra body fat so she can't sink.)

By thirteen she thought she'd look more like her mom, whose hips, thighs, and teeny-weeny shoulders compared to Heaven's are all in angular alignment, walking geometry her dad used to say. Instead Heaven's body bulges out in every direction and is just plain nasty. It sweats when she's not in the water, which means before she gets *in* the water she has to shower, or the girls scream *gross pig!* To have to shower before swimming with all those girls is pure torture, because they see it—how her body is an alien's body, a bubble of surplus flesh instead of skin shrunken tight over bones. It's big and bulbous and unless she's in the water where she's light as a snow cone, she tromps about in her noisy, fleshy, bubble-body like some rubberized robot, bumping into stuff, like a buffoon, Grandmelia called it. "Move more thoughtfully, gracefully, *think* before you step," Grandmelia said, then showed her some modeling moves. *As if!* Heaven is ashamed of the *presence* her body makes. There's no way of hiding it, like in English class when her stomach groaned, and everyone laughed; you just can't control it and she's terrified the rumbles will come out the other end like Robyn's did one day. The others teased him for the rest of the week, Stinkbug they called him, but he didn't seem to care. Everyone farts—he shrugged—it's just a matter of who's around to smell it.

Worst of all, the triangle of hair between her legs, her thighs rubbing together going squish squish and the overlapping popover-belly, Bethany called it, on top of this hair like it's a shelf, drawing attention to the contents below. And stinky underarm hair! She asked Grandmelia if she could shave it and Grandmelia said to ask her mom, but there's no way Heaven's going to take *that* request to the mom in prison. So one day she snakes a razor from Grandmelia's bathroom cabinet and just does it, her legs too, figuring she'd tell Grandmelia that Coach made her do it to swim faster. She cut herself, prickles of blood all down her legs, like putting her skin into a shredder; the chlorine stung like a sonofabitch (Uncle Daniel's word) the next day.

With the hair between her legs she should at least have her period by now, but nooooo, just gunky yellow stuff on her underpants, Heaven checks each time she feels a little moisture down there, which is disgusting. It's nasty enough that Heaven doesn't want Grandmelia's *cleaning professional*, she calls Estelle who comes every other week to do Grandmelia's laundry and household chores (that Heaven hasn't been forced to do!), to see her grungy underwear. Estelle, who has a Spanish accent (*Mexican* Spanish, Grandmelia pointed out, not Castilian, which is what Grandmelia learned in school; useless unless you're in Spain, Uncle Daniel said), wears a white shirt, beige pants, tan flats, and Heaven figures with all that neutral going on she must be very clean. So she hides the disgusting panties in her closet, under boxes of Grandmelia's old shoes she stores there for Heaven in case her own feet ever monster-out into Grandmelia's size eleven, and she wears her bathing suit under her clothes, so the yellow stuff gets washed away at swim practice.

Another worry is that her grandmother, like other MacQueens Uncle Daniel told her stories about, might have a superpower, in this case wishing for someone's drowning, then it happens. Uncle Daniel said before he and his brother were sent off to Goat Island where Uncle Daniel nearly drowned, they'd been roughhousing in the hotel room and got into a tug-of-war with Amelia's favorite necklace and broke it, spraying blood-red garnets all over the room like a murder scene. Their mother was furious when she came out of the bathroom. "I wish I'd never had either of you!" she shrieked. That afternoon was Uncle Daniel's drowning where he came back someone else—still his body but his spirit was different, he told Heaven. Then Heaven's dad years later, but this time she got the body too. Heaven didn't think Grandmelia liked her very much; could she be next? She didn't know how to ask Uncle Daniel about this, so instead she asked him where MacQueens who don't drown go when they die.

"Well," he said, "when Amelia's gone, we'll ship her body to the Isle of Skye and the faeries under the faerie hill will cut out her heart and weigh it on a faerie scale. That's what they do, you see. If it's a weighted heart, full of charity and goodness, her body will be given to the ocean so her spirit might rise out of it in a burst of bubbles. But if it's light as a reed from too little caring or compassion for others, it will become part of the faeries feast, roasted on a spit, and the rest of her will be offered to the giants of Skye. Like a hunt, you don't want to waste any part. In Sleat there are giants who live in the hills, big people they call them. For a giant your grandmother would be but a snack, a handful of nuts before the meal begins."

That night Heaven saw such bad things in the shadow world, killer faeries writhing like snakes and horrible shadows of hungry giants, she had to get up and write *surfboard* over and over on her cool new ocean notebook (dolphins and whales!) snagged from a girl who sits by her in science, to distract her from seeing Grand-melia's roasted flesh, the smell of her burnt hair, like when Peru singed it with the curling iron to give her those "Hepburn waves." Grandmelia had turned to Heaven who was plugging her nose. "If you'd cooperate and let Peru cut your hair, you could have these pretty curls too!"

◆ DANIEL ◆

His window to her window, like a zip line and he's here, waiting for her. She'll look at him, he'll look at her. Eyes that maybe bear the sea, its secrets, what she holds within. Tonight the wind blows hard and he thinks of her loneliness, of his, lonelier when the wind is blowing, like the world outside doesn't exist, just you inside this wind. You, her, the ocean, its push onto the rocky shore.

Yesterday Amelia told him about the baby, said she'd heard it from Mercy's own mother, Anita. Mercy and her husband had wanted a baby but turned out she was too damaged inside, something like that, Amelia said, so she couldn't carry it. Mercy had apparently added its ultrasound picture to her Collection of Broken Things. "Ridiculous in and of itself!" Amelia said. "Who does that kind of thing? Left the husband too, Anita told me, and he was the good one, the second one. Would've stuck with her anyway. Some people are like that."

Daniel had closed his eyes and imagined it, Amelia's voice droning on, the other side of his bedroom door. But he'd heard all he needed to know . . .

Later that night he beamed his signal at Mercy when she got home, one two three flashes and she flipped her light on and off in acknowledgment, then left it on and stood at the window staring out at him. She looked tired, sad, and he felt for her, that empty, hopeless vortex (he knows it well), like nothing or maybe everything will change, and neither matters because whichever way things spin, they won't affect who she is—a thirty-seven-year-old diner waitress living in her mother's garage, he could hear Amelia saying. Then again, who is Daniel? An almost forty-three-year-old man living not only in his mother's house but his childhood bedroom, as Amelia has not spared him pointing this out. I mean, who's the freak here?

It's not like he didn't try to be *normal*, that time in high school when his brother brought two girls home, Amelia in Boston, and Gavin told Daniel to follow his lead, do what he did, the four of them downing shots of Tequila on the sectional sofa. But later, his girl positioned under him on one section of the sofa, same as his brother's on the other, nothing happened. The girl sat up, pushed him off, said, *Screw this!* Apparently, he'd become a boy who felt nothing; no "stirring in his loins," as the nineteenth-century authors they read in English class described it, not for girls or boys either.

After Daniel graduated he was accepted at Bridgewater State. He could've done better, but it had to be in Massachusetts because his brother was still in school and how else could he watch out for him? Barely into his first semester he started having panic attacks. The infirmary sent him to student counseling which rushed him back to the infirmary because he couldn't breathe, told them he was drowning. After a couple of these episodes they sent him home, to his room where everything was calm and flat. A semester's medical leave, then the years passed.

Tonight, waiting for Mercy to come home, things are finally starting to feel different. Like he'd been living in darkness for all those years and somehow, something broke open and light is leaking in. It's later than usual and he wonders if she stopped off for a drink after work, pictures her at the Mill Wharf, and afterward

maybe some man walks her out into the parking lot, the obligatory kiss, but she'll pull back when he slides his tongue inside her
mouth, the taste of martinis and some deeper need, a damp wind
blowing low tide smells off the harbor, sea birds flapping in the
floodlights. Daniel can see it. He just can't be that man. If he *could*,
perhaps she'd be the one who kisses him.

When she's finally home, Mercy puts on her light and waves.
Lifts up her shirt, but this time she doesn't do her little dance,
doesn't make a fist, snap off her light and shut him out. She stands
there, watching him watch her. Then she turns her desk lamp to
its brightest setting and holds up what appears to be a photograph
from her Collection against the glass, what he imagines maybe is
the ultrasound photo, the baby she lost. If she can't look at it, he
will for her.

✦ LEO ✦

Inmate Rules of Conduct
#4 Don't tell a pitiful story. Keep positive! Other inmates have problems too. For a detailed discussion read **"Fraternizing with Other Inmates"** in the *Inmate Guidebook*.
#8 Minimize crying. See Rule #7! Crying is a distraction.

"I MISS SEEING MY TOES," Leo's daughter-in-law sighs, "some strappy little sandal, you look down and there they are. Gladiator sandals, now those were cool! When you see your toes it's like you feel more grounded. My toenails were always painted, red or purple, sometimes green or blue. Here they make you wear these lame-ass Velcro athletic shoes—no ties, what, they think you'll hang yourself with them? Ha ha, well yeah, that's exactly what they think, you know, those skinny-neck types. Plus nail polish is contraband but some of the girls make it anyway. You'd be surprised what you can make from shit around here, chicks who never graduated high school are like effing chemists. You know your son loved my feet? In here you keep your sneakers on. Never know what's on these floors plus it's a good place to hide contraband." She glances up at the CO and Leo follows her look, slouching against the door of the visitor room, his face like it's encased in plastic, frozen into an expressionless expression, the way they used to photograph models before some genius figured out animation, *life*, a more saleable look.

"Cassie," he starts, and is about to ask her why he's here, but she babbles on about the outfit she was wearing when Gavin first saw her, moving from the sandals up to her skirt with snaps down the front, a lacy shirt, her hair. Leo wonders if she's high, the way she goes on and on, waits for what he figures is her real reason for him being here, more money in her account. He'd been tempted to say no when the prison called: "An inmate from RHWC is attempting to contact you. Will you accept the charges?" Why does he always say yes? If he said no that might be the end of it. Cassie could write letters to him. She's not allowed to use email even if he was inclined toward that sort of thing, which he's not; get an email address and you may as well just dial up some Russian hacker and give him your private info. If she was forced to write letters, he could throw them away without opening them. Yet here he is.

"Plus I don't get much sleep at night, the yellow lights in the corridors always on, shine right into our cells, and I'm awake almost 'til dawn sometimes. 'Bedeviled hour' Gavin used to call it, when his failures all lined up, jeered, taunted, then shouted at him. He'd get all restless with regret and he'd want to have sex, or do a line, something to get us through. God what I wouldn't give for a whiff of that salt air blowing across the bay, winding its way up from the harbor, the backwash, into our bedroom window stuck at half-mast no matter the season, rain, wind, fog, sweaty summer night, crickets singing, peepers peeping and we're lying together so close it's like he's me and I'm his spine, his core, the center of him." She closes her eyes for a moment, rocking herself in the chair.

Leo sighs. "Cassie . . ." he starts. But now she's going on about how their wedding was on the beach, not the rocks of Pt. Lobos that Amelia assumed so she wouldn't come. Leo didn't go either, but Amelia seems to have borne the brunt of this. He didn't have much of an excuse, other than once he moved back into his parents place it felt like his life was in retreat, and he really couldn't see venturing beyond the Eastern Time Zone.

"One thing leads to another . . . you have a life one place then you move somewhere else and before you know it you have a life you wouldn't have chosen, like on a multiple choice quiz. Beep! *Maine*, wrong answer. I never finished State, a second quarter sophomore when Gavin came along. You're either part of his orbit or you're not."

Leo nods. That much about Gavin was true. He holds up his hand before she can launch back into it. "So why am I here?"

"Boy, you like to cut to the chase, huh? I was trying to have a conversation with you like a normal person. What I'm saying is I became part of that orbit, but then I wasn't enough." She leans across the table and whispers, "*H* became his soul mate."

"Right, duly noted. Do you need money?"

Cassie snorts. "Well that's a given. But it's not why I called you. What I was getting to . . . I've been thinking things over, and I'm starting to think I *didn't* do it! They based my conviction on having a motive, but the thing of it is, I didn't! Gavin didn't love that meth whore, excuse me, Miss Mary Barbara Smithers. Hell, he didn't even *like* her that much. She was just a distraction when he couldn't get his buzz on or not enough of one, or when he was really wasted; throw a little crystal in and he'd do the first breasted thing in sight. I happened to not be in sight when he wanted it that night, made the mistake of going out to score for us, so when I come back and catch them at it, sure we fight like motherfuckers. Wouldn't you? Like, I go do something nice and that's my reward? I wasn't under some delusion she was taking my place. Smack took all our places a long time ago with our boy Gavin, so why would I suddenly conk him on the head with a board and push him in the goddamn sea? He was my own source for a bump, you know it, since half the time it was your wallet buying it."

Leo feels that tightness in his chest and looks around, wondering if anyone heard, but they're all engrossed in their own visitors, their own problems. He's had plenty of sleepless nights over it to be sure, how much he might've been to blame. But dammit, he knows if he didn't give them money they'd have been on the streets; it wasn't like stopping the flow of his funds would make them quit. "Why are you telling me this?"

Cassie laughs, a manic squeal. "It's not obvious? I need a lawyer, a real one, not a pimple-face, fresh-out-of-law-school public defender. And will you please get Amelia off my back with the confession shit! I'm not confessing to anything I can't remember doing, and now I'm thinking there was no reason for me to do it so why the hell would I?"

"What about the drugs? That's in the court records, you both had a lot in your systems, might've made things escalate in some way, maybe you blacked out."

"So you're saying you think I did it. You're blaming me?"

"I'm not saying *that*. It's just a consideration and given you both have—had—an addiction problem, it could've happened the other way around just as easy."

She snorts, "Like you think Gavin could've nailed me? He was a manipulator and a son of a bitch, but he wouldn't hurt a fly. He could talk the talk, make threats like he's got the balls, but he wouldn't even spank Heaven, even when she'd pull dangerous shit like running into the street, and he wouldn't let me either. I want a retrial, that's what."

"I'm not sure that's possible when they already convicted you for manslaughter."

"Yeah, well, so that's why I need a lawyer! I'll figure out a way to pay you back. Someday when I'm out of here, I will, you know—for everything. All of this crap? This isn't me. I was going to be a nurse."

★   ★   ★

Instead of climbing into his Plymouth and making a beeline toward Augusta like he usually does, grateful to be out of that place, Leo decides to get something to eat, then take a walk on the breakwater where *it* happened. Something about being inside a prison for even an hour makes you want to inhale a gargantuan gulp of air when you're back out, and flee.

Leo's not in the mood to sit among strangers, so he orders his Haddock sandwich to-go from the Rockland Cafe, eats it in his car, then drives to the small parking lot by the breakwater, deciding not to lock his car in case he can't remember where his keys are—he has an extra set hidden in his car for that possibility. Pats his pants leg; they're in his pocket, for now. Heads out.

It's early evening, a slight mist in the air and a rolling fog bank out by the islands, Vinalhaven and North Haven. Figures he has just enough time to stroll out to the lighthouse at the end of the mile-long jetty before it's dark, foggy, and with no lights other than the periodic rotation of the lighthouse light itself, the risk of slipping on damp, uneven rocks is high, particularly for Leo with his bum knees—too many shoots in his earlier years where he had to crouch, squat, all manner of knee abuse for the right picture.

The air smells of seaweed and brine, and the post-sunset light paints the bay in ripples of lavender, pink, and silver, the lights of Rockland Harbor in the distance. A slight quickening in his gut, thinking how this was the last walk Gavin took, half hour away, give or take, from the end of his life.

When he reaches the lighthouse, its sweeping light already on, Leo perches on a large rock, peering up at the structure, then out toward the horizon where an almost full orange moon has risen, soon to be obscured by the fog. It was out here that it happened; the kids who found the board said it was wedged between some rocks by the lighthouse, and that witness said she heard them fighting as she stood at the start of the breakwater, their voices growing more distant, then swallowed up as they moved further out.

It's deep here, he knows that much, deep enough where even if there hadn't been a smack on the head, if Gavin slipped and fell off the rocks, wasted as they were, the sea disorienting at night, he might've drowned anyway. But there *was* a board. A hard whack, and he got into that water, conscious or not, and drowned.

First Cassie said she couldn't remember. Then, what if there's nothing *to* remember? And finally, if she ever *did* remember and she really did do it, she'd kill herself. Now she's saying she didn't do it because there was no reason for her to. Where is the truth in any of that?

Out here, surrounded on three sides by a darkening sea, the foghorn's wail, Leo thinks: What if she did? What if she hit him, nothing premeditated but the board was there, and he knew Gavin could be a jerk to her, he'd seen it—Gavin could be a jerk to anyone as easily as he could charm the pants off anyone—what if Cassie, pushed to her limits, had that violence in her and killed him. Maybe all of them have that violence when push comes to shove; Christ, he thinks, not a good pun. Now Cassie wants a lawyer and a retrial where she denies everything. Amelia will freak. He'll have to go there tomorrow and tell her. He pinches his arm to remember to tell her, remember *something*, the red mark will alert him, though he doesn't usually have trouble with this sort of thing, looming disasters. It's his daily routines, mindless stuff where once only his mind might've wandered, now all of him does. If he doesn't remember to tell Amelia and Cassie does, next time he sees his ex it could be *her* in handcuffs and leg irons for doing in their daughter-in-law!

Leo pinches himself again for good measure, then heads back, murmur and slap of the small waves against the breakwater a lulling sound, this place where their son met his death. If he's being honest—and Leo tries to be honest because, let's face it, he has a hard enough time remembering the truth—does he even miss Gavin, a little? Well, it doesn't matter, Cassie does; whatever she did or didn't do, her pain is real. And Amelia. Leo grins, what do you know, his ex-wife and Gavin's wife have something in common!

✦ AMELIA ✦

"YEAH?" AMELIA'S VOICE AT her front door is without enthusiasm. She's never liked answering doors, you never know what will be on the other side, Jehovah's Witnesses, somebody selling something, or a politician stumping. Rarely was it anyone you'd want to see. She opens it and sees Leo. "What in God's name are *you* doing here?" She peers around him. "It's late. Did you think you'd spend the night?"

"No thank you," he says.

Amelia scowls. "But I suppose you want to come in. Leo, what the hell? Is this about your phone paranoia? I'm telling you, I can only take one crazy person in my life, that's my limit, the limit *of* my limits, and he's Daniel."

"I was at the prison," he starts.

"I'm supposed to give you points for that? I'm up there every other bloody week, and it's a three-and-a-half-hour drive for me— that's *without* traffic."

"It's not a competition, Amelia." He hesitates. She watches him stare into the living room behind her, through the lit hallway. She hopes it looks inviting, her hall table with an arrangement of flowers picked from her garden. Hopes it looks like an orderly, pleasant home, what Leo gave up. Their divorce was mutual, but it's irked her at times over the years how "winning" custody meant she forfeited any dream of her own future beyond a nice home to raise their sons in, and Leo got what he wanted—to disappear.

He shakes his head. "Okay, I'll just come out with it. Our daughter-in-law wants me to get her a lawyer and a new trial."

"She's actually going to confess? Huh, what do you know, my visits are finally paying off."

"Not exactly. She's denying it now."

Sharp intake of her breath like a BB shot. "She does not get to do that! What the hell! Uh-uh, no way, she's already been convicted of manslaughter, which means there was enough evidence. She has his blood on her hands!"

"All right, calm down, yelling isn't going to change things."

"We'll get her a lawyer, all right; we'll get her *my* lawyer."

"She knows who your lawyer is. You've had him up there poking around, trying to needle out a confession. Remember? Look, Amelia, does it really make a difference? At the end of the day Gavin is still gone. Nothing changes that."

"You get her some lawyer to take on this insanity I'll never forgive you. You owe me. You kept giving them money for the drugs. If you didn't . . ."

"If I didn't they'd have been out on the streets, maybe shot, overdosed on bad stuff, who knows? And who knows what would've happened to their kid. At least she's healthy and safe with you."

Amelia fixes him in a cold glare. "This conversation is over. I'll work this out on my own, per usual." She starts to close the door, then peers around him again at her driveway and into the street. "Where's your car?"

He grins. "In your neighbor's driveway."

"Well why in the world is it parked there?"

"Turns out she waitresses at the place where I stopped for some food. We chatted a bit, discovered she's your neighbor. Her car's in the shop so I gave her a lift."

"What neighbor? Oh . . . wait a minute! Do you mean the girl who lives in the garage? Oh my God! Don't tell me, are you hitting on her or something? She's a sneaky one and a failed adult to boot, living in her mother's garage. I mean really, Leo! Are there not enough losers in Augusta, Maine?"

"Her name is Mercy," he says, "and she's young enough to be my daughter."

"When has that ever stopped men? I know what her name is. I can't believe you've come three and a half hours to my neighborhood, and how in God's name you manage to meet . . . *Mercy* next door. Then you're knocking on my door. First your renter, *Mabel*, gets my number and keeps calling me about your wandering, and now you show up here. Why does your business have to be mine too? We're supposed to be divorced!"

"I'm worried about Daniel. Life is passing him by."

"Life is passing all of us by, old man. That's what it does. If you've got some magic bullet, some secret something to get him out of his room, come on in, go for it!"

"What about the child, Heaven? Maybe she can encourage him."

Amelia shakes her head. Her hair is still dyed her signature auburn that used to be natural, and neatly put up. With the soft hall light and the flowers behind her she can see it in her ex-husband's eyes, he's imagining her young again, the way she used to look. Probably framing her in a shot, visualizing it. But that wasn't always a happy time. Instead he'll see evidence of the years passing, fine lines, sag, the inevitable crawl toward the earth like his own face. Like somehow they're still in this together, even though they haven't been for a very long time. Leo *would* like this about older couples, like his parents were, the map of whole lives together written on their faces. Except *they* haven't spent theirs together, not by a longshot, so why is he suddenly more and more reappearing in her own life? Turns up like an old penny her dad used to say. "Ever notice that, Mele?" he used to call her. "You can be completely broke, then you look down and somewhere on the street there's always an old penny. Pick it up, keep it, and the dollars take care of themselves." Sage advice from a gambler who couldn't hold onto his dollars let alone old pennies!

Amelia sighs. "Stop staring, old man. Heaven has her own agenda. Looks like we all do, huh?" She waves her arm toward the neighbors. A light comes on in the detached garage. "Jesus, Leo, she's a kid."

"Her name is Mercy," he says again. "I think she's interested in Daniel."

"I know her name," Amelia tells him. "She likes our son who lives in his room? How in God's name would she know Daniel?"

♦ HEAVEN ♦

Heaven doing laps, stroke stroke breathe, stroke stroke breathe, stroke stroke stroke breathe, flip turn at the end of the lane, careful not to bang her head on the side of the pool, did that once and they laughed, the way her head shot out of the water, *ow!* What a loser, said Bethany, her fingers shaping the L. If it was a meet, Sheryl Chrysler the coach whom they call *Coach* warned, that would've cost precious seconds. Seconds rule, Coach said. Once the *Mariner* ran a "human-interest" piece on Coach, how Chrysler had been a Seahaven 100-meter freestyle champ, earning her a full ride to UMass Amherst, where she made "consideration" for the Olympic tryouts. Now she enjoys her job coaching "young people," helping them to become their "personal best." It's not about being a champion, Sheryl Chrysler said, it's about effort and discipline. All my swimmers are champions. *Gag!* As if.

Shriek goes Coach's whistle, free time! Heaven shoots up for a big gulp of air, then down to the bottom of the pool where no one can touch her because no one can hold their breath as long as Heaven. Coach asked her once for tips for the team; that was a good day, Heaven being asked to tell the others how *they* could do something better. "Show them how it's done," Coach said. Only she couldn't, because when she opens her mouth, out come the bubbles and the fish and the little starry things that live deep down under the water. Now she's one of them hunkered down at the bottom of the pool, carefully expelling a little air at a time (that's the secret), with each bubble we grow a tentacle like a giant squid and the tentacles reach up under Bethany Harrison treading water on the surface. Each bubble's a note like a hum, *hmmmmmmm*, the tentacles stretch up up up, until we've almost got her right between those noodley legs; then Heaven is Heaven again, air released, and she pushes up past those legs, the V, Bethany's triangle of barely concealed fuzz, size B+ boobs, the ponytail of her hair leeching out of her swim cap floating behind her.

They're supposed to tuck their hair inside these caps, but Bethany fed Coach some primo bullshit about how the "tug" of water through the tail of her long hair is like wind through a race horse's mane, making her go faster. Heaven was amazed booby Bethany could come up with that, and even more that Coach bought it, said Bethany must still wear a cap but she didn't have to tuck her hair in. Maybe Coach is a lesbian and Bethany's her crush? Heaven still isn't entirely sure what being a lesbian requires, an internet dictionary said a lesbian is a "female homosexual," but what does that *mean*? Whatever it is she'd like to catch Bethany at it. Once Heaven grows her surfer-girl hair she'll cook up something better to tell Coach, but meanwhile hers and everyone's hair but Bethany's gets crammed under their tight rubbery caps, like wearing a bald guy's scalp. Heaven imagines grabbing that horse's mane and down they go. Timing's everything, Coach said.

★ ★ ★

Back at Grandmelia's she races through the downstairs rooms, open floor plan so nothing gets in her way, Grandmelia's "contemporary aesthetic," a clean look she said; Grandmelia's all about clean as long as it's Heaven or Estelle doing the cleaning. Whoops, fast walk since she's forbidden to run in the house—but it's a good day because Uncle Daniel reminds her Grandmelia drove up to Maine, so guess what, she can run if she wants!

"Damn straight," says Uncle Daniel.

"So my surfboard came?" Heaven's peering at him through the crack in his door, which he opened just enough to talk with her.

He shakes his head. "Not yet. These are our practice sessions. We figure out how often she'll be gone, the likely days, and when a pattern emerges, I'll put in the order. By the way, Amelia said to remind you she left a kale smoothie for you in the fridge."

Heaven makes a face. "Kale looks like seaweed. There's nothing good to eat!" she wails.

Uncle Daniel smiles but she doesn't smile back, because she's mad her surfboard isn't here with Grandmelia gone, feels like grabbing that kale smoothie out of the fridge and hurling it into his room. If she were back in her Rock Harbor house she would. They hurled dishes; if you got mad you hurled. Her dad said there's something satisfying in the shatter of glass. It's just a bunch of sand crystals anyway, he said. But the smoothie is in a plastic glass, a *tumbler* Grandmelia calls it, so forget that. In Maine they got their dishes from Goodwill, nickel a glass and it's real. When you hurl it breaks.

Uncle Daniel has a head like a daffodil with his yellow fringe of hair around the balding part, and a smile that makes his cheeks look like tomato wedges. When she sees him smile she can't get up the what-it-takes, her dad would've called it, to stay mad at him. She walks back to the kitchen, opens the fridge, and tries a tentative sip of the smoothie. "Gag! Tastes like poop!" she shouts. She can hear him laughing in his room.

★   ★   ★

Heaven on her ghetto bike flying down Hatherly Road toward Minot Beach. *Own* that ghetto ride, Uncle Daniel said. She parks it on the concrete path, bolting it to one of the metal rails (even though it's third rate doesn't mean someone wouldn't snake it), scampers down the floodwall, and jumps onto the pebbled sand.

"At high tide there isn't any beach left because of erosion from all the fierce storms with the climate heating up," Grandmelia said. "Mark my words, fifty years from now Scituate and Seahaven will be ghost towns under the sea."

"Did you know there are ghost ships?" Uncle Daniel said, when Heaven told him what Grandmelia said about where they live becoming a ghost town. Heaven said she didn't want to talk about ghosts. She'd had enough of those in the shadow world, but she didn't say that part out loud. Saying those kinds of things out loud can make them real, like in-your-face kind of *real*.

Beyond the rock wall there's a strip of wet sand, the tide's moving in. At high tide there will be big waves and a current, and Heaven knows she'll have to wait for low tide to put her surfboard in, at least until she learns how to surf. Or she could carry it out on the lighthouse jetty, just a few blocks from their house, throw it off and jump on it. But first she has to *get* the dumb board to do any of it.

For now she climbs up on the large Minot shore rocks surrounded by a wash of sea, gulls mewling overhead, and a stiff breeze that smells of fish. Pictures herself in the ocean with her board, surfer-girl Heaven, hair down her back like Bethany's, maybe even to her knees like a mermaid. When it's calm she'll paddle way out to Minot light where the sea is the color of grape juice. She'll practice letting the sea inside her little by little, take a big breath, let it out sloooowly, bring it in, little bit at a time. When she gets really good she'll paddle up the coast to Maine. For now she just sits on the rock and stares out.

There's this look her dad got when he wasn't smoking the glass pipe or sniffing stuff up his nose or his shots. Sometimes he looked at Heaven with it and sometimes her mom, but mostly when he didn't think anyone saw him he'd sit and stare into space, a long, empty look, a look you'd get when your face is only a face, no signs of the person inside it, no sad, no happy, just skin. A nothing kind of look, and Heaven is pretty sure she used to get this look too, when she didn't know what to do and the days spooled out one after the other. Now though, when she feels one of these looks come on she *knows* what to do, head straight to the bottom of Grandmelia's pool to practice. No empty face here—you have to concentrate on letting just the right amount of air out, then hmmmmmmmm. Once she gets this perfect she'll be able to let the water in. Maybe if her dad had known about the drowning song he wouldn't have drowned.

♦ DANIEL ♦

H E DOES THEIR ONE, two, three knock to warn Heaven he's about to remove her father's picture, does this, then sticks his face into the hole, peering over at her on her bed. She's on her back, staring at the ceiling, jiggling her feet and mumbling to herself, upset about something—probably that flock of bitch girls she goes on about. Daniel isn't unsympathetic. He wasn't exactly Mr. Popular in school either and after his almost-drowning, when he was no longer himself, it only got worse. The difference was, by then he no longer cared.

"Hey kiddo, I've got something to show you. It's special. I haven't shown anyone until now."

She sits up. "Is it my surfboard?"

He frowns. "Now, how would I get a surfboard into my room when I never leave said room? It's my private notebook, about drownings."

She yawns, then slouches over to him and he hands it to her. "Is my dad in it?"

He shakes his head. "I'm not finished. I mostly did a particular time period, for now. Also, it's famous people. Your dad was only famous in his own mind. Go ahead, read it. But stop when you get to the final "Addendum," the part about shipwrecks. I want to say a few things about that."

She takes it back to her bed, perches on the edge, and hunches down over his notebook. Sitting that way, the slump of her shoulders, her hair still damp from swim practice and hanging in clumps over her face, makes him feel sad. She looks so vulnerable. He probably shouldn't have said that thing about her dad, famous in his own head (though *Christ*, Gavin!). But she didn't react, and even now, reading his notebook, her face seems passive. She's holding things in, he thinks, probably learned that from Amelia, the queen of passive-aggressive. He watches Heaven mumble over his words, wonders for a moment whether her reading is at grade level, doesn't have to lip-read, does she? Sound out the words to make sense?

SOME FAMOUS DROWNINGS—
Reverse Chronological Order
From the Private Notebooks of
Daniel MacQueen:
Keep Out, *Kapu*

(This means you, Amelia!)

Whitney Houston: American singer, her voice the tongue of an angel. Drowned in her bathtub after a barbiturate, cocaine, and alcohol overdose, 2012. (Addendum, just found out her own daughter has drowned, also a bathtub! Her face underwater for 2–5 minutes and she "lived" in a coma, then succumbed, so a Dry Drowning most likely.)

Rodney King: Famous victim of police brutality, LAPD. Drowned in a swimming pool with alcohol and cocaine in his blood, 2012.

Spalding Gray: Splendidly talented monologist who (ironically this editor thinks!) wrote and acted in *Swimming to Cambodia*. Drowned in NYC, East River, 2004. Probably a suicide, jumped off the Staten Island Ferry.

Jeff Buckley: Singer-songwriter and guitarist, better known as the son of the better-known singer-songwriter Tim Buckley. Drowned swimming in the Mississippi River, caught in the wake of a passing boat and disappeared. 1997. (Editorial addition: 10-year anniversary of his death brought musical tributes from all over the world so maybe he was more known than I thought. I'm just a guy in a room.)

Art Porter: Jazz saxophonist, son of Legendary Jazz Musician Art Porter Sr. Traveled to Thailand to appear in a jazz festival and after the festival his boat overturned in the Kratha Taek Reservoir. 1996.

Robert Maxwell: British media mogul, *presumed* fallen off his yacht in the Canary Islands, but before his death he was investigated for possible war crimes and after his death it was discovered he swindled millions from his companies' pension funds to finance his debt and lavish lifestyle. WHEN IS IT EVER ENOUGH FOR THESE RIDICULOUSLY RICH DUDES? THE CHUMP GOES OFF HIS YACHT. 1991.

Dennis Wilson: Beach Boys drummer. (*Little surfer, surfer girl!* Heaven, this goes out to you!) Dove off a friend's yacht at night after several drinks, popped up once clutching a waterlogged photo of his ex-wife, then down again never to surface. Body found 45 minutes later in 13 feet of water. (These fellas and their yachts, damn! For want of a raft I nearly drowned.) 1983.

Jessica Savitch: Broadcaster, reporter. Drowned with her little dog when the car she was in went off the road into a canal, sank upside down in the mud. 1983.

Joe Delaney: Running back for the Kansas City Chiefs. This was a heroic drowning. He tried to save three drowning children screaming for help. Don't recall if he succeeded in that quest. 1983.

Natalie Wood: One of the world's most beautiful women. Drowned in a suspicious yachting (natch) accident; husband Robert Wagner questioned. I question her choice in husbands. 1981. Note: does anyone drown off a rowboat?

Josef Mengele: Very evil person, war criminal, led the Nazi Human Experimentation Program. Drowned swimming off the coast of Brazil where he was hiding out. Justice served. 1979.

Joe Flynn: Anyone who loved *McHale's Navy* knows this guy! My brother and I used to watch reruns, but Gavin preferred *Gilligan's Island* because Ginger ("the ho") was hot. Drowned in his swimming pool, held under by the weight of the cast on his broken leg. 1974.

Brian Jones: Original guitarist for the Rolling Stones. Drowned in his swimming pool with an enlarged heart and liver from substance abuse. His girlfriend said their contractor did it (threw him in?), but that was never proved. 1969.

Virginia Woolf: Supremely talented writer and sufferer of a debilitating mental disorder (probably bipolar but could've been schizophrenia) who wrote among other great works *To The Lighthouse*, which took place on—yup, drum roll—Isle of Skye. Drowned in the Ouse River, suicide, weighted down her pockets with rocks, then walked in. As a supremely talent-*less* person who also suffers from a mental disorder (agoraphobia, and Tourette's according to Amelia) I empathize, can imagine the heft of those rocks in my own pockets, except I'd have to go outside to collect them and remain outside to do the deed, like dying twice! 1941.

Hart Crane: Also a memorable writer and poet, drowned by leaping from a steamboat off the Mexican coast, yelling "Goodbye, everybody!" Being a writer seems a dangerous occupation for one's longevity, or maybe they just need to avoid water. 1932.

John Jacob Astor and Benjamin Guggenheim (yeah we know these names) both drowned on the *Titanic*. Goes to show even being extremely rich can't save your ass when the ocean decides to take you. 1912.

Percy Bysshe Shelley: Major English Romantic poet, drowned in a storm while sailing. (At least it wasn't a suicide.) 1822.

I can go back further through history but for now we'll stop with a literary character as renowned as if she really did live—the beauteous, mad Ophelia of *Hamlet* fame, drowned in a stream weighed down by her own abundant robes, the flowers she picked and named drifting over her. As Queen Gertrude tells it, Ophelia, floating in the water with her robes and her flowers spread wide around her, appeared "mermaid-like," at home in her aquatic grave.

★   ★   ★

Heaven looks up again finally and Daniel sees her eyes are wet. "Hey, kiddo, what's up with the tears?" he says softly.

"You called me a surfer girl."

He snorts. "*That's* what you took from the whole thing? And, for your info, I thought you'd be honored. The Beach Boys were big-time."

"Well I don't even know all those people. Why did you even write it?"

"Because it's important. It's a way to, you know, witness, commemorate. They lost their lives this way. By drowning."

"Nobody commemorated my dad."

"Well, maybe we will. You know, figure something out. Did you stop reading where I told you to, before the final Addendum?"

She nods. "I don't really want to read about famous people drowning."

"Bring me the notebook. This last part is different, and it's important. It involves your heritage."

She gets up and walks over, hands him the notebook through the hole in the wall.

"Listen to me. I'll read it aloud."

She shrugs, "Whatever. Can I go back on my bed?"

"This will take two minutes. Just hold on! It's your heritage, dammit, it's who you are, who the MacQueens are. Your grandmother, for instance, is a royal pain-in-the-butt, but she comes from strong Scottish stock. Which means so do you."

He begins: "Addendum, to the notebook of Daniel MacQueen: You cannot document historical drownings without including Shipwrecks. What follows is a list of pertinent shipwrecks that happened in our area of the world, and one in particular from which the story of the MacQueens was born. Super-Secret, not for you Amelia, not yet. Heaven, as you're reading this, please know I have researched it thoroughly, and the last one I mention here, what I know from family stories, my research, and in my heart, is what likely happened to your great-great-great-aunt Maggie MacQueen."

Daniel stops for a second, peers at Heaven's face to make sure she's listening.

He reads: "So, the area off Scituate, Massachusetts is known as the graveyard of Massachusetts Bay. The rocky ledges there and the meager lighthouses historically served more to lure vessels in than as a saving grace. They said by the time ships saw Minot Light and the Scituate lighthouse it was too late, they were already on the rocks. That's what happened to the brig St. John, a famine ship they called it, carrying a hundred starving Irish to their watery graves in 1849, two years after the Loch Sloy, a Scottish vessel, had her first maiden voyage and was wrecked that first time off Seal Island, Devils Limb in the Maritimes, which has seen 25,000 ship-wrecks over its history.

"The Bay of Massachusetts on up through Maine and into the Canadian Maritimes is known for its violent nor'easters. Scituate alone has seen more than its share of devastating storms; one of them, the Portland Gale in 1898, changed the course of the North River, cutting off forever a part of town known as Humarock, and creating Seahaven, our own little satellite town. That storm damaged or sunk 350 vessels, from Provincetown, Massachusetts, to Nova Scotia, and over 500 people drowned, including those on the Boston Harbor pilot schooner, *Columbia*. She had displayed the number 2 on her mainsail and thus was considered a lucky vessel. Her luck ran out during the Portland Gale, driven ashore on Sand Hills in Scituate, none survived."

Heaven raises her hand. "Is that like our neighborhood here, Sandy Hills?"

He shakes his head. "Sand Hills is Scituate. We're four beaches south, Seahaven. But close, right? What I'm saying is this entire region, from up above where you lived in Maine, the Canadian Maritimes, to down where we are now is deadly for shipwrecks.

She raises her hand again. "You said only odd numbers are lucky, but they thought number 2 was lucky."

"Yeah, well they wrecked, didn't they? Now listen."

"In 1851, some months before Abigail and Maggie MacQueen's crossing, after the family was "cleared" from their home on the Isle of Skye, it was the Minot's Ledge Light that got destroyed, the first lighthouse there, and claimed the lives of its keepers. They had scribed a note in the eye of the storm saying the light tower "won't stand over night" and rang the bell wildly. Then the folks on shore saw the light go off and the bell silenced as the tower fell into the raging sea. The light keepers had stuck the note in a bottle and a Gloucester fisherman found it; only one of their bodies was ever recovered.

"In 1852, the *Allen and Brown* sailed out of Glasgow, Scotland, bound for Halifax, Nova Scotia, to pick up more cargo (and void itself of its illicit cargo, the emigrating Gaels), and then on to Boston to unload its listed cargo, a barque carrying lumber and dry goods. What were the odds of it meeting its end in the same place the Scottish *Loch Sloy* wrecked?"

Heaven shrugs, rolls her eyes. Daniel frowns, continues:

"Seal Island has had its share of shipwrecks. A ghost from the wreck of the SS *Ottawa* in 1891 is said to haunt the island still—a stewardess, Annie Lindsey, believed to have drowned when the ship went down, washed up on the island, then placed in a coffin and buried there. But some believe she must've been buried alive, come back from drowning to suffocate inside her coffin, and now she'll forever roam the island, seeking her stolen life."

Daniel stops reading again for a moment, watching his niece's eyes grow big at the image of a stewardess ghost. "Thought that might grab your attention," he says. "Listen, I want this final part to sink in . . .

"So, the ship bearing your great-great-great aunts would not reach Boston, not even Nova Scotia if you count Halifax as its destination. Your great-great-grandfather Charles made it all the way to Boston on *his* vessel, where he decided to stay, most likely because he ran out of the means to get up to Maine where the shirt factory was. That was to have been his job, or situation as they used to call it. Instead, he found a job as a manservant to a banker. The banker must have noted our great-great-grandfather's potential, his intelligence and bearing, for I have it on good faith that he taught him numbers, eventually promoting him to clerk at his bank. A good thing, for if history had determined a different fate, the rest of our story could not have happened."

Daniel puts down the notebook, backs away slightly from their hole in the wall, his eyes still locked onto hers. "That means you too, Heaven, my brother's daughter, my beloved niece. We would not be here, but for Charles MacQueen; he is our ancestor by blood, our direct line of the MacQueens. But listen, Heaven, listen carefully, because this is something I know in my heart, from things my grandfather told me, but can't prove. Not being able to prove it, however, doesn't make it any less real. Do you understand? The ship from Scotland bearing our great-aunts went down. One of them was rescued, the other was not. But the thing is, they both lived."

MAGGIE MacQUEEN,
♦ 1852–1853—THE CROSSING ♦

DEAR DIARY, GUESS WHAT! I've got sea legs! And guess who said it? A boy, a real one, not in my mind, Charles's age so almost a man he is. What's been dread and loneliness, leaving my family and knowing in my heart I won't see them again (except for Abigail, who, I'm grateful is with me, though she's felt so poorly in her stomach she wishes it not so), finally things are starting to feel a wee bit more like an adventure. Not that when I dreamt about adventuring off the Ise of Skye I could've ever imagined this!

Three weeks out on the Allen and Brown, and we're pitching and rolling—not a storm, explained the captain, just your average winter swell. We left Glasgow late in November, and the captain predicted a six- to eight-week voyage, depending on the weather, which could kick up, he said, in the winter, but that for his two pence, December was a better crossing than February. Tell the Gaels that for comfort, though, you'd get none. The lot of them, including Abigail, moaning in their berths day in and out, can't hold down food, which is a blessing, perhaps, as we had little.

The old woman, Mrs. MacNaughter, whose berth was beside mine, kept giving me slices of her salt pork. Occasionally she even slipped me a scone from her creel, convinced that her feet would not touch dry land again, and why waste good food on a stomach that's doomed? We had packed a stack of oatcakes Ma cooked up days before the eviction, for the purpose of sending them with Charles, Abigail, and me when we left for the new world (not letting any of us touch a crumb, even after the milk was tossed by the factor and we had nothing). Elizabeth, our Glasgow cousin's wife, had packed us vegetables—carrots, parsnips, and onions mostly, as nobody had potatoes in those days due to the blight, not even in Glasgow. We'd brought three lemons to prevent scurvy, and though they tasted foul and eventually their rinds sprouted prickles of mold, we dutifully ate a sliver each day until these too were gone.

The stench in the hold became overwhelming, particularly at night when they closed the hatch at the top of the ladder leading up to deck, airless with the bunks lined up one against the other, thin slabs of wood so unfinished you'd get splinters in your hands if you weren't careful, with lumpy straw mattresses that slept two for the size of one, all of us packed like herrings in a cask, as Da had warned. The stink of everyone getting sick, and only buckets for our slop, with no way to see where we're aiming at night, this odor could turn even a starving person off their meals, meager as these were.

Back to the boy and the sea legs! That's what he spoke: You've got sea legs, said he, as I was climbing the ladder to the upper deck when we were allowed back on, everyone else too sick or tending to their sick in the hold. I've got what? I asked him. Sea legs, means you're a natural sailor, born on the sea, he said. I was born on Skye, I told him, and he laughed. Such white teeth I thought, then blushed thinking this, for to think of a lad's teeth is to notice his mouth, and there seemed something a bit unseemly in that. So it's a bird you are, the sky your home? I can perhaps determine if you have wings through your jumper, but that skirt of yours hides your sea legs. Let me see your legs, and I'll tell you which you are:

bird or fish, he said. I started to hike up my skirt—not so indecent as my woolen stockings were on and my shift under the skirt, and Ma after all used to tie us lassies' skirts up with twine so we could go about the croft picking barley and oats, potatoes before they blighted, not the cleanest toil. And when gathering peat in the bogs, you'd wish you were a lad in pants, our woolen skirts dragging through the muck.

Then two other sailors walked by as I was hoisting my skirt, and they looked at this boy, then at me, and what I saw in their eyes was like nothing I'd ever seen; certainly the Suisnish boys never looked this way at me, with or without my skirt hitched. I wasn't sure what to make of it, these looks, and saved them up to think about later that night in my berth, Abigail moaning with sickness on one side, old Mrs. MacNaughter snoring on the other, and everyone else in the room wrapped up in their own misery such that I could rehearse in private how it went: their eyes shifting up and down me like they're fixing to make a purchase of me, examining every limb and skin of me and picturing the rest, I suppose, under my woolens that they could not see.

I didn't feel a fright over it, but rather it was like I had a secret about me, one so private not even I could fully know it, but it gave me a kind of power it seemed, in retrospect, over them. Such that for the moments when they were all three of them staring at me that way, just then I could get them to do anything I wanted, the only problem being the other side of that look, whatever it was I'd have to do in return. Because of course that's the way things work; you give to get, and if you want, you have to offer. Simple rules of the trade and barter, any crofter's kin knows this. I wasn't sure yet what it was I had to offer, but from what I saw in their eyes as they gazed at me, I knew they fancied it and therefore it must be good.

Mind you, I wasn't even sure what I looked like, and not just to others. We had no such thing as mirrors on the croft, having nothing that couldn't be put to efficient use. Sometimes when polishing up the large silver platter Ma owned, her only silver but for some cutlery (our cooking pots and tools were iron), I'd see the outlines of my face in it. A curious thing, it would seem to me, long, sharp, a bit too defined—the look of hunger Charles called it, in the years of the blight, as by then we all had it. I knew my hair was good, thick and long to my waist when it wasn't pinned up, night colored, the wee ones liked to brush it before bed. And of course our eyes were all the same, sea eyes the sailor might've called them, their bluish-aqua (though but for the rare sunny days of our winter crossing, under a dank sky the Atlantic was much grayer and darker than our eyes would tell it). Still, the convention was that Abigail, older and a beauty with her Nordic bearing, would husband first, and I would follow with whatever remained. Yet it was me the sailors looked at, perched near the top of the ladder, my skirt partway up calves hardened from toil on the croft, tight as whips in my indigo stockings.

The following week or maybe more—it was hard keeping exact time on the vessel, as December daytime there's not much to see but dismal light over a sea colored the same, then the darkness comes and you feel the roll of this sea, smell the sick in the hold, until the light brings it all back in focus again the next morn. It felt on and on in other words, nothing seemed to change. Anyway, on one of those days I was picking through the throwaway bins for discarded food, as it seemed I should force my sister to eat more than the oat gruel that had become our suppers, if she was to get strong again. The sea still pitched and rolled, but this once the sky was fair, and the plan was to take whatever food I scavenged to Abigail, then climb back up again to feel the sun on my face. I liked standing on the deck with the wind in my hair, cold as it was, the way it stung my ears when I neglected to pull my scarf down over them. Liked looking up at the three giant masts with their sails flapping, then turning around and gazing at the water, endless it seemed, and finally calm on this day, a glassy plane all the way to the horizon.

On nice days the sunsets were particularly pleasing, what with nothing but the sea, sky, and the orange, violet and reds of it reflected in the water like the ocean had swallowed a rainbow. It was a comforting sort of barrenness, as I was used to the barrenness of Skye, its treeless hills and bogs, a huge expanse of green land with not much on it, just the crofts here and there, cottages dotting the hillsides.

Will you be fish or fowl today? The sailor spoke suddenly behind me. Or canine, said he, since you're picking through the garbage. My face flamed. This I did not like.

We're hungry! I told him, jutting my chin out in that defiant way Ma wouldn't have approved of, not a lady's face, she'd say (though I learned it watching her). Da might've thought it showed spunk.

The sailor's cocky expression changed, I thought at first to concern, but then his eyes, which were bluer than mine, no green or aqua, just an icy lightness like a wolf, became crafty, his grin to match it. How about a kiss for some food then?

A kiss? I shrugged, imagining the pecks we gave Ma on her cheek; what harm in that? Holding my breath I stood on my tiptoes and brushed my lips to the side of his face.

But he shook his head and I noticed his fair curls under his cap that moved when he did, and with the same rhythm, snuggling up to his neck. I had a sudden desire that made me blush, to *be* those curls, touch that neck, see how it felt, warm like his cheek where my lips touched or cool like his eyes?

He grinned, at my own flushed face, I should think. You've not kissed a lad before, done any of that?

I wasn't sure what to answer. I'd kissed Da, after all, Charles and wee Robert, but that didn't seem to be what he was implying. Suddenly he stepped close enough to me that I backed away, startled, but there was only the bin and after that the wall, and that's what he led me to, away from the sight of others coming and going. His hand cupped my shoulder then around my neck, pulling my mouth into his. With his lips pressed against mine, I knew once again I'd have to capture the experience to think about later, as for now it was a mash of so many things—his smell, a musky ripeness on his breath I knew was tobacco, and the salty sweat of his underarms, me being much smaller, my head near inside them, and with the ship's roll pushing me into him all the more, such that I had the strange sensation of becoming him, that this was his intent, a kiss that would swallow me and make me him. Not such a bad thought at that moment, to be a cocky, wolf-eyed boy who sailed the seas, rather than a pence-less lassie heading toward a strange land, at the mercy of whatever situation is found for her.

Later that night I lay beside Abigail, sleeping more peacefully now, about our fourth week out, and half the Gaels that had been sick were no longer. I knew she'd be up and about in time, and I determined if I was to see the sailor again, it had to be soon, as I had a feeling my sister would not approve. What I felt was that power, conjuring up the memory of it, him melting into me, quivering and seeming to feel such urgency in our kiss that were I to suddenly slip under his arm and disappear, he'd be begging for me to come back. I wondered at that need, how vital it felt, and found myself doing what I never dared at home, three of us lasses to a bed, which was to explore my own body under the cover I shared with Abigail now, not lifting my shift in case she awoke, just strolling my hand over flesh caught under its thin weave, wondering at how this might feel if my hand were not my own.

The next day clouds were gathering again, and the pitch became a hard chop, heaving to and fro, as the vessel lurched in its grip. The sky looked dark for midnoon, and the sailor had to be on deck most of the day hauling lines, setting the sails, scrubbing down the decks as saltwater sloshed on to them. He was doing all this despite having told me, after our kiss, that the captain held no sway over him, that he was doing the work for the adventure of it, on his way to the new world to go to university there, and then he'd be in finance. A banker most likely, he told me, lighting his pipe, its smoke circling over my head. I knew by that confession we were of different worlds and were it not for us both on this vessel, where one's world is limited by what could be propelled by three giant masts their sails run up, we would not have had much to do with each other.

And yet I wanted to see him again. Things were erupting in me that I had not known were part of me, strange feelings and wonders and a sort of restlessness and a craving, though I was still

not certain for exactly what. It was a muddle, these emotions, and I
knew not what to think about them. He had said he would take me
to a viewpoint where the passengers weren't allowed, only crew,
said he, for a horizontal kiss, he called it, where we would kiss side
by side and not be on our feet. But the weather kept worsening and
it wasn't until the following week that things calmed enough for
we Gaels to be allowed out of the hold for more than the minutes
it took for a breath of fresh air. The calm between storms, the first
mate warned, get out while ye can.

All day I roamed about looking for the sailor and for food, as
our stack of oatcakes was so low it was not even a stack, but a tiny
wedge, and the oats for our porridge so scant it was gruel we were
eating, morning and night, more water than oat. There's a supply
room below in the hold, the captain had told us, separate from
where we were lodged, that would keep our extra parcels and any
food that could not be boiled by the cook or stored with us on the
crossing. I lingered outside that room, knowing there was food
in it, but as it was locked I couldn't see how I'd be admitted. My
stomach was howling, but other parts of me had a kind of hunger
too. I traced with my fingers where the sailor's lips had been on
mine, and my mouth felt like someone else's. To be thinking about
touching the sailor's mouth that way, I got all tingly then bold, and
determined to investigate what he'd offer for that horizontal kiss,
when next I saw him.

★   ★   ★

He had promised me we'd climb to a place where only sailors were
allowed. Maggie the goat he called me, as truly did I crave those
higher views, sea legs solid as on land. Although we did not have
many trees to climb in Skye, we had hills with steep cliffs and the
Cuillins themselves, and perhaps it was these I was missing when I
found him in the corridor adjacent to the galley, said yes to that
horizontal kiss. But instead of a climb it was back down to that
storage room we went, only, he assured me, he had the key. Before
this he had bragged about getting access to a cabin, which I knew
were saved for any wealthy passengers, traveling lairds and

merchants, Brits that could pay many pounds for their passage and wouldn't be carting their own food on board.

He peered about him before sliding the key into the storage room lock, so I figured he wasn't supposed to have it, but the difference between us was he knew where to get it from and where to put it back. There's food in here, Maggie, he whispered in my ear, to your heart's desire, and all for that horizontal kiss!

Aye, I told him, and my stomach rumbled, but I could not take it from the other Gaels, I said, all those poor souls stuck in the hold. Would there be ship's food perhaps? I did not object to the thought of this, food pilfered from the outsized belly of some laird, or even the first mate's substantial pouch.

Ah Maggie, said he whose name I did not yet know, as he kept telling me to guess it and I refused—too many names possible, said I, rather I call you the one you'll answer to. The food is indeed the ship's, salt pork, salt beef, potatoes not rotted, peas, onions, all from the new world where there's no blight whatsoever, giant heads of green cabbage, even pudding. Much more than what you Gaels could bear! he said, cocky, I thought, but mattered not if my hunger would be fed.

Blood pudding? I asked him, gazing about the windowless room after he shut the door tight, for a light source beyond the small lamp, its wick dull, above the topmost shelf, which might illuminate this banquet. I was starved for protein, felt its desire in my blood right along with some other excitement that was happening there, when suddenly he grabbed my hand. He was leading me to an empty shelf of all things, but full sized, bigger than the bunks we slept on in the hold.

Any pudding you fancy, said he, then took off his pea coat and spread it on the shelf, instructing me to lie down. Ladies first, he said, which I giggled at, because at home the only time I was called a lady was on Sundays when we were to go to church. Dressed in our washed skirt and white cotton jumper, Ma was afraid I would play round-around with the wee ones, or just wander outside through the bog, happy for one day out of the week not to be cutting and gathering peat from it. You'll get dirty she warned, a lady keeps herself clean on Sundays. I got sad then thinking of Ma and the moors, the great land that was Skye, and how I was not likely to see it nor her again. My eyes must've watered as he kissed them first, then his mouth was on my mouth, his tongue inside my mouth, and I suppose mine was happy enough to greet it, as it was doing a jig with his, the two of our tongues dancing together between my lips.

The storage room was dark and crowded with containers of food, I imagined, though I had not a moment to investigate this enticement, and perhaps if I wasn't engrossed in that kiss, much longer than its previous, though I'm unsure how to count as they came one after the other and with each his tongue pushed deeper inside my mouth, his body pressed more firmly against mine, as if not just our lips kissed, but all of him against all of me; perhaps if not for this wonderment I might've felt the sea growing more wild underneath us, as suddenly the ship lurched sharply to the left and we were off that shelf onto the floor, the closeness of his body shielding mine from the impact. We heard the whistle, the all-hands-on-deck command, and in between his lips stuck on my lips and his tongue swimming over my tongue, I tried to ask him does that not mean he must go?

But he ignored my efforts at speech and the whistle too, which was shrieking over and over, and the slide of the waves under us so insistent, like they were making the ship go one way too fast and that way was not to its liking. Crates and casks and parcels came rolling toward us, but the sailor seemed unbothered by it, because suddenly he was under my skirt and my shift, and I neither helping nor hindering as it had not occurred to me he'd end up there— the place I'd kept secret from all except Abigail, who when I first started to bleed helped me arrange the rags such that they could soak up the blood each month when it came.

Once again I didn't know what to feel, as there was a whole rush of sensations racing through me like my veins were ignited, a searing sudden pain, then something else inside me that wanted this fire, begged for it, was willing to succumb to it and be scorched over and over, a sense I was no longer entirely me but something so raw and alive every skin cell was lit, yet frightened of it at the same time such that I imagined I was whispering no, no, must've been saying it, but as my lips were consumed by his, who would hear me anyway?

The whistle kept blowing and the sailor kept on me, boxes and parcels, this and that sliding all around us. I heard people shouting and I thought it was Abigail's voice calling to me, Maggie, Maggie, where are you! I tried to answer but the sailor's hand pressed over my mouth. Shh! he commanded; you'll get me hung for this. I wasn't sure what *this* meant, being in the storeroom where the captain said no one should go? Not answering the all-hands-on-deck command? I wanted to ask him, but his mouth was on mine again, the rest of him moving in me while the ship pitched to and fro, and I grew scared and started to cry.

Shh, Maggie, he whispered, again placing his hand over my mouth but not quite so hard this time. It's only a storm. Just then there was an enormous crunch, as though the ship had suddenly anchored itself on one of the beauteous icebergs we saw in the northern part of the passage, looked like floating Cuillins made of ice, the sun sparking off them like flint, and at their centers the most lovely aquamarine, as though it were blue hearts they bore. But this couldn't be as we'd left the icebergs a long while back and were closer to Halifax, maybe a week weather granting, the captain had said, just days ago. Could we have arrived already and too roughly docked? Then the ship pitched violently to the right, the whistle wailed its final cry, and everything went black.

PART IV

SUMMER

◆ AMELIA ◆

Visitors Rules of Conduct

#5 Keep cursing at a minimum: Visitors should comport themselves with courtesy and decorum and not use excessive foul language. Examples: the F-word, S-word, and "damn" with "God" in front of it.

L AST NIGHT A WIND kicked up, whipping her shade about through her open window, Amelia in bed glaring at it, willing it to stop, how can she sleep with that racket . . . then the flapping of some night bird—an owl?—lifting off from the bushes outside. Suddenly she's falling through water like it's air, drifting down, though how is this possible? Remembers asking herself this, ever practical, analytical, *you don't take after me*, her father said, she's a two-feet-flat-on-the-ground kind of person, no nonsense, no non-*sense* person, water rolling her about like a storm's on its surface and she can't breathe! Mouth filling she reaches out to a shape . . . but it isn't him! *Was it her?* Why in God's name was this even in her head!

Woke up feeling the worst kind of hangover, like when she used to have one too many gin and tonics, that dullness, a sense of dread with nothing *real* to base it on. Five hours later, three cups of coffee and no food, a dull throbbing at her temples, sour throat, and a tremor in her hands, has not put her in a charitable mood for this confrontation with her daughter-in-law.

"So!" Amelia starts, "I want to disabuse you of this retrial nonsense."

Cassie snorts, "*Disembowel?* Shit Amelia, can't you *pretend* you're for real? I could say no to your visitor request; they can't make me sit here and talk to you."

"Well whoop-de-do. Aren't you the tough gal. You're in no position to decline anything, I should think. Everything you've got is through our graces."

"*Our?*" Cassie mutters, "Leo's you mean. You have my kid."

"And what a blessing is that! Look . . ." Amelia stares hard into Cassie's eyes. They're red rimmed like she's been crying, or maybe drugs! She takes a deep breath, rubs her own eyes, careful not to dislodge her contacts. Her ophthalmologist told her she should consider glasses, her astigmatism is becoming too pronounced for contacts, but Amelia likes to face the world sans buffers. Besides, the sea-green shade of her eyes is one of her few attributes that hasn't faded over the decades. "I slept poorly and I'm a little cranky. Let's start again. Would you please explain your intentions, *please!*"

"*Cranky?* I'm going with the b-bomb, rhymes with witch. I didn't do it, how about that. I want a lawyer. I told Leo I'll pay him back when I can."

Amelia feels her blood pressure rise, heat pulsing in her veins, flushing her cheeks. "You swore you couldn't remember what happened that night! How is it you suddenly remember that you *didn't* do it?"

"Nah, I still don't remember, that's right. But the *motive* they based my conviction on is wrong. That prosecutor—what a cyborg. I'd have confessed to the crucifixion to get out of that courtroom. That bitch had me believing I did something, and I wasn't even sure what the fuck she was talking about! Yes, I said, I don't deny it, and in my head I'm going please, please, just get me the fuck out of here, I'll trade places with Gavin, just fucking get me gone!"

Amelia tugs at a lock of hair that has come loose from her French twist (inadequately secured by a plastic comb, sans the bobby pins they go to pieces over in this place), taps her fingernails against the table. "Why do you have to talk that way?"

"What the fuck?"

"*That* way. It sounds so low class. Why the barrage of four-letter words? Gavin didn't speak like that."

"Oh, sure, your son was the perfect gentleman. Why do you talk the way you do? Who do you think you are, anyway, the manners police? I can think of a lot of folks with a lot more class than you, Amelia, and they don't have a penny."

"It's not about money; it's about refinement. If you had it, you'd know."

"No way, it's *always* about money. You think you're better than me, better than a lot of folks because you have it. Gavin told me about the MacQueen bucks. I figured he'd hit you up for some, but he went to his dad instead."

Amelia laughs like a shot. "Hah! Because I would've said no! Did he tell you my father squandered this so-called fortune on the horses? Oh yes, and if they weren't racing, any slot machine would do in a pinch. He even bet on bloody greyhounds."

"So that's where Gavin got the addiction bug. They say there's a family history lots of times. Not me. My folks didn't even drink. I figured Gavin's rubbed off on me."

Amelia shakes her head. "For your information my great-great-grandfather came from Scotland with nothing and made something out of it; his son and grandson, my grandfather, had a head for business, which my father did not. He had a good heart. Everyone ran all over him, mowed him down, then he finished the job. After he died it took every cent of what was left of the MacQueen estate to cover his debts. My mother gave up before that, her heart just quit. So much for inheritance. I'm a self-made woman. Everything I have I've earned."

Cassie leans forward and grins. "Me too. What you see is what you fucking get," she says, sweeping her arm toward the prison walls.

"Well this is what I'm talking about! All these four-letter words are coarse and unnecessary. We're not on the streets."

"Jesus, look around you lady! Are we at a tea party here? I'm an addict and so was your son. *Refinement* was a clean bag of smack. My dad worked in a factory, but we did okay. Stockton used to be a nice place, then they shut some of the factories down like they've done all over this damn country, shipped jobs to China and India where probably twelve-year-olds do them for fifty cents an hour. My dad's a dying breed and I don't even know if he's still alive! Stopped calling him after getting with Gavin, figured he wouldn't approve of what we'd become. He doesn't even know he has a granddaughter." Cassie's eyes fill and Amelia looks away toward the guard, a brittle man with a scar across his face like a cracked mirror. *I will not feel bad for her!*

"Point is I wouldn't have done what that cyborg said I did out of anger or jealousy or any of that shit. Gavin was *everything*. Loving him meant you just put up with him being a son of a bitch. I knew that from the day I walked in on him—I'm nine months pregnant, mind you—and he's snorting coke off some skank's inner thigh. Now there's *refinement* for you."

"I really don't need to hear this . . ."

"You do, Amelia, dammit, you know it's true. Gavin had that *thing*, that charm or whatever that made everyone want to be around him no matter what. He didn't have to work to make folks love him, they just did, even when he didn't deserve it."

"He had an innocence . . ."

"That's total crap. He was a conniving, manipulative prick and he got whatever the fuck he wanted. I put up with it. I was in his orbit like everyone else. Figured as his wife, *most* of the time at least I could orbit a little closer to him. So suddenly that night I decide I'm not shamefully codependent and desperately in love with my husband because we're fighting and strung out? Hate to break this to you but that wasn't exactly a rare thing. Look at you, mother of two sons and you loved Gavin more than the other one. Everyone knew it. Even Daniel probably loved him better than he loves himself. You think that kind of mother worship didn't have consequences? Gavin thought the moon followed him and him alone."

Amelia struggles to not let the tears in her eyes roll down her cheeks. This woman doesn't deserve that, to see her broken and think *she's* the reason, that she's had an effect. She growls, "What I don't get is what he saw in you!"

Cassie's face pales, her lips tremble. For a moment Amelia regrets having said that, though she did wonder—he was so beautiful he could've had anyone, just like Amelia could have. They both settled was the upshot, though at least Leo was a nice guy. He wouldn't be on the other side of this table convicted of manslaughter; Amelia would've gotten to him first if anything! Somewhere a buzzer goes off and Amelia hears the clang of an electric gate shutting tight. She shivers.

Cassie leans in closer. "So then why would I kill that, huh? Why the fuck would I? I don't care how wasted I was, he was—any of it. Who else would love me that way? I didn't do it, I swear. I couldn't have," she whispers, "I loved him more than my life."

"But they found the board, your prints were on it, his blood. Are you saying someone *else* was out there, or maybe a sea monster rose from the ocean and conked him on the head, then dragged him into the water? Listen to me." Now Amelia leans forward almost touching Cassie's hands. Cassie flinches, jerks back, and Amelia pretends not to notice. "Can we barter? That's what you do in here, right? I've seen prison movies, shows; I'll give you this if you give me that. Am I right?"

"You don't know jack shit about how we are in here," Cassie snarls.

"Yes, okay, of course not. But listen. I wanted a retrial too, but with different results. I wanted you to come clean so we could publicly clear my son's name. But I get it now, no one cares, the trial is over and you're in here, he's in the ground. So maybe it's about me. *I* need to know what happened in the last moments Gavin was alive. I need it like I need my own blood; he was my son! You say you don't remember, but I need you to be my eyes, ears, all I could've been if I was with him, you see? I'm his mother! He's part of me. If I could arrange it through my lawyer, would you be willing to take a lie detector test? Maybe we could bring in a hypnotist too, if I promise the results would be only for you and me. No retrial, just personal."

Cassie shakes her head. "You are a piece, lady. A *hypnotist*? You don't seem the sort who'd go for that voodoo shit. Why the hell would I believe you anyway, that it's only for you?"

"We'll sign a contract, have it notarized. The lie detector will only prove that you don't remember that night, so if that's true you have nothing to hide. And for your information hypnotism is medically valid. Maybe a hypnotist can discover what really happened. Don't you want to know? If you say you couldn't have done it, you've nothing to be afraid of."

"I don't know," Cassie says, her voice thin. "What's in it for me?"

"You'd get me off your back, for one. Once it's done, whatever the results, I'm through here. Except for Heaven's visits, of course."

Cassie snorts, "That's incentive all right. But if I do, I might need some . . . compensation."

Amelia rolls her eyes. "Yes, naturally. I'm sure we can arrange something. Aren't you regularly tapping the spineless Leo anyway? This would be cheaper than him buying you a lawyer, so I'm sure we can make it worth your while."

Cassie stares over Amelia's head at the brick wall. "You don't get it . . . that was the worst night of my life, even if I can't remember it, worse even than losing my mother! My husband *died*. Why the fuck do I want to relive that?"

"At the trial you kept saying you didn't deny anything, but you couldn't remember, and yet you pled not guilty at your arraignment."

"I was still in shock, Jesus! Twenty-four hours Gavin was gone and I'm in jail. Then at the trial the way that bitch summed up all the blah blah blah evidence against me made me think I really *must've* done something. My pubescent lawyer was like *duh*, can I lick your shoes? to that dyke. Now that I've had some time to digest I'm thinking uh-uh, not true. That whole motive thing, not happening, never could."

A buzzer blares. "Visitors let's wrap it up!" the CO barks. Amelia stands and for a moment, tall as she is, she feels her power over Cassie still slumped in her seat. She needs to remind herself she has this power, the power of the free. Get convicted of something in this country and that's it, right or wrong you've crossed some line forever. Far as Amelia's concerned Cassie is guilty as hell, but it wouldn't matter, her future is trashed regardless. Amelia takes some small satisfaction in that. "Just think about it. You can let me know next week. I'm coming a week early, so we get some closure on this."

"Don't bring Heaven," Cassie says, rising, staring into the chaos of the room, visitors lining up at one entrance, inmates the other. "I don't want her here anymore."

"Court mandated, once-a-month visit. You're her mother!"

Cassie shakes her head. "This place . . . how can I be a mother to her now?"

"You just *are*, end of story."

"No, you don't get it. She didn't have to testify against me or be at the trial, but she knows I'm here for *some* reason. How do I keep sitting here with her thinking all the while whatever it is she thinks I did to be here?"

"Well she doesn't talk about it."

Cassie shakes her head. "Okay!" she snaps at the CO motioning her to the door.

"*Now* inmate," the CO barks. "You move your butt this minute or visiting privileges are revoked for the next six months."

"Like I fucking care," Cassie mutters. "Oh, and Amelia, the four-letter words? What can I say, you bring out the bad in me!"

Amelia gets a whiff of a kitchen spice, nutmeg or cinnamon and a sharper, more bitter scent under it as Cassie brushes past her, ambling toward the guard who lunges at her in a menacing fashion. That smell, like she's trying to cover something up.

Back outside in the parking lot Amelia climbs into her car, inhales deeply, closes her eyes, then she's sobbing so hard she chokes. "You're a narcissist," her mother once told her, "you care only about yourself." Well if she didn't take care of herself who would? A melancholic, hypochondriac mother and a yarn-spinning "punter" dad who sold out her inheritance to whatever he could place a bet on. He didn't try to hide it, as though betting on horses was a perfectly reasonable way to support a family. No wonder she resents Daniel's Skye stories; they are forever associated with gambling loss, their family having to "batten down the hatches" her dad would say, until his "winning streak" kicks in. Next time's the charm! he'd tell them, winking. Meanwhile he's spouting stories about seal-people, conniving faeries, and water-horses ("no no," he'd admonish her, "not *seahorses*, kelpies, *killer* kelpies!"), while cooking up packages of instant broth for their dinner. "Let's save a cow's life tonight!" he'd say, like they're choosing to go meatless, like their grocery money wasn't instead fed to his bookie. Her mom, feigning one of her "fatigues," would rarely come down to eat.

Her mom . . . who when she thought she was dying the first time, whispered that it wasn't so bad, then didn't die. Years later a heart attack took her just like that. One minute she's staring at Amelia (who'd brought them over some food) with that impenetrable look—was it longing? disappointment? regret? or . . . nothing—the next she'd stopped breathing, prostrate on the floor. Sometimes Amelia catches herself in a mirror wearing that look and orders herself to "batten down the hatches." Now she takes a tissue from her purse, wipes carefully under her eyes, starts up her car, and heads home.

Four hours later in a golden evening light, Amelia pulls into her driveway and sees it. Perched on her roof like a weathervane, something that's supposed to be there. An owl, curved beak, tufted ears, its yellow eyes blink when she brakes. Then it takes off, flapping its massive wings.

★   ★   ★

It's past dinnertime when Amelia opens the back door, stomach rumbling, head pounding. She'd sat in her car awhile after parking it in the garage, thinking about that owl. Uncanny coincidence? Portent? How, right before her dream or vision, whatever that was last night, she'd heard it flapping . . . *hadn't she?* In the end she decided it was just an owl. Has she become the sort of person who believes in portents? No, of course not. And of course no dinner smells! She'd left take-out stroganoff in the refrigerator with instructions for Heaven to microwave, but the girl subsists on white foods, everything pale and fatty: cheese, macaroni, sugary cereals, fries. A high-protein dinner is a teaspoon of marinara sauce over a massive plate of noodles, slathered in parmesan; or cheese shreds on a slab of white rice. For tonight's entrée she probably grabbed a bag of chips.

In the living room Amelia stops cold. Heaven and two Seahaven police officers, a man and a woman, are seated around the sectional sofa, a plate of Oreos on the coffee table, which no one besides Heaven seems to be touching. The cookies are clearly a Daniel move, her son either a dimwit or a genius, telling Heaven to serve Oreos to the police on Amelia's designer china. The girl sits calmly munching, but in between stuffing cookies into her mouth she's rubbing her legs, a sign, Amelia knows, of her stressing over something. Strange the things she's begun to understand about this child, more than just the ways she's like Gavin and the ways she isn't—the ways she's her own *Heaven* person, often an annoying one at that! Amelia looks out the window for their cruiser and sees it parked on the other side of the road; she'd been so intent on that owl she didn't notice it. "For crying out loud, now what?"

"Amelia MacQueen-French?" Both officers stand up.

"You're in my home so I suppose we can assume."

"We need confirmation, ma'am," the woman officer says.

Amelia nods. "I go by MacQueen since my divorce, sans *French*, and that's been for quite some time. What's this about?"

"You're the guardian of Heaven French?"

"*Temporary* guardian," Amelia and Heaven say at the same time, then stare at each other. Heaven calmly takes another bite of her cookie and Amelia frowns.

"Heaven was caught shoplifting from the Postee," the woman says.

"From *what?*"

"It's the nickname the local kids use for the Egypt Country Store," the male officer pipes in. "They used to post mail from it, before the North Scituate post office branch was built."

Amelia glares at the three of them. "A history lesson with some colorful local factoids, fabulous. What in Sam Hades is going on here?" This she directs at Heaven who shrugs, then reaches for another cookie. "Stop eating those bloody things! I want an explanation," Amelia snaps.

"She was caught on a security camera," the female officer says, "which confirmed what the manager witnessed. He said she stuffed various candies and packages of chips into her backpack. When she denied it the manager called us. We asked her to open her backpack and she refused, but the camera has proof."

"Open your backpack this instant!" Amelia commands.

Heaven's eyes start to fill, and Daniel calls out from the crack in his bedroom door: "Remember your protectors."

"Oh for God's sake!" Amelia marches over and grabs the backpack. "I don't think this is the time to call upon your uncle's faeries! My son and my . . . Heaven have a fantasy world," she tells the officers, unzipping then dumping the contents of the backpack onto the carpet. "Well whoop-de-do, what have we here? Candy bars, chips, gummy bears, and—what's this, some red rope imitation licorice *plus* a bottle of Coke?"

Heaven sticks out her chin. "I bought the Coke."

"Are you out of your mind? A sugar nightmare, eat this junk and it's hello plus sizes after the dentist pulls out all your teeth. What's the meaning of this?"

"It's for our trip," Heaven pouts, her lower lip quivering.

"What trip?"

"To Maine. You never feed me in the car or stop for food and it's a long ride," she whines. "I don't like granola bars, they're nasty and that's all you ever bring."

"Look," the female officer starts, shaking her head, her tiny comma-shaped ponytail sticking out from under her cap. She seems to be the one in charge, Amelia observes, glowering; *yeah women.* "Normally we would take Heaven immediately to the station—that's protocol—but because of her age and this being her first infraction, we're willing to leave it in your hands this time, as long as you make restitution to the Egypt Country Store. The merchandise should be returned, of course, and anything missing paid for. We'd like to see some retribution for her behavior, so Heaven understands the seriousness of what she did, that there are repercussions. You could revoke the privilege of going to the Postee for one, and maybe some sort of service could be offered."

"Officer!" Amelia snaps. "With all due respect, I've raised two sons. I don't need a parenting lesson. Are you even old enough to be a parent? Heaven! What do you have to say to these officers who have kindly chosen not to arrest you?"

"But it's my arsenal!" she wails. "For the trip to Maine." She sticks out her lower lip like a two-year-old.

"You won't need it!" Amelia hisses. "You're not going to Maine. Your mother doesn't want to see you."

✦ HEAVEN ✦

Heaven in bed two hours later, no dinner just the rest of the cookies snuck into her room while Grandmelia lectured Uncle Daniel through his door about the day's *events*, and the *protocol* for housing a thief, what one does when the police come to the door. "Rule number one: You don't suggest Heaven serve them cookies on my good china!"

It's not like it's the first time she pinched stuff, just the first she's been caught. And on top of it all she had a terrible swim practice today, the *worst*. Bethany Harrison called her bubble butt when she told Bethany and the others about the surfboard that was coming for her by Federal Express, then called her a liar. "No one would give a fat turd like you a surfboard," she said. "You'd drown." "Yeah," fish-face Brittany piped in—"you wouldn't drown *on* it 'cause you'd sink it!" They all laughed, and Bethany lunged at Heaven like she was going to slap or punch or do something embarrassing like give her a wedgie, but then she pulled back going "*EWWWWEEEE* don't touch her, her fat might be contagious." At that point Heaven dove into the pool even though it wasn't free time, to escape them, down, down, slow exhale into the drowning song, imagining how she'll sing Bethany in, maybe all the B-bitches, sing sing sing, bubble bubble bubble, *hmmmmm*, and when she finally popped up Coach shrilled her whistle, ordered Heaven out of the pool to *sit on the side for the rest of the practice for her insubordination*; so she plunged in again, pretending not to have heard before Coach could blow her whistle the second time. Second time's the killer, done for, maybe even kicked off the team.

Knock, knock, knock, one, two, three on her wall. Heaven jams the last Oreo into her mouth, four five six, then seven eight nine, distress knock, and Uncle Daniel peers at her through their secret hole. "Once upon a time . . ." he begins.

"Wait, is this about me being bad? Evil faeries, killer kelpies, or anything else bad? I'm sick of bad stuff."

"She didn't mean it," Uncle Daniel says. He scratches his chin, scruffy with a day-old, maybe even two or three days old unshaven beard. He looks like one of those cartoon drawings of a wimpy guy, with his balding head, his scruffy chin, and his big sad eyes that look even bigger and sadder when he forgets to put on his glasses, like now. "That part about your mom not wanting to see you, Amelia didn't mean it."

Heaven shrugs. The mom in prison is a placeholder mom; *someone* has to be there in that prison, though she won't say it, not even to Uncle Daniel.

"Once upon a time . . ." Uncle Daniel starts again. *Dear Mom!* Heaven goes in her head to the *real* mom, *such a bad bad sucky sucky day*, wiping the tears out of her eyes but they just keep falling down her cheeks, dripping onto her lap as she sits on her bed, and she wishes Uncle Daniel would sit here too instead of staring at her through the wall like some owl. Maybe if she keeps crying she'll drown in her tears. That'll show them. Grandmelia will wish she'd fed Heaven some dinner and been nicer to her, and maybe the B-girls will get suspended from school for being evil bitches.

"Have I told you about the magic birds of Skye?" he says, blowing a kiss at her like she's a little kid, which right now is what she wants to be, a little kid whose mom and dad are putting her to bed, telling her a story; sleep now, no worries, it'll all be okay.

"They're known as the Birds of Bride. In Loch Eisort, below where the MacQueen home stood, there were three little kids who fell asleep in a boat and woke to find the tide had risen and the boat broken loose from its mooring. They had no oars and they'd be too small to use them anyway, so they drifted further and further into a wild sea. They wailed and cried for help, then exhausted from weeping grew silent, sure that no one had heard them, and they'd drown or be smashed into the rocks of Kyle at Lochlash. But the Birds of Bride heard and like gleaming white crosses flew to the Chapel of Kilbride on the hill overlooking the loch, in search of their mistress. Soon the children saw a lovely lady in white walk across the sea, her arms full of bog cotton. When she arrived at the boat she dropped the cotton inside and told the children to curl up on it and sleep. The tired little ones slept on their cotton bed and the lady and her white birds bore their boat to shore."

"That's it?" Heaven asks.

Uncle Daniel nods. "Happy ending. You asked for it."

She sighs, swipes cookie crumbs off her sheets onto the floor, then gets up and walks over to the hole in the wall, peering in at Uncle Daniel, eye to eye. "I don't believe in magic birds," she says. "Why would birds need magic? They can just fly away."

★ ★ ★

The next morning Grandmelia picks her up from swim practice and drives her to the Postee. Here's Heaven returning *almost* all of the chips and candy—managed to snake a Mars Bar because she loves marshmallow and chocolate and because she's hungry and pissed. It's not like this was an easy haul, stuffing all that crap in her backpack, slipping them in when the clerk was occupied. Stupid cameras, she didn't figure on more than the one she'd already scoped out above the door—like this isn't an electronics store, smartphones, something valuable!

"Okay goodbye," she says to the guy who runs the place, but Grandmelia, who's panting behind her like a pit bull pinches her elbow. "Um," Heaven goes, "Oh yeah. I'm supposed to offer to do something, like unload boxes? I'm pretty strong. I've got major biceps from swimming the breaststroke." She shows off her guns under her T-shirt and he actually smiles. She thought up that one about the boxes because she's betting there won't be security cameras back in their storeroom.

The man shakes his head. He's somewhere around Grandmelia's age, or maybe Uncle Daniel's; it's hard to tell because old people just look old to Heaven. "I pay a boy to do that," he says. Grandmelia clears her throat and they exchange a glance; the kind Heaven knows won't go well for her.

"Would you like to sweep out, run a mop over the floor on Friday?" the man asks, like he's offering her a treat. "She'll do it," Grandmelia says. "Good thing it's summer vacation!" she snarks as they walk out to the car.

"Indeed," Heaven says. She got that from Grandmelia, who uses it ironically, Uncle Daniel said. Heaven is beginning to get what that means. *Ironically* doesn't go well for her either.

It gets worse. A week later they're in Grandmelia's Volvo heading down the Driftway to some medical building and in that building, Grandmelia says all sweet-like, is someone Heaven can talk to.

"Talk about what?" Heaven asks, fakey-sweet herself. Because she knows and she's not having it. She overheard Grandmelia making the calls, first to Leo, Heaven's grandpa she hasn't met, and then to a *therapist*! They don't get how she's always listening. She learned to do that living with her parents, always listen so you know what to expect. People coming and going all day into the night, and Heaven would need to figure out how to get herself some food, and if a party's going on, where she could sleep, people stumbling around her in her crate like she isn't even there. Sometimes her dad said she could sleep in their bed, but even then she'd sneak back out, so if they did the shots, lit the pipe, or sniffed powder up their noses and winked out, she could watch over them.

Grandmelia makes a sharp left into the Driftway Park, shuts off the engine in the parking lot, and stares out at the marsh. Gulls are wheeling over it and a blue heron perches at the end of the dock, staring at the water like he's debating whether to swim or hang out. It's a *stellar*, Grandmelia called it, July day, sky a shade of blue

Uncle Daniel calls cerulean; he said the sky over Skye was either cerulean or gray and misty. But that's not why they named Skye that. He said some believe it was named after wings and others for the woman warrior, Scáthach. Heaven likes that one. If she were a warrior she'd beat the crap out of Bethany Harrison.

"We're early so I thought we might chat a bit first," Grandmelia says.

Oh great! Heaven thinks. Grandmelia doesn't *chat*. She doesn't trust Grandmelia's smile, a smile that shows her teeth, which Heaven notes have a smear of lipstick on them. She won't tell her. Grandmelia's always going on about looking *presentable* when they go places, so let her discover it for herself. "I'm concerned that you haven't properly mourned your father. Do you know what that means?"

Heaven frowns, not the territory she was expecting. She thought it would be about the Postee thing, Heaven's *criminal tendencies*, Grandmelia called her behavior.

"Mourning is how we express our grief when a loved one dies."

Yeah, duh! Heaven thinks, but she won't say it. In fact, better not look at Grandmelia at all right now because tears are suddenly in her eyes. She blinks them back and stares at the heron. It's enjoying the sun, but if she were it, she'd dive in even though there's only about two feet of water, lie flat on the silty bottom and hold her breath. She stares out at the marsh leading into the North River, and in the distance the houses on a cliff overlooking Peggotty Beach. From there it's smooth sailing, the Atlantic ocean all the way to Maine then on up into Nova Scotia, where Uncle Daniel said her great (times at least two more *greats*, as in way old!) aunt went down with the ship that wrecked on the rocks off Seal Island.

"You loved your dad, didn't you? Well of course you did, but I haven't seen you mourn him."

"What would that look like?" Heaven says, then immediately regrets it. Grandmelia will think her fresh, or worse she might actually answer the question with a to-do list of sorts—Grandmelia is famous for these: How to Mourn, one hundred steps, check off each using the chores chart on the refrigerator! *What would that look like?* It's just a cool way of talking, all the kids are saying it.

"Well, there's no one way people mourn (whoopee, she's going for serious; Heaven glares at the heron, Save yourself, dive to the bottom! she orders it in her head). But I'll tell you what it *shouldn't* look like, and that's the way you've been behaving. That's called acting out. People act out when they're keeping other emotions, like grief, imprisoned within."

Heaven rolls her eyes, but not so Grandmelia would see. "So that's why I have to see a therapist?"

Grandmelia shoots her a barbed look. "So you do know where we're going. Yes, in a word. Whatever your problems are, she can talk to you, you to her, and then maybe I won't be raising a thief! Besides, a girl your age should set her sights on shopping at Macy's or a boutique, a pretty dress, a nice scarf, like that, not the Postee for *candy*."

"You mean I should steal clothes? I *like* candy," Heaven fake-pouts.

"Oh for crying out loud you know what I meant! Look," Grandmelia starts, stops, stares out again at the marsh, gulls swooping and mewling overhead. "*I* loved your dad. He was my son. Ask most women if they had to choose between their husband or their son who they'd pick, and if they're honest they'll tell you their son. That's because a husband is a stranger. You meet him and the two of you try to bind in such a way that you're *not* strangers, but the fact remains you're from different worlds. Your son comes into *your* world already bearing half your genetics. He *is* you, do you see? So when you lose him, you're losing part of you."

"You have Uncle Daniel," Heaven offers.

"Yes. I do. But, you know, one son doesn't replace another. They're not lightbulbs." Grandmelia starts up the car, backs it out, and right before she turns onto the Driftway she looks at Heaven and Heaven sees her eyes are wet. "I'm not saying he was perfect. I'm sure you had your challenges living with him and your mother. Your mother is a pip. You should be properly mourning your dad, but I don't know how you should be dealing with . . . the other. That's why you need to talk to this therapist. Let her help you figure it all out."

Heaven shrugs. Maybe her mom in *prison* is a pip, whatever that is, but the *other* one isn't. "Is proper mourning the same as plain old mourning?"

Grandmelia snorts. Heaven can tell she's re-armored, no more wet eyes or *chats*. "Proper mourning is not robbing the neighborhood convenience store so you'll have plenty of fatty snacks to stuff down your throat on the way up to Maine to visit your incarcerated mother!"

"Thought you said she doesn't want to see me no more," Heaven says.

Grandmelia sighs. "Anymore—she doesn't want to see you *anymore*! It's the principle of the thing," she says, turning into the Driftway Medical Arts building, then parking the Volvo. "Okay!" she chirps. "Let's go make you behave, shall we?"

It goes something like this:

T (for therapist—she has a name but who gives a crap?): So, Heaven, can we talk about your parents?

H: Yes.

T: Do you miss your dad?

H: Yes.

T: Are you angry about what happened to him?

H: Yes.

T: Do you worry about your mom being in prison?

H: Yes.

T: Do you think maybe your recent behavior has something to do with missing your dad and worrying about your mom?

H: Yes.

T: Can you talk to me about what that feels like?

H: Yes.

T: Can you use your words, Heaven, and please respond to my questions?

H: Yes.

T: Okay, let's look at something else here. When you were living with your parents, did you see anything going on in your home that made you uncomfortable?

H: Yes.

T: Could you tell me more?

H: Yes.

T: You are angry, am I right? You want to hurt yourself and sabotage your chances to heal because you're angry?

H: Yes.

T: How about others? Do you want to hurt others? Me, for instance?

H: Yes.

T: This is going nowhere. If you can't cooperate and talk to me, Heaven, I'm afraid I won't be able to help you.

H: Yes.

On the way home Grandmelia scolds Heaven, who's sitting in the front at Grandmelia's insistence, her earbuds in and her iPod up to maximum. "Take those bloody things out of your ears and listen to me!" When Heaven doesn't respond, Grandmelia reaches over and slaps her thigh, lurching out from the spandex shorts Heaven wears over her swimsuit.

Heaven scowls, pulling the earbuds out but leaving the iPod on so Jonestown Massacre wails in the background, their song about how screwed up and useless school is, and Heaven couldn't agree more. "You're not allowed to hit me. My dad said no one is allowed. It's child abuse."

"That was a slap, a slap is not a hit, it's called getting the attention of an annoying little girl who is rude to have those things in her ears in the first place and too chubby to be wearing those shorts! I want to talk about the hour we just wasted along with my eighty dollars. You never, ever get it back you know, time wasted. Just wait until you're my age and you'll see how much of your life is gone, never to be recovered. That therapist told me not to bother bringing you again because you're unwilling to meet her halfway and do your part. You have anything to say about that?"

Heaven shrugs. "I was totally positive."

"I beg your pardon! You care to explain that comment in light of what I just told you?"

"I said 'yes' to her. Uncle Daniel said to be positive."

"Oh and he is of course an authority on these things, Mr. Good Humor Man himself!" Grandmelia pulls into her driveway, the perimeters of her small garden lined with midsummer blooms, mums, asters, and dahlias (Grandmelia told her their names, what does Heaven know about flowers, the Rock Harbor yards in their neighborhood grew weeds and dog poop). The rest of her yard is a bunch of stones, the ocean wailing in during a nor'easter, spitting beach rocks all over the place. Grandmelia punches her garage opener on the visor so hard it falls onto the car floor mat. "Oh for crying out loud, can nothing work properly?"

When the car is parked she presses down the auto-lock button so Heaven can't get out. "I know you have swim practice tomorrow morning and I won't take that away; it's a commitment and we honor commitments. But until breakfast you are to stay in your room and think about lost chances. Life is full of them and when you get older like your uncle, they start turning into regrets. Middle age is when it starts, not being able to take things back. When you're my age it's entirely too late. You just lost a chance to work with someone highly regarded in the field of adolescent mental health. I told the police in return for them not arresting you I would take you to a therapist. You have enough criminals in your family, don't you think?"

"Yes," Heaven says.

Inside she slams the door to her room and Grandmelia immediately opens it again, tells her, *Do not ever slam this door!* then slams it shut. Luckily Heaven has her stash from the kitchen, forged late last night when Grandmelia was getting her "beauty sleep"—Cheez Doodles, Doritos, Oreos, and the chocolate granola bars, which are the worst, but Heaven figures she better eat something healthy since tomorrow she has to race Bethany Harrison freestyle, which isn't fair since that's Bethany's stroke and Heaven's is breaststroke.

Coach said they have to be able to master another stroke just in case and put them in lap pairs for Friday's practice. Bethany pitched a fit when she heard Heaven was the other half of her pair, and Coach made her dive in and do extra laps. Later Bethany slammed Heaven up against the locker room door. "I'll whup your fat ass," she hissed.

Then at this morning's practice during the relay race when all of the lanes were filled with swimmers doing their strokes, Heaven looked to her left over the float line for just a moment to see if she was beating whoever was swimming there and saw it was Bethany. Bethany saw her too and on the downward stroke of her freestyle she reached under the float-line and scratched Heaven's leg, causing Heaven's eyes to smart under her goggles and she lost two seconds, which made her team come in third out of three.

Everyone was mad at her in the locker room, her team and Bethany's groupies, her gaggle of skanks, which is what Heaven calls them in her head, like a gaggle of geese. "Look!" Grandmelia pointed out one day in the marsh off Hatherly road, "a gaggle of geese!" Heaven refused to shower, despite being so cold after swim practice she got chicken skin. That's what Uncle Daniel calls the cold-skin bumps, said he learned it as a kid in Hawaii before he nearly drowned. The practice pool in the summer is outdoors, and later in the morning when the sun is high the water feels good, but that early it doesn't. She knew if she took her suit off the girls would tease her about her fat, but if she didn't they'd torment her saying, "How come you're not taking your suit off—because you're so fat?" It's a no-win, as Uncle Daniel would point out.

"I'm getting my cool surfboard any day now," she told Bethany.

"You're too fat to surf."

"Yeah, she'd roll off it and float like a beached whale," one of the skanks said.

"How can a beached whale float?" Heaven said. They were not only a gaggle of skanks, but a gaggle of *dumb* skanks.

"So where *is* your awesome surfboard? You said it was coming last week!"

"My uncle decided to have it made special for me, at a place in Maine that builds wooden surfboards like they used to use, hand-crafted with my initials on it."

"H. F. for hog farts?" Bethany bellowed. The skanks gig-gled and Bethany grabbed the towel Heaven wrapped around her shoulders, throwing it down on the wet floor. Heaven shivered and Bethany got right up in her face, so close her little pale eyes looked like chunks of ice. "Made in Maine, huh? Where your mother is? We heard they locked her away up there. What for, being crazy?"

Heaven shook her head. "She's not crazy. She's an astronaut."

★　★　★

Now Heaven sits on her bed and rips opens her treats. I was *totally* positive with that therapist, she thinks, her beagle snout and her glasses perched so low Heaven kept wanting to push them back up over her big nose, but why stop there? Shove them into her forehead, through her skull until they're sitting on her brain and maybe *then* she could see Heaven, who Heaven really is, not just a bunch of symptoms. That's what Uncle Daniel said shrinks do, which is why they call them shrinks, he said, because they shrink your brain down to the size of a bean with their platitudes. In the end, he said, all they really want is to drug you, so you'll pay them, then shut the fuck up and go away.

The faeries want positive, Uncle Daniel told her, or they might play a trick on you. Like the man who thought he'd help himself to the stones of Gharsainn to build a new house with. When he was warned the faeries under the hill protected these he said he didn't believe in faeries. So he carted away two loads of rocks and when he went back for the third, a strange light glowed from inside the hill and a voice called out warning him about "the vengeance of evil things." The next day his horse died, his cattle sickened, his crops failed, and his boat sank.

Uncle Daniel said faeries could be nasty because they're little people and little people don't like being little. He said one theory is that they used to be the original occupants of the Hebrides, but then the giant blond Nordics came, conquered Skye and the darker little people had to take to the hills and hide. "So now they play tricks on you if you're not like them," he said.

Heaven's huge and pale as a worm. Maybe *that's* why her surf-board's late. Maybe some cute little mean-girl faeries pinched it so big fat Heaven can't ever have it.

◆ LEO ◆

AMELIA CALLED EARLIER THIS evening, three times until Leo finally answered. "You *want* Moscow in your business?" he said. Immediately she's going on about *the* granddaughter, like he hadn't even spoken. "The granddaughter is a thief!" she said, "Plus she wouldn't cooperate with the therapist, who quit. I took her there as restitution for the police not arresting the girl. She must take after her mother!" Amelia snapped.

Leo reminded her Gavin was a drug addict, thus in the eyes of the law, a criminal. "Well he wasn't caught," she said.

Wasn't that his former wife in a nutshell? Innocent until caught! "What do you want me to do about it?" he asked, bad move.

"You figure it out. Why does this all have to be on my shoulders?"

Leo choked back what he's wanted to say for years—because Gavin is *your* son. It's a matter of principle that he can do it, staunch what would become kerosene on long-smoldering coals. And it wouldn't change a thing. Instead he said, "Because you have court-ordered custody of his daughter."

And now a call from the prison! Why does he even pick up? Some perverse guilt, he supposes, like he owes it to Gavin's wife for the money he gave them that maybe helped put her there, and who may or may not be a murderess! *An inmate from Rock Harbor Women's Correctional . . . will you accept the charges?* Then Cassie's on the line sobbing so hard she's hiccupping. "Calm down," he tells her, "I can't understand a word." Eventually he gets the gist. She'd been in seg for forty-eight hours; another inmate ratted her out, that *ghetto ho*! But it's not why she's calling.

"How much?" he asks.

"No, they froze my personals! Can you believe it?" she whines. "Like what kind of punishment takes away tampons!" She wants him to take some pictures for her, she tells him. "Something inspirational, with people."

Out the window Leo sees in the moonlight a slick of something floating up the Kennebec, more solid than slick, some kind of detritus? bobbing and dipping like a seal. Ever since they removed the Edwards Dam there's fish in the river, big sturgeon and it's healthier, not the open sewer of his youth, so maybe a seal got lost where river meets estuary and is just following its dinner. *Really* lost, he thinks. "I don't do inspirational," he tells her.

"You have to! You don't get it. They found an envelope in my pocket because of that crack whore snitch. They're forcing me to get clean. Making me go to the prison addicts anonymous or whatever that shit's called." She starts crying again. "It's all such crap and on top of that Amelia's going on about a lie detector. How much more do I have to take? Without Gavin nothing is worth anything to me! Doesn't anyone get that? Why the hell wouldn't I do drugs, it's all that holds me to this fucked-up world."

"Jesus H," he mutters. "Cassie, honestly. You're being made to clean up is a long time coming, don't you think? Do it for your kid, if not for you. Anyway, what do my photos have to do with any of this?"

"I need something on my cell wall, something to focus on. Otherwise I'll just blow up inside my own head. There's stuff in there I really don't want to see."

"How about I buy you a nice poster? Bluebirds, rainbows, a snow-capped mountain, squirrels in a birdbath. That's inspirational for most folks."

"No!" She starts crying again. "I want people, Leo, real people. Can't you please do this for me? Gavin showed me some of your photos and you're good, he was proud."

"Right," Leo says. "I'm sure, in between his works, he was proud. How could you two live like that? And *why*, did you ever ask yourself that, why you did?"

She exhales into the phone like she's been punched. "You think I wanted this life? I played softball. Lived in a decent neighborhood. My folks stayed married and they were nice to me. It sucked having my mom die when I was only thirteen, but parents can get cancer and die. When you need something to get you through you don't think, am I a good person? Why am I doing this? *Who the fuck am I!* You don't get all existential, Leo, it's not a choice for fuck's sake. I need something on the wall because it's too messed up in my head."

Leo sighs. "Okay but listen. I take pictures of buildings, ruined ones, broken down, desiccated, decayed stuff. I don't do models anymore. When I look at a model now I put forty years on her, tragedy, sickness, some kind of soul-sucking struggle and only then is her face of any interest to me. Physical beauty is transient. What rose lasts? If I take pictures of people, they won't be pretty."

"Most people aren't. Just Gavin. Gavin was pretty."

"And proud of me you say, huh?"

"He would've liked to do what you do, make something solid, you know, before the shit hit the fan."

"Or his veins . . ." Leo whispers, but not so she'd hear.

After they hang up Leo stretches out in his recliner that faces the old analog television, turned off, maybe even unplugged—he hasn't watched it for a while, perched on a 1950s TV tray, its metal legs bent but stable enough, in front of bookcases overflowing with books stacked every which way. He loves his books: ancient hardbacks with chewed-up and faded covers, paperbacks, their pages brittle, yellow with age. Sometimes he'll pick one up and just hold it, attempt to mentally assemble the world inside its pages that he can't mine much anymore—he has trouble remembering each night what he read the night before, but if he thinks about it, really concentrates, he can mostly recall the story itself, the emotional heft of it, gist of its information if it's nonfiction, the impact it had on him however many years ago. His test for any book, artwork, his photographs for that matter: Is the world a better place for these being in it? He couldn't always answer a definitive yes, given the horrors so many face just trying to survive, war, violence, poverty, hunger, humanity's tragic failures to be *humane*, but if it was any good at all, he'd know *he* was better in some way for it, its story a part of him.

Opposite the bookshelves are file cabinets filled with his photographs, the ones he never sold, and then he stopped trying to sell any of them, even the ones people asked for. Most recently a gallery in Pittsburgh wanted to do a "retrospective" of his work, like he was already dead. What was the point? He didn't *aspire*, as Amelia once told him; she meant it critically, but it was true enough and Leo rather thought it a good thing. He had no interest in recognition; he had that in the fashion world long ago and look what it got him: the Egg Me! girl. Now his file cabinets are plastered with sticky notes, reminders of things he has to do each day that he worries he'll forget, like putting his keys in his pocket when he goes out for a walk, or even just to check the mailbox, and the door slams behind him locking him out. Then he forgets to look at the notes. Too bad, because one of the notes is a reminder to unlock the door *before* he goes out for the mail, and another note suggests he replace the doorknob lock with a deadbolt that only locks from the inside with a key. Which means he'd have another key to forget.

Now Leo gazes out the window at the river and sees that *something* again, a small disturbance in the calm expanse of the Kennebec, lit up by the moon. It occurs to him whatever it is has reversed direction, moving back now toward the sea.

✦ AMELIA ✦

AMELIA PERCHES ON A stool opposite the kitchen counter, watching Heaven make pancakes. She'd come home from swimming practice *starving*, the girl claimed, *always* claims, and asked Amelia if she could have pancakes for her breakfast. Amelia had told Heaven numerous times she should have breakfast *before* she goes to practice, but according to Heaven she never gets up in time to eat. Amelia wouldn't know because her reason for buying that damn bike for her granddaughter was so Amelia wouldn't *have* to wake up early! She'd been about to say no to the pancake request, explaining yet again to the girl how bad white flour was, no nutrients, no fiber, plus it makes you bloat, when she suddenly remembered Gavin around the same age as Heaven, telling Amelia that her "default" to every request was always "no." Was that true? Amelia hadn't thought so, but now she finds herself frequently saying no to Gavin's daughter.

"Okay," she said instead, and Heaven's eyes practically popped out of their sockets.

"Seriously?" Heaven said.

"On one condition, you have to make them yourself."

Heaven shrugged. "Well do you have mix? I made them before at my parents' house with pancake mix. My mom made them once with a mix, then I did it after."

Amelia snorted. "She couldn't afford to clothe you properly, yet she bought pancake mix? No I don't have the mix, but I do have a cookbook and all the ingredients, even white flour and sugar, if you insist on those." She thought Heaven would fuss about having to make them herself but instead the girl grinned, said "Cool!"

They'd looked through the cookbook together, found a recipe, and Amelia braced herself for a messy enterprise. Now she's surprised to observe Heaven carefully measuring the flour, sugar, and a teaspoon of baking powder into a sifter, then sifting it over the bowl, no spills. She measures the milk into a cup, pours it into a separate bowl, and is now carefully cracking two eggs, then beating them with the electric mixer.

Amelia says, "Maybe I should let you cook more often," and Heaven nods solemnly, concentrating now on spooning the batter neatly into the pre-heated frying pan. Her dad would've never been this meticulous with a cooking project, or to be honest, any project, Amelia thinks, and is suddenly struck with a memory of Gavin and Daniel (years ago!) making ornaments in California. The memory is so clear it's practically a vision.

It was almost Christmas, seven months before Daniel's accident. Home after the final Egg Me! shoot before the holidays, she'd walked into the dining room of their Silver Lake adobe late in the afternoon. It was that good Southern California coastal light, the Santa Ana winds had blown the smog out to sea and rays of sunlight streamed into the window over the table where Leo, Daniel, and Gavin sat making ornaments out of foil, pasting on colorful bits of confetti and glitter. Daniel would've been eleven, Gavin seven, and already people stared at Gavin on the streets, in the market, wherever they went. His long flaxen hair, the perfect ovals of his radiant eyes, a face that looked angelic. Except he wasn't,

not by a longshot, but Amelia adored him, and the vision of him
at that moment, lit up under the late afternoon light was luminous.
She'd walked over to the table and stood behind him, fawning over
him, stroking his hair, touching his arms, his hands that were busy
destroying whatever ornament he'd attempted to make. Bam Bam
Bam! he cried, hitting it with his fist, then shredding it. Amelia
laughed.

But when she glanced up, it was Daniel's face that caught her
breath, causing it to seize up like the air in her lungs had turned
suddenly to ice—Daniel studying his brother, then looking at his
mother, was this the moment he recognized his own exclusion?
Because of course it was true, though she would've never admitted it then. Daniel watched, almost impervious it seemed, his face
showing nothing but a sort of acceptance beyond those eleven
years: this is the way it is, his expression said; you have beauty, and
you have absence. What happened next makes Amelia, this many
years later, want to cry. After Gavin's own ornament was destroyed
he reached for Daniel's perfectly cut and decorated tinfoil star, and
Daniel let him take it, put it in his hand.

Later, after the boys had gone to bed Amelia was sitting on the
patio with a glass of wine and Leo walked out, stood beside her
chair. They both gazed into the distance at L.A.'s lights. "I was
thinking about the beach," he said, "out past those lights where all
that darkness is. How the ocean keeps washing up on the shore like
it's done for thousands of years, before humans made such a mess
of things, this city based on some absurd notion of the American
Dream. Legions of people came from all over to settle in it, the
vision of a starstruck life filled with riches and ease, which one
percent of them might achieve with good looks, good luck, and the
rest would fail utterly."

"Jesus, someone's in a mood! Happy Christmas to you too. Sit
why don't you," Amelia said. "I don't like people hovering over
me."

Leo crouched down beside her. "You smell like wine," he said.

Amelia snorted. "God, Leo, you complained before about
me drinking too many gin and tonics, so I switched to wine, for

chrissake. I told you, I drink to keep from eating too much, to keep my figure. My job depends on my figure, our family on my job!"

Leo laughed, joyless. "You found a convenient excuse, didn't you? Remember Gavin this afternoon, when we were making ornaments?"

"Yeah, did you notice that ray of sunlight, like a halo over him?"

"Right, and his destruction, *bam bam bam*. Then Daniel handed over his perfect star, like this was what was expected of him, his place in our family."

"Yes, Leo," Amelia had sighed. "I was there. I know what you're getting at. I don't think we should make a big deal out of it. He's only seven years old."

That's when Leo said something really cruel to Amelia, and recalling it now makes her shudder. "We never talked about abortion," he said. "Why is that?"

She remembers her sharp intake of breath, and how in the glow of the patio light she saw a play of emotions cross his face, trying to control some sort of deep anger, she realized. Amelia had felt confusion, then stricken. "How dare you!" she'd spat. "You'd do that to me, would you?"

"Well, you see, right there is the problem; you thought it only involved you. It didn't," Leo said, "it doesn't. You saw that impassive look on Daniel's face, knowing if he didn't offer his star Gavin would take it anyway. He's going to grow up in the shadow of his brother's more luminous light, and as undeserving as Gavin is, as undeserving as most of the celebrities people worship, their skin-deep shine glowing by the grace of good genes, entitled childhoods, and expensive cosmetic interventions—that's the way it will be. So I'm just wondering, Amelia, back when you realized you were pregnant with Gavin and that he wasn't my biological kid, how come you didn't consider abortion?"

"We're talking before *Roe versus Wade*, so I guess that would've made it an ideal solution for you, four months along and under the knife of some back-alley hack, two for the price of one," she'd sputtered. She figured Leo was about to retort something sarcastic and mean, which had become their way, but when she glanced at his face she noticed how beaten he looked. She felt it too, hollow and broken, and they both swallowed whatever nastiness had been on their tongues.

"I'm going to bed," he said, and she said nothing, just stared out past the lights into the vast darkness of the sea.

★   ★   ★

Later in the afternoon, the fried scent of Heaven's pancakes still lingering, her lawyer calls and Amelia wants a cigarette so bad she can taste its burn. She hasn't smoked in years, not since the end of Egg Me! and her discovery she'd been retired off the modeling circuit, aged out at thirty-nine. "You're TV-identified now," her agent explained, "we *maybe* buy you a year in mature skin commercials, gray coverage does us a couple, but forget high fashion, darlin,' that train left years ago. Detergents could have you to forty-five, but even these have a longevity clause." *My career reduced to a longevity clause.* Her agent had shrugged. "Human capital, name of the game."

"What do you mean we can't bring in a lie detector, Bub?" Her lawyer's name is Bob Robbins, but everyone calls him Bub. A gay man called "Bub" like he's some beer-guzzling jock. Jock*ey* more like it, Bub said. "It's a prison for lord's sake, they should have them available as rentals."

"Amelia dear, I can't bring a polygraph inside without a court order, and the French case is closed."

"Look, I used to think sixty was old before I turned it, but now I'll tell you what, I'm a goddamn *elder*, so you best hear me out! This case is *not* closed, far as I'm concerned. Either you find a way or I'm talking retrial and they *make* her take a polygraph."

"Who are *they*? We can't just ask for a new trial without more evidence turning up. You have any? She was convicted of manslaughter. Last time we spoke you told me she's outright denying it now, which will not, I assure you, get the results you're after."

She hears him suck in a breath, fortify himself. Amelia's always put Bub a little on edge, and she's always thought that's not a bad place to have your lawyer.

"Look Bub, that woman can deny until the cows come home but she still claims not to remember anything. That's what I want to find out, if she's lying about not remembering. I told her I'm not trying to get her upgraded to murder-one, I've given up on that. I just need to know what Gavin's last moments in the world were like. Was he in pain? He got smacked on the head with a board! I brought him into the world; I was there when that beautiful little face emerged. I need to know how he went out. Can't anyone understand that?" Amelia sniffles for effect, but in seconds it's real and she reaches for a tissue from the box on her coffee table. Bub clears his throat.

"So what about a hypnotist then," she sniffs, "can we bring in one of those?"

He laughs. "Sure, and how about an astrologist while we're at it, do you know her sign? Not exactly my specialty dear, I'm gay not whacked, and there's another problem. Cassie's privileges were revoked and that includes visitors. They let me see her for ten minutes as your lawyer, only because you have custody of her kid. She didn't look good. Had the shakes, greasy hair, skin the color of meat gone bad and it looked to me like she'd dropped ten pounds, which she can't afford, she's the girth of a corn stalk. I asked her how she was doing, and you know what she said?"

"I won't hold my breath in anticipation!" Amelia snipes, wishing again for cigarette smoke in her mouth, blowing it out, curlicues, smoke rings—she used to be able to do those—inhaling those tasty toxins down her throat.

"Well my dear, your daughter-in-law told me she's clean, they made her get clean and now she has nothing to live for. What about your child, I said? What about Heaven? You know what she said?"

"Bub, this isn't the ten questions game; I'm not in it for a new dishwasher!"

"Fair enough, but I need you to see what we're dealing with here, why these notions of yours to first make her confess, then to bring in a lie detector and, God help us, a hypnotist to wring some sort of truth out of her won't work. She tells me, I would have you note after saying she's clean . . . looks me straight in the eyes, her pupils the size of my thumbnails . . . Mr. Robbins, she says, I'm an addict. No telling what I will do."

Amelia rolls her eyes, a good eye roll, her granddaughter would be impressed, full-on *duh* with that tinge of arrogance. "Whoop-de-do, yesterday's news! What *are* you saying?"

"I'm saying this woman is an unreliable witness to her own culpability. She's an unreliable witness to her own life, Amelia dear, you really must try to forget all of it."

After they hang up she massages her scalp, her forehead, cheeks, runs her hand over her mouth, leans back against the sofa and squeezes shut her eyes. *Do not cry!* she commands herself, *that woman is not worth your tears!* She breathes deeply, then transports herself backward in her life before all of this, all of them. February 1967, she's a young, sought-after model and it's Fashion Week in New York. A month later her agent will book her first Egg Me! commercial in L.A., and she will fly to the West Coast with renowned photographer Leo French. But for this moment, though the war in Vietnam is heating up, folk singers in the Village strumming its evils and hippies in Washington Square chanting "Make love not war," Amelia's on the runway and she's a star.

Amelia MacQueen in a Hubert Givenchy "little black" backless evening dress, her auburn hair rolled on top of her head, slant of those sixties cat eyes with the false eyelashes out to *there*. Never mind catwalk, she *is* the cat, slinking down the runway, the fluidity of her motions like water, like music, the seductive thrum of the wind. She's a goddess and this her world, and not once did it ever occur to her that her life at this radiant moment, with the photographers' flashes popping, strobe lights flashing, people clapping, whistling as she pivots on the balls of her high-heeled shoes and sashays back toward the dressing room, that this glorious moment was built on ephemeral beauty, the fleetingness of youth, the transitory nature of life itself; and the person she believed she was, the bright shining future she assumed was unconditionally hers, would forever disappear.

♦ DANIEL ♦

TWO AM, A KNOCKING on his window, he knows who it is. Flashed him three times before coming over—she got that right, a prerequisite for going any further with this thing. But what *is* this thing? Is it a thing?

Daniel cracks open the window three inches, one, two, three, enough to hear her voice.

She says, "Are you there?" No points for intelligence so far, who opened the window if it wasn't him, there? Plus her voice is jarring. Lower than he would've figured, husky, but it's not that so much—more that it's an actual voice, which confirms a person, a female person, is attached.

He clears his throat, a way to get started, like a drummer's tapping or warming up the car before pulling out. "I need to ask you something before we engage. Amelia said something about Leo giving you a ride home. I'm curious how you know him?

"Leo, yeah, strange coincidence. He stopped at The Seagull for some food before coming here to talk to your mom. Fortification, is my guess, confronting Amelia! He sat in my section and we figured out the connection. My car was in the shop and I would've had to wait a couple hours for my sister to finish her shift, so he offered. Nice guy."

To her credit she knew who he was talking about and didn't pretend otherwise. She might be smart enough after all.

"Are you going to let me in?" she whispers through the screen, a buzz in his ear.

"If you're an angel you could float through this wall, beam yourself in."

"What, like *Star Trek*? It's ghosts that go through walls I think and believe me I'm no angel. Leo told me about your room thing. I won't touch anything, I promise. He told me you're sweet but a little odd. I can do odd unless you're like psycho-odd." She laughs and he likes her laugh, not forced or projectile.

"I don't know about *sweet*. I reject that. It's not supposed to happen this way, you crawling in the window while I watch you do it. It's all wrong." He inhales a sudden whiff of her scent through the screen, a musky mix of something herbal, something fried—she'd been at work earlier and didn't shower to come see him. Which is fine. He likes her smell.

"What the hell, Daniel? You expect me to crawl through your window?"

"No, that's what I mean. You were supposed to just appear in my room. Maybe you crawled through the window, but I wouldn't know it. If I know it, I can't allow it, because nobody comes in my room."

He hears her sharp intake of breath, whether a sigh, or maybe she's trying not to laugh, he can't be sure. "I guess the front door's out of the question?"

"I'd have to leave my room to open it." Maybe she isn't as smart as he thought.

"Yeah, duh. I sure as hell don't want your mother opening it."

"No one would."

"Then could you at least open the window more and put on your light so we can talk face-to-face, like an actual conversation? It sucks that I can't see you."

He slides the window up a few more inches, one, two, three, then pushes it down one of those inches so that the cumulative opening is five, an odd number. He keeps the room dark. Sees her standing near the motion sensor light, staring into his dark room. He could tell her how if she stays perfectly still for three minutes the light will go off and she'd be in the dark too, but he likes this dynamic, him seeing her. He likes her looks, black hair pulled back with a clip, nothing flashy, her face has an uncertainty about it he can relate to, like Jell-O that hasn't found its mold. "What if you don't like my face?" he asks.

"Well it's not like I haven't seen you from across the yard through your window, also your dad has a photo in his wallet of you and your brother. He showed it to me when we figured out I'm your neighbor."

"Anything that has my brother in it would be too old. I don't look like that anymore. I may not even be the person you think's in the photo."

She snorts. "Who *is* in an old photo? It caught you then and now is now. You could've been someone. I mean like someone with a life outside your room. I googled your parents after Leo dropped me off. They were rock stars for chrissake, celebrity model and a renowned photographer."

"My mother modeled eggs."

"Yeah, well, my mom just keeps marrying, thinks if she does it enough maybe someday it'll take. Though I should talk. I've got two failed to her four under my own belt. I'll probably be a waitress for the rest of my life. I get mad at stuff, then I say bad things or break things; once I even slugged the manager at this bar, Dragon Lady we called her. She was that kind of woman who hates other women. We took bets on how long each of us would last, figured the prettiest would get canned first. The other girls thought I'd last the longest, like Dragon Lady wouldn't think I was a threat. I was out on my ass in two days because I called her a bitch, which she was. I hit her when she canned me, she was such an asshole about it; wouldn't even pay me what she owed, said it was a trial period, some bullshit like that. Not a slap across her face,

I'm talking punched her out. Would've had me arrested only the publicity would be bad for her biz."

He's watching her mouth say all this and wondering about it, full lips, no lipstick, sort of pouty but not stupid pouty, more like there's some actual sorrow there. He likes that, but this life she's talking about is nothing he would imagine her having, gritty, rough around the perimeters. Can an angel do grit? "What color are your eyes?"

"What color do you think? I'm not a blue-eyed white-girl, or didn't you notice?"

"I don't know," he says.

"Okay so forget my eyes. I want to show you something, but I need to see your face, so I know how you react."

He nods. This makes sense.

"For the record, I think your dad is pretty cool. He's got genuine talent and he's nice about it."

Daniel nods, "I agree, but don't tell him that. When people know they're admired, they stop being admirable." He stands face-to-face with her through his window, beaming a flashlight under his chin; he's not ready for the full-on ceiling lamp, they haven't gotten there yet. He and Gavin used to do this when they were kids and slept out in a tent sometimes in the backyard. They'd shine lights under their chins and make faces. One Halloween when nobody wanted to go trick or treating with Daniel, after Gavin got home he shared his candy with Daniel in the tent. The ones he didn't like, Good & Plenty, yellow Lifesavers, Dots that got stuck in his teeth. But it was still nice. A good memory.

"The flashlight's a little weird," she says. "Is that like the only way you communicate or something?"

He nods, his chin in the flashlight's light bobbing up and down. "Or something."

"Okay whatever, watch." She slides off the platform shoe like she's done for him so many nights through her window, but not with a kick this time. Then she puts it carefully on the ground beside one of Amelia's decorative garden-rocks, placing her bare foot on the rock, the foot attached to the shorter leg, sliding her short skirt even further up her thigh than it already is. He tries not to look at her thighs, a creamy brown in the light, because he knows what she wants him to look at.

"So, what do you think?"

"It's a homunculus."

"A *what?*"

"A homunculus is a perfectly formed miniature human, so in your case you have a perfect miniature leg."

She stares at him for a moment then nods, pulls her skirt down, slips back into the platform shoe. "Good answer. I mean what's the big deal? It's all relative, right? Who says what the correct size is, who sets these standards? It's only relative to my other leg that this one doesn't measure up."

"You could be a selkie."

She looks at him like he has bees flying out of his nose. "A . . . come again?"

"Half woman, half seal. Sometimes they get caught in the transformation phase, they're ninety-nine percent woman but they have whiskers, for example, so maybe your homunculus leg is a flipper in another carnation, which makes you magic. You have the power to transform."

She laughs, but sounds friendly enough, like she isn't totally shutting off the possibilities. "You're probably crazy, you know that, right? You think I'm a seal? I don't dig the ocean, man. You don't spend a lot of time on beaches in a swimsuit with this *fin*. If I knew magic I'd transform my butt right out of this life and into somebody else's, someone with money. I wouldn't be a diner waitress, that's for sure. Or if I was, it would be at the kind of upscale place that calls waitresses *servers*, only those are mostly dudes."

He guesses he must have passed whatever test this was, because she's inched up closer to the window. He can smell her better now, a soapy smell like she washes her hands a lot, and that something fried he'd smelled before, but fainter like it's wearing off.

"So, here's the thing. I need a favor, your dad's phone number."

"Why?"

"When I googled him, like I said, and it turned out he used to be famous, I realized we had one of his prints on the wall. Belonged to my first husband, but I loved that photograph. It probably saved me from total debasement by my husband, like I'm talking lying on the floor at his feet, grabbing his legs and begging him not to leave, just-kick-me-instead kind of debasement. The kind where you don't even recognize yourself anymore. It was a picture of a famous folk singer. Her eyes stared out like she got me, got what I was going through. That picture made me feel a little less alone."

"Sure, I understand that. But Leo's a photographer. Not Mick Jagger. You know how many people care about photographs unless they're in them? And now with smartphones and digital photography, everyone thinks they're a photographer."

"Not like Leo, they aren't. They're doing effing Instagram updates; he's an artist. I want to ask him if he'll take a picture of my collection. I showed you some of the stuff through the window. The Collection of Broken Things, I call it."

He nods. "Amelia told me its name. You must've told her, or maybe your mother did. Why do you collect broken things?"

She shrugs. "Not sure, really. Give them a new life? We live in a throwaway culture. I'm saving them from the dump."

"There's something Japanese called *kintsugi*, where broken objects are repaired with powdered gold to display their cracks. It means to patch with gold."

She laughs. "How do you know about weird things like that, dude-who-stays-in-room? I don't repair my collection, that's the point. To appreciate brokenness for what it is. That's why I want Leo to take its picture. For posterity, like, in case my stepdad kicks me out and I'm on the street. Can't take it with me if I'm homeless."

"You could live here." He squirms a bit after saying this. What is he opening up? More to the point, is he actually flirting with her? He remembers Gavin flirting with all those girls back in high school. They seemed to love him for it, but Daniel thought the whole thing pretty demeaning. Gavin had a reason for doing it, getting into their pants he said, but Daniel isn't sure what he wants out of this, and again what *this* is!

She's smiling as if she likes what he said. "Would I have to crawl through the window when you're not looking every time I came home?"

Daniel shrugs, *nonchalant*, he hopes she thinks, because he's feeling anything but. "Anyway, Leo doesn't like phones. Me neither, by the way, unless it's an emergency."

"Oh. Well . . . Hey, change of subject, you know what I like to do? Go to furniture stores and lie on different beds, pretend I'm testing them to buy them."

"Why would you do that? You're not going to, are you, buy them?"

"Of course not. I live in a garage. But it's like trying out different lives, you know? Beds are about as intimate as it gets, a portal into someone's soul, the sort of bed he'd sleep on. You can't do that because you never leave your room."

"Which do you like best, memory foam, pillow-tops, or waterbeds? I'd go for the waterbed myself, but Amelia's afraid they'll wreck her floor."

She shakes her head. A wavy lock of her hair that's fallen out of the clip slides across her cheek like a question mark. "You are a strange one. Tell you what. How about a trade? You get a hold of your dad and tell him I need him to call me. I'll give you my number to give to him. Tell him it's business, about his photography. I can pay him. It would be worth some extra shifts to have a picture of my collection taken by Leo French. Say you'll get him to call, and I'll show you my breasts."

Daniel's cheeks grow hot, even his neck is flushed, but she won't notice in the flashlight's thin light. "I've already seen them, through the window." He hopes Heaven in the next room hasn't heard any of this. He knows Amelia won't because she often turns on NPR to fall asleep to and he can hear it now. For the first time in a long while Daniel feels like he might have something in his life worth hiding.

"Well, you know, they're better up close. What the hell, I've got nothing to lose." She lifts up her shirt and Daniel turns off his flashlight so she can't see his blood flowing out of his brain, his cheeks, his chest, his stomach, making a beeline toward his groin; switches it back on again, one two three. Something catches in his throat like a chunk of meat and for a moment his breath is stopped. He swallows hard. "What are those marks on your arms?" he says, avoiding the breasts now, which are nice, though he doesn't have much to compare them to, but this other . . . red slashes like she'd had a run-in with a cougar. They're on the insides where he'd guess her skin is sweetest, away from the sun, from all eyes but his! lifting up her shirt for him.

She shrugs, pulls down her shirt. "I cut myself sometimes. Mostly with a razor, sometimes a knife. Helps me keep, I don't know, grounded. My sister thinks it's a sick teenage trend, that's what she called it, and disses me for it. But she doesn't get it."

He nods. "Marks of the saint. Maybe you really *are* an angel."

She laughs, loud and sharp like a bark. "If I'm some angel I'll tell you what, I'm an avenging one, for the wrecked, the humiliated, and the freaks!" She grins at him; he can see her teeth gleaming in the motion sensor light like little animal eyes. "Angels don't have this mouth," she says, pressing her lips against his window screen. "Someday maybe, if you're very nice to me, I'll show you what I can do with it. Goodnight strange man." She makes a kissing sound then heads back across the yard. He watches the light go on in her garage, then off again, pictures her climbing into her bed, not a waterbed, not a pillow-top, a cloud. Or kelp. Maybe kelp.

♦ HEAVEN ♦

AFTER HER MORNING SWIM practice, Heaven's at the back of Grandmelia's yard, peering over the fence to where the garage girl lives. Grandmelia called her that. Heaven's swimsuit under her shorts and T-shirt is still damp, and she hopes Grandmelia doesn't come outside and call her in to change. Suddenly the garage door opens, and the garage girl steps out, staring at Heaven.

"Hey!" Heaven says, trying desperately to remember her *real* name.

"Hey yourself. Can I help you with something?"

"Well, I need to write a paper to get into eighth-grade bio, so I'm looking for cool insects. Got any in your yard? That's one of the topics, describe an insect survival behavior. I'm probably going to write to the question about how sea animals breathe, 'cause that's my thing, but my friend Robyn said he wrote about a cool insect. If I find a cool one maybe I will too."

"Your thing, huh?" She walks over to the fence and sticks her hand over it for Heaven to shake. "I'm Mercy. You're Daniel's niece, right?"

Heaven nods. "Do you like my uncle?"

"Yeah, kind of. Is that okay?"

Heaven shrugs. "I heard you talking to him last night. He doesn't know I heard. I always hear the stuff people don't want me to hear."

Mercy tosses back her head and laughs. "Talk about a survival skill!"

Heaven likes Mercy's neck, tan and long, like a deer's neck. She tries to picture Mercy with her uncle. She's a lot prettier than he is. Her skin looks caramel against her white waitress shirt, and Uncle Daniel is pale as a marshmallow. "He won't come out of his room, you know."

Mercy nods. "I've heard. Well, I can tell you a survival thing I happen to know about a kind of insect, if you'd like. It's kind of cool. Ever seen a tiger bee fly?"

Heaven shakes her head.

"So after the tiger bee fly mates, the female looks for carpenter bee nests. When she finds one with carpenter bee eggs inside she flies in and lays her eggs there too. Her larvae are parasites; once they hatch they look for the hatched carpenter bee larvae. Then, the fly larvae attaches itself to the bee larvae and feeds on its insides."

"Eww," Heaven says, "that's so gross! How do you know stuff like that?"

Mercy shrugs. "I'm into entomology. Wouldn't have thought that about me, huh? Your diner waitress neighbor is a science geek. If I'd been born into a different kind of life, I might've even gotten a PhD in it. Just call me Dr. Mercy!" she says, and laughs. "I've got to get to work. Nice meeting you!"

Heaven nods.

Fish have gills to take oxygen from the water. Antarctic sea spiders breathe through their pores. Whales, seals, porpoises, and dolphins have lungs. A sperm whale can hold its breath 90 minutes, the beaked whale for two hours before they come up for a breath through blowholes at the top of their heads. Blowholes are like whale nostrils, also porpoises and dolphins have blowholes. Seals can hold their breath under water for usually an hour, but the elephant seal can hold it for two hours! A study found that seals, whales, and dolphins have an "oxygen-binding protein" in their muscles, which is maybe why they can stay underwater so long. Seals sleep under the surface by letting their body float, called bottling. They are completely underwater except for their snouts, so they can breathe. Unfortunately for whales the Navy uses sonar underwater, which is like a giant wave of intense sound and whales will dive down so deep to escape it they bleed from their eyes and ears. Humans can't stay under water more than a few minutes without mechanical help such as from oxygen tanks (except if you practice a lot, like me!). Otherwise, they drown.

By Heaven French: "Discuss how different ocean animals breathe."

In the end she decided to write about ocean animals to try out for eighth-grade bio, the *cool* science class taught by Ms. Diaz, a cool teacher. Hopefully she'll get in, or she'll have to take eighth-grade *lame* science, a survey class taught by Mr. *Lasagna*, something Italian like that. Seems nice enough, but Robyn said Ms. Diaz's bio was way cooler and Robyn rules. They were given a choice of four different topics to write a one-page response on, due tomorrow, a month before school starts. Heaven picked the ocean animals because she's all about breathing in water, plus, what Mercy told her about those cannibal insect larvae creeped her out.

Later that night she tries to fall asleep, but she can hear through the wall Uncle Daniel's weird electronic music he listens to sometimes, which makes her feel jumpy in her head instead of sleepy. He calls it punk music, but Heaven thinks it sounds like *junk* music. Thinking about breathing in water now, she remembers when they lived in California, driving with her mom and dad from their flat in San Francisco to Monterey Bay. Her dad had given Cassie a scuba lesson for her birthday, but Heaven's mom didn't seem to want it.

"I want you to do something brave for your birthday," her dad had said.

Her mom turned around and spoke to six-year-old Heaven in the backseat like she was sixteen, telling her that her dad was in his manic phase. "That's what this is about," she said. "Manic you do coke, and crazy things like making your wife dive a hundred feet down into the sea, then when the depression hits you do everything else. But he's happy today, Heaven. Don't want to diss happy, do we?"

"If you're brave you can do anything," Heaven's dad kept saying.

"Christ, you're a broken record!" her mom said.

They still had her mom's VW Beetle then; Heaven remembers they even had a car booster seat for her in its tiny backseat. They had packed a basketful of food. "Sodas for the kid, blow for mom and dad," Cassie snarled. "Wow our act is *down*: a car that runs, a picnic, our child strapped safely into a car seat," she said, as they headed down the winding coast highway, indigo ocean on the right, cliffs with wind-twisted trees on the left. Monterey. "There's a cool jazz festival in Monterey," her dad said.

"So why the hell can't we do *that* instead!" her mom snapped.

Her dad said, "You're hot when you're brave," running his hand up her leg. Heaven saw him do that between their two front seats, stroke her mom's bare leg. What was his deal about being brave? she wonders now. Of course, she didn't ask. She knew not to ask things when her parents got like that. Remembers sucking her soda through a straw, that loud *sluuurp*, her mom turning around and glaring. Heaven was all about orange soda back then, remembers how its sweet, bubbly flavor made her burp, which made her and her dad laugh.

"Bright young couple with their adorable child on an outing!" Her mom kept saying things like that, nice words, but from her mom's mouth they didn't sound so nice, and with each declaration her voice got louder and sharper. Heaven sucked at her soda and stared out the tiny VW window. She remembers feeling nervous and kicking the back of her mom's seat, until her mom reached behind and lightly slapped Heaven's leg. "Quit it!" she said. "Don't hit her!" her dad said. Heaven slurped her soda through the straw so fast and hard she felt sick. Finally, they arrived and checked into the motel by the beach.

There were six people in her mom's scuba class, which began in the motel's pool. They practiced putting on and using the equipment: wetsuit, mask, fins, gloves, weight belt, nitrox tank, regulator hose, and pressure gauge; practiced breathing from the regulator, sucking in through the mouth, then exhaling slowly—*inhale, exhale, pause*—before hitting the ocean. Her dad explained the various pieces of equipment to Heaven as they watched. Where had he learned about these things? Heaven never thought to ask. She waved at her mom from behind the pool fence.

For the ocean part of the class they walked down with Cassie to the shore. There's even a picture somewhere, Heaven remembers, of her mom cinched into the skin-tight wetsuit like sausage casing, leaning down toward Heaven who'd wrapped her arms around her mom's waist. *Do we look like the All-American happy family goes to the beach, or what!* Then things got weird. Her mom and dad sneaking behind a pile of rocks (sniffing their drugs probably), Heaven alone on the sand, waiting for them to come back.

Soon enough her mom's in the icy ocean with the rest of the class trying it all out, the wetsuit, fins, her mask that "keeps clouding up!" Cassie shrieked, breathing air through the regulator, trying not to obsess over how she's getting this air and what if the tank springs a leak? Heaven remembers her mom worrying about those things, and her dad laughing, like it was some kind of joke for Cassie to be nervous. Heaven laughed too, but not because anything was funny. Nervous parents made Heaven nervous.

When her mom waded back onto the shore for a break, flopping down next to Heaven on the beach, yanking the regulator out of her mouth and inhaling gulps of "real air," her dad knelt beside them and told them about his brother (Uncle Daniel!) who nearly drowned. "He was never the same after that," Heaven's dad said.

The instructor, Mick, who looked like a long-haired surfer, started up the motorboat, motioning Heaven's mom and the others flipping about in the shallow water to climb aboard. "Shit!" Cassie muttered.

"Be brave!" Gavin called out to her as she struggled her equipment back in the water, then climbed into the boat.

"We're going deep!" Mick said, after everyone was settled onto the fiberglass benches stretching from one side of the boat to the other. Then he turned the boat around, and Heaven watched as they roared out toward open water.

Heaven pieced the rest of the story together from things her dad and mom said to each other on their drive back to San Francisco. They never did spend the night in the motel, even though it was paid for. She remembers fussing a little about that, had been promised a swim in the motel pool, take-out food in the room! Now Heaven would've recognized the signs: her dad's increasingly dark mood and her mom's jumpiness, flashes of anger, later the tears. She'd get it now. They'd run out of drugs.

After Mick anchored the boat, her mom said, he told them to jump in with their equipment and get used to the water's temperature. He showed them the rope secured to the buoy he'd anchored the boat to, explained how it was tied to a chunk of coral sixty feet down, and that if they go down holding this rope, they would understand it—what a scuba diver does, "letting the equipment breathe for us, trusting it." He had apparently stared at Heaven's mom, bobbing in the freezing water, her mask pulled up on her forehead, then grinned. "How about you first, miss, you seem the adventurous type."

Cassie was not adventurous, not at all, but as she told Heaven's dad, hopped up on blow she figured what the hell, somebody had to go first, though it usually wasn't her. *Be brave,* Gavin had said. Her mom kept repeating this, and even now in the dark Heaven can remember the sneer in her voice, as she repeated it in the car, *Be brave!*

The ocean felt like pea soup, thick and opaque. Mick said it was because of all the plankton. "Monterey Bay is one of the richest oceans in the world," he said. Cassie grabbed the rope with her gloved hands, pushed the mask down over her eyes then started down, her heart hammering. Whoosh of her breath through the regulator, *in, out, pause.*

But the crazy thing was, she said, the further down she descended, the more she relaxed; this thing was breathing for her! Felt like the ocean was speaking to her, whispers of tiny fish darting about the rope, grainy sediment making it too cloudy to see much but she could hear its voice the way the wind carries voices, almost but not quite lucid . . . *"Don't you want to release that cumbersome tank from your back, your waist? Go ahead, drop the weight belt down, does bravery require so much equipment?"* She'd imagined the belt's black straps winging out like a manta, something that belonged there. Forty feet, fifty, the water growing colder and darker.

They had watched a show once, Heaven sprawled out on their living room floor, her mom and dad smoking on the couch, about the crazy thoughts divers had in the depths. Mick had said when they hit sixty feet the rope would stop. Could crazy happen at sixty? Heaven remembers her mom talking about the sting of icy water through her wetsuit, the deeper she went. Inside the dense skin of it she'd imagined herself weightless, had wondered if she let go of the rope would she float free? *"Take off the mask, become an eyeless thing, you don't need air, the rope, a piece of plankton cruising the richest ocean in the world."*

A tug on the rope, Mick's signal to come up. She'd reached the end where it's tied to the giant head of coral, little fish swimming in and out of its crevices. She should be afraid down there, why wasn't she more afraid? She's not brave, not by a long shot, never been accused of that, even playing softball she'd duck if the ball winged too close. "Was *that* brave or stupid?" she snarled at Heaven's dad, during their drive back.

Her mom had sat down on the coral, she'd said, the rope tugging harder. Heaven closes her eyes now and pictures her, where the water is clear and dark. Fish swimming by, grazing her wetsuit, nibbling a little maybe? Or maybe she was part of the coral, swaying back and forth with the current. Rope tugs again, hard enough to burn through her thick gloves, her mom said. Heaven reaches her arms out in the dark of her room, her dad's room, like she too could've held on, held on to her mom. In ten minutes Cassie's nitrox tank would be out of air. Heaven feels it—the frigid water, her breath through the regulator; if she presses the purge button that would be it, her last gulp of air before kicking it all off, the tank, weight belt, regulator, mouthpiece slipping from her mouth.

Heaven remembers it clearly now, can hear her mom all over again. Later that night, as they got closer to San Francisco, its bright lights milking the sky in the distance, her mom, no longer snarly and irritated had become subdued, almost peaceful. Heaven had to lean forward in her booster to hear her tell it, the final part of her story. With ten minutes left of breath, her mom had thought back to what Heaven's dad told her on the beach, about his brother almost drowning. How Daniel had said it wasn't the drowning part that was so bad; the trouble began when he realized how much he wanted to live.

◆ MAGGIE, 1853 ◆

IT HAPPENED ON NEW Year's Day, though I would not know this
until much later. Christmas came and went, with nothing to
give or receive, but in those days it was not such a celebration
among Highlanders, who believed it a Papist holiday and banned
in much of Scotland. Rather Hogmanay, our New Year's Eve
was celebrated, when we gathered, kin and neighbors. In Suisnish
a bonfire would be lit, and first footing paid heed to, which is
that the first foot to enter your home after midnight should be a
dark-haired male's, perhaps because the Vikings were mostly
blond and that meant trouble. This man should bear with him
shortbread and coal, a bit of black bun and whiskey, and with
these things came good luck—a clearing of the old, fortune for
the new.

Our dark-haired Da was the one who entered for our family,
and Charles being fair, I wondered, with his life in the new world,
who would enter his home at Hogmanay for luck. Though as it
turned out he must've found someone, perhaps his own son, as he
ended up making fortune a plenty, in banking no less, to pass down
to the rest. Da would've been pleased, if he had lived long enough

to know it, that Charles, and Abigail too, brought the MacQueen name to the new world and did it proud.

On Christmas we knew it only in retrospect, because the ship's cook, who normally would cook only for the crew, any cabin passengers, and those few emigrants who had the forethought and means to purchase some meals (or more likely to have brought him their own food to boil), made biscuits for us all. We were grateful of course, though many of us were in greater need of a bit of meat, or a section of orange for the scurvy. On New Year's Day the Captain might've remarked to us all that it was a new year, but as I was so consumed looking for food or the sailor, whichever came first and most preferable to find both together, I wouldn't have heard it anyway.

So Hogmanay was not celebrated or even acknowledged the evening before, no dark male to step over our threshold, as we had no threshold, only the ladder leading down into the hold, and the only male I had eyes for was fair, those pale curls leaking out of his sailor's cap like tendrils of ivy. So perhaps because of this, instead of blessing ourselves with good fortune for the year, with goat or cowhide wrapped around sticks, ignited to keep the evil spirits away, we brought upon ourselves a most ill fortune, and many of us would not be around next Hogmanay to set things right.

★　★　★

Abigail shouting me up the steps, slick with the water rising, swirling around them as I climb and climb into her waiting arms, is one way it could've gone; it was her voice, after all, I thought I heard above all the others, their screaming and crying, calling to me before it went black. Or the sailor takes my hand, pulls me up off the floor that had become our bed, bearing me in his strong arms through the rising water, then the two of us race up those steps toward a new life together, is a way I might've longed it to go. Perhaps there is after all a hidden window in the windowless storage room, and he hurls one of the crates against it, breaking its glass so we can climb out of it—except, of course, when a ship is taking on water and a part of it already tilted and submerged, the last thing you'd want is to allow a new place for more water to rush in. So this version is hopelessly flawed.

In my least favorite adaptation, the one I most fear, the sailor, when he's finished doing what he's done to me, leaps up at the final call of the ship's whistle leaving me on the floor, with the ache between my thighs, a greater one in my heart, and water rising such that I'm soon afloat. I swim to the door and find it locked from the outside when he slammed it shut after him.

What likely happened is I made it up those steps myself. I can almost remember the feeling of that, slippery and soaking wet underneath my feet, the reel and lurch of the vessel causing me to grasp onto each stair over the one I climbed, the darkness making me as a spider, arms and legs blindly scrabbling about searching for a foothold, up to the deck where I spy in the distance a giant wave rising high and cone-shaped above all the rest in a wild sea, sharp as the old Man of Storr mountain peak, and as it loomed closer it appeared like the world had tipped and an immense black sky was about to fall upon us. 'Tis a rogue wave! someone shouts. The wind too shrieks this news, and with the vessel's raw tilt, its masts groan under a sudden new weight, that of a wall of water. The night black as pitch and I am aware of a smell: a briny salt, with the ocean spraying about, and something else—fear maybe, hopelessness, people getting sick, others partly submerged in water that has covered every inch of the deck, their bowels loosened as it rises ever higher to greet its kin, this enormous, granddaddy wave. Dear Lord, we are doomed! a woman cries; aye, someone answers, as if this needed affirming.

This wave will end up swallowing what remains of our vessel, its hull slashed open on the rocks off Seal Island; in just another day we'd have been at Halifax, so close after all. But with its fatal split when the New Year's Gale, the storm will later be called, pushed it aground on the island's rock ledge, like the strike of an axe into a tree where any moment it will crash, this wave would finish what is left.

It was my skirt took me down, long and heavy like being draped in bricks, such is wool in the water. I tried to slide it off but became tangled up in it, and briefly thought it was too bad that sailor who wanted so dearly to be under this skirt, and did eventually find his way there, had not just torn it off. The water rising and me with it going up, up, then down and down and down some more, then for a brief moment up again where the ocean filled my mouth instead of the air I desperately sought, and down down down, water frigid as an ice bath, until I no longer had breath for it, this fight to rise yet sinking more and more, still trying to untangle my legs from the skirt, growing weaker every second. Neck tipped back, arms floating out, which is the posture of a drowning person—I've learned it since—and while my chest felt it could explode for want of breath, at the same time I began to feel oddly comfortable, even a wee bit warmer as I drew down further beneath the surface, its wind-whipped waves and turmoil. Eyes opening, I figured I'd at least witness my own ending, the last I'd see; said a little prayer, though I wasn't quite certain how or by whom it would be answered at this point, Ma would've thought me blasphemous, but what was I praying for? I knew it was too late for a rescue that would bring me back to the land, which was nowhere in sight. Though dark, with eyes now wide open I was surprised to discover not only could I see, my eyes felt comfortably familiar in this underwater world. I was startled to make out shapes below me, torpedo shaped like the cigars I'd seen lads smoking on the Glasgow dock before we embarked on this doomed crossing, yet curved too, glistening, their shadows luminous in the dark water.

They were under me when the air in my lungs completely expired and I couldn't not do it, open my mouth and inhale another breath, which was water of course, not the oxygen I should have needed. I kept doing this, couldn't help the want for it, great gulps of seawater pouring into me, mouth like an open vessel to receive it, expecting any moment the life in my body would slip away, as I would be but ocean now having drunk so much of it. The shadows were below me and above me and around me and it seemed we were traveling together toward a massive shape, like a whale it was, an island underwater, and above the rest of it. When we reached it and I could rest and be sheltered in its underwater folds, I thought

perhaps it was my deathbed they brought me to, that these silvery
shapes floating around me were angels. Yes this must be so, I soon
determined, having no more desire for breath at all.

★ ★ ★

Abigail will tell any who'd listen in the years to come, throughout
her life's journey from Prince Edward Island to San Francisco and
on to Honolulu as a nurse, where she'd marry a missionary doctor and bear children, that she could've sworn I was behind her.
Though the steps were tar black, the ship having lost all its light,
lamps blown out, their wicks extinguished with the sudden tilt
and on-take of water, and gratings for natural light useless as was
none to be had. Listing so badly, the vessel almost on its side such
that climbing those steps was a trapeze act. But Maggie was a good
climber, so surely she was behind, had called out to her, didn't
she? and thought she'd answered. Though with so many others
between them, perhaps she did not hear after all, the chaos, yelling
and wailing, fear, despair, and all of it resulting in such pushing
up those stairs Abigail's own feet barely touched each step. When
she made it to the deck, three meters sunk into the sea already, the
mammoth wave had not yet hit.

It wouldn't have mattered, as it turned out, even if I *was* right
behind her, as there was not enough time to launch more than one
lifeboat before that wave would strike. After Abigail was pulled
onto the boat, the last person on it, the crew oared away from the
sinking vessel at a furious pace, outstretched arms of the others still
on deck screaming them back, the oars heaving frantically, outrun-
ning what Abigail saw too, that giant wave. Saw it rise like a sea
dragon over the Allen and Brown as the lifeboat caught its crest
and was able to turn out just in time to be saved from its fall.

When first light broke, the lifeboat was in a calmer sea, headed
on a new course toward Prince Edward Island, chartered by seabirds, an oarsman's hunch, and a survival instinct to row away from
the doomed ship and the storm that sunk it. In the clearing sky,
Abigail looked back and saw Seal Island at a distance, a long blue
hump like a whale breaching. No sign of the Allen and Brown.

No sign of her sister and so many others, including the captain who heroically went down with his ship, attempting to save his cargo—the Gaels, of course, though history will make nothing of it, as there was no manifest to claim our names. Was my sailor on it when it sunk? I did not learn his fate, though I suspect he was the sort, unlike his captain, to save himself if he could. What the fortunate souls in the lifeboat did see were seals swimming about their boat, as if they were guiding it onward. The oarsman who had become their provisional captain said it was a good sign, that it meant land was close. They live for both, he said, able to spend an hour underwater with enough oxygen for that, surface when they must for a breath.

PART V

AUTUMN AGAIN

◆ HEAVEN ◆

Bird cruising high over the pool, little white sail in a sky so blue could be the sea. Here's Heaven hitching a ride on its back to Minot, where it joins the gang that hangs out on the rocks, a gaggle of gulls—can gulls be a gaggle like geese? Peers into the water with its sharp bird eyes and sees . . . hmmmmm . . . Heaven on her super-cool surfboard now, paddling out into ocean the color of the sky . . .

"French, look alive!" Coach barks, "or you'll get extra laps! Meeting time all eyes on *moi*, got it? Little ladies," she starts, Coach's version of trash talk, like they're not *real* athletes, "school starts tomorrow so our practices begin at five thirty AM. On September twenty-second, fall equinox, folks, we're back inside."

The girls are seated around the edge of the pool, dangling their legs in the water under a strong morning sun. Heaven joins in the chorus of groans, only her groan is less about the hour or the indoor pool, and more because school's about to begin and still no *real* surfboard! Last night Uncle Daniel assured her it was almost finished, but there was a problem with delivery, the shop in Maine doesn't mail their boards so Heaven must be patient until he figures out a way to get it down here.

"What about when Grandmelia goes up to the prison?" Heaven asked.

"First off, you'd have to *tell* her about the surfboard, and how much you want to bet she'll say no, and second, your mom has no visitation rights until the end of the month. It's a conundrum," Uncle Daniel said. Heaven just scowled. She'll start eighth grade with everyone thinking she's a liar.

"Five minutes everyone in, practice breathing!" Coach yells, shriek of her whistle.

Heaven's favorite. She dives to the bottom then scoots along the tile, counting the blue and white patches in the checkerboard, swimming her breaststroke without coming up for air, frogging she calls it because it looks the way a frog swims, legs scissoring, arms pulling, shoulders less fatty now after a summer of practices, biceps, triceps, her arsenal. Through all of those practices, the sting of cold water in the early mornings, breath seizing at the first dive in then hmmmmm, exhale into it, she imagined herself on her surfboard paddling out, the waves off the lighthouse jetty at high tide, rolling and crashing, Heaven blowing through them like a dolphin.

When she reaches the center of the pool with its big drain, she tugs up on the drain cap, which lifts about a half inch before she lets it slide back into place. Shoots up for a breath, sees Bethany in the lane beside hers, doing the back float, the tail of her hair freed from her cap, spreading out like a fan. Heaven swims back down to the drain to practice, hmmmmm. It takes a while to perfect all of this, timing is everything, super-sized inhale, pull, pull, pull those arms, scissor-kick scissor-kick, holding her breath and lifting up on that drain simultaneously, *hmmmmmmm*; she has just two more weeks in the outdoor pool, then they'll have to go inside. She doesn't know about the drain in that one, whether it will move at all.

She pulls up the drain cap once more, setting it down, singing her song, face up where she can see that hair, Bethany's legs

scissoring now, her backstroke. Heaven studies those long thighs
as they open and close, open and close. Sees that white bird again
winging it to Minot, Heaven's surfboard waiting on the rocks
where the white bird lands and she follows him in, the gaggle of
them shuffling and parting as she makes her way up to the top,
grabs her board then leaps off the rocks where it's deepest and wild-
est just in time to catch a wave. Heaven shooting through its blue-
green curl, up her board pops on the other side, Heaven riding it
until it's spent and Bethany, her skanks, Robyn wearing his favorite
purple skirt, the mom in prison, Grandmelia, even Uncle Daniel
comes out of his room for the occasion, all on the beach watching
her perfect form.

Last week on her way home from practice she pulled her bike
up in front of Our Lady of Sorrows Catholic Store and pretended
to be *shopping for her mom*, she told the lady, a birthday saint perhaps?
She'd listened to this lady, whose face was a jowly bulldog face, tell
another lady, with a long scrawny neck like a giraffe, about bury-
ing St. Joseph in her backyard. You bury it upside down, she'd said,
then ask for his blessing to sell your house. Leave it in there until
you get an offer, she said. Oh, said Giraffe, does it work? Of course,
he's a saint, said Dogface.

Meanwhile here's Heaven inching up to a row of plastic two-
inch-tall Jesuses and right behind it the little angel—spotted her
from the moment she walked in the door, her white fabric dress
with a gold ribbon tie around her waist, and a halo of gold too,
attached to her pretty little shoulders, under her wings. She's holding a white dove in her hands like she's offering it, the bird of peace,
her mom told her. When Dogface rang up the St. Joseph, Heaven
snatched the angel and a Jesus too for good measure, stuck them in
her hoodie's pouch then beat feet out. Nobody followed her. She
figured there weren't a lot of security cameras in the Catholic store,
because they're Catholics, right? Watched over by Jesus and Mary
and all those saints, the ones with animals and the ones you bury
upside down in the dirt.

Heaven placed the angel and Jesus on the shelf over her bed,
toward the back where Grandmelia wouldn't notice if she came

sniffing around, to watch over her while she slept, protect her from any bad faeries or killer kelpies in the shadow world and to help her with her quests. She prayed to them every night, hands folded, eyes shut. Uncle Daniel has his angel, now Heaven has one *and* Jesus.

✦ AMELIA ✦

Aᴍᴇʟɪᴀ ᴀɴᴅ ʜᴇʀ ʟᴀᴡʏᴇʀ are sipping chilled Chilean chardon-
nay on the patio, the house finally quiet with Heaven back in
school, whoop-de-dee! She's arranged a tray of French Brie, rye
crackers, and purple grapes, thinking *good lord*, has she become the
kind of person who spends afternoons with her lawyer, consuming
imported wine and cheese by the pool? Though not particularly
bothered by it. A golden September afternoon, radiant with just a
hint of the coming fall, bright red sumac against her white fence,
ivy turning, asters, mums, their glowing colors, even the ragweed
growing randomly between scatters of beach stones flung across
her yard by last winter's nor'easter looks acceptable, Amelia thinks,
trailing down to the salt marsh, also with yellowing grasses.

"How about this for a new approach," says Attorney Bub who's
been no help so far whatsoever. "Win over your daughter-in-law's
trust. Get her feeling like she really does belong, part of the *fam*,
then maybe with her new sense of responsibility to you she'll be
more willing to come clean. Wasn't it President Johnson who kept
using that phrase for the Vietnam War, 'winning their hearts and
minds'?"

"Yes and look how *that* turned out!" Amelia snipes, but Bub babbles on, proposing that Cassie was likely suffering from trauma-induced amnesia, which Amelia looks up on her phone and reluctantly agrees is possible, though, she reminds him—"We're dealing with a murderess. Let's take the sane-person cards off the table."

"She's insisting she *wouldn't* have done it, dear. She asked me to represent her. If she were a man, I'd say she has balls, but in her case maybe hallucinations."

"So, what I don't get is why the hell she didn't just deny it at the get-go then?"

"Or could be the drugs talking." He clucks his tongue, bites into a cracker slathered with Brie.

"Whoop-de-do, old news, they made her clean up. How is she *still* on drugs?"

"Oh, come now sweetheart, surely you aren't that naive. Prison is ideal, a captive audience, converts sympathetic to the cause. You can get drugs anywhere, anytime. We're a stoned culture. Boomers introduced the proclivity, then half of us became right wing, holier-than-thous, punished the rest who indulged. But they can't staunch the flow, no little Dutch boy with his finger in *this* dike." Bub sighs, sips his wine.

"Here? Right now, this afternoon in Seahaven? You can get me some, I don't know, something fun, not too streety! I hear Ecstasy is a kick."

"Give me twenty," he grins, making like he would leap out of his lounge chair, and Amelia laughs. She has a slight buzz from the wine, the sunshine, and the quiet! God she's missed the quiet of her own life. Not that her granddaughter is a chatty girl; in fact, usually it's Amelia trying to get Heaven to talk, prying things out of her, the girl stubborn and recalcitrant about her former life (which was Gavin's life, so she'd like to know a few things about it, why can't anyone get this?). Sometimes Amelia visualized poking pliers down Heaven's throat and yanking the information out of her. It was just that having her around all summer—the child didn't seem to have any friends and the few times Amelia

suggested a get-together with someone from school she panicked—made Amelia feel there was always a presence around her,
a shadow behind her, over her shoulder, watching her, or else
someone Amelia should be watching, interacting with. It was a
kind of parental pressure Amelia had gladly given up when her
sons were grown.

Only swimming took Heaven out of the house, but those practices were so excruciatingly early Amelia was just enjoying her second cup of coffee and the girl was back, slamming her gym bag
with its wet towel down on the kitchen table. Thank God she'd
acquiesced on that bike! The thought of crack-of-dawn carpool-
ing, ugh. Though sometimes Amelia did set her alarm, just to get
up and have an hour to herself. Now that school's begun again,
she's guaranteed an eight-hour day, all hers.

She sighs and stretches, her body long and languid, though
mostly covered up from the sun; still, she saw Bub eyeing her legs
peeping out of her wrap and for a second imagines leaning over
her chaise into his and kissing him. How would he react? Are we
sure you're gay? she'd whisper, Bub still in his lavender shirts from
back when this was a *statement*, and still cute, the angular planes
of his face, even though his chin is slacker. Gay or not he was
enchanted with her before and maybe even now? In the past it was
enough to have someone attractive charmed by her to light something inside, but now all of that just seems . . . gone. She closes
her eyes.

"Anyway," Bub says, "your daughter-in-law could drum up
some trouble, but I wouldn't worry. There were no other witnesses, no one there but her and the victim, and they don't tend
to take the testimony of drug addicts all that seriously. They're
supposed to, of course, but there's that perception of unreliability,
a taint. It comes down to the indisputable fact that somebody who
wasn't your son picked up that board and cracked him on the head,
and that somebody's fingerprints were on it."

"Jesus, Bub!" Amelia snaps, downing the last of her wine,
"more old news! Either way I'm still not getting any answers,
am I?"

He sighs, sniffs. "I'm sorry dear, but the truth is maybe you won't ever get any answers. Whatever that woman remembers or doesn't, it's her word, her version, and it's all we've got."

"Well, I'm sorry too, but that's just not acceptable to me. Heaven will be home soon. Shall we call it a day?" She considers saying how she'd never imagined being seventy and waiting for a child to come home from school, meaningless chatter to fill the sudden void in their afternoon, but she's too vain to announce her age, to *speak* it out loud, put it on the table with the empty wine bottle, like some sort of finality.

★   ★   ★

Four hours later, in a dying violet light, it's Leo at her front door. He's carrying a box with punched out air holes and something moving inside. A pale paw pushes against one of the holes. "Oh good lord, now what!"

"It's Farley. For Heaven."

Amelia places her hands on her hips, blocking the entrance. "What exactly *is* a Farley?"

"Farley the cat. My tenant's been leaving food for him on her porch and she finally managed to trap him."

"Let me get this straight. You have a *feral* cat in that box, and you want to give it to our granddaughter?"

"Feral Farley." Leo grins, still that boyish smile, used to make Amelia think he'd been up to something, until she figured out that was *her* role in their marriage. "He's one of those big orange ones, cuddly looking. She can sleep with him."

"Oh my God!" Amelia shakes her head. "You're encouraging interspecies bed habits for your granddaughter with a wild animal. Is this some sort of penance or payback or some ridiculous notion of God knows what goes through your head these days? We're supposed to be divorced!"

"Couldn't you invite us in at least?"

"Us? You and that cat are an *us*? We can talk right here. I'm under no obligation to take your tenant's stray. Why on earth did

you think this was a good thing for Heaven? What does that creature look like?"

Leo removes the towel he placed over the top of the box and
opens the flaps slightly, enough for them both to peer down and
see two mean-looking yellow eyes staring back, then a low growl
and a hiss."

"Well that's just great! You brought her an attack cat or
something?"

He shuts the box, pulling the towel tight over it, puts the box
down by his feet. They can still hear it growling. Scratches his
chin. "I don't know. Seemed friendlier in Augusta. Heaven left a
message on my voicemail, something about could I bring her surfboard. I don't have a surfboard."

"So, you thought instead you'd bring her a wild beast? And
what's this about a surfboard?"

Leo shrugs.

"Of course you couldn't call back and ask, the Russians or
drones overhead? I'm surprised you even checked your voicemail."

"Don't usually, I don't get many messages. Thought maybe
it was Daniel, though he's not much for phones either. Mabel
said Farley needs a home. Heaven needed a home and you gave
that to her, so I thought maybe they'd, you know, click with one
another."

"This is bull-pucky. Your tenant's getting back at us for all the
times she's had to deal with your late-night wanderings, the cops
bringing you back, waking her up because you forgot your keys,
or even where you live sometimes. Knock, knock, is this the crazy
guy's residence? Are you out of your mind, Leo? A feral cat? You're
just lucky Heaven's at a swim meet practice and doesn't know what
she can't have!"

"Maybe they'd like each other. She's kind of feral herself, right?
Maybe they'll be kindred spirits. What about letting Daniel keep
him for a little while, break him in. He likes cats. Maybe he can
socialize Farley." The cat makes scraping sounds against the box,
desperate paws on the air holes, a lunge and a hiss.

Amelia snorts. "Our son the agoraphobe, *socializing* that animal?"

"I'll do it!" Daniel calls out from the crack in his door. "Bring him to me. Leo what are your intentions with Mercy? She said you didn't call back."

Amelia scowls. "Mercy? What's a Mercy? Wait . . . the garage girl?"

"Mercy the avenging angel!" Daniel says. "Dad promised he'd take a photograph for her, then didn't follow through."

Amelia stares at Leo in the porch light, his hat tipped low on his forehead like he's playing detective, the sky behind him dark now. Farley rakes his claws against the side of the box, yowls. Amelia shakes her head. "What the hell, Leo?"

"Right," he sighs. "It just slipped my mind."

★   ★   ★

After dinner Amelia suggests Heaven retire to her room and do her homework.

"It's done. Sixth-period study hall."

"Where are those common core standards when you need them?" Amelia mutters. "Fine, then just go to your room."

"You're punishing me?"

"Who said anything about punishment?"

"Well I don't care if you send me to my room, because I have a new quest! Do you want to know what it is?"

"Does it involve me?" Amelia asks. Heaven shakes her head.

"Good. I'll take your quests on a need-to-know basis."

Heaven shrugs. "Whatever, I'm going to ask Uncle Daniel when I can see his cat." She stands up and makes a show of pushing her chair into the table (having been chided numerous times for leaving it out), so tight it's rubbing the wood, then heads to her room after dumping her plate in the kitchen sink.

Amelia rises, is about to call her back to *rinse* her plate, then thinks better of it. She slides Heaven's chair back an inch, glances at the mahogany to make sure there's no mark, picks up her phone, and walks to her own room. She calls Leo's cell twice. The first time he doesn't answer, but she knows if she just keeps dialing his number he'll pick up; *he* knows she'll just keep dialing. It's been over three hours. He should be home by now.

"Right, Amelia," Leo answers, third ring. "I know you want something, or you wouldn't be calling. You know I don't like phones."

"Well I wasn't going to discuss the weather! A family portrait."

"Come again?"

"I've been thinking about this since Daniel said you were supposed to take a photograph for our neighbor. I want you to do a nice portrait of our family for Cassie. You, me, Daniel, and Heaven. It needs to be here, obviously—Daniel won't go anywhere. You owe me. That beast is under my roof, running roughshod all over Daniel's room. And of course you didn't think to bring food or a litter box or anything people who give feral cats to other people should have thought of. So now I have to go out and get those."

A long silence, Amelia tapping her fingernails against her bureau, then Leo grunts. "You can't be serious!"

"About which, cat supplies or the photograph?"

"What is this? I'm suddenly a people's photographer? Did I wake up in a different life? I don't do portraits, I don't do 'real people,' our daughter-in-law's request. I do buildings falling apart. Cities coming undone. Histories unraveling. Decay, rust, ruin."

"Cassiopeia wanted a photograph of real people?"

Leo sighs. "Right. I found out in her AA, NA, or whatever their addicts anonymous prison version is, required apology to me that she'd intended to swap it for drugs. Apparently one of the inmates found an old photography book in the prison library with some of my shots, figured I must be famous. Cassie tried to leverage that and got caught. But now that she's clean she *treasures* it."

Amelia snorts. "Since when are your pictures drug trade! Lord, I guess Bub was right. He said she never stopped using and here's me waiting for some cogent memory from a druggie. She's completely untrustworthy. What in God's name did Gavin ever see in that person?"

"Right, and he was of course a paragon of trust. So now you want to give her a family portrait?"

"Yes," Amelia snaps. "So she'll think twice exploiting her family by lying to us."

Leo laughs, a hard caustic laugh that Amelia doesn't appreciate. "Because *our* family members never lie to each other!"

"Since when are *you* the cynic? I thought if she had a nice photo of us, one with her own daughter in it, she might feel something for us, something a little more than random 'real people'!"

"And this out of the goodness of your heart?"

"I told you! So she'll stop all the lies. I didn't pretend it was for any other reason." Amelia hears the suddenly loud monotonous beat of some whiny pop music coming from Heaven's bedroom. Leo must've heard it too because he turns up the jazz he'd been listening to. After the truth of Gavin's conception was revealed Leo not only stopped photographing rock stars but gave up their music too, blaring progressive jazz throughout their house instead, speakers wired from the living room stereo to the kitchen, family room, patio, bedroom, penance for her transgression no doubt. Amelia surprised him by liking it. Its dissonance reflected her moods, the emotional muddle in her head. Besides, she'd figured jazz was a better image for the Egg Me! model, more refined. Remembering this now she feels silly, so young. That's one thing she misses about Leo, his music. These days her house is silent or Heaven.

"You realize that you're not just asking me to take a picture. You're asking me to drive from Augusta, Maine, three and a half hours, then back again."

"Well isn't that your usual trek these days? This afternoon was the second time I've seen you in what, a month? You need to be in it, or I'd get someone else to do it."

He chuckles. "Thanks for the endorsement. So if I consider this, and I'm saying *if*, I'm going to need something from you."

"What, pay you?"

"Nope. A confession, or maybe more of an admission."

"I'm not having an affair, Leo."

Leo grunts. "Right, you flatter yourself, love, to think I'd care at this point. I want you to admit Gavin was a drug addict."

"What on earth, Leo!"

"Say it or I'm hanging up. Gavin was a drug addict and was every bit as responsible for their problems as Cassie."

"Well he didn't conk himself over the head with a two-by-four!"

"No, but I'm sure his behavior went begging for a good whack on the noggin for a long time. Too bad he was on the breakwater when he got it. You've been blaming her, and whatever they were or weren't, they were both addicts and in it together."

"I want her to know who she's hurt! It's not only about her. The family! Me."

"Who *they* hurt, Amelia."

"Fine," she sighs.

"Say it. Our son . . ."

"Our son . . ."

"Gavin . . ."

"Gavin . . ."

"Was a drug addict."

"Yes," she says, then starts to cry.

"Did you note I said *our* son?" he says quietly.

"Must you always take the high road, Leo?" she sniffs. "I really don't have that much more to lose."

"You have Daniel. And Heaven. MacQueen and French. Your family."

♦ HEAVEN ♦

Later that night grandmelia flounces into Heaven's room, just as Heaven falls asleep, switches on the light, and marches over to her bed. She sits down, telling Heaven to scooch over a little. "About our names," she says.

Heaven sits up, blinks the sleep from her eyes, and moves over so her grandmother's face isn't on top of hers.

"He was Leo French when we married and always will be Leo French, because back then men didn't change their names, and he liked his name, your grandfather told me. I became Amelia MacQueen-French at the altar, then shortly after dropped the hyphen because I didn't care for its look aesthetically, then I dropped the French professionally. An almost supermodel who had a following as the Egg Me! girl needed to maintain her own identity, I decided. And the whole tradition irked me, the idea when a woman marries she trades her father's name for her husband's, like her dad abdicated his ownership of her and now she belongs to her husband? Give me a break. I made more money than Leo from the get-go. Once we were divorced, I legally expunged the French. Our sons have both names on their birth certificates,

Daniel MacQueen-French and Gavin MacQueen-French. Do you see where I'm going with this, child?" Grandmelia asks.

Not a clue, Heaven thinks, but she won't say it to her grandmother. Grandmelia has never woken her up for anything and Heaven figures it's best to just listen and nod.

"Well, when your dad grew up and moved out to San Francisco he dropped the MacQueen (though not legally—Gavin never bothered with legalities), becoming just Gavin French. This slayed me, really, and I'm guessing it was a triumph for your grandfather, though he never said it. Daniel moved back home after only one semester in college and became just MacQueen, but I knew better than to think he was honoring me—it was his Isle of Skye obsession, the abandoned ancestral home.

"Cassiopeia Grabber, your mother, was only too happy to give up the Grabber part of her name, after a childhood of name taunting: grab *bottom,* and other body parts grabbed. Cassie French sounded more exotic, like a brand-new person. I know this from things your father told me, back when he still bothered to call or write to me.

"Your father also told me that you were named just Heaven French, not even a middle name, because, he said, how could you one-up *Heaven?*"

Heaven nods. "He told me that too, but I kind of wanted a middle name," she says. "But that's what my dad said. How can we do better than Heaven?"

Grandmelia stares at her, furrowing her brow. Heaven notices Grandmelia hasn't gotten ready for bed yet, or washed her face, because she still has her penciled-in eyebrows to furrow. "Do you still want a middle name?" Grandmelia asks.

Heaven nods again. "I mean, like, having only two names when everyone else has more, not even having a middle initial, makes me feel maybe I don't *matter* as much."

Grandmelia shakes her head. "Well that's just wrong. You do matter and we can fix that. It occurred to me earlier, that since Gavin, my son, was *legally* still a MacQueen-French, this should make his daughter, you, a MacQueen-French too, regardless of what they put on your birth certificate. You are a part of me and my family history and should be labeled such. Heaven MacQueen-French. What do you think?"

Heaven smiles. Her cheeks are flushed, and she's aware of her heart racing for a moment. She isn't sure what she's supposed to say.

"I want to show you something." Grandmelia reaches into the pocket of her cardigan, pulls out her wallet and digs around in one of the sleeves, then hands Heaven a photo encased in its own plastic sleeve. "I've been meaning to give it to your mother, it's of you and her, but I just . . . haven't. It was in your dad's wallet. I suppose the reason is because your dad, my son, took the picture and would've been just outside the frame on the same beach with you and your mom, under that bright sunshine, *alive*! And he'd been carrying it around with him for who knows how long. It was in his water-logged wallet, which after the trial was returned to me along with the clothes he'd been wearing. It wasn't in great shape, but I took it to a place where they restore old photos and they managed to get most of the image back."

Heaven stares at the picture, trying to remember the day, *any* day like this one. A beach—Grandmelia points out the Cliff House in the background, "where your mother used to work, a cocktail waitress," her sneer. Heaven is maybe three years old, holding her mom's hand. "My mom is beautiful! Way prettier than Bethany's mom. I saw her pick up Bethany from a swim meet once in super-tight jeans. Her hair was scooped into a messy bun stuck up on her head. It looked like a sprouted onion."

Grandmelia snorts at the bun description, pats her own tidy French twist. Heaven stares at the picture. Cassie in a black swimsuit sleek as sealskin, one of the straps down and her head tossed back, coppery hair loose on her shoulders, laughing. Heaven in a two-piece swimsuit with frilly bottoms, a red pail in one hand, looking as sure of her place beside her mom as any three-year-old who's dependent on the adults she belongs to, certain they'll care for her. Love her. *Heaven imagines it, holding her mom's hand, a warm sea breeze blowing (though her mom said San Francisco was usually foggy and cool), her mom's laughing, so her dad taking the picture probably is too.*

Heaven doesn't remember much laughter in Maine, but maybe there are other pictures showing a happy life they had before the falling-apart house in Rock Harbor, its cold and rocky beaches. Blue ocean, red pail filled with white sand, her pretty mom, and her dad would be so proud of them he takes their picture and keeps it in his wallet.

"So, do you want to make it official, *Heaven MacQueen-French*? I'll need to find out from that social worker where your birth certificate is. I would've thought they'd have given it to me when I signed the custody papers. I don't suppose with what-all they had going on your parents kept track of it. Do you know?"

Heaven shrugs, then nods vigorously. "I want to be MacQueen-French."

"Fine, so that's what we'll do." Grandmelia gives her a quick, dry peck on her forehead, snaps off the light, and walks out of her bedroom. Though she won't notice or even think to look, Heaven has closed her eyes and, still clutching the picture from her dad's wallet, falls back asleep, grinning.

✦ HEAVEN ✦

There's a new girl in the eighth grade, new girl in math, new girl on the swim team, new girl to sit with at lunch, whisper secrets at their lockers, walk together in the hall, what *friends* do, someone she could even text if her phone would do that, but guess what? The new girl's phone's a dumb one too! And she isn't pretty, isn't do-my-homework smart, rich, or wears cool clothes (so no interest to the B-bitches!), but she's nice to Heaven, Heaven's nice to her and thinks (hopes?) she might have a friend.

First swim meet of the season, with Cohasset Saturday morning, Heaven and the new girl whose name is Meagan ride their bikes to the Cohasset pool together, parking them side by side at the bike racks outside, red bike, blue bike, friends. Just as they step inside the Center, Bethany blows in, and in front of all the other swimmers, their parents, grandparents, sisters, brothers, even a dog (Heaven caught a tail wag out of the corner of her eye!), yanks down Heaven's shorts and tugs up her tank suit, giving her a wedgie. Meagan laughs. Probably everyone else does too but what Heaven hears is *Meagan's laugh*, who wears braces even, SUV smile, yet Bethany invites her to hang with them after the meet to get back at Heaven. For what? Being bloody alive, as Uncle Daniel says.

To make matters worse, Heaven doesn't place in her division, breaststroke, seventh- and eighth-grade girls, fumbles the push-off then a lopsided flip turn coming back. Luckily the rest of her team didn't do great either, not even Bethany, or else the tormenting she'd get in the locker room would kill her. Heads down, swim caps still on like a row of mushrooms, Coach lectures them on the bench outside the locker room, how they need to be *better*: swim *strong*, swim *hard*, swim *win*! Heaven sliding downcast eyes to her right, stares at Bethany's pale legs the blue-white of milk, gazes at the little mound between Bethany's thighs overtly emphasized by her tight swimsuit. Something twists in her stomach. Uncle Daniel in her head whispers *"Focus on your quest."*

When Heaven finally exits the building, alone, Grandmelia's car is in the parking lot and she's standing beside it, shading her eyes, looking for Heaven. With her hair loose about her shoulders, blowing in a breeze that's kicked up off the harbor she could *almost* pass for a mom. Heaven wheels her bike over.

"How about a ride home? We'll fit your bike in the trunk."

Heaven shrugs. "Did you see the meet?"

"Part of it. Your part."

"I didn't do good."

"*Well*, you didn't do well." She places her hand for just a second on Heaven's shoulder, warm under her thin T-shirt from the noon sun. "Look, I know you don't get this yet, but it won't matter in the grand scheme of things, child. Over a lifetime an eighth-grade swim meet is but a blink, barely worth that."

Heaven says nothing. It's the kind of thing Grandmelia says that's supposed to be reassuring, the *grand scheme of things*, but it's zip to Heaven. Grandmelia drones on, but Heaven's thinking betrayal. Maybe she should sing drowning songs for Meagan too.

When they get home Grandmelia tells her that her grandfather will be coming next weekend from Maine to take their picture, a family portrait, that finally she'll be able to talk to him in person. Heaven claps her hands—she needs to act excited, which she is!

But not for the reason Grandmelia thinks. Big whoop. She can barely wait for Grandmelia to go away, make lunch, do *something* so that Heaven can check out her grandfather's phone number again in Grandmelia's contacts list, let him know he has another chance to bring her surfboard from Maine.

The solution to the delivery dilemma, as Uncle Daniel called it. Once at their house it'll be too late for Grandmelia to say no. Here's Heaven on her super-awesome handcrafted board with her initials, H. *M.*(M for MacQueen!) F., paddling into the waves. Meagan will be soooo sorry she chose the wrong friend. As for Bethany, she better enjoy it while she can, steal Heaven's friends, be a "middlebrow, nouveau riche, pampered little slut-in-training," Uncle Daniel called her when Heaven told him about Bethany. "Those kinds of girls graduate from cheerleading to cellulite and alcoholism," he said. Heaven could give a *rat's ass*. She's that much closer to her quest.

★　★　★

Later that afternoon Heaven's about to ride her bike to the beach when she notices Mercy's car in her driveway. It's Saturday, maybe she doesn't have to work? Impulsively, Heaven rides out of her driveway then into theirs, parks her bike by the side of the garage (the part not facing Uncle Daniel's room in case he's watching), knocks on Mercy's door.

"Hello there," Mercy says, peering down at Heaven on the stoop. Heaven sees she's still in her bathrobe. Mercy follows her gaze, laughs. "I wasn't expecting company. Welcome to my concrete palace. Want to come in? I don't have much. You like seltzer?"

Heaven follows her into the room. "It's big," she says politely.

"*Two*-car garage," Mercy snarks. "I've got a mini-fridge and a microwave for my culinary needs." She opens the refrigerator, pulls out a bottle of seltzer, gives it to Heaven.

Heaven takes a sip and makes a face. "It just tastes fizzy, no flavor?"

Mercy laughs. "I bet you mean no sugar!"

Heaven shrugs. "That's okay. My grandmother doesn't like me eating sugar. Uncle Daniel puts all my favorite ice creams on her shopping list, pretending they're for him. Then we share them."

"He seems like a good guy. Sit down." Mercy points to her one chair by a small table, then sprawls out on her bed, pillows behind her back.

"He thinks you're an angel," Heaven says.

Mercy laughs. "I'll tell you what, he's got to be the only person who's ever thought that about me!"

Her robe has slid up her thigh and Heaven notices long scratches on the side of her leg, all about the same size, like she'd been raked, or got attacked by an evil faerie with long fingernails! Mercy tugs the robe back down over her legs. "It's a bad habit, Heaven, don't ever start, okay?"

Heaven frowns. "You mean you did that to yourself?"

Mercy sighs. "Look, I have a lot of pent-up anger, and sometimes I do unhealthy things to release it. I don't recommend this, but I have to say it's better for me than drinking a lot of alcohol or . . . other bad behaviors. I'll leave it at that."

Heaven nods. "I get angry too. Like today at the swim meet, a girl I thought was my friend laughed at the joke this other really mean girl did on me, then she hung out with those girls instead of me."

"Girls your age can be more vicious than a pack of wild dogs. Wish I could tell you it gets a lot better when you're older, but I'm still waiting." She grins, which makes Heaven smile too.

"Hey!" Mercy says. "Want to see the pictures your grandpa took for me? He didn't even charge me. You know he used to be famous, right?" She jumps off the bed and walks over to a set of utility shelves near the window, grabs a manila folder, slips two photographs out.

Heaven says, "He's coming here next weekend to take a portrait of our family for my mom." She stares at the two pictures Mercy's holding.

"This one's of my collection. Cool, right? I'll tell you about it sometime, maybe. And this one he took of me at The Seagull, that's where I work. Heaven stares at the one with Mercy in it. She's in her uniform, standing on a chair, and she's hitched the black skirt high up her legs, like she's showing off her legs. Her face glows, looks almost triumphant. Heaven knows that expression. She had it when she placed at a swim meet. Otherwise, she knows her face doesn't look like Mercy's here, like she's . . . really happy.

Mercy leans over Heaven in the chair, points at her legs in the photo. "Because of that short one I never wanted to have my picture taken, used to pitch a fit if anyone did. But your grandpa asked if I'd also like a photograph of myself. I thought about it, then said 'let's do it!' Even told the damn cook to shut the F up when he said we couldn't do that in the diner. Like, nobody was even in there, what the hell? My whole fricken lifetime trying to hide the thing and now, dammit, look at me flaunting it. Your uncle thinks it's magic, but to me *this* felt like winning, you know?"

Heaven nods. But the truth is, she isn't sure what to feel. Good for Mercy, of course, but also a little sad. Will it take Heaven this many years before *she* likes herself?

✦ AMELIA ✦

Five PM and Amelia watches out her window as Leo pulls up at the curb, turns off the engine, then sits in his car. He's staring at her house, white and glowing in the late afternoon light. She imagines how it looks to him, the gray thatch of ocean on the other side of the street, in between a row of beachfront houses. It annoys her that even though she can barely see the ocean from her bedroom window, and a view the width of a pencil from the living room, nonetheless because of climate change, the increasing severity of storms, and beach erosion, her home was put in the flood plain when the maps were redrawn, and now she has to come up with sixty thousand a year in flood insurance. "Neighbors are listing their homes for sale right and left, but no one's buying. We're a storm away from homeless!" she complained to Daniel. Of course, her son just laughed, then described his image of her crashing in an alley under newspapers, panhandling change, dumpster diving for her meals. Which made him laugh louder.

Picks up her phone and calls Leo. "We see you out there, did you forget to put on your invisible cloak?"

"Right," he sighs, climbs out of his car and heads up her path.

Heaven opens the door, gives Leo a frank up and down, which he returns. "Grandmelia said to let you in."

"Right, Grandmelia." Leo smiles, more of a grimace, steps inside.

Amelia, standing in the living room entranceway, nods curtly at him.

"How many years since I've actually been inside here?"

"Eighteen months, Leo. Gavin's funeral, remember?"

"How come I wasn't at my dad's funeral?" Heaven places herself between Amelia and Leo, hands on her hips like she's looking for a fight. My granddaughter, Amelia thinks, almost smiles.

"You were still in Maine," Amelia tells her, which was true enough. But the *real* truth was, at the time, Amelia didn't want to have anything to do with Gavin's life in Maine, as if even the place was implicated in his death. It hadn't occurred to her that his daughter should probably come down for the funeral. She wasn't even sure where Heaven was, probably foster care, and of course had never met her. If she had seen the child, other than the color of her eyes, Amelia would've never guessed she was a relation.

"Why don't we sit for a moment in the living room. Daniel agreed to tether the attack cat, then open his door, as long as he doesn't have to step more than the length of his foot beyond the threshold. We'll take the picture there. Heaven, I told you to put on something nicer and here you are still in shorts and a T-shirt."

"But they're new ones!"

"Maybe where you come from that's considered appropriate dress for a family portrait but not on my watch. This is for your mother; don't you want to look nice?"

Heaven shrugs. "Can we go see your car?" she asks Leo.

"Why?"

"You *know*! I want to try it out before it's dark."

"My car?" he peers over at Amelia.

"I can't imagine why you need to *see* his car any further then looking out the window. See? At the curb, in front of our house. Now go get changed so we can get this over with, then you can do what you wish. You all can, far as I'm concerned," giving Leo one of her laden looks that's supposed to speak *volumes*, she used to tell him.

"Right," he says. "As for me, I'll be hitting the road."

★ ★ ★

After several tries, Heaven refusing to smile because Uncle Daniel wouldn't, Amelia gives up and settles for solemn. She plasters on her Egg Me! grin. "I'll smile for all of you!" she growls.

Leo sets the timer so he can leap, arthritic knees and all, back into the picture and pose between Amelia and their son, who hasn't spoken a word to either of them, before it goes off. Heaven in front of them in a denim skirt, which she immediately peels off, her shorts underneath, the moment Amelia announces they're done, tearing out to Leo's car.

Within seconds she's back inside. "Where is it?" she demands. "Did you put it in the garage already?" She races toward the door before Leo can say a word, but Amelia stops her as she's about to open it.

"Halt this instant! What in god's name are you up to, Heaven?"

"You know!" she looks back at Leo then Daniel, still hovering by his bedroom door where they stood for the shot. "My surfboard, where is it?"

"For crying out loud! What on earth are you talking about? The surfboard thing again? Leo—your grandfather—doesn't surf. Does he look like a surfer to you? Do you see what I have to put up with here?" Amelia barks to Leo.

"You were supposed to bring *my* surfboard!" Heaven wails, tears welling in her eyes. "I was going to call but Uncle Daniel said he'd tell you."

They all stare at Daniel who rubs his head, pulls at his chin, looks sheepish—or maybe he's trying for a look of regret. "I'm sorry. Forgot to tell you, the shop was closed when I called so I wasn't able to arrange it. I'll have to contact them again."

Heaven looks stricken, tears rolling down her cheeks. "I hate all of you!" she squeals, runs into her room and slams the door.

Amelia throws up her hands. "I'll have that door taken off its hinges, I swear!" she shouts after Heaven. "What's this about a surfboard?" Pins her gaze on Daniel, slow and piercing, another speaks-*volumes* look. "That child is not getting a surfboard. I am not allowing a thirteen-year-old to have any such thing. You think we live on Waikiki beach? The surf here is a climate-change disaster, smashing on jagged rocks, for lord's sake, wiped out any semblance of the beach we used to have, homes too, as you well know. It's way too dangerous! Don't you think this family's suffered enough drowning and near-drowning? I suppose you figured a seal could rescue her!" she hisses, then marches out of the living room.

◆ DANIEL ◆

DANIEL CASTS A FORLORN look at Leo, then shuts himself back inside his room. Forlorn because he really does hate it that he's upset his niece—that damn surfboard! What is he supposed to do about the situation?

"May I join you?" Leo calls through the door.

He sighs. His dad probably figures Daniel's a better bet if the alternative is an empty living room with a she-wolf in the wings who might reappear at any moment. Of course, Leo could pack up his camera equipment and split, but he never was that kind of guy who exits at the first hint of trouble. His dad waited until the hints were not merely *in* his face but on top, smothering him. "Please?" Leo repeats.

Daniel opens the door, motions Leo to stay where he is on the threshold, then squats on his floor mat, staring at his feet. "Look, I just wanted to do something nice for her birthday. I've been meaning to do it. I know I have to make that call, but I don't know who will answer. Plus, I might need to get a credit card. I'm not sure how to do that, since I don't have a consumer history. I'd have to talk to *several* people probably, maybe even make several calls." He can feel his cheeks burn; he tugs at his shirt, swallows hard.

Leo nods. "It's okay, I understand."

Farley sits hunched at the top of the bookcase, glaring at the intruder with yellow-eyed disdain. "Cat working out for you, son, doesn't try to escape?"

Daniel shrugs. "He's acclimating. Not a moment here he's not wishing he was someplace else." Stares up at his dad, attempting to mimic Farley, leveling Leo in a glare. His dad once told Daniel he had a certain look he acquired after his accident, *"a way of looking at someone as if you're looking through them, like staring into water,"* Leo had said. "You heard about the drowned kingdom coming up on a beach in Borth, Wales?"

Leo knits his bushy eyebrows like he's considering this out-of-context, off-subject, not-remotely-related-to-anything-he-recognized turn in the conversation. Daniel suppresses a smile, watching his dad try to keep his straight, concerned face. "I don't think so."

"It's been exposed due to all the coastal flooding washing away the sand, an ancient kingdom, complete with the ghosts of forests, prehistoric stumps of trees, animal and human footprints, artifacts, the works. There's a poem kids in Wales learn about a sunken kingdom called Cantre'r Gwaelod, swallowed up by the sea and everything drowned. On a quiet night you can hear the kingdom's church bells ring."

"Right," Leo says, "but what does it have to do with a surfboard for Heaven?"

Daniel turns away for a moment and stares out the window where the sky has become the salmon pink of an Atlantic sunset. Mercy will be home in less than an hour unless they put her on cleanup after the dinner shift. "Do you remember when I almost drowned?"

The seminal event that changed their lives, does Leo *remember* it? Daniel watches his dad gaze at him, his face a moving pane of emotions like a slide projector: sadness, fear, pain, perplexed, his son, forty-two years old, balding, a mostly unmarked face, skin the starched smoothness of someone who's never in the sun, the way his shoulders lean in, sitting cross-legged on his mat the way a child might, or maybe Buddha, someone who does yoga, Daniel thinks. That's what his father sees. Above him on the bookcase Farley yawns, closes one eye, the other half opened, still fixed on Leo. Who nods. "Right, I do."

"Yeah, well, I thought the reason I was saved was so I could become a better person. Why else? People drown everywhere all the time, even in their bathtubs. It should've been like a thunderbolt comes down and smacks me on the head. Here's why *you've* been saved, now go out and do good. But it didn't work. Same old jealousy, not wanting to share my stuff, but if I didn't Amelia would get mad and Gavin would pitch a fit, so I'd let him have whatever he wanted. But in my head sometimes I'd wish him dead because Amelia loved him more."

"That's not true . . ."

"Oh, come on! She still does, even his ghost. I think she believes if I drowned then maybe he wouldn't have had to."

"You were twelve years old, Daniel."

"Yeah except I didn't get any older in my head, just bigger. Not only didn't I feel like a better person, I didn't even feel grateful, didn't feel like *me*, didn't know who *me* was anymore. People drown every day. I'm alive, I breathe air, but the ocean's inside me. Do you see? Do you get it? I've been slowly drowning all these years. What do I have to show for my life? Never mind consumer history, I have *no* history. Can't leave this room. I've got an ocean inside me, but I'll never go *in it* again."

Leo rubs his chin, lifts his gaze until he too is looking out the window at a pink sky. "You did though. That time with Gavin and his friend with the boat? It was a while ago, before Gavin left for San Francisco and you . . . well, that's when you retreated to your room. Did you actually try to . . . Gavin said you were free-diving?"

Close your eyes, let it come back . . . hot sun gleaming off the Atlantic, Gavin asks him along, his friend's speedboat (Doug?), sandwiches, beer, Get a life! Gavin said. Anchor off some submerged rocks, Gavin and Doug smoke a joint; Gavin, golden hair, tan chest, yellow trunks, his brother's the sun and Daniel a moon-thing huddled in the corner, but the beer when they crack it open is icy cold. Beginning to feel relaxed as he allows himself to be, then with the motor cut he hears it. At first like somebody humming and he peers sharply at his brother, Gavin messing with him, his friend? But they'd baby oiled their skin and are languid on the deck, snagging the rays as they put it. No, more than a humming he can make out words now, a language he doesn't know in a lilting soprano. So he dives, no thoughts other than if it's HER he wants to see her, and maybe something in him wants to test it—with the ocean already inside him could he swim into its heart and be part of it? The underwater world is frigid and dark, a bursting in his ears, his head, firecracker sounds going off like his veins are popping as suddenly he rises again, Gavin swimming him up and up, when they break the surface he sputters and gasps, Gavin's hoisting him onto the boat, chewing him out for making him dive in—"So fucking cold not to mention a waste of tanning oil!" Then he slaps Daniel across his heaving shoulders. "Hey big bro! Now look who's saved whose ass!"

Daniel stares at his dad. "Leo . . ." He hesitates. "Mercy told me you took a picture of her along with her collection. That was nice of you, but, just so you know . . . she might not be who you think she is. She might not even be entirely human."

Leo sighs. "Or she might be a little *too* human. I had a feeling that girl could use a confidence boost. So, what about that lost kingdom in Wales? You never finished the story."

Daniel rises, walks over to the window, turning his back to Leo. Peers out at the darkening sky over Mercy's garage, also dark, nobody home yet. Turns back around and is struck by the look on Leo's face, anxious, tender, his father's compassion, how ineffectual if well meaning it is. Daniel walks toward Leo, arms out as if to embrace him. But he doesn't; the MacQueen-Frenches aren't huggers.

He shrugs instead. "That story doesn't have its ending yet," he tells his dad. "A work in progress, a cautionary tale, about the ways our world keeps showing us that it's drowning, and nobody seems to care."

◆ HEAVEN ◆

HEAVEN IN THE LOCKER-room bathroom before afternoon swim practice, late on purpose because that way she can change out of her school clothes and into her swimsuit without the others teasing her about her bubble thighs or her itty-bitty fatty boobs. She goes into the bathroom to pee and wait for the others to leave. Out the crack of the door she can see Bethany preening in front of the mirror, white legs, bands of even whiter skin below the half apples of her butt, curve of her hips in the team swimsuit, a spandex tank that flatters Bethany but not Heaven, her surplus flesh pooching out of it like raw dough.

From outside the locker room the sound of Coach's warning whistle and the girls scatter, leaving Heaven to quickly climb into her suit. She glances into the toilet just before flushing and sees a swirl of red, and on her underpants, which she'd shed without looking, a dark red stain the size of a baby's fist. "Good lord!" she cries, sounding like Grandmelia. She presses her hand against the door, feels for a moment like she might pass out then tugs down her suit, plops down again on the toilet, staring between her legs.

Earlier in the summer Grandmelia had left a package of tampons and a box of pads on Heaven's bureau, a scrawled note tucked underneath: *For when it begins*. No discussion, and for sure Heaven didn't want to initiate one. Now she's scared and doesn't know what to do. She'd been carrying around one of the pads tucked into a pocket inside her backpack, but if she puts it on, with the tightness of her suit it would stick out like a lump and everyone would know. She can't go home because she'd have to pass through the glass hall by the pool and Coach would see her and call her on it. Coach said at the beginning of the season their periods were not an excuse to miss practice or, God help them if they did, a meet. "Plug it with a tampon," she said.

But how would she "plug it"? Celine, one of the girls on the team who occasionally spoke to Heaven when no one was watching, had whispered that her mom said tampons could pop their virginity. Coach's second whistle shrieks, no longer a warning, Heaven's officially late and starts to cry. Who will teach her these things? She thinks about families, how they're supposed to function as a unit, but she remembers how even before her dad died and her mom went to prison, with two parents she felt her separateness. It was a them-versus-her sort of thing, like at night when they made her go to bed and she'd be alone in the dark, just that thin bar of light under her door (when she still had her bedroom, before they rented it out for money!), hearing their voices, the drone of their TV, it was her parents together, Heaven in the dark of her bedroom.

She's feeling sick and it's the mom in prison she's missing, remembering the last New Year's she spent with her mom, just months before everything Heaven believed true in her life would be destroyed, and her mom let her drink a whole carton of eggnog. She didn't say Heaven would get fat like Grandmelia would say. Let her drink all of it then held her head over the toilet, pulling back her hair when Heaven puked. Her dad wasn't there and when she asked her mom where he was, she said he was out "slutting and bumping." Which sounded like a dance or a sport, or some weird combo like line skating. "Don't ever get married for love," her mom warned, who was also drinking eggnog but hers was mostly whiskey, "it will break your heart."

"Heaven French! That you?" She sees Coach's black flip-flops, thick ankles, and her man-muscled calves from under the stall door. "Don't bother answering, I know it is! You're late to practice and I chose *you* to lead the relay. You going to let me down?"

"No," Heaven mumbles.

"Then move your butt out there! You get ten extra laps starting now. This is your second late demerit for the month, French, three you're benched!"

The minute Coach leaves the locker room Heaven yanks up her suit, grabs her swim bag with her clothes stuffed in (considers throwing away the bloody underwear but someone might find it), tosses it inside her locker. Quick snitch-check for unlocked lockers, found an awesome barrette once, a push-up bra that almost fit if she had more to push up and "De*lips*cious" watermelon lip gloss, then makes a dash for the pool, praying the blood won't trickle down her leg before she hits that water.

Forgetting she was supposed to take a shower first, which earns more snarling from Coach and a chorus of *gross piglet!* from her teammates. Better than blood, Heaven thinks, a sick wave in her gut and a sudden stab of cramps—*You're a Woman Now!* the pamphlet in the school nurse's office chortled, describing periods almost like they were monthly treats, five days of ice cream and the minor *discomfort* of cramps. Pushes off from lane 5, extra laps, breaststroke best stroke, hums as she pulses along, not looking in the lane beside her knowing it's most likely Bethany. It always seems to be, whether Coach does it alphabetically, which makes Harrison follow French, or just to make Heaven's life suck even more. When she reaches the halfway rest after ten, her hand on the side of the pool, tangy stink of chlorine circulating from the filters, glass walls on either side of the deck fogged with the pumped-in heat like a hothouse, Bethany pulls up in lane 6, places her hand over Heaven's, pinching hard.

"Ow!" Heaven wails.

"Oh, excuse me," flashing her fake grin. "Waiting for your pretend surfboard again, that why you're late?"

"I told you. My uncle has to figure out delivery from Maine."

"Why doesn't he just contact the pretend mail carrier at the pretend post office? Maybe a pretend airplane could fly it down!"

"French and Harrison! Someone give you permission to chat? Get on the laps."

"Like I'd *chat* with Bubble Thighs," Bethany snarls, pushes off.

Heaven heads out after her. She can see through her swim goggles Bethany's hair trailing out of her cap in a blond wave, the fluid motion of those spaghetti legs, then Heaven feels something loosen between her own fat legs that makes her stop swimming and pop her head up out of the water.

"French!" Coach yells. "You are really trying my patience today. I should demerit you for raising my blood pressure. Swim! This is not free time."

She does. It's all she wants to do, the only thing in the world she *can* do she's any good at. In the next lane Bethany is so far ahead she's a watery blur and Heaven knows when she turns and heads back, she'll see it, blood flowing uncorked from between Heaven's legs. She won't ever be able to show her face in school again and they won't let her swim either. Bloody Piglet they'll call her, and Heaven feels the sting of tears in her eyes under her goggles, making the chlorine's burn worse. Though they can't accuse her of crying, everyone gets red eyes the way this indoor pool maxes out on the chemicals.

She'd been waiting for a sign, something that would tell her it's time to complete her quest, praying every night to plastic Jesus and the angel but they haven't answered. Because she snaked them? That's probably what Uncle Daniel would say, who hasn't been much help lately since he's been staring out his window at Mercy 24/7. She'll have to take things into her own hands.

From underwater Heaven sees the smooth arch of Bethany's freestyle on its approach from the other side. It's all in the timing; she has to make sure she and Bethany are in the middle of the pool at the same time, the lanes separated only by floating lane lines.

She's calculated all of it in her head so many times—diving under the lane line the moment Bethany's beside her, quick yank on that hair, then swimming her down to the bottom toward the drain in the middle (same kind she'd practiced on in the outdoor pool, turned out)—that when Bethany approaches Heaven decides not to let her get close enough to even *see* the blood. Lifts her head for a second, then a quick scissor kick after a deep inhale, dives under the floats and grabs Bethany's ponytail dragging down.

It's all in the speed and surprise, not letting Bethany kick out on the surface to attract attention and with Heaven behind her she won't even know what happened. She can feel her struggling, stronger than Heaven figured but Heaven's got the power of breath and begins her song as they approach the drain. *Hmm . . .* She's practiced this maneuver during free time, angling down like a shot, pulling up on the cap. Of course, it can't come up much with the weight of the water, but just enough to catch Bethany's hair, release. Bethany's thrashing like crazy now but they're too deep to draw attention, all the other girls splashing in all the other lanes. *Hmm*, wants to tell Bethany it will be okay, the water is sacred, though it's the pool not the ocean so no selkies, no kingdom in the coral, no magic at all and Heaven almost feels a little sorry for her.

For just an instant, her fist wrapped around Bethany's blond hair, she sees her dad, middle of the night in the ocean's blackness, his blond hair on the surface a golden-white light bobbing for a moment, like one of those floating lanterns they saw when they still lived in San Francisco, at some Buddhist festival on Ocean Beach. *Obon* it was called, you sail a paper lantern out into the ocean with a lit candle on it.

The thrashing is beginning to lessen, and Heaven knows she doesn't have much time. But as she's lifting the drain cap with one hand, grasping Bethany's hair in the other, there's a sudden splash and a dark shape grabs Bethany around her neck, Heaven releases her hair, and Coach swims Bethany to the surface just as Heaven runs out of breath, pops up gasping.

"Her hair got caught in the drain, I was trying to help!" Heaven shouts.

Coach leaps out of the pool with Bethany in her arms, lays her flat on the tile, turns her face to one side and straddling her pushes down on her stomach over and over until a squirt of water drools out. Again, more water. There's a hush around the pool, where everyone has either climbed out or is standing in the shallow end watching. Bethany coughs, gasps, and Coach sits her up wrapping a towel around her shoulders. "Everyone to the showers," Coach orders, no whistle, her voice grim and flat.

Heaven is the last to climb out and they all stare at her as she walks up the three stairs in the shallow end, chill of the air against her wet skin, trying to squeeze her fat thighs together, one . . . two . . . three steps. "Psycho-bitch!" someone whispers. A rivulet of blood runs down her leg.

♦ AMELIA ♦

AMELIA GLARES AT THE group sitting around the rectangular table in Principal Keagan's office. Keagan, her hair in a knot at the base of her neck like a drawer handle, some satchel-faced woman introduced as president of the School Board, and a grimacing, pudgy little man, the school psychologist for the district. And Heaven, staring out over everyone's head like there's something to see, one small window in the middle of a row of bland portraits of bland people, probably former principals.

"So," Amelia says, sliding out the chair across from her granddaughter, "I'm given to understand this is a disciplinary hearing. Should I be calling my lawyer?"

"We're not labeling it that," Principal Keagan says. "We've already decided on a course of action. Heaven is being suspended until after the holidays. Given the circumstances we think this is more than fair, and the district will provide her with a home tutor so she doesn't fall behind in her classes."

"We also believe her actions are a cry for help," the psychologist chimes in. Amelia cuts him off. "Can you be more cliché?"

"Excuse me?"

"Mrs. French," the principal interrupts and Amelia shoots up her hand. "MacQueen, and certainly not missus. You haven't done your homework," wagging her finger.

Principal Keagan tightens lips thin as toothpicks. "Look, this isn't easy for any of us. But the facts are—"

"What facts? From our phone conversation I gathered you really don't know the facts, and yet you are suspending her on what some other child says?"

"Bethany Harrison claims Heaven was trying to drown her. We aren't clear exactly what happened under the water, but Bethany was observed to be swimming along fine, then she disappears, and the Coach notices some sort of struggle underwater. There were just two girls involved, Bethany and Heaven."

"I was trying to save her!" Heaven says, pouting.

Amelia glares at her. "Let me handle this."

Principal Keagan nods. "So you said, Heaven. At any rate Mrs. . . . Ms. MacQueen, the girl had to stay overnight in the hospital for observation. She swallowed a fair amount of water and that's serious. In addition to this incident, when we searched Heaven's locker, we found missing items that belong to other students and school personnel. Heaven insists she doesn't know how they got into her locker, but I'm pretty sure if we involve the police, we'll get a different story."

"I didn't take anything," Heaven whines.

"Hush!" Amelia orders Heaven. "Why did you search her locker? You're calling her a thief?"

"Protocol. And we're calling her in serious trouble," Principal Keagan says. "Her locker contents alone are basis for suspension, and the pool incident on top of that is of grave concern. Dr. Butler, our district psychologist, has written a report which he'll share with you as it will be included in her file."

The psychologist nods then leans forward, gazing at Amelia intently. "I understand from Heaven's school file in Maine she had a father and mother, and Heaven told me her father is *gone*— that's the word she used but I'm aware he's deceased—and that her mother, according to Heaven, is an astronaut in Texas. I also know the location and situation of the mother. In a nutshell I'm recommending psychological help for Heaven. She clearly has had some trauma in her family life and her behavior could be interpreted as acting out as a result."

"Been there, done that, didn't work," Amelia says. "You are one for the clichés, aren't you? In a *nutshell*?" She stands up, towering over them, at least she hopes that's the perception. Somehow her height at seventy doesn't carry the same impact it did at forty. "Since it seems everything has been decreed, I see no point in wasting my time at this hearing, by whatever name you call it. My lawyer will look over the file and your report. You will be hearing from him. I assume the tutor will contact us with Heaven's assignments."

"Say," the school board president suddenly pipes in, "weren't you that model from those old egg diet commercials? I remember them from when I was a little kid. I didn't recognize you until you stood up."

Amelia smiles at her, slow and cold. "Indeed. If I had an egg to offer you now can you guess where I'd suggest you put it?"

★ ★ ★

On the way home Amelia manages a frosty silence for three minutes tops then turns on the girl, whom she insisted sit in the front seat beside her, no hiding out in the back with earbuds plugged in. "You really can be stupid, can't you? Stupid, stupid, stupid. I'd been giving you more credit. Figured you'd realize now that you have a stable home you have something worth behaving for! What's the matter with you?"

Heaven wails, "I *had* a home. I want to go home to *my* home!"

"What you had no longer exists. You can't go there, nobody's home."

Heaven starts to cry, and Amelia reaches out, her hand hovering over the girl's shoulder, but she's not sure of its impulse, to caress or slap! She withdraws, taps her fingernails painted an eggplant-purple, utterly wrong for the moment yet somehow comforting at the same time, against the steering wheel. "Look, I'm trying very hard to make this work for you, can't you see that? I didn't ask for this situation either, but here we are. We have to make the best of it. And making the best of it does not include drowning people and stealing from them!"

"I didn't!" Heaven sobs.

Amelia pulls the car over to the side of the road, shuts off the engine and glares at her.

Heaven sniffles, head down, avoiding Amelia's eyes. They're parked in front of the Lawson Tower in Scituate, that Amelia had once overheard Heaven tell Daniel she thought looked like the Rapunzel castle, with its turret and tiny windows: "Like Bethany the pervert-princess could stick her head out one of them, dangle her long blond hair, and I'd crawl up her hair, snipping as I go." Amelia had laughed quietly at that. Her granddaughter has spunk, anyway, no one would say otherwise.

"Here's where we're going to start being honest with each other, beginning right now. There's been too much lying in this family," Amelia says.

"Okay," Heaven says. "So is Uncle Daniel ever giving me that surfboard?"

"Of course not. Don't expect anything from him. He's not capable of fulfilling anyone's expectations."

Tears well up again in Heaven's eyes making the blue in them deepen into what Amelia remembers as the intense aqua of Gavin's eyes, then tears are in her eyes too.

"But why did he tell me he would? I told everybody. Nobody likes me already and now they'll all think I'm a liar. Why did he do that?"

Amelia sighs. "He wants you to love him, that's why, and he doesn't know how it's done. A kind of prolonged shock maybe? Post-traumatic stress? That school psychologist of yours would provide a label no doubt."

"I thought either you love someone, or you don't," Heaven sniffs.

Amelia laughs, a sharp yip like a coyote. "It's like autism dear, a spectrum disorder. The severely love disabled on up to the functional enough to get by."

Tears are rolling down Heaven's face. She stares at the tower. "I should've just cut off Bethany's hair in seventh-grade math. Robyn would've loved it; he'd say I'm fierce and maybe he'd even be my friend."

Amelia reaches out for a moment and touches her granddaughter's arm. "You know, people have said I'm fierce. I'm not sure it's necessarily meant as a compliment. Okay, I was honest with you. Now it's your turn. Did you do the things they are punishing you for at school? If you did, you'll take the punishment, it's only fair. We reap what we sow. If you didn't, we turn it over to my lawyer. Which is it? Answer me."

She shrugs, sniffles again, wipes her nose. "I wasn't trying to *kill* her. It was a drowning song. If it worked, she'd be a selkie, swimming in the sea forever."

"It's a swimming pool for God's sake! Are you as delusional as your uncle?"

Heaven rubs her eyes. "I want to go home."

"Where's that?" Amelia hisses, scowling out the windshield. It's starting to rain, big fat drops and the sky has clouded over, dark and ominous looking. A sudden gust of wind blows leaves against the car, swirling for a moment like a dervish. Amelia remembers they're predicting a nor'easter. She'd meant to prepare, should've at least taken in the patio furniture, made sure the generator was gassed up in case the lights went out, but then all this *other* blew up. She starts up the car. "We need to get going. A storm's predicted and because of that damn meeting at your school I'm unprepared. You better hope it doesn't take out our house, then none of us will have a home!"

◆ DANIEL ◆

IT'S EARLY STILL BUT the sky is darkening with a storm coming. He knows it's coming, can feel it in his bones, under his skin, his body's slow, all-over ache. Tomorrow October, today the last of September, hurricane season. He doesn't want any dinner tonight, doesn't even want to talk to his niece, and certainly not Amelia. He shuts out his light, lies down on his floor mat, and stares as darkness spreads over his window like a giant hand, closing out the daylight. He closes his eyes.

When the angel comes, he will tell her this: how he imagined it and then it was true. First on the outside, then moving through the wall, window, glass and she's flesh, she is here. And it's okay that she's here, because she's an angel. She tells him to lie down on his bed, then she is beside him. He lets her touch him and he's never been touched, not like this, like it means anything at all. Love making is perhaps like drowning; you lose yourself, you can't catch your breath, but maybe you discover you don't need to breathe, that she is in you and you are in her like the ocean. When the angel leaves the floor where she stood will be cold as the sea, but in his bed it will finally be warm.

✦ MAGGIE ✦

*D*EAR *DIARY,*
    How long you'd be by now if you were on actual paper, scrolls and scrolls, century and a half, going on two. Who would read you? Who would care? Dear Diary, this section shall be called—What I Miss:

    Boys, wondering about them, dreaming of a life that would involve them in a way I had not yet understood, but felt that craving of it nevertheless when the sailor first kissed me, touched me in that tingly way unknown but for my own stealthy hands. Dear Diary, I miss my breasts, as they had been growing larger, a wee bit sore too, and these I would stroke secretly at night, my hand slipping under my shift when on either side my sisters, Abigail and Molly, slept. I would pinch my cheeks, make myself stay awake, my only chance to be just with me. We did not get much privacy on the croft, and if we complained about it Ma would instruct us to do more work, her solution to all our dilemmas, the thing mattering most to her that our bellies be full.

    I miss hot porridge when there were berries to put on it, sea buckthorn, a delightful orange berry along our coast, a bitter yet satisfying citrus contrast to the porridge, particularly when we were low of milk. And Ma's Sunday scones when there was oat flour leftover from the bread and oatcakes baking.

I miss my beautiful long dark hair, and while the silvery gray I sus-
pect has its own beauty, I do miss wondering at the woman I might have
become, whether I'd favor fair Ma, her thin lips, brittle ways, or more likely
Da whose hair was the color of mine, our skin rosy.

At times I get to missing the ghost tree so much it hurts inside, where
underneath 'tis yet all heart. The way it would bring our family close I sup-
pose is the reason, it being one of the few trees on our croft. In the mist which
blew in from the sea or down from the mountains, this tree rose up stark
and otherworldly, its branches swaying like a ghost. At night Da would tell
stories of faeries and kelpies, those devilish water horses, formidable giants,
and all manner of sprites and spirits that roamed our island beyond death,
living as ghosts, he said. Ma, ever practical, her evenings spent mending or
weaving would shake her head, not even look up from her loom or thread,
and tell us only the Lord could bestow life after death, and if we were good,
she'd say, it would be Heaven for us, not wandering the moors of Skye. Ah,
what little we knew . . . as if this was an either-or choice.

★   ★   ★

Last night the wind rose over the ocean and with it a full-moon
tide bearing waves that crashed against the Scituate jetty, spraying
up and over the light-tower. I kept my eyes on their house in Seahaven, its whiteness aglow between two other houses closer to the
shore—which shall be no more with what is coming. I know it,
can feel it in my blood and the sea itself, which has begun to thrum
with its building. I know this wind. This wind carries voices on it,
sometimes in song but more often in warning. Imagine it banging
against the wood of their house, shutters knocking about the windows like they're of want to come in, rattling things inside, doors,
cupboards, clicking and clacking. We had but stone and thatch for
our cottage, and yet I understand wood, its vulnerabilities. The
child and the grandmother slept, but I knew the other was awake.
He wondered at the wind, what it meant. His blood remembered
what he could not, another wind over a century and a half ago, the
way it roared, whipping up the fires, burning roofs, that acrid stink
of thatch and peat, the smell of endings.

Though within some endings there is a hint of a new beginning . . .

There are those who believe we lure seafarers into the brink with our songs, keeping them under until they drown. Others say never save a drowning man, as he may have our mark upon him. We are swimmers, shaped for speed and agility, with a woman's heart. We retain our human longings and memories. Our magic is that we do not die. Our tragedy is this as well: we are not able to forget our past but cannot hope for a future that bears its intent. No doubt the tales have come from such, the way she might follow your boat and stare so mournfully at you, like she is peering into your soul.

For a while we retain our own language in our heads, each of us from different circumstances, bearing different lands in our memories. Eventually we lose it. I no longer can speak Gaelic, though not a pure Scot, nor English, nor American neither. We lose what we were; our despair is not being able to forget what we lost. For a long time, I asked, why me? Why not old Mrs. MacNaughter, who was right about her feet never touching land again, or a brave Gael lass who did not make it to the lifeboat for saving someone else? But magic is mercurial, if there were answers it would not be magic.

I often wondered if Abigail knew. She'd sit on a Prince Edward Island beach before leaving the province for the States, near the Point Prim Lighthouse—Pinnette, where the lifeboat bore the Gaels who survived, guided by the lighthouse's light. With its stark tower above her she'd gaze out, her long legs folded, spine straight, red cliffs rising behind her like sails at sunset, staring at the ocean as if it might tell her something. She'd peer intently into its waves, a wash of red like rust or blood from their constant churning over the red sand, and it reminded me of the way we used to also stare out, perched on the cliffs over Loch Eisort, watching the seals and dolphins swim below us. Those days I'd look past the cavorting sea life toward the Sleat peninsula, knowing beyond was the bigger world, the United Kingdom, and other lands so distant they were but a dream. Don't be foolish Maggie, Abigail would warn me when she'd see it in my eyes, the longing for something more.

There is some contentment to be sure, and gratitude for not having been entombed in a sunken vessel, where thousands of shipwrecks, many that history never recorded have come to rest ten thousand, twenty thousand, even thirty thousand feet down. Crypts they are, where the ghosts of human life and its artifacts rest undisturbed by the concerns of a world so temporal. I know they are there, these graves, see the occasional specter of some sunken ship in a clear stretch of ocean when sunlight hits it just right, covered in barnacles and anemones, sea creatures staking their claim.

Truly there is joy to be had in sun-dappled water on a fine Atlantic day, when the sea reflects the clarity of the sky, the occasional cloud-shadow blooming like a giant rose in its depths. We embrace our youth on days like these, without the burden of aging we don't have aching bones, failing joints, a body shutting down. Aye, but other times it's a feeling you are but a ghost ship, crew disappeared, left to float on and on through time, no direction, no purpose, no record of having ever existed.

I swim, from the Canadian Maritimes to Penobscot Bay in Maine, Massachusetts Bay, off Scituate, and the occasional very long swim to Hawaii, to check on my sister's progeny who've settled there. Otherwise it is Charles's heirs I watch, for this does not change, our craving for family. The wee ones I lost track of alas, the two that survived, Molly and Dottie, having moved to an inland province. I remember their small hands brushing my hair, and their giggling, and Molly's cold little feet beside me in bed. Wee baby Robert and Mary, the youngest lassie, did not survive their crossing, along with Da (as previously mentioned but alas, my heart never recovered from its sadness). The three of them in a winding sheet, Da's hand clutching that Skye soil, committed to the depths.

Ma lived to be an old woman on Prince Edward Island, and I watched her pace the same beach Abigail once sat on, her last years with a cane picking her way over the red sand and rocks, no idle strolling for Ma. Consumed she was with her anger at The Clearances, the loss of her family and home, burnt out to graze sheep no less, she kept muttering to any would listen—and of course the

Maritimes had more than its share of displaced Highlanders, a Scottish diaspora it would come to be called, so she had sympathetic ears. She lived long enough to learn of The Crofter's Holdings Act in 1886, when the Gaels fought back, the newspapers having reported the brutalities of the landlords. The law made the forced evictions so many of us suffered illegal, and even offered some land with more generous terms, such that many crofters were eventually able to purchase their own crofts. Ma passed on with peace in her heart, justice served, if too late for the MacQueens.

If I could go back it would be to a time when my family was still whole, one of the rare and precious sunshine days when the Isle of Skye, with its mountains and jagged cliffs, its heather-covered moors, green valleys, and windswept hills shone with a brilliance unlike any I've since seen. It is summer and the light with us close to midnight. We have toiled long on the croft, but supper was plenty, and we are satisfied. The crickets start up into the evening quiet. Da takes his pipes and joins into their song, and though it's late we sit, all of us outside our cottage watching the play of colors in the sky as the sun goes down. Even Ma has put up her mending, a wee one asleep on her lap. We are before the eviction or even the threat of it, Ma's rage and Da's heartbreak, the rupturing of our family. The world above us shimmers, and here and there a falling star blazing across the darkening sky, before burning up and disappearing into the night.

◆ AMELIA ◆

THE NIGHT HEAVEN DISAPPEARS a nor'easter howls in with winds so fierce it's upgraded to a category-one hurricane. "We can't call it a nor'easter anymore," a local news anchor said gravely before the electricity blacked out over all of Seahaven and most of Scituate. Sirens wailed as the tide rose in a fifteen-foot storm surge with twenty-five-foot waves swamping the coastal neighborhoods, exploding over the Scituate seawall, the seawall at Minot Beach, racing through streets in a saltwater river. North Scituate to Cedar Point, and Seahaven to Humarock, neighborhoods are evacuated, along with what's left of the homes still standing on Peggotty Beach after Hurricane Sandy. The Scituate lighthouse parking lot is swamped under five feet of seawater, both jetties completely submerged in gigantic waves, and a twenty-foot siege of ocean crashes against the beachfront houses in Sandy Hills, after roaring over a makeshift seawall residents had pieced together since a prior Nor'easter destroyed their permanent one. A state of emergency is declared.

Winds are clocked at ninety miles per hour with gusts to one hundred, tearing shingles off roofs, twisting off gutters and launching them like missiles, knocking down trees and closing off access roads, including Hatherly Road, where an ancient oak blows down on top of the street, luckily smashing pavement instead of a house, but blocking off a major evacuation route from the coast. The sound of its impact like a shotgun blast, and Amelia jumps out of bed, grabbing her battery-powered lantern to illuminate the hall toward Heaven's room to see if the girl is all right. She never did get the opportunity to buy extra gas for the generator and was kicking herself for not doing it, putting most of the blame on yesterday's idiotic disciplinary hearing where her granddaughter had already been tried and condemned, the principal with her hair and no doubt her panties too in a knot, the psychologist spouting clichés, and the ridiculous school board person who had nothing to add beyond a jab at Amelia's age—saw those commercials when she was a *little* kid, she said. It seemed like the storm had stalled, was taking its sweet time to start pummeling the town, so Amelia spent the day talking to her lawyer about how to proceed, instead of preparing for the nor'easter accelerating. She'd made Heaven stay in her room all day as punishment for her part in yesterday's drama, for vexing Amelia.

Heaven is not in her room now, her bed still made, something Amelia insisted on from the start after discovering that the girl had never been taught to make a bed (then again, she'd been sleeping in a box!). Okay, don't panic—she checks the bathroom, not there or in any other room in the house, which Amelia races through, shining the lantern in front of her so as not to stumble in the dark, lurching out onto the patio, the shrieking of the wind outside masking her calls. "Heaven? Heaven where are you?" God, Amelia hates that name. How could they do that to a kid? "Heaven? Answer me for lord's sake!" The evacuation siren is a steady wail and she can hear police beating on the doors of her neighbors, shouting into their megaphones; any minute they'll be here too forcing them to leave. She hears the crashing surf, smells its briny breath on the wind.

Rages into Daniel's room, shining the lantern at his face; he's lying on his floor mat wrapped in the ruglike Nepal blanket that

Leo bought from some Portland street vendor. The cat curled up on the edge of the blanket leaps onto the bookcase hissing. "Wake up!" she shouts, and Daniel pops up.

"I'm not asleep, for chrissake. Am I in bed? Why are you in my room?"

"I can't find Heaven!" Amelia's heart hammers and a sour taste slicks her throat, fear, or maybe her bloody dinner coming up, white food for the girl, spaghetti noodles with butter and frozen peas for God's sake, no time to prepare anything substantial before the nor'easter wailed in. She shines the lantern in his face again.

"You aren't supposed to be in my room. I reject you being in my room!"

"Did you hear me? I need sane Daniel! I'm telling you she's missing! She isn't in this house and the phones are out, the landline and the cell tower too, all down!" She stamps her foot, then suddenly she's crying. "I don't know what to do! I don't know how to be a mother to her any more than I was to you. She's headed down some criminal path at the age of thirteen and now she's disappeared!"

Daniel stands up, touches Amelia's shoulder. "You're not her mother."

"I am tasked with raising this child and they're telling me she tried to drown a girl and has been stealing from people for who knows how long. Seems I can't even keep track of a thirteen-year-old because I can't find her! It's a bloody hurricane, what am I supposed to do? We have to evacuate, and I can't leave without her. What did you say to her earlier? I know she asked you about that damn surfboard. Why do you do these things, Daniel, tell her she's getting something you have no intention of getting for her?"

"I do have the intention. I told her I would."

"Oh, stop that. You will not. Intentions are not the same as the deed. Probably the worst criminals in the world had good intentions at some point. That child thought she had a friend in you, someone she could trust. She's been let down by everyone in her life, do you realize that? Her parents most of all, with a mother in prison for murdering her father who . . . Christ, Leo's right. They were addicts, both of them. Gavin a drug addict and you're a forty-two-year-old who believes in faeries. Some family. Others in my generation raised lawyers, doctors . . ."

"Serial killers, child traffickers, rapists, luck of the draw."

"Well what have I got to show for any of it?"

Amelia's crying and Daniel puts his arms around her for a moment, inhaling her scent, remembering how as a kid he used to sniff the perfume on her vanity sometimes when she was gone, as if smelling it would bring her back. "You've got me," he says.

She rubs her eyes, wipes under them for mascara runoff. "You're only here because you're afraid to be anywhere else. You'd leave me if you could."

"I can help look. I doubt she's far. She's probably hiding close by just to give us a scare. Remember when Gavin was her age and told you he swallowed a bottle of aspirin because he was mad you wouldn't let him go see some R-rated movie?"

Amelia sniffs. "Yeah, I got to the bottom of that one giving him the blow-by-blow on stomach pumping. Anyway, you never go out of your room. What are you talking about, a thorough investigation of the patio around the pool through your window? I already looked there by the way in case she was dumb enough to swim in this weather."

"It's a start."

Amelia sighs. "I'll put on my raincoat. I can take Leo's waterproof camping flashlight he left with us. Like we ever camped. I don't know what he was thinking. The police will make us evacuate you know—even you. They'll be knocking on the door any minute. It's dangerous out there. Before the power went out I heard a lot of the streets are flooding, not just our neighborhood, creeks, the marsh, the river, everywhere there's any water it's rising. I have to find that child!"

"I'll stay here in case she shows up."

"We need to leave! Can't you hear it? The tide, waves, we may get swamped!"

He shrugs. "Maybe that's not such a bad thing. Who decided when our ancestors crawled out of the sea to breathe air, grow legs, and build lives on the ground, that's the way it's supposed to be? Then when they go back in the water, the sea claims what belonged to it in the first place."

"Darwin," Amelia says.

"What?"

"That's who decided, Darwin."

Just then a loud knock, pummeling the door. "Police! Anyone in there?"

Amelia races out of Daniel's room, grabs her raincoat from the hallway closet and opens the front door to a blast of wind, needles of rain pelting her face. The officer in his black raingear blends in with the darkness, no streetlamps, just the flashlight he's holding illuminates the area where he stands, water inching past the soles of his boots, roar of the wind making him shout to be heard. "You have to evacuate, ma'am! The tide peaks in an hour and waves already swamped the houses by the ocean. Seawall broke through."

"My granddaughter is missing!"

"We'll look for her, but you have to go! This is a mandatory evacuation."

"She's thirteen!" Amelia screams after him as he moves on to the next house. "A big girl!" But maybe not so big, she thinks, feeling like she might cry again, but there's no time for that. *Steel yourself!* she hisses. Sees the pale shine of water swirling in her driveway and toward the beach more of it, a river racing through the dark street like it belongs there. Sirens wailing, the wind howling, but she's hearing something else too. At first, she thinks it's her neighbor's dog barking, but it's too hoarse and in an almost rhythmic cadence, with pauses, higher then lower. She hears it moving closer, as though it's on the flooded street where the tide swells under a new set of waves, propelled by a wash of water. Its sound seems to rise above the rest, and it's this insistence she hears over the sirens, the wind, even the sea itself.

"A seal," Daniel says calmly, standing in the open door of his bedroom. "That's the barking of a seal."

◆ HEAVEN ◆

SHE POUNDS ON HER door and when Mercy opens it, in the light of her lantern she looks smaller than Heaven, even though Heaven knows Mercy's bigger.

"What the hell?" Mercy says. She opens the door wider. The growling of the wind and rain is thunderous, a waterfall's roar. She grabs Heaven's hand outstretched for another knock, pulling her inside. "Why are you here? We're supposed to evacuate. It's an effing hurricane!"

"You owe me!" Heaven shrieks over the roar of the storm.

"How you figure?"

"You made the angel go away!"

"I *am* the angel, of the broken and the humiliated. Your uncle didn't tell you?"

Mercy slams shut the door, the storm pounding on it like it wants to come in too. Holds the lantern higher to fully illuminate Heaven. "Jesus, aren't you a sight."

Heaven stands there dripping little puddles on the concrete floor. She digs her hand into her soaking wet jean pocket, pulls out a plastic Jesus. "Had an angel too. Uncle Daniel likes *you* now and now my angel's gone. I want to go home! My *real* home!" she moans, then bursts into tears.

Mercy shakes her head. "You mean Maine? Look, I know your history, okay? I'm not sure your home is there, you know. I mean your folks aren't in it, right?"

Heaven stamps her foot, the slosh of her wet sneakers on the concrete. "It's there!" sticks out her chin in defiance. "You know what it's like to lose your home?"

Mercy sighs. "Yeah, as a matter of fact. I'm living in a fricken garage, after all."

"You told me my grandfather took those pictures for you. He lives in Maine too. Maybe if you take me there you could visit him. Anyway, like I said, you owe me."

"Look, I don't owe you a thing, let's get those cards off the effing table. But . . . I'm not unsympathetic to your situation. I was a castoff too."

"What's that?"

"When they don't know what to do with you, so they hand you over to someone else. Or you marry someone else, and he doesn't know what to do with you . . . but you're not there yet."

Heaven's crying harder now, it feels so hopeless. Why did they make her leave her home in the first place? Even if her parents weren't there she could take care of herself, she isn't a baby. If they knew how much she'd had to do to for her parents—even shop for food then cook it sometimes when they were too drugged, maybe they'd let her stay. Everyone hates her here, at her school for sure, but now she's *disappointed* Grandmelia again (I'm *so disappointed* in you, she said) and probably Uncle Daniel too.

Mercy shakes her head. "Okay, I'm going to ask myself later why the hell I'm doing this—am I a complete idiot? Look at you shivering and shaking like some bedraggled puppy—here." She gives Heaven a dry T-shirt, hoodie, and sweatpants, then tosses her an afghan to wrap around her shoulders. "A yard sale find, someone's mom in someone *else's* family made it."

Heaven sniffs, rubs her eyes, shivers, and pulls the blanket tight around her like a cocoon. "My mom wouldn't make this either. Some moms just aren't blanket-makers."

Mercy laughs. "Yeah, guess not. Well damn, they're forcing us to evacuate anyway, though that's not a reason for driving your ass up to Maine. I must be out of my ever-lovin' mind!"

"But we're friends, right?"

Mercy sighs. "Yeah, I suppose we are. Just don't go accusing me of stealing your angel, okay? I've been a fuckup a lot of my life, but an honest fuckup. Proud of that."

After changing into the dry clothes Heaven follows Mercy to her car, wind slamming against them, the blanket dragging over a flooded driveway. The engine starts up on the third try. Then they're sloshing through streets more river than pavement, half of them blocked off, the ocean with its fifteen-foot storm surge, waves rising like black ghosts behind them. Sirens wail from all directions. "Don't suppose you told your grandma where you are?" Mercy asks.

Heaven stares out the windshield, pretending not to hear Mercy's question, and at that moment the car is lifted up on a sudden burst of water, a roadside creek or maybe just the drain ditch overflowing. When they're set back down again, the engine, lights, radio (which was mostly static), everything at once winks out.

"Sonofabitch!" Mercy growls, bangs her fist against the steering wheel, then peers over at Heaven gone quiet. "Got a plan B?"

★ ★ ★

First they try the train, but it's not running. "Tracks flooded," the ticket man says. When Mercy asks about the Hingham commuter boat he says, "It's a hurricane, ya know? Think boats run in a hurricane?"

"No?" Mercy says. "Ya think?" stepping into the storm again, slashing rain, a wind so strong for a moment they have to grab a stranded car not to blow over. "Stay here!" Mercy commands, pushing Heaven back against the station overhang where it's out of the driving rain, though not exactly dry. "I have to figure this out. Can't see how we can get anywhere in this bullshit let alone all the way up to effing Maine. Tell me again why the hell I'm doing this?"

"I want to go home!"

"Right-on." Mercy shakes her head.

The night is black, a roar of wind, rain like a sheet of glass. No streetlights or lights anywhere except for police cars and other emergency vehicles flashing by. Heaven hangs low, pulls the hoodie over most of her face. What she didn't tell Mercy is Grandmelia's looking for her, she heard her yelling, which means by now the police are too. Though maybe they're too busy saving people. She considers walking out to Minot and watching the storm, imagines the giant waves rolling in and how if she had that surfboard she could ride them, and everyone would think she's fierce. Or she could paddle out beyond them, hang on and let the current carry her up the coast. She wouldn't need a ride, the water could bear her home.

But who is she kidding? She's not getting that board. Not until she's old enough to buy it herself, or figure out a way to snake it. And what makes her think she could surf? She's Bubble Thighs, whom everyone hates even more now for the Bethany murder thing (that's what someone yelled in the hall when she got sent to the principal, hey murder-girl!), plus pinching their shit. She's an eighth-grade geek—no, make that creep. Geeks are cool like Robyn. Geeks don't care what people think of them. She wishes she were like him, or that he'd *like* her. He isn't mean to her anyway, and a couple times he even smiled at her. She told Uncle Daniel about how when she got her surfboard, she'd paddle Robyn out and he'd think she was *dope* for being able to do that. "Robyn's my boyfriend," she told Uncle Daniel and he didn't give her that look people do, like she sprouted an extra ear.

Heaven tries to keep an eye out for Mercy but it's like she melted into the storm. Wait, what if Mercy disappeared to get the police! She'll tell Grandmelia, rat her out; why did Heaven think she'd help her? Mercy called herself the avenging angel, and then Heaven's little angel on the shelf over her bed disappears. She'll hitchhike to Maine, that's what she'll do.

Heaven fights her way through the storm out to 3A heading toward Boston, through the spanking rain, wind screaming in her ears trying to knock her over, leans into it and pushes on. When she reaches the highway, she sticks out her thumb even though she can't see if any cars are out there, wind growling like a serial killer, rain ripping across her back and shoulders; she could as easily die in this storm hitchhiking as get murdered doing it. She knows the drill, has seen the *Lifetime* specials, except when a TV girl hitchhikes it goes two ways: either a cool guy picks her up, falls in love with her, and becomes her boyfriend. Or else something really bad happens, the girl is saved in the nick of time but learns a lesson. Anyway, Robyn will never be her boyfriend because Heaven will never be able to set foot in that school again, what with the drowning song, the blood dripping down her legs and the booty they found in her locker. She's toast, as her dad used to say when it was too late for everything.

Sudden flood of headlights and a car fishtails to a stop. A woman driving, Mercy in the front seat struggling to open the door, wind slamming against it. *"You drag me out in this shit, then you fricken ditch me at the station? Jesus, you're as crazy as the rest of your family!"*

"Sorry," Heaven mumbles, climbing into the back beside an empty car seat.

"You're soaked!" the driver says as Heaven settles in, water running off the seat, onto the floor. "Sorry," Heaven repeats.

"This lady was nice enough to give me a ride to find your ass!" Mercy snarls.

"What are you doing out on a night like this? I wouldn't usually stop for y'all, but I was worried someone else would. It's not safe, hon! You folks in a car somewhere broke down?"

"I'm going home. To Maine," Heaven adds.

"You're headed into Boston, you said? We can get the bus there," Mercy says. "If the damn things are even running." She turns around and scowls at Heaven.

"I don't live far from the station. Wouldn't be out at all but the lady I clean for in Scituate kept saying oh, just stay 'til it ends. Like I don't have my own family to tend to. Likely as not someday this town's going to wash away, every storm takes more of it."

"Do you know Estelle? She cleans for my grandmother."

The woman pulls carefully back out onto the highway, glances at Heaven in the rearview mirror. "We don't come in a pack, hon. You folks hear about the flooding? Parts of 3A washed out near the coast."

Heaven shrugs. "I'm a really good swimmer. I can hold my breath under water longer than anyone."

The woman shakes her head, her hair short and springy; it barely even moves when her head does, Heaven thinks, like she has her own cloud of it above her. "I can't think how holding your breath will help much in a hurricane, hon."

★ ★ ★

The woman, Geraldine Blakely she tells them, insists on waiting with them inside the bus station. "It's not safe at this hour; gracious, can't believe your folks would approve. You take care of her or something?" she asks Mercy, looking her up and down.

"Or something," Mercy says.

"It's a surprise," Heaven says, after she buys her ticket to Rockland (no Rock Harbor stop, the ticket lady said, this bus the only one running at all!), hiding the wad of cash she pinched from Grandmelia's wallet, tucking it into the pocket of her hoodie, the one Mercy loaned her because hers was wet, now this one is too. She'll have to remember to transfer it into her backpack on the bus. "Because my mom's, like, sick."

"Well it won't be a good surprise if something happens to you. Be careful hon. It's a wounded world we live in, folks desperate. Makes them behave bad sometimes."

Heaven nods. She knows about the wounded world.

When the bus arrives, Geraldine shakes Mercy's hand, instructs them to sit in the first open seat that's closest to the driver, then asks the driver who's busy loading suitcases under the bus to watch

out for them. "Am I a kid?" Mercy mutters, "or is this crip care."
The driver nods curtly, doesn't even look up. Heaven could be
anybody and that's okay by her, because by now the police are
probably looking all over for her, maybe searching cars and busses
heading out of state, she's seen those shows as well. Geraldine hugs
her goodbye like a mother would, enfolding her in her arms; Heaven's so surprised she forgets to hug back. She imagines going home
with her, maybe they'd have a cup of hot chocolate, then Geraldine
would put her to bed in a room that's clean and warm, filled with
nice things. Or maybe not, Heaven doesn't need Geraldine's things
she can pinch her own, the storm raging outside.

Mercy tips her head back against the seat as the bus pulls out
of the station, accelerating toward 95, the slick road causing it to
shimmy wildly until its wheels take hold. The driver curses. Mercy
nods, "Yup, we'll probably break down in this fricken thing now.
You might've fooled that lady, kid, but you don't fool me. I know
where your mother is. I don't know why the hell I'm doing this."

"Maybe you can visit my grandpa. Grandmelia says he's got
some screws loose."

"Hate to break this to you, kiddo, but your grandpa is like the
effing Gandhi of sanity compared to the rest of your family."

"Sanity is overrated," says Heaven sagely, leaning against the
window.

"Wow, who made you the cynic?" Mercy shakes her head,
stares at Heaven beside her hunched into her hoodie, or rather
Mercy's hoodie. "Look," Mercy says, "I only know your situation
from what your uncle said, and I get the wanting to go home bit,
but like, you know it's not the same up there, right? Your uncle
loves the crap out of you, and while your grandma can be damn
scary sometimes, I'm sure she loves you too. So, what's the deal?"

Heaven shrugs. "I just don't want to be here anymore, school
sucks here. Nobody likes me. I want to go home!"

Mercy sighs, "Jesus. Look, I get how you feel. You've got a face
like a sleeve, wears its hurt. I know about hurt. But for me, I just
get mad. Really, really mad."

"What, like you break stuff?"

"Pretty much. Broken beyond repair."

The driver announces the hurricane's been downgraded to a nor'easter, but there's still a lot of wind, rain, and flooding, so they should plan on a longer arrival time and should keep the noise down so he can concentrate on the driving conditions, which are *bad*, he emphasizes. "You're lucky they didn't cancel the route," he says. "Or unlucky if we don't make it!"

"Ha ha," Mercy says, "a funny guy. Okay girl," she nudges Heaven, "wake me when it's over." She closes her eyes.

The ride is long and the bus overheated, which Heaven is okay with since it dried out the clothes Mercy gave her to wear, even the bills in her pocket she forgot to transfer. She fingers them now, the lights of the Piscataqua Bridge glowing, New Hampshire into Maine. Home, she goes in her head, tries to think of a good image for it, home, *home*, but what comes back is her dad's OD. Which she's tried *not* to think about, but when she's thinking about *not* thinking about it, bam, that's when it wails in. It was like he fell asleep on the living room floor, arms splayed, like a crucifixion picture she saw where Jesus even looked like her dad, her dad's long hair and his beard, sunken face, his wrecked, skinny body. Her mom's slapping his cheeks, screaming at him, *Wake up! Wake up!* Call 911! she shrieked to one of the others in the house, Heaven can't recall who, a blur of faces, never knew who'd be on their couch when she came home from school. Heaven was hiding under the counter separating the kitchen from the living room; she was supposed to be asleep in her parents' room, but no one noticed her much anyway.

"Do you get what's happening here?" her mom screamed to some woman. "He's shutting down! That's what happens in a smack OD, you stupid cow, his body is dying in front of us." The woman was wailing and crying, Heaven's mom slapping her dad's face, blowing air into his mouth, *Wake up! Wake up!* until the ambulance came, and everyone scattered. Heaven alone in the kitchen where she stayed the whole night, curled up under the counter until it was time to get ready for school. It's not that she liked school, just that her name on the register meant she belonged there. "Home,"

Heaven whispers, wiping tears from her eyes. She rests the side of her face against the cold window and sleeps.

Hours later they're at the bus stop outside the Rockland Ferry Terminal, last ones off the bus. The terminal is closed, not even a dry bench to sit on to get out of the rain, softer now, almost a mist. The tide is high, dark water covers the rocks, slapping against the dock where Mercy and Heaven sit cross-legged, staring out. It's an hour before dawn, cold enough to see her breath, and she remembers how to walk to her house from here, the next town over, but who would be there to open the door? Would anyone even know Heaven lived there? Tears run down her face as the rain, suddenly harder, pelts against it.

"It's okay kid," Mercy says. "We've come this far, for chrissake. Why cry now?"

Heaven sniffles, how does she even say it? *What happens when everyone is gone?* Staring out into the harbor she knows where the breakwater would be though she can't see it in the darkness, no moon or stars, only this stinging rain. Somewhere out there her dad drowned. They think because no one told her about it that she doesn't know her mom's accused of hitting her dad on his head with a board, making him fall into the water. What universe do they think she lives in? One where you don't hear people talking or you don't google stuff in the computer lab? But remembering how her mom needed her dad to live after the OD, *Wake up! Wake up!* Heaven knows it can't be true. Not on purpose, anyway. Maybe she was holding the board and it slipped? Or her dad fell on it, hit his head, and they blamed her mom because who else was there to blame?

"How about we see if we can find anything open, grab a cup of something hot. Get out of this effing rain."

"My dad drowned," Heaven says.

Mercy nods. "I never knew mine. Checked out before I could even sit up."

"Was yours murdered?"

Mercy laughs. "To hear my mom tell it, someone should've! He figured I was defective, a handicap girl, because of my little leg. Didn't want to deal with it so he booked. Some parents are just fucked-up, you know? Maybe they don't know the difference between decent and fucked-up. That's why I've decided I don't want to be one. How could I know I'd be any good at it?"

Heaven slips off a shoe, dangles her foot in the water off the dock, feels the sting of its coldness, imagines her dad sinking under this freezing black water and her mom screaming after him, *Wake up! Wake up!* He'd hear her voice calling him back, feel that water like a blade, so cold like it's knifing him, but he keeps sinking under the weight of it, she couldn't save him this time, he's going down in all that blackness and he'd be so scared! More alone and scared than even Heaven's been.

"I want my mom!" Heaven cries.

Mercy puts her arms around Heaven, tentative at first like she's afraid the girl will resist, then tighter into a hug. "How about we get out of here." As they stand up a sudden noise in the water below like a hard slap, a swivel, then a dark shape surfaces. "Hey, what the eff?" Mercy says. "Shit, is that like a shark or something?"

Heaven stares into the water and it's staring at her. She sucks in her breath, leans over the edge of the dock but Mercy tugs her back. "What the hell, kid! You looking to be next or something?"

"It's a seal!" Heaven says. "Oh wow, Uncle Daniel's right! Look at her eyes!

"How can you see eyes, for chrissake, it's too dark."

Heaven shakes her head. "Look, you can totally see. They're shiny. You know why? They're blue, that's how come. Blue-green like mine and Grandmelia's, Uncle Daniel, my dad too."

"Seals don't have blue eyes," Mercy grunts. "What, you're saying your cousin is a pinniped? Most kids your age would claim a celeb as family, Beyoncé, or maybe in your case Miley Cyrus, a white girl like that. It's an illusion. Some light somewhere is shining into them, or who the hell knows. Come on kid, put your shoe back on, let's ditch this place. You got me into this. I'm not hanging around with some freaky-eyed seal in the fricken rain."

★ ★ ★

By the time they get to the prison it's early morning, misty and damp. Heaven's hungry, cold, tired, and her feet hurt so bad from the long walk she could scream. She knows they won't open the entry gate for her, no one *wants* to live inside those brick walls, but they won't let you *get* inside either, even if you want to, without the permission set up in advance Grandmelia goes through each time before coming here. They're probably being watched from the watchtowers, either side of the roof—Grandmelia pointed out the guards inside them the first time she brought Heaven, plus radar, motion detectors, security cameras, the works. You couldn't steal from this place even if there was something worth pinching. You can't get in to try.

Mercy leans against a scraggly parking lot tree, snags a smoke from her sister's pack she *forgot* to return, she said, lights it, and lifts her face toward the sky like there's sun in the dank gray, something warm up there. "I'll hang here. Do what you got to do."

Heaven walks further up the driveway staring at the huge building, like ten Lawson Towers crammed together, only Bethany won't be letting her long blond hair down from it, or anywhere; Principal Keagan told Heaven she'd cut it all off. "Aren't you ashamed of yourself?" Keagan said. "She was scared of getting it caught in the drain, of someone doing what she says you tried to do." Heaven wishes again she'd just cut it off in the first place, sitting behind Bethany in that math class, snip snip.

She sees movement in a barred window two stories above, then a hand presses against the thick glass; she can just make out the shape of fingers through the bars. She can't see whose hand it is but shouts anyway just in case. "Mom? Mom?" Then she's crying, "Mom! Mom!" The hand in that window smacks against the glass. Heaven can't hear it, but she sees it, sees that the hand sees her. *"Mom! Wake up, Mom!"* Two guards, a woman and a man come running out, the gate swinging open, then clanging shut behind them. They grab Heaven under her arms on either side and half lift, half drag her away from the building, screaming, "Mom! Wake up, Mom! Wake up! Please Mom, wake up!"

"What the hell is this?" Mercy yells. "Let her the fuck go!" She tosses her cigarette still lit on the pavement and hurtles toward them.

"Get away lady or you'll be in big trouble," the male guard growls.

Heaven's still screaming, "Mom! Mom!" Mercy tries to grab her, but the female officer pushes her back, calls for reinforcements.

"Fuck you, cunt!" Mercy shrieks.

Immediately a team of beige uniforms pours out of the prison, clang goes the gate; they grab Mercy who's kicking, yelling, swearing, batting them off, more kicking, punching, shrieking, and Heaven pauses her own wailing to watch. Holy crap, she's never seen anyone go ballistic like that in real life that's not on TV. Her dad didn't get mad, just *snide*, her mom said, and her mom usually sulked or stomped off somewhere. Heaven feels honored and a little in awe that Mercy's doing this to help her.

The officers force Mercy down on the ground into a chokehold then slap handcuffs on her, but it took eight of them to do it, Heaven counted. "You're under arrest," the female guard says, panting, then adds, "and for resisting arrest too!"

"Whore!" Mercy hisses when they release her neck. "Fuck all of you bunch of low-life, institutional robots. Kid wants to see her mom! You pigs don't have mothers?"

Which reminds Heaven, who starts wailing again, *"Wake up, Mom!"* Please, please wake up.

✦ AMELIA ✦

WHEN AMELIA WALKS INTO the social worker's office, third floor of an old Victorian mansion turned Department of Health and Human Services, Heaven's sucking on a lollypop. Amelia feels a wash of anger and relief. Exhausted from the all-night search, then unanticipated drive to fetch her granddaughter, but watching Heaven work that lollypop, her tongue stained red in its wake, she's aware how much of a child her granddaughter still is.

Peggy Howell shakes her hand. "Amelia. Please have a seat."

Amelia glances at her options: two cane chairs with pillow-top seats facing Peggy Howell's desk, Heaven in one of them. She sits in the other, then looks over at her granddaughter who isn't meeting her eyes. "You do realize how foolish and dangerous what you did is? Your uncle and I were beside ourselves when we couldn't find you. I reported it to the police. In a hurricane, for lord's sake! Were you out of your mind? Do we need to put you on lockdown like your mother?"

Peggy Howell sticks up her hand. "Just a second, Amelia, let's take a time out. Heaven has something she'd like to say to you," her syrupy voice.

They both peer at the girl who pulls the lollypop out of her mouth, gazes at it in her hand, then finally meets Amelia's eyes. "I'm sorry," she says.

"And?" Peggy Howell coaches.

"And I want to come home with you," Heaven says.

"Well of course you'll come home!" Amelia snaps. "Where else would you go? You're lucky we have a home to go to! The basement took on five feet of water, but the rest seems okay—your kidnapper's garage didn't fare so well."

"She didn't kidnap me. I asked her to. Who would kidnap me?"

"Good point," Amelia says.

"It's not that simple." Peggy Howell wags her finger at Amelia. "The state can keep her legally, you have court-assigned temporary custody. When something happens that makes such an arrangement not beneficial to the child she goes into foster care until a suitable situation can be worked out."

"That's ridiculous!" Amelia explodes. "*Suitable* situation? Her mother's sentence is fifteen years. Heaven will be through college, maybe even married by the time that woman gets out. What's not beneficial? I'm her grandmother! She has a home with her uncle and me. We are her family."

Peggy Howell nods. "Yes, good, Heaven also said this. She understands now that she ran away from home, whereas she had convinced herself before when she did what she did that she was *going* home. Do you see?"

Amelia rubs her temples where a headache threatens. The room is stuffy, typical overheated state building that charges the taxpayers for petty bureaucrats' comfort. *Did what she did.* These linguistically challenged psychology types! The girl has begun sucking on her lollypop again, but with less enthusiasm. "Heaven, your home is with us. I'm sorry . . . if that wasn't completely clear before."

"Good," Peggy Howell says, "good good good. And Heaven has agreed that on the condition she be *allowed* to go home with you, she will go to counseling again, this time making a serious effort. I think we need to plan some sessions that include you as well, some family counseling.

"What is it with you people? Every time the slightest thing goes off you send us to *counseling*. Are there no other options?"

"Do you have a suggestion?"

Amelia sighs, looks over at Heaven who's working the lollypop again. "I suppose not."

"Well then. What about her uncle? It's best to have the whole family involved."

"He doesn't go outside," Amelia says.

"Not ever?"

"Never."

Peggy Howell looks puzzled, frowns. "I don't believe I have that in my records. I'll have to update them. Well, another thing we need to consider is enrolling Heaven in a different school. Her present situation is causing her a considerable amount of anxiety. It appears she was being bullied and her behavior, in part, was in response to that."

"You think?" Amelia snaps.

Suddenly the girl tosses her lollypop into the rubbish can beside the desk, shoots out of her chair and runs into Amelia's arms, which are barely open wide enough to receive her. Sharp intake of breath as Amelia leans back in her chair to bear the weight of her granddaughter, who's climbed onto her lap now, sobbing. "I'm sorry!" she gulps, hiccups. "I'm really sorry, Grandmelia, I didn't mean to make you mad or worry you or anything. I just miss my mom and dad so much!"

Amelia slides her hand down Heaven's spine, awkwardly at first likes she's petting a cat, but then she gathers her into her arms, sagging a little under the girl's heft. "I know you do. I don't hold you entirely responsible. A certain neighbor of ours, who should've known better, was your accessory and is in jail now as a result."

Heaven wipes her eyes, slips off Amelia's lap and stands staring at her, then Peggy Howell, then back to Amelia. "Mercy's in jail?"

"Disturbing the peace, assaulting an officer, abusive language, resisting arrest, pick your poison. She's one certifiably angry person. There's a bail, which I have no intention of paying."

"She was protecting me," Heaven sniffles.

Amelia scowls. "I hardly think helping a child run away in a hurricane across state lines is protecting you."

"She had my back," Heaven says softly. "That means when someone's watching out for you."

Amelia sighs. "I know what it means, Heaven. I'm the one who does that for you from now on, okay? State of Maine decreed. Ask your caseworker here. But don't worry, your grandfather will probably bail your friend out of jail, if she thinks to call him. And if he answers his phone. He's a veritable *bank* for the criminally inclined."

★ ★ ★

After slogging through a number of documents (legalese bullpucky and Amelia wondered briefly if she should call Bub before signing, but she was too anxious to get Heaven out of there), it was dark when they were finally on their way. While Heaven's in the restroom at a Main Street gas station ("Why on earth didn't you go at the Department of Health and Human Services?" Amelia couldn't resist. "Taxpayers pay for *those* bathrooms to be kept clean"), Amelia calls Leo in Augusta and asks if they can spend the night. As usual she has to hang up and ring two more times before he finally picks up. "Good lord, Leo, it's nighttime, your spy drones are asleep! It's either you or a hotel, and I suspect you're closer than any I'd want to stay at. I'm too exhausted for that long drive back home tonight."

"Why sure thing, Amelia, it's been an awfully long time since you asked to spend the night with me."

"Oh for God's sake I'm worried about the child. I'd rather not have her in a strange hotel, do you realize they almost kept her, a ward of this bloody state? I'm not going to sleep with you. The couch will do just fine."

"Pity," he says. "Come along, I'll see if I can scrounge us up some dinner."

"Something healthy and low-fat for Heaven, please. She's been eating lollypops and god knows what else for the last twenty-four hours. Did you hear from your paramour in jail?"

She can hear him chuckling. "Paramour? Why you flatter me, Amelia. She's out. On a Boston-bound bus."

"That was fast."

"Did you know you can pay bail on a Visa card these days?"

"You can have a funeral on Visa, old man."

The ride up Route 17 is dark and empty, the twisting road, a waning almost full moon coating the spines of hills on either side, the occasional lake or pond paling in its wake. About halfway to Augusta Amelia looks over and sees Heaven hunched into herself, her shoulders shaking. She inches her arm over, close enough for the child to recognize she's there, but not quite touching.

"Why do people have to die?" Heaven sniffs, rubbing her eyes.

"Well, for one, we wouldn't want everyone else's people to live forever, would we? We want our own folks with us but what would it be like to have Hitler still in the world, for instance?"

"Or if Bethany Harrison lived forever," Heaven adds.

"I suppose, so it's only fair that everyone, good or bad, has to eventually die."

Why did Uncle Daniel lie to me about the surfboard? I asked him and he kept saying he didn't, but he did."

"I tried to tell you before. He just wants to be loved."

"I'd love him even if he gave me nothing."

"Well you're in luck then," Amelia laughs. She gives Heaven's hand a quick squeeze, warm and a little sticky, and something seizes inside Amelia's chest. *Flesh of my flesh . . .* "Your dad was the opposite. We gave him everything and it wasn't enough."

"I gave my dad a dead butterfly once for his birthday, put it in a box with cotton under it to protect its wings from breaking off. A monarch, they're the coolest. Monarch means king and queen of butterflies. It looked perfect, like if only it was alive it would fly. My dad said Monarchs are endangered because idiot humans want weed-free lawns, so they put chemicals on their grass that kills milkweed, the monarchs' food source."

"Well how about that, my son the environmentalist."

Heaven nods. "I'm going to tell Uncle Daniel I don't want any more bad stories. Selkies are okay, maybe not sirens, though I think sirens are *kind* of cool, but no evil faeries and killer kelpies. I'll tell him a story about a girl who swims all the way to Maine using her superpower breaststroke. Who needs a surfboard when you swim good?"

"Well," Amelia says. "Swim well."

⋆ AMELIA ⋆

S HE SEES LEO WATCHING from his front window as they pull up to the duplex. Across Water Street the Kennebec ripples and shines like a sheet of tinfoil in the moonlight, as if in the daylight it had a shot of being scenic in *this* neighborhood, where abandoned, boarded-up factory buildings and other failed businesses have yet to be turned into condos for "revitalization." When that happens her ex will be out of here, gentrification with its three-thousand-dollars-a-month artist lofts that real artists could never afford, Starbucks, Trader Joe's, galleries, and art theaters. None of that would hold any interest for Leo. But where will he go? Life sheds people who can't adapt like they're dead skin cells. His dad used to work for Edwards, textiles, mostly *Canucks* in their neighborhood, Leo said, employed by the factory until it burned down. Then there was nothing.

Amelia climbs out of the car, then Heaven, who looks a little stunned. Amelia peers around as if to find her bearings, but she knows where she is, she always knows where she is, even when she doesn't. Leo used to tell her he admired that confidence, a way of putting her feet down in the world and claiming it, he said. Amelia and Heaven start up the stairs. The porch light is out, and Leo opens the door so his hallway light will illuminate the entrance.

Amelia shakes her head. "So, this is where you've been hiding. You've heard about Thomas Edison and the invention of the lightbulb?"

He grins. "Keep forgetting that one. You know my folks' building, you were in it."

"A lifetime ago, they were still in it too."

"Hello again," Leo says to Heaven. "I hear you had quite the adventure."

Amelia glares at him but Heaven nods. "I got soaked."

"Right, well have you dried out by now? I've got some dinner. Hope you like spaghetti and meatballs."

"Oh lord Leo, you still eating red meat? You know your doctor told you to watch your cholesterol."

Leo winks at Heaven. "Told me to watch my sugar too, so for dessert we have ice-cream sundaes. Can't properly watch something unless it's sitting in front of you, right?" Heaven grins.

★   ★   ★

After dinner Heaven asks to watch TV and Leo tells her he only gets three stations. "It's a pretty old set," he says, wiggling the ancient rabbit ears. "These are more for decoration, but it's an analog signal."

"And she knows what analog is," Amelia says.

"I do," Heaven says, settling in on the couch, "it's like the old way to run stuff." Hyperactive blond hosts of *Entertainment Tonight* burble trivial celebrity minutia. What a despicable culture we've become, Amelia thinks, no wonder Leo felt no need for a *real* TV. Heaven pulls the comforter Leo placed there over her and within minutes she's asleep. Leo turns the drivel off, pours two more glasses of Pinot Noir, and they sit in the overstuffed chairs near the window, other side of the room, the moon winking in and out of clouds over the dark snake of the river.

"Looks like she's down for the count," Leo says, Heaven snoring softly.

"Yes, an overfed, exhausted child. Two sundaes, Leo, honestly. You wonder why she snores; kids aren't supposed to snore if they're fit. I bet that was supposed to be my bed, huh? Was this your plan? No guest room and just your own bed left?"

Leo grins. "I said you could spend the night. I didn't invite you to sleep with me."

Amelia takes another gulp of the Pinot Noir. "I might've said yes, old man, you never know, ply me with enough of this wine."

"Right, and since when have you wanted to have sex, starting oh, forty years ago, give or take? At least not with me, anyway."

"Leo," she leans forward closer to him, imagines him inhaling a breath of her perfume, same musky jasmine scent she's worn all these years. "We didn't promise each other monogamy, remember? We eighty-sixed *faithful* along with honor and obey right out of the ceremony. It was 1968. Who believed in monogamy? We never even imagined ourselves past forty and here we are."

"I thought we were in love."

Amelia shakes her head. "I don't think what brings two people to marriage has much to do with love. I think it has to do with the abyss, facing the fear of dying, not wanting to do it alone. Of course, when you're young you can't know this; it's more a sub-conscious thing, but maybe that's what drives us to the altar, the subliminal hope that this is the person who will be there with you at the end."

"Kind of deep thinking there, milady. Got a copy of Nietzsche or Camus in your purse? You usually just insult me and we're good to go."

He'd probably expected her to at least crack a grin, retort back, but her eyes tear up. "It's just . . . I felt something for her in that school principal's office, everyone dug in around the table like an inquisition, all dead set against her; she'd been condemned to hang by the time I walked into that room. And Heaven's sitting there, those round shoulders held straight up under bad vibes so overt if their eyes were scissors, they'd have cut her to shreds; she's just staring into space. She needed me, Leo. Not to protect her, she's shown herself pretty capable of that, but to be her advocate. Of course I yelled at her, made her stay in her room all day; it was a damn stupid thing she did, plus all the stealing! I mean my lord what is up with that? You have to tell her what's what, right? Then the child takes off, assisted by that garage girl, to bloody Maine in a hurricane. Scared the bejesus out of me and I'm mad as hell, but God that took some guts. She's a fighter, Leo. I have to respect that. Goes about it all wrong, but what chance did she have? How could Gavin have ever thought he could do it, raise a child when he never stopped being one himself?"

They both look across the room at Heaven, a lump under the plaid comforter, clumps of her stringy hair flung across the couch pillow like a mop.

Amelia sighs. "I might be too old to be a mom again. Took to it like a fish out of water before."

"Heaven has a mom. Be her grandma."

She sniffs, wipes under her eyes. "I don't exactly like the sound of that one either. Like one of Daniel's old witches or crones."

"So why name it? Just be the person she's safe with."

"Is she? I raised a drug addict and an agoraphobic who believes in faeries."

Leo shrugs. "Faeries are pretty harmless."

"You haven't been introduced to our son's, apparently! They've got attitude and a bad temper when things don't go their way. They can wreak all sorts of havoc, then disappear in the blink of an eye."

Leo laughs. "Sounds pretty close to home, Amelia. You haven't sprouted wings by chance, have you?"

"Ha ha, very funny." She holds out her empty wine glass and Leo divides the rest of the bottle between them. "You're not going to bug out on me, are you, old man? Wander out of this place and never find your way back?"

He grins. "If I do, I won't remember. We let him down you know, Amelia. We weren't there for him. It was always Gavin demanding the attention so that's where attention went. I think Daniel sort of fell through the cracks."

"Yeah, to another world! Look, I know when you say *we* you're really saying it's me. But I have to live with him for the rest of my life, isn't that penance enough?"

"You've got a point. Guess he puts a crimp in your swinging lifestyle?"

"Oh sure, everyone wants to make it with the seventy-year-old chick! You know what though? Daniel actually tried to go out with me and look for Heaven. Tried so hard he broke out in a sweat, started gasping for air speaking of fish out of water, soon as his feet left the front porch and I told him to go back to his room. Even though it was a mandatory evacuation, I think he figured he had a better shot with the ocean. Just out of curiosity, you didn't really react when I said that thing earlier about sleeping with you. Not that I'm saying I would. You teased me, that's all."

"Right, your vanity eating at you, my dear? You were never someone anyone could say no to."

"Why would they?"

"Uh-huh! Well try this. That was a shitty thing you did, Amelia, and you know what I mean so don't give me that look. I know you never liked talking about it, but we're here now, Heaven's clearly going nowhere anytime soon, and this is something I've always wondered: Would you have ever told me if you weren't forced to by circumstance?"

She stares out the window, the river, a swath of moonlight cutting over it like a scythe. "Circumstance, as in you wouldn't have bought an immaculate conception? I'd like to think I would. Anyway, Gavin was your son in the ways that count, just not your genetics. He *was* beautiful though.

"He looked like you, but you have grit, a spine. His beauty was fragile, maybe from the get-go it wasn't built to last."

She shakes her head. "You sound like a car commercial. Still, you were a decent father to them both. Even when you didn't live with us you were the one they went to."

"I gave Gavin money, remember? You said you'd never forgive me for that."

"No one could save him. I'm getting that now or admitting it maybe. I've decided to give up on the thing with his wife, my heart isn't in it anymore. I think she's guilty as hell, but what's the use? If she can't recognize her culpability, what are we going to get out of it? Plus . . . I don't think it was intentional. Getting to know her a bit, I don't see it in her, that she could be that evil. I don't want to believe Gavin would love someone who could. I phoned Bub on the way to Maine, asked if it was too late to drop some of the charges from her trial. He said I should forget that boondoggle, his word, and that if she stays clean she'll likely get her parole when it comes up. Which won't be for quite a while, thank God, I still think she should serve most of her time. Maybe that's punitive, but two of them went out that night and one came back, wrong one far as I'm concerned. I guess we'll never know the truth of how it happened."

"If there is one truth."

Amelia nods, tearing up again. "I'm tired, Leo. I didn't expect things would turn out this way, did you? A dead son, an emotionally crippled one, and now I'm raising a kleptomaniac granddaughter who may have tried to drown a bully, and who probably has all kinds of other wounds I haven't seen yet. This growing old. You figure on the aching joints, the faded looks, hope for some wisdom, but I didn't expect the heartbreak. I'm just bone-tired." Amelia stands up, staggers, and Leo jumps out of his chair, cursing the pain in his knees and grabs her, steadies her, then lets her go. "I don't want to die, Leo."

He picks up their empty glasses, stares into them, then at her face. Amelia pictures the way she'd look to Leo now. The lines around her eyes and on her chin like someone had etched these in, but still her graceful neck, at least—heron he used to call her, her intricately structured face and body, gaunter now, a lattice of brittle bones. She remembers when he told her how he'd *really* felt, during that frantic ride from LAX to the studio for their first major gig together, after the late flight from LaGuardia, a six-hour plane ride. How sitting so close to her, her scent, even the touch of their elbows on the armrest caused a buzzing in his ears. She'd thought he was nervous because they were late, but it was her, it's always been her, Leo said. Even in the years of their anger, hurt, a despair so vast he could barely look at her, there was no one else. She'd felt conflicted when he said it. There'd been times during their marriage when she actually *wished* he'd have an affair, so she wouldn't have to bear the weight of her own deceit alone. And yet, while she's unlikely to confess this to him, in the years that have passed since their marriage ended, she never found anyone either. Not that she looked very hard; it just didn't happen.

"You won't die," Leo says now, putting their glasses back down and grabbing her elbow to steady her again. "You're too stubborn. But if you do, you'll make it look so great everyone will want to do it. Remember the throngs you had buying eggs? The most tasteless, boring, gross food on this planet, fertilized you're chowing on zygotes." He wraps his arms around her, pulling her against his chest.

"Careful old man," Amelia says, but she doesn't resist.

"Don't you know?" he breathes into her hair. "Everyone will want to go to heaven if Amelia gets there first."

◆ DANIEL ◆

DANIEL HEARS THEM PULL into the garage, a moonlit dark and the wind off the ocean has picked up, the tide moving in. His lights are off so he can stare outside his window at the waning moon, three nights past full but still aglow. It seems particularly bright this month, casting its light down on the storm devastation in their neighborhood. Nobody says a word when they pass his door. Maybe they think he's asleep already? He left his room again today, after Amelia called and said they were spending the day in Augusta. Broke into a clammy sweat firing up the generator outside the garage so they'd have electricity (Amelia bought gas for it before she left for Maine, made a point of telling him that), then crept down to the basement to run the pump. Pumped out almost five feet of saltwater and began the slow process of cleaning up all the sand and debris. He won't tell his mother. She'll discover it eventually and want him to continue. The neighborhood is closed off to local traffic only, and Daniel could see through the windows that their house fared better than most, including Mercy's. Storm damage is arbitrary, Amelia will say, and he'll say maybe not.

He hears Heaven's door shut. She doesn't knock on the wall or even yell goodnight to him, probably still mad about the surfboard. He'll set his sights a bit lower next time, a skateboard maybe? He knows she's okay. "We almost lost her to the state of Maine," Amelia said when she called, "but she wants to come home."

He hears his mother go into her bedroom on the other side of his and he imagines her rummaging around in her closet. She doesn't know that he knows what's on the shelf in the very back. She does this at night sometimes, particularly after her trips to Maine, closes her door and he can tell by the quiet in her room what she's doing, then the sobs she can't quite stifle.

Daniel did it too once, when Amelia was somewhere else, more out of curiosity than grief. Geared himself up for the short venture out of his room, counted the steps, eleven to her door, something that felt necessary, holding, touching, smoothing over and smelling the clothes his brother drowned in. Forensic kept them until after the trial, and Daniel guessed since Gavin's wife was convicted and incarcerated, they wouldn't go to her. Heaven was a minor, so the police (or court? he wasn't sure how these things worked) sent them to Amelia along with the wallet that had been in his jean pocket.

He'd pressed the denim jacket, flannel shirt, even the jeans to his face and inhaled, thinking he could still smell it, the ocean that claimed his brother. Though it didn't seem likely after months spent in Forensic, tested for fingerprints, DNA, and all matter of body fluids—there are what appear to be faint bloodstains around the collar of the shirt—then zipped into a plastic bag. He imagined his mother doing this, trying to pick up the scent of Gavin, and since neither of them had seen let alone *smelled* Gavin in well over a decade, Daniel wasn't sure what Amelia was hoping to find in his clothes.

He pictures her doing it now, rifling through the wallet: three saltwater-pocked dollar bills, a debit card, maxed out and no doubt closed at this point, scraps of paper with traces of phone numbers, addresses, pretty much erased by the sea, a saltwater blemished photo of Gavin's wife and Heaven as a toddler, you can still see them smiling like they do in wallet photos, and a Maine driver's license. Did he even have a car? It seemed they were living on the edge of a cliff, saved from the fall by Leo. Until they weren't.

Daniel imagines Amelia staring at the photo on the license, what you can see of it from the water damage. He knows Gavin called her a few times over the years, her birthday when he remembered, but less and less as he became more drug addicted. He never visited, never invited Amelia to visit after the wedding invitation decline, and Daniel pictures Amelia sitting on her bed, tracing her thumb over that face staring out from the grainy, destroyed photo, trying to reconstruct Gavin's life from it. Those lost years. It occurs to Daniel that *this* was Amelia's heartbreak, her son's deliberate desertion. Gavin's death only made it unredeemable.

Then he hears the splash.

✦ AMELIA ✦

SHE HAD PUT HIS clothes on, the jeans which fit surprisingly snug—her son must've shrunk more than just brain cells with all that dope—his shirt, then the jacket and headed out to the pool, itself drowning in a saltwater mess from the storm tide. She didn't turn on the outside lights; power lines were still down throughout the town, and while clearly Daniel slunk out of his room to fire up their generator, she isn't sure how long its power will last. Anyway, it would've been dark when Gavin went in and she wants to mimic his ending as close as possible, except for the obvious—hers is a chlorinated pool and her son drowned in the ocean, with a blow to the head. She needs to do this, feel what he felt, his final moments. Would the clothes have held him down? The heavy cotton in the denim jacket becoming water-logged, keeping him under like a weight vest, or perhaps the cloth buffer between his skin and the water might've buoyed him for a few more seconds of air before the descent. And of course, his shoes, which they did not return, maybe they were lost before his body was recovered. Amelia had put on a pair of ankle-high leather boots figuring he'd either have worn Doc Martens or athletic shoes, the only shoes he wore as a teenager, and this the closest compromise she owns. That the pool will destroy her Italian leather boots makes the whole excursion more appealing, a penance of sorts. She jumped in and immediately sank to the bottom.

Now she tries to imagine his fear, her fear, opening his mouth, her mouth and the water rushing in. Would he have been able to kick his legs, her legs, the shoes, pants, his head throbbing from the whack with the board, the weight of dark water as he goes down? Opens her eyes to the sting of chlorine and the mess from the storm, that fierce ache, the need to breathe, fighting to stay down at the bottom as her body begins its instinctive rise upward toward breath. Then a light shines over her and it's all wrong, unless this is salvation and she too has drowned?

Her feet push off the bottom as a hand yanks her up. Breaking surface she gasps for air, want so thick in her throat it feels solid, something sustaining that he wouldn't have had—this right here is the difference and she gulps it in again and again. "I can't do it," she tells Daniel when she's able to speak; he's pulled her out of the pool and she sits dripping beside him on the patio tile, chest thrust out to breathe, breathe, "my body won't let me. I can't drown."

"Jesus Christ! Why would you?"

She shakes her head, leaning to one side to let the water trickle out of one ear, then the other, twisting her hair, wringing it out like a dishcloth. "I wanted to feel what he felt, if he was scared, if he had time to think at all. Thought I could at least know this. I've given up on everything else."

"He probably didn't feel a thing, if he was even conscious after the crack on his head and all those drugs. Maybe it was like a big wet blanket covering him and he just fell asleep."

"I used to do that, didn't I? Cover you? Tuck you boys in when you were small?" Amelia is quietly weeping, and Daniel lets her lean against him. "You came out of your room again," she whimpers.

"Yeah, special occasion, my mother tried to drown herself. Lucky I heard you or you might've found out more than you'd ever want to know about drowning. Hope you appreciate it, because every cell in my body's shrieking to be back in my room." He starts to shake, for emphasis she figures.

"I wasn't trying to drown as in *die*. I'm not the suicide type. I just wanted to get a sense of it, how he felt. But my body wouldn't even let me go *that* far. It flat-out refused to even fake-drown. I must not be a true MacQueen."

"You're just nuts. I thought *I* was the resident cuckoo."

Amelia pats his leg. "Your title is safe, son. By the way, I saw that big owl the morning after the hurricane, perched on our roof again, just sitting there. Isn't that supposed to be some sort of omen, seeing an owl in the daylight?"

"What owl?"

"The one that's been coming around here. You haven't seen it? I thought you were supposed to be the authority on strange things."

He laughs. "Amelia, far as I know an owl isn't strange. It's a predator bird with amazing eyes. Ever seen their eyes up close? Almost human-looking. Those *strange* birds, as you say, have eyes with emotional depth, like they can peer into your soul."

"When do you ever see an owl up close?"

He laughs again, having quite the joke at her expense, Amelia thinks. "I was just messing with you, Mother dear. It perched on a bush outside my window this morning, until Farley saw it too. Pounced at the glass like he figured it was air and he could leap through it. The owl just stared like Farley was an idiot, then took off. It's a portent."

"That something bad will happen?"

Daniel shakes his head. "Nope. That something bad already happened, humans encroaching on wildlife habitat, clearing trees to build gigantic homes, paving the forest, poisoning fields for crops so wildlife has no choice but to be in our yards, on our roofs. With global warming these too could be history. Humans are the planet's bad news."

Amelia sighs. "The male Cassandra who lives in his room. But you came out, for me." The wind has picked up again and the salt scent of the sea mingles into the chlorine odor off her body and hair, and now Gavin's clothes, the last he'll ever wear will smell of their pool. "Do you think he thought of me at all . . . in the end?"

Daniel shrugs. "Maybe. You know what they say about your life flashing before your eyes. Pick a good memory with him, maybe it's the one."

"How am I supposed to do that?"

"Just remember. I'm guessing you had some wine before you did this crazy thing. I'm hoping you wouldn't just leap into your storm-contaminated pool in Gavin's clothes sober. Relax. See what comes up. Be quick though as I'm close to losing whatever resolve made me able to come out here and save your ass."

Amelia gazes at the moon, about to slip out of view behind a thick cloud. She closes her eyes and tries to picture the face that's stared out of his driver's license, the times she's looked at it since they sent his clothes to her. Gavin grown up, husband, father, drug addict. Her lost son.

What comes back is his childhood, all of theirs really, before their lives were fractured so irreparably after Daniel's accident and Amelia and Leo's divorce. There had been cracks, of course, how not after her infidelity? Not that she's apologizing, more like acknowledging . . . it took its toll. Leo had been a "nice guy" back when that had become a little boring. First, she loved him for not seeming smitten by her looks, for seeing something *else* in her, then punished him for that same nonchalance. In this memory there's none of that. Daniel's ten and Gavin six, two years before the near-drowning and they've all accompanied Leo to the South Carolina Lowcountry where he has an industry shoot for a seafood company. "We'll make it a family vacation," he said. He'd rented a beach house on Hunting Island, but it's the tidal marshes that entrance the boys.

The memory isn't particularly unique, Amelia thinks, other than she can count their "family vacations" on two fingers, and she has to stop herself from editing it, as if Daniel had tasked her to find "the" memory and what if this isn't the one? But there it is, she and Leo sitting on the wooden dock, dangling their bare feet over the edge. The tide is out and below them there's no water at all, just long marsh grasses waving from mud that's caked and speckled with crab holes, their kids scampering about trying to catch the crabs as they peek out of their holes, antennae waving, eyes staring up from their stalks. Daniel manages to trap one with his red fishing net and they both peer over the rim of the net staring at it, before dumping it into their bucket. When they're ready to leave it will be Daniel who insists on letting the crab go, "so it can live" he'll tell Gavin.

Meanwhile the sun beats down and she can hear cicadas chattering from the honey locust and palmetto palm trees that line the marsh. Overhead a brigade of pelicans head to the shore, and from somewhere chirps and whistles, the shrill cry of an osprey. Leo is humming some tune, and she lifts her face toward the sun, eyes shut, and when she lowers it and stares out at her sons it's as if they've been illuminated, their shirtless bodies, the concaves of their chests, their tan shoulders hunched and glowing in the sunlight as they peer down into the bucket. A small tableau to a vision of peace they didn't get enough of, and Amelia, for the moment, revels in it.

CODA

FOUR MONTHS LATER

◆ DANIEL ◆

A KNOCK ON HIS WINDOW. Peers out into the darkness as if he doesn't know who it is, as if she isn't partially illuminated in the reach of the motion-sensor light, as if there were anyone else in the world. Slides the window open partway, then turns the flashlight on her face. Her eyes look hawkish, not repentant at all. "You mad at me?" she says.

"Disappointed. You're proof angels aren't real, not the ones on land anyway."

"Avenging ones are. We're everywhere things get fucked up. Look, to be clear, I went to Maine the night of the hurricane because your niece was practically hysterical and asked for my help. When I came back my stepfather and mom had gone somewhere else and the house was trashed. I even found crabs scuttling around and a fish swimming in the toilet. Looked like a fricken beach in the garage. My Collection of Broken Things was ruined which, okay, I can appreciate the irony in that, and my car died its final death in the storm. That's why I haven't come by. Had to move in with my sister just to get rides to work. No redemption anywhere. My folks are selling the house. Good luck with that, who wants to buy into a neighborhood that's getting eaten by the sea? My sister said I can keep living with her but I'm not sure I want to do that."

"Why not?"

"What do you think?"

Daniel walks over and switches on the lamp by his bed, then points up at Farley, grooming himself at the top of the bookcase. "That cat and I leave each other alone. We pretty much pretend the other doesn't exist. We have an agreement. I keep him fed, and he doesn't scratch my eyes out when I sleep. It works. He was supposed to be Heaven's, but everyone agreed he's better suited for me." He switches off the lamp and walks back to the window, shining the flashlight first in her face, then lets it travel the length of her down to her feet, the sneakered one, the one in the platform shoe, then back to her face.

"Can you still believe in me?" she asks. "Even if I'm no angel?"

"I believe your homunculus leg is magic."

"What, like it casts spells?"

Daniel snorts. "Shows what you know. Magic happens when things go out of kilter. When you can't predict results."

"So why don't you let me come in then? I can do out of kilter, I'm damn good at out of kilter! All you have to do is open the window wide enough for me to crawl inside. We can start with that. I know about you and your mom out by the pool. My folks were in their house sorting through the wreckage and they heard you. So, I know you can come out of your room."

"That was an emergency. I saved her from drowning. That's my job. When a person nearly drowns, to reclaim their soul they need to save someone else from drowning. Pay it forward. It's in the contract."

She shakes her head and he sees her little ponytail he likes swish about her neck; a few loose strands remain on her ears like they're stuck there. Her ears look like halves of cowry shells. "You are seriously whacked, you know? But I like it, I think. Open the window."

"What's up with my dad? Amelia said you called him for help in Maine. I think she's actually a little jealous of you."

Mercy snorts. "Leo is still in love with your mom. He's para-noid about drones, wiretapping, computer hacking, can't remember where his car is or even where he lives sometimes, but he remem-bers everything about her. He bailed me out of jail, dude. He's a fricken savior. I'm saving up to pay him back. They're making me take anger management classes and I can't come within a mile of RHWC. Yeah, like I want to hang out at an effing prison! He got them to drop the other charges, even the cunt guard who claimed I kicked her in the shin and made a giant hematoma. Like we don't know hematoma's just a fancy word for bruise. Who the hell *hasn't* been bruised? So, Daniel, here's my bottom-line: I can't consider dating you if you won't leave your room. I don't do bedroom dates, not anymore. I want to go to the movies then out to eat like people do. Or the park. We could just take a walk in the fricken park."

Daniel almost chokes on his saliva. "I'm agoraphobic, diag-nosed. Look it up."

"You weren't born in your damn room. You got yourself into it so you can get out of it. Can't you at least open the window wider so I can stick my face in or something? I don't know why I'm here. I don't know what I am to you."

She looks anxious suddenly and he feels bad for her, but he isn't used to feeling bad for women, isn't used to women when you got down to it, at least not women in his age group, and definitely not one who wants to take a walk in the park with him. He doesn't know what he's supposed to say. "You're Mercy, who used to live next door, who may or may not be an angel."

"What about the kid?"

"What about her?"

"She's a swimmer. Don't you worry about the drowning thing? Her mom's in prison for smacking her dad with a two-by-four, then he drowned on top of it because they were so fucked up on drugs. And then there's you. I thought *I* came from a whacko fam-ily. Why do you think I tried to help her go up there? I felt sorry for the kid. Just slide that screen and open the window more. I want to show you something, here's a preview." She lifts up her shirt. "Want to touch them this time?"

Daniel turns red but she can't see. He shines the light on her breasts, first one then the other. They're good, any fool could see that and he's no fool. Yet he still doesn't have a clue what he's supposed to say. "I don't know. It's a commitment."

"No!" she shakes her head, tugs her shirt back down. "No commitment at all if you don't let me in right now."

"I've got a mean feline in here."

"I can be pretty mean too, if the situation calls for it. I'm seriously badass now. I've been in jail. Open the window, Daniel, first things first. It's all we've got."

So he does it, slides the screen up and opens the window all the way. Heart hammering, he steps back and watches as she climbs through, first the perfect little leg with its great big shoe then the rest of her. She's smaller than he expected or maybe he's taller than he knew, because she only comes up to his neck; which means when she puts her arms around him and draws him to her, he can smell her hair under his face and it smells like strawberries, which is also a surprise. He likes wild strawberries. He remembers picking them in some field Amelia took them to when he and Gavin were kids, still unencumbered enough to enjoy things like that. "Strawberry fields forever," Mercy whispers, like she hears his thoughts. The way his heart pummels his chest as she presses in tighter against him, maybe she can hear that too. He wonders about this, and if that field is still out there somewhere.

♦ HEAVEN ♦

WHEN HEAVEN COMES HOME from Thayer Academy there's a package on her bed. "From your mother," Grandmelia calls from the living room, "but I'd like you to wait for me before you open it, okay?" That's how Grandmelia has been punctuating her demands, with an "okay?" at the therapist's suggestion, to give Heaven the illusion she has a choice. "How was school today?" Grandmelia adds, which is also new, Grandmelia taking what the therapist calls an *active interest* in Heaven's day-to-day. Heaven is okay with these things because Grandmelia is sending her to a private school, where so far she hasn't made any friends, but no enemies either. The days slide by and if she stays out of trouble and makes good grades, she'll be allowed to swim again, on the Thayer team.

It's a private school that costs a fortune, Grandmelia said, so no more stealing, she said, and at the first report of anything missing Heaven will have to pay for the school herself. Heaven's okay with this too, because the therapist, Matilda ("Call me Matilda," she'd said, all fake-friendly), gave her an awesome red leather diary with a gold key, and told her every time she feels like taking something that isn't hers she should write a story about it instead. So now when Uncle Daniel starts up with his Skye stories, Heaven has stories of her own to share, about a thirteen-year-old girl with superpowers who can make things disappear by holding her breath.

Uncle Daniel told her she's a natural storyteller. Heaven feels good about this because she's never been a natural at anything, except being able to hold her breath underwater longer than anyone. It's too cold now to practice that in Grandmelia's pool, but in the summer she will, though she won't sing the drowning songs. She and Uncle Daniel made a pact: they agreed to always be true to each other; he won't tell her she's getting stuff that she isn't, and she won't do things that could get her taken away from him and Grandmelia. She'll *try* not to anyway. "One day at a time," Matilda said. Grandmelia rolled her eyes at that one.

Heaven sits on her bed and stares at the package. *Contents Inspected by Rock Harbor Women's Correctional*, the prison address stamped in the corner. She picks it up and shakes. It's light, nothing rattles. She knows it's from her mom, because, for one, who else does she know in prison, plus she recognizes her mom's handwriting on the address to her, a loopy scrawl a lot like Heaven's. When Heaven learned how to write cursive her dad used to tease that he couldn't tell her handwriting apart from her mom's, except that her mom's looked like a guinea hen wrote it. Which sounded kind of mean, but he was smiling, and her mom was too. That made it a good memory.

"It came in today's mail," Grandmelia says, walking into Heaven's room, then sitting in her desk chair opposite the bed. "I thought we could open it together?" The question again, softening what Heaven knows is not a choice. She nods, and Grandmelia hands her a pair of scissors.

It's a medium-sized box, heavily taped—"to cover up that the guards opened it even though it says *contents inspected* right on the package, for lord's sake," Grandmelia points out. When Heaven tugs open the flaps there are two letters stacked beside what looks like a cross between a paper boat and a bird. Heaven lifts it out carefully. "It *is* a bird!" she says. "But it looks like a boat too."

"Read the letters. Do you mind sharing them?" Question without a choice.

Heaven picks up the first letter, "letter #1" it says.

Dear Heaven,

I need to tell you something, Amelia too, because I'm pretty sure she'll be on you to show her this letter. Anyway, you both should know the truth about what happened that night. I wasn't faking it. I really couldn't remember. Psychogenic amnesia, *prison shrink called it. But the weird thing is, after I got sober my memory started surfacing again. Little at a time at first, then last week I was in Dr. Woo's office for my six-month bullshit visit, and she was droning on about how it seemed I had never grieved my own mother's death, then suddenly like a shot I was back on the breakwater that terrible night. I'm going to tell you about it. I don't want to hide things between us anymore, Heaven. You have a right to know what happened to your dad, and my part in it.*

The fog was heavy and moist that night, like some humongous giant's breath, rocks wet and slippery from the rain, high tide lapping against them. I was chasing your dad, trying to catch up with him, screaming at him. I could hear it in my head all over again, the echo of the fog horn, sounds drifting on the wind from Rockland Harbor, boats groaning in their moorings, another boat honking as it circled the harbor, and the wind biting my face, whistling in my ears.

When we reached the end of the breakwater I was shouting at the back of his head, telling him I was fucking sick of it, the way he'd been behaving. Sorry about the four-letter word, your grandma is probably reading this over your shoulder, but that's what I said. Then he said, I'm too trashed for this shit, Cass, give it a rest. So I told him again in detail about everything I was sick of—and you know some of this Heaven, I know you do: the dope we couldn't get enough of, your dad going after all those other women, how we couldn't have a normal home. I was so sick of it, I told him.

He laughed at me, Heaven. Imitated me, said, Oh, are you sick, Cass?

You know I hate it when people laugh at me. I told him to fuck himself (sorry!).

He was standing on that large flat rock we used to sit on, end of the breakwater, hot summer days when we hadn't crashed yet. Remember? You'd be playing on the rocks behind us, a gentle ocean glistening on either side of the breakwater. But that night the ocean was raw, black, slapping up, then sucking back against the rocks.

Your dad said, I'm gonna wail on you Cass, I swear, if you say another fucking word. He thrust his arms out, feinting like he was air-punching me.

I told him again to fuck himself and that I was so sick of his games. I never felt so goddamn lonely! Then I kind of lurched toward him, I guess, stumbling on the board before I saw it but in the next breath I picked it up, smacking it down against the rocks. Sick sick sick! I screamed. Because by then I was feeling it, a coldness in my blood, pain in my stomach, and I knew the crash was coming soon. I started to cry, sobbing and smacking the board against the rocks. He kept taunting me, sicksicksicksick! he mimicked. While that was going on I became aware again of all the chaotic noise: the foghorn's belches, that boat horn wailing, then the foghorn roared like it had gotten inside my head, and the wind was stabbing at me, whipping me so hard I almost slipped on the rocks. Then the rain started up again, spitting in my face.

Your dad shouted: Fuck those rocks, hit me with that thing if you're so bloody sick of me! Let's see what ya got. Hit me goddammit, grow some balls! So, I did, Heaven. I felt like I was going crazy with all that noise, plus the wind and rain. No intent to harm—they asked me that at the trial, did you intend to harm your husband? No, that wasn't the fucking point, was it! How can you harm someone who's already broken? First on the leg, he only laughed harder. Pussy! he sneered, then turned away. It was his turn that caught it. I remember that now! I meant to lob it across the back of his shoulders with all my might, but suddenly he moved a little or bent over, it was hard to tell in the darkness, and when I smacked him again, hard as I could, it was across his head, that awful whap sound like when a batter hits a homerun. The lighthouse light rotated just in time to catch his surprised look. Because of course he was surprised, right Heaven? I'm not a violent person! And I'd put up with this shit for how many years?

He staggered a bit on the rock, close to but not on the edge, not where he'd fall. God, you see, he did not fall! Sweetie, he said, rubbing his hand over his scalp, you've gone and made me bleed, your darling boy. Why would you do that? He's shaking all over and I was too, so cold. Was that blood running down his forehead as he rubbed his head? I was in shock! I remember this now. Then he grinned, white stripe of teeth shining in the darkness. For my next act! You'll like this, he said. Watch closely now!

Whether it was the number of drugs in his bloodstream (even more than our usual together, and who knew what he had with Mary Barbara when I left them alone), or maybe he wanted to teach me a lesson. Maybe all of it and the knock on the head rattling his brains such that he couldn't think it out, recognize the danger. But in the flash of the lighthouse light I saw the arc of his beautiful body, arms stretched out in crucifixion pose, hitting the icy black water when he jumped.

He jumped, Amelia, your son jumped. I don't think he meant to drown, or even thought about the consequences. We were so trashed, and I'm so sorry about all of this, Heaven. Amelia, I'm not telling you this because I want a retrial, I don't need anybody's redemption. We were both at fault, if you can call it that. But I feel more at peace now, and someday when I get out of here, I want to make a new start. I hit him with the board. He jumped.

Heaven sits there holding the letter, avoiding Grandmelia's eyes. Her own eyes have tears in them, but she doesn't think she's going to cry. She's not really sure how to feel. Her mom *didn't* murder her dad, but she did hit him really hard with a board. Her dad jumped, but he didn't mean to drown. *He didn't mean to die.* She picks up the second letter, shorter than the first, and starts reading it aloud before Grandmelia tells her to:

Dear Heaven,
I hope you don't hate me after what I just told you in the first letter. I made this paper thing in the box for you, on my six-month anniversary of sobriety. I go to these meetings to help me stay clean. I can't promise I won't screw up again, but I'm going to try every day to not, you know. Anyway, on the half-year

anniversary they ask us to give something special to someone we hurt. I don't have any money to buy anything, and we don't have much you'd like in our commissary anyway plus what's there is a total rip-off. I made this from a piece of construction paper. It's origami. I learned it from my mom long ago when she was sick in bed and wanted to do something with her hands. She didn't last long so we only made origami one time, but I remembered how to do it.

It's a crane, which is supposed to be good luck or something. This one needs to float, because it's also a lantern, so I made it out of heavy paper. Remember when we lived in San Francisco, and we saw that Buddhist ceremony on Ocean Beach? Their departed loved ones were with them, then they released their spirits into the ocean so their loved ones could sail on to the afterlife and be free. Plus, maybe it frees you from the pain of having them with you, but in a way you can't touch. Maybe you were too little to remember, or to be honest maybe I was too high to remember if you'd remember, but theirs were square lantern-shapes or lotus flowers, which I guess is traditional. But my mom taught me to make a crane and I think cranes are better anyway because they can float and fly. It sort of looks like a swan too and you don't want to mess with swans, they can be mean SOBs. What can a lotus do except be a flower?

You'll need a candle, the tea ones with the tin base fit perfect in the fold I made and won't burn the thing up, then you light it and set it sailing on the ocean when the tide goes out. Say some words, a prayer, or whatever, then the water carries it away. I know it sounds weird but on Ocean Beach there were a lot of people doing it. I figure they couldn't all be Buddhists. Or maybe they were which means there must be something to it. Anyway, I was thinking maybe it's time we set your dad free.
Love Cassie, Your Mom.

P.S. I'm taking "parenting" classes here for something to do, this place is boring as heck (your grandma hates me using those four-letter words, but what do you know, heck has four letters too!). Maybe

I'll get some tips for your next visit. I hope soon. But remember to
use the door instead of shouting up under the window. Lol ☺
P.P.S. I'm not a smiley-face kind of person but the ones you put
on your letters to me are nice so figured I would do one back at you.

Heaven looks at Grandmelia expecting her to say something, but she doesn't. Heaven can't think what to say either. They both stare at the paper crane.

◆ AMELIA ◆

AMELIA AND HEAVEN ARE driving up Hatherly toward Minot after waiting for the sun to go down and the tide to start heading out. Daniel had given them a candle from his stash. "At one time he dabbled in Buddhism, Taoism, transcendental meditation, anything remotely spiritual he could practice from his bedroom," Amelia explained. "Didn't take, but we now have a lifetime supply of candles and incense."

She made Heaven wear her old clamming boots and a down parka, but when they get there it feels warm for a late January evening, a few degrees above freezing. The full moon lights a path in the water, with enough light from the post-sunset sky to pick their way over the rocky beach to the shore. The air smells like salt and seaweed.

"See if you can release that thing on the moon path," Amelia says. "Then we can watch its progress."

The first couple tries fail, the candle blows out, then a small wave shoots the lantern right back to the shore. "Maybe my dad's spirit doesn't want to go," Heaven says.

Amelia nods. "It would be like him. If you wanted him to stay he'd leave and vice versa. He wasn't so accommodating to other people's agendas. See where the tide slides back into the ocean after the tiny shore break? Get it on that, see if it does the trick."

"Do you think if it makes it out he'll be immortal, like a faerie or a selkie?"

"Oh for God's sake, your uncle's fed you a steady diet of nonsense. The one thing you can depend on in life, child, is comes a time when it will end. We're sailing a paper bird into the Atlantic to free your dad's spirit, isn't that enough silliness? When you go to college you best be a science major, learn how to think constructively about the natural world and save our derrieres. This planet is in a lot of trouble from our arrogance and foolishness."

"Were you a science major?"

"I was a model, my own business. The next best thing."

Heaven lights the candle once more, steps further into the icy water, then releases it on the outgoing tide. This time the lantern sails off. They watch the light flicker and sway in the current as it drifts further out.

"Oh crap, I forgot to say something! Weren't we supposed to say something?" Heaven wails, lumbering back onto shore, her boots squishy and wet.

Amelia squeezes Heaven's hand. "Your fingers are frozen, should've made you wear gloves." They watch the light dip and bob, growing fainter as it sails further out, then darkness, the empty path of the moon.

"What if a wave knocked it over or swamped it?"

"Don't worry. He can only drown once."

"But I wish I said something! Maybe it's bad luck or something."

"It's okay. I said it for us."

"I didn't hear you say anything."

"In my head, you know, like a prayer, what your mom said to do."

"What did you say?"

Amelia sighs. "Well, I thought about telling him how it would've been better if he'd done things different, that maybe if he'd lived a different kind of life, he'd still be with us. I thought about praying, since your mom mentioned that, but it's a bit late for divine intervention, don't you think?"

"So, what *did* you say? This is frustrating, Grandmelia! I feel like something's supposed to come next, like a drum roll, THE END scrolled in the sand. The light is out. But what happens now, like for the rest of my life?"

Amelia shrugs. "I told him we love him. Then I told him not to screw it up this time and wash back up on the beach."

It's completely dark now but for the moonlight. Amelia switches on the flashlight to walk up to the street, then drops it on the sand, wrapping her arm around Heaven who's still staring mournfully at the ocean. "Look, to be perfectly honest I didn't know what to say. We're not Buddhists. Do I look like a Buddhist? It'll be okay. You have me, your mom, Uncle Daniel, and, God help us, Leo, if he can remember where home is."

"Probably just telling my dad we love him would've been enough," Heaven says.

Amelia nods. "Right." She tightens her arm around her grand-daughter's shoulders, slips her other hand into her coat pocket, running her fingers over the little figure she's kept there since she took it off the shelf over Heaven's bed, cold to the touch, as plastic is. She's considered confronting Heaven about it, asking her where it came from (obviously the Catholic Store, but make the girl tell it to her straight), yet it seems that time has come and gone. Plus, what could she say when Heaven asks how come *she* took it, or maybe why she took the angel and left Jesus? Amelia doesn't know—impulse? She's rarely impulsive anymore, a gift of age; think things through, she's told Heaven. Anger at the girl for stealing it in the first place? Or maybe placing her faith in myth instead of Amelia, for whatever it was the child hoped for! Nothing is gained at this point returning it to the Catholic Store. Some-where a factory in Beijing spews out hundreds of these little figu-rines; they won't miss this one, and Amelia's grown accustomed to the firm feel of it in her pocket.

Also, and this is a little harder for Amelia to admit, but it felt good for once being the person who just does something for the hell of it. When she was young, she had that freedom, or so it seemed—Gavin's conception was proof of that, but somewhere along the line, maybe after Leo stopped contributing income, after their divorce, she had to become the responsible one. He got to be *the artist*, while she paid the bills, took care of the kids, took care of her parents; when did she have the time or the freedom to do some silly, irresponsible little thing that had no meaning other than *she* did it, and nobody's the wiser?

Amelia stares out toward the horizon, what she can make of it in the dark. Imagines she sees something, flash of light, a movement. Probably the moon's illumination, the tide doing what it's always done, flowing forward, pulling back. A breeze blows off the ocean, cold and salt smelling, then suddenly warm like a breath. Amelia stiffens. She gazes out to where the lantern was when darkness consumed it and suddenly, for just a moment, she sees her. She's not much older than Heaven, hair black as the night sky and her eyes are the sea, as Amelia's dad and her grandfather before him had always sworn they'd be, a face beyond myth, wisdom, the reckoning of time itself. Then she's gone, the silvery curve of a wave.

AUTHOR'S NOTE

M Y INSPIRATION FOR THIS novel came from two occurrences. The first was discovering that my great grandmother's family (MacAulay) had been part of the Highland Clearances in the late 1700's and 1800's, Isle of Skye. They lost their home forcing them to emigrate to the "New World" of Prince Edward Island, where two generations later my great grandmother was born. I knew she was Scottish, but somehow managed to go through a lot of my adulthood not knowing what had happened to her family and hundreds of other families, who'd been evicted (often violently) by wealthy landlords so that the more profitable sheep could graze the land. Maggie in my novel is not her, although the reference to her sister Abigail does touch upon my great grandmother's amazing life's journey. She was part of a big farm family in PEI, with too many mouths to feed. So, along with her sister she trained as a nurse, then traveled on her own to San Francisco where she landed a job as an ailing William Randall Hearst's private nurse to help him make the voyage by ship to Honolulu. There she met my great grandfather, Doctor John Pratt of Honolulu, and the rest is, as they say . . . history!

After researching The Clearances on the Isle of Skye, I originally thought the timing was right for her family to have been part of the clearings of the two villages depicted in this novel, Suisnish and Boreraig. When I was on the Isle of Skye doing physical research for my novel, I felt I needed to find the sites of these villages. We parked as close as we could, but it was a ten-mile trek to get to the ruins. I did it alone, in the misty rain so prevalent on the Isle of Skye. When I finally got there I had to climb over a big cattle fence to get in. Wandering around I stopped inside the rocky perimeter of one of the ruins, and suddenly had an overwhelming sense that this was it, what was left of my ancestors former croft. I stood there in the rain, staring out toward the ocean that bore them to the New World, and wept. Later, I learned from my son-in-law's impeccable genealogic research that my ancestors would've already been in PEI at the time of those notorious "clearings," though perhaps at one time they'd lived there. Or, maybe I was feeling the collective grief of all who'd lost their homes, their land, and their livelihoods.

The other thing that happened is I suffered a near-drowning off Goat Island, Oahu, as depicted in this novel. I grew up there and was as confident and comfortable in the ocean as one could be, yet this occurred while swimming alone in a strong current. I wasn't rescued by a mythical creature. . . . However, I *was* rescued by three "angels," two young men in a canoe and a strong swimmer who saw from the beach that I was in trouble. Having been rushed to the hospital by ambulance, I never had a chance to thank them, or the woman who helped me on the beach, then notified my family. Perhaps they will read this novel! I owe my life to them. Incredibly, my great, great, great grandfather Captain Angus MacAulay, a ship's captain who helped ferry emigrant families from the Isle of Skye to PEI during The Clearances, drowned after falling overboard off a small sloop in Charlottetown Harbor, Prince Edward Island.

Sources consulted for inspiration and information on: Isle of Skye, the Highland Clearances, Celtic Mythology, Borth (Wales), Prince Edward Island, Shipwrecks, and Scituate, MA.

Books:

Craig, David. *On The Crofters' Trail—In Search of the Clearance Highlanders*. Birlinn, 2006.

Hall, Thomas. *Shipwrecks of Massachusetts Bay*. The History Press, 2012.

MacDonald, Jonathan. *A Short History of Crofting in Skye*. J MacDonald, 2007.

Monaghan, Patricia. *The Encyclopedia of Celtic Mythology and Folklore*. Checkmark Books, 2008, 2004.

Murphy, Alan. *Skye & Outer Hebrides*, 2nd edition. Footprint, Footprint Handbooks Ltd, 2014.

Newton, Norman. *SKYE*. D&C, David and Charles—F&W Media Inc., 1995–2009.

Scituate Historical Society. *Images of America—Scituate*. Arcadia Publishing, 2000.

Swire, Otta. *Skye The Island And Its Legends*. Birlinn, 2006.

Williams, Paul. *Walks Isle of Skye*, 31 Walks. Pocket Walking Guide. Hallewell Publications, 2003.

Other Helpful Sources:

"Come Find Your Island." Prince Edward Island 2018 Visitor's Guide.

"Go To St. Kilda Adventure Guide".

"Boreraig".

"Lighthouses of Prince Edward Island". Prince Edward Island Lighthouse Society.

"Prehistoric forest arises in Cardigan Bay after storms strip away sand". *The Guardian*.

"Clothing in the Highlands and Islands in the 19th Century".

ACKNOWLEDGMENTS

I AM GRATEFUL FOR SUPPORT in the various stages of writing this novel, early drafts to numerous revisions, from: Dorland Mountain Arts Colony (much thanks to Janice and Robert!); Split Rock Cove Artist's Retreat (thanks, Sandy!), and The Hambidge Center for Creative Arts & Sciences. Also Susan Campbell Bartoletti, who let me use her lovely lake house for a two-week intensified revision. For funding travel to the various sites this novel is set in, much thanks to Binghamton University, in particular the Harpur College Dean's Office and the Peter Mileur Faculty Development Grant, and the English Department's Newman Grant. To my agent, Eleanor Jackson, for keeping the faith in me, and for reading and offering invaluable feedback on various drafts of this novel. To the hard-working staff at Alcove Press, my editor Jenny Chen, Production and Publishing Assistant, Melissa Rechter, and Madeline Rathle, Marketing Maven (as Jenny called you), all of whom were bombarded by emails from me and still retained their professionalism and put out a lovely book. The copyeditor, Jill Pellarin, was meticulous and encouraging. To Sheryl Johnston, independent publicist and wonderful friend—can't imagine a book without your expertise. My good friend and colleague, Libby Tucker, Distinguished Service Professor, Binghamton University, gave valuable feedback on several chapters in this novel, and to my English Department and Creative Writing colleagues at Binghamton University, who have all been so supportive, along with my various writer-friends scattered across the globe—you give me hope and inspiration (sometimes even letters and blurbs!) every time we communicate. My son-in-law, Rui Gomes da Costa, whose in-depth genealogical research into our family tree was inspirational. Last but never least, to all my family, from Hawai'i to Portugal and all the places in between, I couldn't do it without your support and love. Thank you!